THE
CHOSEN
— OF THE —
MANIFOLD

THE STARSEA CYCLE BOOK FOUR

KYLE WEST

1

THE RED SUNLIGHT of the Psyche sunset bathed the dunes of the Burning Sands the color of blood. Four figures entered the cool twilight from the desert Spire under a baleful sky dominated by the white gas giant Cupid. Unlike the former furnace of daytime heat, the air now held a dry chill, and would only get colder as evening faded into night, leaving only the pearlescent luminescence of Cupid above. The cold was far more preferable to the heat. Cupid, half-obscured by shadow, provided plenty of light by which to see.

Lucian, Serah, Fergus, and Selene headed east toward the *Zephyr* crash site. After mounting the first crest of the dune, a wall of sand surrounding the Spire created by the Psionic storm, Lucian spied the wreckage of the Queen's former flagship. It lay broken, scattered, and half-buried in red sand. Shattered boxes and crates spilled their contents throughout the still-warm sands. Most of the massive envelope was empty of helium by now, and only a tiny portion connected to the stern contained enough gas to remain buoyant. It feebly tugged at its lines, a broken thing that wanted nothing more than to be free. But the debris of the ship buried in sand prevented its escape.

"*That's* a right mess," Serah said.

Selene slid down the face of the dune, not waiting for the others to follow. As Serah stared after her, her eyes narrowed. "*What* in the Worlds is she doing?"

Lucian watched Selene for a moment, her gem-studded train trailing in the sand. "I don't know. She's doing something, that's for sure."

"I *still* think the Queen's controlling her," Serah said.

Lucian didn't bother contradicting her. The Queen was as good as gone. The Orb of Psionics had seen to that. It held a power that not even Ansaldra could withstand. That power terrified Lucian, even more so because it was his to command. He suppressed a shudder.

When he picked up Selene's trail, the others followed. She weaved around the debris, seeming to make right for the half-filled envelope. She extended a hand toward it, her hand glowing with orange radiance.

"She's blowing it up!" Serah said.

But to Lucian's eyes, it seemed she was doing nothing of the sort. The entire envelope glowed with orange radiance for a few seconds. Once the light had dissipated, Selene lowered her hand and turned to address Lucian. It was as if he was the only one there, the only one worth speaking to.

"Sir Lucian, I'm trying to get a sense of our helium supplies. Looks like a good amount survived the crash. Enough, perhaps, for me to flux some helium into hydrogen and create water if need be."

"*Sir* Lucian?" he asked, perplexed. "I'm just some guy, no Mage-Knight."

Selene blinked in surprise. "Oh. I figured from your clothing and the way the others seem to defer to you—"

"I defer to *no one*," Serah said, proudly. "Noble blood ain't worth a bucket of warm piss out here."

Selene glanced at her, annoyed. "Forgive me. Mage-Princes often travel with squires or retainers. If I have offended you, then I retract my former statement."

When Serah rolled her eyes, Selene's cheeks colored in indignation. Lucian had to step in before it could come to blows. He had to keep everyone focused on the problem, not each other. "We're all equals here, Selene. All of us got our clothes from the Sorceress-Queen."

"I . . . see. You play the part of the prince well if you don't mind me saying."

Lucian ignored that, especially as Serah's gaze had gone colder. "So, about this helium. You can make water from it? Wouldn't that just cause a giant explosion?"

"Not with me controlling the stream," Selene said. "Fluxing is easy enough, and I can bond it to the oxygen in the atmosphere, even skipping the nasty exothermic reaction bit."

Lucian had to admit that could be useful. It would help them survive for a lot longer. How much longer, he couldn't say.

"Perhaps you can do that," Fergus said. "Then again, it's more practical to search the wreckage for water and food first. As an Atomicist, can't you detect traces of water?"

"I . . . can," Selene admitted.

It was obvious she hadn't thought of the idea, which was probably the source of her embarrassment.

"*If* we find water," Fergus continued, "it still doesn't solve the problem of actually getting out of here. We're stranded, and unless someone picks us up—"

"Lucian, you told me you had an escape plan," Selene interrupted.

"I do," he said. He still needed to let Selene in on his plan, as much as Serah might hate it. She and the noblewoman would not be the best of friends, that much was clear. "Vera is on her way to Psyche right now with her ship. I don't know how long that will take, but probably three months at least. No matter how much food and water we find in that wreckage, or how much helium Selene can flux, it won't be enough to survive this place. Fergus is right. We have to find a way out of here, as impossible as that might seem."

"Who's Vera?" Selene asked.

"A powerful Psionic I know," Lucian said. "A powerful ally. If she can get past the Warden blockade, she's our ticket off this world."

Selene gave a light laugh. "You're delusional."

"Well, you're welcome to stay here, but no one's coming to rescue you. At least, not fast enough to save you. The point is, we need a way out of here, to get somewhere we can survive long enough for Vera to pick us up. Frankly, Selene, I don't care what you do once we're out of the Burning Sands. Until then, though, we need to work together if we want to survive. What's our path out of here, realistically?"

"It's impossible," Selene said.

"Let me rephrase," Lucian said. "What's our path here, assuming it *isn't* impossible?"

"Well," Serah said. "We have to cross one thousand kilometers of bone-dry dunes. There would be no shelter during the day, so we would roast alive. Even if we found the odd rock or mesa, the shade wouldn't do much. We'd have to keep a Thermal ward up at all times. With four mages, we might cycle it, but none of us are Thermalists, though we have two mages who have Thermalism as a secondary. That's too much strain. Not to mention we'd have to carry everything ourselves on our backs, including food and water, because we'll find none. There's no way we can carry enough food and water. The Burnings Sands is a barren wasteland. There may be water sources on the periphery, but not this far out."

"Psyche's a small world," Lucian said. "Is going west a possibility until we reach the Riftlands?"

"The Riftlands are on the exact opposite point of Psyche," Fergus said. "There's nothing to the west but more dunes. Probably a thousand kilometers of them, followed by the Rift Sea, which is several thousand kilometers wide. After that, you'd reach the eastern extent of the Far Riftlands, but still have a few hundred kilometers to go before reaching Deeprift."

"The sea isn't passable?" Lucian asked.

Serah laughed. "There is no passage by sea on Psyche. Cupid's gravity produces unreal tidal forces. Waves tens of meters high. You'd have to fly, but one storm would kill us, and storms are constant over the Rift Sea."

"That's a no-go," Lucian said.

Fergus nodded. "That leaves east, back the way we came. Even assuming we cross the entire Burning Sands, we have the Fire Rifts to deal with. We can't walk that, or at least, I don't think it's possible to walk it. Lucian would need to Bind everyone across."

Selene's eyes widened. "*That* would certainly fray you."

Everyone went quiet. Fergus had slipped a bit, but from his expression, he was doing a good job of hiding it. One thing was for sure: it would not be easy for Lucian to keep his two Orbs a secret. Not for long, anyway. Lucian didn't want to tell her about them yet, but he would probably need to use them at some point if they were to have any hope of surviving.

There was only one actual solution, and that was to tell Selene the truth. Serah's expression seemed to warn him not to, but she was going to find out anyway, and telling her now might help win her trust. Something they would need to survive the journey ahead.

"It's time I told you why we're really in the Burning Sands, Selene. I won't go into specifics. Not yet, anyway. But I have the Orb of Binding, and after yesterday, the Orb of Psionics."

SELENE'S green eyes widened at the revelation. It was strange to see that reaction on the face he associated with the Sorceress-Queen.

"I guess that shouldn't surprise me. Why else would we be out here? Everyone knows that part of Arian's prophecy, that the Amethyst of Starsea lies somewhere out here. That said, I will need to see proof to back up such an extraordinary claim."

"You will see proof soon enough, I promise," Lucian said. "For now, you just have to believe me."

"Well, if that's true, it changes the equation substantially. Why, if the words of Arian about the Orbs *are* true, then you have unlimited power with those Aspects!"

"Not unlimited. In theory, their power is unlimited, but my Focus still gets exhausted if I stream too much."

"Still, I have an idea that just might work."

"What idea?" Serah asked skeptically.

Selene seemed to brood. Lucian could almost hear the gears turning in her head. "I wonder. With the four of us, plus sufficient supplies of food and water, plus the intact section of that hull, and the amount of lift provided by that helium. Would it be enough to carry us across the Burning Sands?"

Selene watched the broken airship, her eyes seeming to see something that wasn't there. Lucian watched her with growing amazement. Did she think they could *repair* that thing and get them out of here? Impossible.

After some time, she spoke again. "We wouldn't need the entire ship, of course. Just a flat enough expanse of it. It would be more like a raft or a skiff than a proper airship. But if we can lift that skiff with the helium we have, it *should* be enough to float us, along with any supplies we bring. Carrying anything more than ourselves, food, and water, plus perhaps a tarp to shelter us from the sun will just weigh us down. If Lucian truly has the Orb of Binding, he should have no problem pulling us along, right?"

Lucian could see it now. "That . . . sounds like it could work. Assuming we could cobble a ship together."

"It wouldn't be hard at all," Selene said. "We are mages. We can make quick work of it. We just have to assemble the components."

"All right," Serah said. "How long would this take?"

"Not long at all. We might have most of the work done tonight, even. Most of the needed pieces are already above the sand. The trick is getting the right amount of lift for the right amount of wood, supplies, and our collective weight. If the ship sinks because of helium leakage, we can just drop excess weight. All the resources are here. They just need to be marshaled. The only unknown is whether Lucian can keep up the tethering all day, multiple days in a row."

"I don't see why Lucian can't just pull the four of us across the Burning Sands *without* the ship," Fergus said.

"That would be too draining," Lucian said. "If I do every-body one at a time, it would take less magic, but it would be slower than this air skiff. And if I did everybody at once, it would be too strenuous. Even if the raft and us on it is more mass to move, I would only need one tether for it."

"That would still be more than any Binder in the Worlds could handle," Selene said. "Six or more Binders working in confluence pulled *Zephyr*. The hardest part is getting it up to speed, but after you reach a certain point, all you have to do is maintain its momentum."

"Makes sense," Lucian said.

"And this skiff would be enough to pull us across the whole Burning Sands, and with luck, the Fire Rifts and the desert Westlands?" Fergus asked skeptically. "I suppose if we are high enough, the temperature would be tolerable, with a tarp as you said. Would we be able to go as fast as the *Zephyr*?"

"Faster, more likely," Selene said. "The Queen had six Binders to pull the entire ship and could use twelve at a time if needed since the Binders worked in two separate shifts. This would just be Lucian, but the mass would be far less than the entire *Zephyr*. I'm sure he could get it moving pretty fast with the Orb of Binding."

"Assuming this skiff holds together," Serah said.

"Yes, that remains to be seen," Selene said. "But Lucian asked for a way out of here, and I gave an option. Perhaps our only option."

At this, Serah went silent.

"Well, I don't have a better idea," Fergus said. "And time is running out."

"I suggest we get started immediately," Selene said. "Just do as I say, and we'll have something workable by the time the sun comes up."

2

SELENE WAS as good as her word. When dawn broke over the eastern dunes, the heat was already incredible, but they had something of an air skiff made. It wasn't pretty, standing about ten meters long and half again that wide, looking as if it might fall apart at the slightest breeze. Lucian wasn't keen on piloting this thing, but it's what they had to work with.

So he had to make it work.

The first thing they had done was dredge up the broken stern. Lucian kept the ship in place with a Binding stream, so that the still attached envelope didn't pull it into the sky and out of reach. They then loaded the ship with weight until there was enough to keep it in place without Lucian streaming magic. Only then did Fergus stream a green laser to cut away most of the ship, which they didn't need. The goal was to get it as light as possible, so it would be easier for Lucian to pull while allowing for more cargo to be piled on.

By the time they finished, about ten meters of the ship's stern, two masts with rigging, and the part of the envelope still filled with helium remained. The helium tugged at its lines with surprising force, and all they had to do was drop a little weight to get the skiff into the air.

They had scrounged plenty of food and water—Ansaldra's stores had not been lacking. Even if sand ruined most of it, plenty remained for them to survive the journey. All that remained was to tie down the cargo to the deck with repurposed rigging.

The sun was well above the horizon, and the heat sweltering. They had to decide whether to embark immediately or rest until evening.

"We must get moving," Selene said. "We've been lucky so far to have no moonquakes or storms, but either could happen at any moment."

"I agree," Fergus said. "I know we're tired, but once we're up in the air, it should be cool enough."

"Lucian?" Serah asked. "Are you good to go?"

Truthfully, the work had exhausted him, especially the Binding stream to keep the ship aground long enough to pile it with cargo.

"Let's just see if this thing flies. I'll try to get it going, but no promises."

"It'll fly," Selene said. "I've balanced the mass and buoyancy perfectly. I even allowed for some leakage."

"Wouldn't it just go straight up, then?" Serah asked. "What if Lucian's knocked out of commission somehow? Then we're screwed."

"Why would that happen?" Selene asked. "We need some leeway, otherwise we might crash, and that would certainly spell our doom."

Before Serah could get her own rebuttal in, Fergus cleared his throat, probably trying to distract the two from arguing. "Perhaps we should practice first and then sleep the day off in the Spire. We have plenty of supplies, so what's the harm?"

Selene's eyes narrowed. "The *harm* is moonquakes and

storms. The skies are clear and we would be fools not to take advantage of that."

But Lucian's exhaustion was such that the mere thought of having to pull the rig all day long under the heat of the sun was almost enough to make him pass out on the spot. He knew Selene had a point, but he just didn't see it happening.

"I have enough energy to test her out, first," he said. "All this is theoretical until we know she flies beyond the shadow of a doubt."

"That's simple," Selene said. "As soon as we're on board and drop some cargo, it'll lift off, and we've already prepared the mooring lines. Finding something to tie them to will be the hard part if we need to land at some point. There's nothing but sand out here."

"All the more reason for Lucian to rest," Serah said. "He might not get to stop for hours or even days."

"Let's just get moving," Lucian said. "We'll cook if we stand out here any longer."

The four of them climbed on board, the shade of the tarp providing some marginal relief from the harsh sun. Lucian hoped they'd secured the crates well enough. If he caused the skiff to pitch, he wasn't sure the rigging would be enough to hold everything down. He looked around doubtfully. What a sad, ramshackle thing. The railing didn't even completely cover the sides, while there was no protection from sliding off at the end, where Fergus had cut it.

This was all they had, though. For that reason alone, it would have to do the impossible. Despite the fact that it could disintegrate in midair with absolutely no warning, they had to trust it to carry the four of them over a thousand klicks east.

"Let's just try to fly her over to the Spire for now and tie her up," Lucian said. "One of those broken pillars should work."

Everyone clasped the railing as Lucian drew a centering breath.

"Throw off some of those crates we're using for weights," he said.

They did so, one at a time. By the twelfth crate, the ship shifted perceptibly, lifting off from the sandy ground. Lucian quickly tethered the point of the stern; like the former bowsprit, this was also carved in the likeness of a wyvern's head, only this one was half-broken. He set the focal point for the top of the dune just before the Spire. The tether worked perfectly fine, pulling the skiff directly forward while rising slightly into the air. To Lucian's surprise, this did not take as much magic as he thought it would. It was nowhere near as draining as tethering four people. The only question, of course, was whether he could keep it up all day. For now, it seemed he could, though of course, his need for sleep might be a hard limit.

He didn't know if he could pull this skiff hundreds upon hundreds of kilometers with no rest. But he also had to do what was necessary to survive, whatever the cost.

Lucian settled on tethering the outmost column of the Spire, pulling the skiff toward it. He slowed the stream as they neared. He didn't want it to crash into the sand and break apart on impact. The ship touched down gently. Serah and Fergus were already climbing down the rope ladder they had fashioned on the ship's starboard side. Each carried a coiled mooring line looped around their shoulders. Fergus wrapped his line around one column while Serah wrapped hers around another, each making sure they hitched their knots tightly. Lucian felt the skiff tugging against the lines taut, but they held strong, with no chance of fraying. Once he deemed it secure, he let his Binding stream go. The skiff floated about half a meter off the ground, while the ladder provided easy access to the ground beneath.

"This might work," he said. He stifled a yawn. "But I definitely can't go any farther today."

"Now, we just have to hope there aren't any storms," Fergus said, once back on board. "Hard to imagine a moonquake being rough enough to trouble the ship."

For now, the sky was blue and the threat of a storm seemed quite distant. Out here, though, that meant nothing. All it would take was one storm while they slept, and that meant certain death.

But Lucian had to put the possibility out of his mind. He couldn't go on without sleep, and he had to hope the Spire, and the depression it was in, might provide protection.

"What should we name her?" Fergus asked. "Seems bad luck to set out without christening this hunk of junk."

"Maybe we can name it that," Serah said. "Hunk of junk."

Selene's cheeks colored. She did not appreciate Serah denigrating her handiwork.

"*Endurance*," Fergus said. "That's a fine name."

Serah blew a raspberry. "*That's* a boring name."

"You've got one better?"

"I've got twenty better," she said. "How about *Wyvern's Blood*, or *Ansaldra's Bane*?"

"Well," Lucian said, "the ship was Selene's idea, and without her, we could have never built it. I think she should name it."

She stared for a long while, seemingly in the distance, the harsh sunlight reddening her pale skin. Lucian wasn't sure she'd heard him.

"*Vengeance*," she said. "That's her name."

They watched her in silence for a moment. Then Lucian nodded. "*Vengeance* it is, then."

With that, they went back into the Spire, their last rest before the long journey ahead.

———

DESPITE HIS EXHAUSTION, Lucian simply couldn't sleep. Every time he closed his eyes, he felt the Orbs' presence, like twin black holes burning at his consciousness. It took all of his willpower to keep from reaching for them, from feeling their collective power right at his fingertips. Just to stream a *small* amount of magic would feel nice, and the mere fact of knowing that streaming Binding and Psionics couldn't fray him made the temptation almost too much to resist.

He kept thinking back to his battle with the Sorceress-Queen. Would he ever have a challenge like that again? Even if he had almost died, he also wanted to relive the feeling of raw power. If that power was only *two* Orbs, what would it be like to hold more, even all Seven?

"Lucian?"

Selene's soft voice nearly made him jump out of his skin. He stood hastily, finding her standing not a meter away, her green eyes shining with curiosity. How long had she been watching him?

It was as if she had expected this question. "I could tell you weren't sleeping. I need to discuss something." She looked toward Fergus and Serah, who were sleeping round the small fire. "You know, without being heckled to death."

Lucian motioned her away from the fire, toward the base of the crystal stairs. She followed him there.

"What's going on?" he asked.

"I feel as if you're the only one I can talk to here. But I hardly know anything about you."

Lucian had the feeling there was something more she wanted to ask, but it would take her a while to get there. "I tried to talk to you about myself two nights ago, remember? What's changed?"

"That was before," she said. "I thought you were some Mage-Prince, still loyal to the Queen. Now, however, I'm not sure *who* you are. I would like to know where I stand with you. If . . . we're friends or enemies."

"I . . . suppose that's fair."

"You are someone of great importance. That much is clear. Or at least, Queen Ansaldra thought so, enough to bring you with her on this expedition." Her voice took on a note of distaste at the mentioning of her name. "That has me curious. And you hold two Jewels of Starsea . . ." She shook her head. "If you'd just come out and said that from the beginning, I might have taken you more seriously."

"You should've done that anyway instead of judging me on appearances."

Selene gave a gracious smile. "Perhaps I should have, but try to see things from my perspective. It *was* an honest mistake to make. When you're someone like me, there are a lot of grifters who are just after money or favor. You can't give the time of day to just anyone. So, you learn to stand back and let people prove themselves first. If you had been born into power, Lucian, you would understand this simple thing. I daresay you will know what I mean one day."

"I suppose that makes sense. I wasn't born into power. That much should be obvious. I guess I took your actions as . . . *snootiness*, I guess. Especially around Serah."

"I'm doing my best," Selene said. "I won't lie. I'm used to having things done a certain way, and I'm used to people following my orders. That's in my mage's blood, and that's not likely to change. I make no apologies for who or what I am. I'm of the nobility of Dara, and it is our part to rule Psyche. On that one thing, I agree with the Queen. You, though. You're different. If you have two Orbs, then you must be the Chosen of the Manifold. The one Arian wrote his prophecy about."

It was hard not to betray his surprise. "Does *everyone* on this rotting moon know about this stuff?"

Selene shook her head. "The mages do, of course. We are

well-informed regarding *The Prophecy of the Seven*. Many study it out of great personal interest."

Lucian wondered what the point of all this was. "Can't this wait until tomorrow?"

"Listen," Selene said. "Queen Ansaldra holds the truest copy of *The Prophecy of the Seven* in her library. If you are indeed the Chosen, such an item would be of great use to you."

"The truest copy? What does that even mean?"

Her eyebrows arched in surprise. "You don't know? I thought you might be well-versed in such things, or at least have a somewhat accurate copy of the prophecy yourself, being the Chosen and all. It's said during the Mage War and even before, the Aspirants for the Orbs highly prized any translation of the prophecy, accurate or not."

"I don't know about all that," Lucian said. "And I'm not Chosen yet. At least, not according to the Oracle. According to what I know, the Chosen is the one who holds all Seven Orbs. Until then, I'm just some guy."

Lucian knew he was underplaying it. In the technical sense, he was a Vigilant, the same as the Lords of Starsea from hundreds of millennia ago. The last thing he wanted to do was inform Selene of that fact, however.

"The Chosen is not just the one who holds all the Orbs," Selene said. "Fate dictates he is to gather them all. He may not know he *is* the Chosen, but he still is. Since you have gathered two already, it is exceedingly likely that you are the one which Arian prophesied. No more or less."

"But it could still *not* be me."

"You hold two Orbs," Selene said, with forced patience. "Perhaps that's not indisputable proof, but you're the closest thing to the Chosen that has ever walked the Worlds. My question to you is, do you have a highly pure version of *The Prophecy of the Seven*?"

"I don't know what you're talking about. Why would you think I have a copy of the prophecy?"

Selene's cheeks colored. "You truly don't know?"

"I would tell you if I did. Again, does this have a point?"

Selene blinked. "You . . . have a coarse way of speaking with a lady. I wouldn't bandy words with you, but this is far too important. I only wish you would take this more seriously."

"Just as I wish you would take my friends seriously," Lucian said. "I trust them with my life."

"Again," Selene said, "I don't much like that Serah. She's rude, and she jeers at everything I say, even after I've proven my worth. Would you at least give me a chance? You saved me from Queen Ansaldra, and you must have done so for a reason. Was that reason to distrust me? Is that the nature of Serah's dislike, that you took the harder road and spared my life, while she wanted my head lopped off?"

With that observation, Selene knew far more than Lucian would have guessed. He truly hoped she wasn't an enemy, because if she were, they were all in trouble.

"You've gotten to the heart of it," Lucian said. "I won't say I didn't think about doing it, but deep down, I knew it was wrong."

"You are a gracious man," she said. "A suiting Aspirant for the Seven Orbs."

"If you genuinely believe that, then please listen to me about my friends. I've been through thick and thin with them, and I don't want there to be any conflicts. I can talk to Serah, too, but the last thing we need is for there to be arguments when we just need to survive."

"I couldn't agree more. Fergus seems a noble and . . . dutiful man." Her cheeks colored slightly. "Serah, I will do what I can, but much also depends on her."

"That's fair. I guess I was just guarded around you after our first conversation. You're right that Serah doesn't seem to like you, and I trust her a lot. You need to realize that Serah doesn't like it when people act like they run the place. Especially those she had a hand in rescuing. She doesn't give a rot about mage blood. She's a mage, too, just like you. Aren't you supposed to respect mages wherever they come from?"

Selene's face relaxed a bit. "Well, I must admit I hadn't considered that. Again, I know how to do things, and I can do them very well. My old master told me often that I had a big head, but that's only because I'm usually right. It would be far simpler if I led the expedition back to the Westlands. The skiff was my idea, after all."

"I'll be leading the expedition, but I'm glad for your contributions. We need each other, and this is the arrangement."

Selene smiled. "Of course."

"Okay, then. We're a team. Just as I have talents, Serah and Fergus do, too."

"And yet, they look to you to take the lead, do they not?"

Lucian realized that was true. Fergus had been the leader of the expedition at the beginning, but somehow, imperceptibly, the onus had fallen on Lucian's shoulders, about the time the Sorceress-Queen had taken them captive.

It was hard for Lucian to look Selene in the eyes because all he saw was the Queen staring back. Her remarkable good looks hardly affected him, such was the association she had with the Sorceress-Queen of Psyche. Even if the person behind those eyes was different from Ansaldra, it was almost enough to give him the chills.

"As long as we agree," Lucian said. "Now, what did you want to say about *The Prophecy of the Seven*?"

She cleared her throat. "Well, I thought I might educate you a bit about Arian's prophecy since it seems you are . . . ignorant of it, if you'll excuse my saying."

Lucian resisted the urge to roll his eyes. "By all means. Educate me."

"Now, you probably already know *The Prophecy of the Seven* reads . . . differently, depending on who is doing the reading. That's because Arian wrote the original prophecy in a state of Psionic hypnosis. While his mind was delving the Manifold, his hand remained here, relating his revelations. The words come out garbled, but each reader sort of *hears* something different. Most of it is unintelligible, but under Psionic hypnosis, there can be a reason to the madness."

"Okay. I follow that."

"Now, no one knows what happened to his *original* prophecy, but several scribes made copies of it in the twilight of Arian's life at the Volsung Academy. Only the words became . . . less *pure* if you will. This is not merely a translation error. Since the words heard in the mind change depending on who is reading, what the transcriber writes turns out to differ from what was there originally."

"So why couldn't mages just transcribe the words exactly as they appeared without Psionic hypnosis?"

"You can't do that with an alien language," Selene said. "I mean, you *can*, but it's of no use to anyone but the one who speaks the language. And of course, no one in the Worlds except for maybe Arian could speak it."

Lucian frowned. An alien *language*? That one time he had read the prophecy, he had heard it in his mind in his language of Standard-English, or what he *assumed* to be Standard-English.

"I thought they were *all* Standard-English translations," Lucian said. "At least, the one I read was."

"Those exist, but they are practically useless. A pure copy can only remain true to the original language, written under Psionic hypnosis. What you read was likely an interpretation of the translator's. That said, among dozens of translations, certain things line up, what has become *common knowledge* about Starsea. Things like the Orbs, the Immortal, the Chosen of the Manifold, and some details about the Starsea Cycle, all of which you seem to know. And on Psyche, a unique line exists, relating to the Orb of Psionics. I'm sure you're familiar with that line, otherwise, you wouldn't be here."

Lucian had always known the words of the prophecy were sheer madness on the surface. But to know that the madness was different depending on who translated it was another matter entirely.

"So, what do you mean when you're talking about the *purity* of the translation?"

"Less pure translations will corroborate more pure ones. And preferably, the translators never came into contact with each other. A purer translation will have that, along with additional information not conveyed in other copies."

"Okay, I follow that."

"A corrupted translation, however, will have few translations agreeing with it, and perhaps even none. So, that's what I mean when I say the Sorceress-Queen probably has one of the purest translations of *The Prophecy of the Seven* available in the Worlds. Many less pure translations agree with it. Ansaldra's translation even gives the unique line relating to the Orb of Psionics. And as we both know, that turned out to be true, meaning that *this* translation is second only to Arian's original. Which, of course, passed out of all knowledge long ago."

Lucian immediately saw where she was going. If Ansaldra's translation of the prophecy had given a unique line about the Orb of Psionics, then it might have clues about the other Orbs, too. It might be the key to everything.

"What are you suggesting, Selene?"

"Don't you see? If you had that translation, Lucian, you could find the other Orbs. Arian wrote *The Prophecy of the Seven* for the Chosen. Assuming you *are* the Chosen, then it should speak to you personally. You need only use the power of the Orb of Psionics to unlock the meaning."

"Okay. That begs the question. Where is the original, the one Arian wrote?"

"*That*, no one knows," Selene said. "After Arian's fourth and final delving of the Manifold, his most famous, he immediately frayed. He disappeared from the Volsung Academy, and no one knows where he went. And he took with him his masterwork and left behind only imperfect translations. It's from those copies that all our knowledge of *The Prophecy of the Seven* comes."

"I see." Lucian was much too tired to think about this now. And he didn't like the implication. If the Sorceress-Queen had a highly pure translation of *The Prophecy of the Seven*, and he was the Chosen, then it meant he was beholden to go get it.

And worse, the Sorceress-Queen would know that. And would wait for him.

"If you're suggesting we go to the Golden Palace, I won't have anything to do with it. My goal is to get *off* this world, not get ensnared in the Queen's schemes."

"I understand that, but Lucian, we're talking about the purest translation of *The Prophecy of the Seven* in existence, aside from Arian's original."

"How would I even go about getting it? It's impossible, and she'll be expecting me to come and find it."

"Everyone knows about Ansaldra's library," Selene answered. "She has almost every book from the first colony. They were this group of religious Luddites where, after their spaceship got them here, didn't want to use any technology from beyond the nineteenth century. They kept all their knowledge in books."

"Religious Luddites? What does this have to do with anything?"

"Only to explain why this library exists. It is Ansaldra's true treasure. From its tomes, she has kept all the knowledge that has built her civilization. And its crown jewel is her prophecy,

kept in a central display case for all to see. While the translation is under guard, it is also available to study for any mage
with the proper papers. Ansaldra always hopes more Psionic
readings will lead to an even purer version. Any mage can
request to read it, provided they share their findings with
Ansaldra. Many have tried, over the years, but no one has
improved upon it."

"Getting it would be impossible," Lucian said. "The Golden
Palace is surrounded by walls and towers, and guarded with
Mage-Lords, Mage-Knights, and hoplites. The Palace is the *last*
place we should go."

Selene gave a small, patient smile as if he were a student
who just wasn't getting it. "Yes, it is dangerous. But even if
escape from Psyche *was* possible, what would be the point of
escaping if you don't know where to go next? You need *The
Prophecy of the Seven*, Lucian. I only mention this because I
want to help you. You are the Chosen, or at least, are likely to
be. Finding the *Prophecy* could be your destiny."

"I *hate* that word. My only question is, why should you
care?"

"Remember what I named the ship? The Queen took everything from me, so now, I want to take what's most precious from
her. That is, before I kill her, of course."

Lucian would have laughed, but for the deadly seriousness
in her fiery green eyes.

"All I say, Lucian, is think about it. All of this is pointless if
we don't make it out of here alive. But I've heard it said that as
long as you know where you're going, you can make use of any
wind, favorable or unfavorable."

When she walked away, he let out a sigh of relief. She had
given him far too much to think about at a time where he was
least prepared to process it. He just wanted to get off this moon,
to hide out in a pleasant spot with plenty of food and water
until Vera picked him up.

But if everything Selene said was true, then Lucian couldn't do that. He had to go back to the place he least wanted to go. The thought made him sick to his stomach.

He reached for his Focus, feeling at each of his Orbs. Even holding them in his mind without streaming magic was a comfort to him, and he could set his fears aside. At least for now.

Selene was right about one thing. All of this was pointless to think about until they got out of the Burning Sands, and that was not guaranteed.

3

AS THE EVENING faded into night, they left the Spire well behind. The night was clear, a stroke of good luck. Despite the danger of piloting such a small, rickety vessel, Lucian felt something of a thrill as he allowed the ship to gain some altitude. As he created tether after tether, aiming for the top of each dune, he faced doubt. What if the Orb decided not to obey him?

He had to trust he was doing the right thing. The Orb wanted him to escape this place. At least, that was what he hoped.

The others clung to the railing as the vessel picked up speed. They were flying fast now—far faster than Lucian would have thought possible. Which made sense, given the power of the Orb of Binding and how little the skiff weighed compared to the *Zephyr*.

"Damn," Serah said. "At this rate, we'll be out of here in just a few days!"

Lucian had to temper her excitement. "Well, that's if I can keep this up. I'll do what I can, but my Focus has its limits."

"Pray those limits are high," Selene said. "We need to move

as quickly as possible. A storm can fall upon us at any moment."

Because of the sharp curvature of Psyche, the desert Spire was out of sight in less than fifteen minutes. Once up to full speed, it took little magic to maintain the *Vengeance's* course. Lucian had never held an active stream for hours on end, as Queen Ansaldra's Binders had aboard the *Zephyr*. He didn't know if there was a time limit to the Orb's power. For all he knew, it might shut off after a few hours of constant use. He supposed he'd learn the answer to that as they went.

From time to time, the sands below shifted from moonquakes, creating cascades of falling sand. That let Lucian know that, even without the heat, a journey overland would have been impossible. Setting the ship aground was simply not a possibility. He didn't trust himself to brand the ship to the sand overnight. He wasn't sure how stable it would be with the constant moonquakes. And so far, he hadn't seen so much as a stand of rocks around which they could tie their mooring lines. It was nowhere near time to stop, so maybe the landscape would change over the next few hours. They had to find something before dawn and hope the shade of the tarp kept them cool enough.

The journey was mostly quiet. Selene remained aft, sitting near the drop-off between two crates, seeming deep in thought. Fergus walked about the ship, doing inventory, while Serah also elected to sleep by the mainmast. And Lucian pulled the *Vengeance* from one starlight-dappled dune to another, under a sky dominated by Cupid above. The scene was beautiful, in a bleak and mournful way, and the breeze blew dry and cold. He stopped counting dunes after the first ten. This desert truly seemed to be endless. Without this ship, all of them would have been as good as dead.

Of course, they still could be if things went wrong.

Fergus joined him at the bow. He stared up at Cupid, its

bloodred eye staring down balefully. It was hard not to feel like the planet was alive, an omnipresent god somehow marking their moves.

"I don't know where to put down for the morning," Lucian said. "Dawn's a few hours away. If we don't find some rocks to tie the ship to, then I'm going to have to keep going in the heat."

"I've told Selene and Serah to rest. Between the two of them, they can hold a Thermal ward over us all day. You can travel by night and rest by day, and the women can stay awake in the day, warding us against the heat."

"Can they do that without murdering each other?"

Fergus chuckled darkly. "In that case, we might be doomed."

Lucian shook his head. "It's hard to say, but it'll probably take three more days to get out of these dunes. And in the end, it might not be the weather, wyverns, or moonquakes that kill us, but internal dissent."

Fergus shrugged. "Humanity has the nasty inclination to turn on itself when things get hard."

Before Lucian could respond, the dunes rumbled beneath. A great cloud of dust rose from the sand, but wouldn't reach high enough to cover the skiff.

"Selene and I had an interesting conversation last night," Lucian said. "I don't suppose she told you anything about that?"

"Not at all."

"Well, maybe you can tell Serah when you get the chance. After I'm done explaining, I'm probably going to be too tired."

"Sure. What did she tell you?"

Lucian told him then about *The Prophecy of the Seven* and her suggestion that it might be a good idea to get a hand on the Queen's translation because of its purity. Fergus's expression darkened, and once Lucian had finished, he shook his head.

"You *are* trying to get us killed, aren't you?"

"You haven't figured that out by now?"

THE CHOSEN OF THE MANIFOLD

"Well, I can't say you didn't warn me. Is it truly needed, though? Do you have any idea where these other Orbs are? Might your friend know? This . . . Vera."

"If she did, she probably would have grabbed them by now, don't you think?"

"Maybe." Fergus stared off into the distance. "Rotting hell. It *is* down to us, isn't it?"

"Seems like it. If Selene's right, then it's probably something we need to get. But no one's forcing us to do it. We have to decide for ourselves whether it's worth the risk."

Serah walked up to join them. "Whether what's worth the risk?"

"You should sleep," Fergus said.

"I can't," Serah said. "Besides, it's a beautiful night. What am I missing?"

When they caught her up, she chuckled.

"I *said* this would happen."

"Said what would happen?" Lucian asked.

"When I told you to finish the job back at the Spire. She's working for the Queen and wants to serve us up on a silver platter."

The thought *had* crossed Lucian's mind, but something about it didn't add up. "Why would she be helping someone who took full control of her? When she talked about the Queen, you can see how much she hates her. She named this ship the *Vengeance*, for rot's sake."

"There are other reasons she might want to help her," Fergus said. "Reasons that aren't clear because we lack information."

"Exactly," Serah said. "Lucian, if you go back to the Golden Palace, there is no help for you. I want no part of that."

"I never said I wanted to. It's just . . . a possibility."

"Please don't be stupid. Let's just find some place to wait for Vera. Otherwise, you're just going to get us killed."

"Nothing's decided yet," Lucian said. "I thought it was at least worth the discussion."

"This is what we do," Serah said. "We fly this rig past the Fire Rifts and find a nice source of water and food in the Westlands. All we have to do is wait a few months for Vera. No need to risk anything."

Lucian glanced toward the back of the skiff. Selene was still fast asleep. Was she just trying to play him, as Serah had said? That was probably the reason she had wanted to talk to him alone. Fergus and Serah were too skeptical to give her a chance.

"I wish Cleon were here," Lucian said. "He'd know what to do."

"Maybe," Serah said, though she sounded doubtful.

"*The Prophecy of the Seven* is real, all right," Fergus said. "Unless you think Elder Jalisa a scoundrel. She believed in it. While she doesn't own a translation that I'm aware of, she has deep knowledge of it. We could discuss the possibility of getting it, I suppose."

"We have to survive this, first," Serah said. "Otherwise that conversation is pointless."

"Progress is going well so far," Fergus said. "If we can just keep this up . . ."

Lucian looked out ahead at what appeared to be a line of mountains.

"Look," he said. "We've made it! That was quick."

Fergus's eyes widened. "Surely, we haven't come far enough yet. Something's wrong."

As Lucian stared at those mountains under the light of Cupid, he saw something *was* off. They were *moving*. And lightning was flashing within them.

"Sandstorm," Serah said. "It's running north to south as far as the eye can see. And coming this way."

"Turn around?" Lucian asked.

"Yes!" Serah said. "If we enter that, we're dead."

Selene, awakened by the others' elevated voices, approached. Her eyes instantly found the threat.

"We'll never outrun it," she said. "Turn south. If I'm remembering my maps correctly, a ridge of the Bone Mountains should extend this far west. That can shelter us."

"Are you fraying?" Serah asked. "There's nothing but dune out that way!"

"It's beyond the horizon," Selene said. "It's our only chance because there's nothing back the way we came, and certainly nothing to the north. South is the only option if we want to live."

Lucian didn't have time for arguing. He angled the *Vengeance* south, increasing the rate of his stream from the Orb of Binding. He'd need every bit of ether to race this ramshackle skiff across the Burning Sands.

4

AS THE SUN rose above the dust storm in the east, Lucian was beyond exhausted. The storm was nearing, perhaps a kilometer away. Even if they could have outrun it, Lucian's Focus was getting tapped out. Their only hope was getting beyond the horizon and in sight of the Bone Mountains. So far, there was not a sign of them. He knew it was a gamble. A big one. And it had to pay off, or everything was over.

"Come on," Lucian breathed.

He streamed more ether from the Orb, latching onto a distant dune and giving it all he had. The air skiff zoomed ahead, racing over the sand. The timbers beneath creaked under the strain. The wall of dust and lightning seemed to advance faster. They had minutes left, and there was still no sign of the mountains.

"We're dead," Serah said. "Dead!"

Lucian drew even more deeply of the Orb. Reality faded and was replaced by a matrix of blue streams, all of which converged on him, a shining blue light. Delving the Ethereal Background was a dangerous thing indeed, even with the Orb.

THE CHOSEN OF THE MANIFOLD

But he needed to tap into its power directly to have a chance of saving everyone on this ship.

He manipulated every one of those blue streams into a single, powerful blue tether. The skiff roared ahead, and he could only hope everyone was holding on to something. The wind became a din around his ears as the timbers of the deck groaned in protest, threatening to rip apart. The helium envelope dragged at its lines, straining them and threatening to break loose. He couldn't keep this up forever, but there was no other way to escape the storm.

The sun shone down hot from above, and the storm was just a few hundred meters away.

And on the horizon, Lucian could see the first sign of the mountains, the barely perceptible sharp points of their peaks.

"There!" he shouted.

He reached with everything to bridge the distance between the ship and the closest peak. To his surprise, he found a focal point there. If he could just stream harder, get enough magic into the tether, they would make it.

That was when the Ethereal Background itself fell away, replaced by a dark plane. A dark plane where Lucian stood alone in a world of silence. There was nothing here—only himself, his thoughts, his body, and a nameless fear. Something watched him from this darkness, a dread he knew very well.

He had delved too deep.

Too much, the Voice taunted. *You are still too weak to be playing with so much magic.*

Go away.

It's too late. The Orbs will not suffer your insolence. Not for long. I will let you leave this prison . . . but only because I need you. Always remember. The Orbs belong to me. It is your lot to gather them. Play your part. You've sealed your word to me. Never forget that . . .

Lucian screamed as the darkness departed, returning him to the deck of the *Vengeance* to find a scene of chaos.

Wind and sand ripped across the deck. Fergus, tied to the mainmast, held onto Lucian to keep him from flying away. Serah and Selene had tied themselves to the second mast, barely visible from the sand blowing sideways. Looking above, Lucian could see the envelope had punctured and that the ship was going down. But such was the force of the wind that it didn't matter. They were being carried somewhere, somewhere far away, at the wind's complete mercy. Timbers split from the deck while crates dislodged despite their lashings. The railing and supporting banisters peeled off, one by one, the storm of sand carrying them away forever. Every minute that passed, there was less boat than the minute before and more sand.

How long they endured that hell, Lucian didn't know. But eventually, the wind lessened and the not-so-aptly named *Vengeance* began going down. The bow pitched forward into the maelstrom.

By this point, Fergus had somehow tied Lucian to the mast with him. There was nothing left but to hope that when they landed, they wouldn't do so too roughly. And perhaps a rough landing would be better because at least that death had the potential of being quick.

But Lucian could leave nothing to chance. He reached for the Orb of Psionics, hoping to create some repelling force around the skiff right at the moment of impact. But his Focus refused to work. Whatever he had done with the Orb of Binding, he had exhausted himself. All he could do was hope for the best.

When the ship hit, Lucian closed his eyes, perhaps for the last time in his life.

WHEN LUCIAN CAME TO, the full heat of the day was baking him from above. The tarp had been the first thing to go. His skin broiled under the intense radiation; the day hadn't progressed long enough for Cupid to eclipse the sun. He struggled against his ropes and couldn't undo the knot. Fergus would have to do that, but he seemed to be knocked out.

Or worse.

"Fergus." Lucian's voice came out at a rasp. "Wake up. We need to get moving."

When there was no response, a cold tendril of dread snaked in his stomach.

He stamped on Fergus's boot, and to his relief, the big man jerked, hacking a few times.

"Confound this blasted dust!"

"Fergus! Untie us. We need to find some shade."

"Yes, I know that," he rasped. A moment later, his hand emitted a thin green laser that instantly cut the ropes. Lucian broke free.

His first instinct was to check on the others. He found Selene struggling against her restraints, her pale skin already flushed from the desert heat. Serah's head lolled forward, her mouth agape and lips parched.

"Just a minute," Lucian said. "Fergus, can you—"

There was no need to finish. Fergus cut the thick rope with another laser. Selene fell forward into Fergus's arms before she hastily stood on her own two feet. Despite the sunburn, she seemed fine. Serah, however, didn't wake up as Lucian caught her. He checked for a pulse. There was a heartbeat, steady and sure. Just knocked out, then.

"Alive," he said. "We need to assess this damage, get it back into the air . . ."

Selene scoffed. "With what helium? All of it's gone."

Still holding Serah, Lucian just now noted his surroundings. The *Vengeance's* two masts had broken in the middle, while half of the canvas envelope had splayed out behind them, still partly connected to the masts with whatever rigging that remained. The other half was somewhere out there in the desert, and the helium it held was long gone. Only a few of the crates they had secured remained. Three, by Lucian's count.

Now, the *Vengeance*, if they could still call it that with no sense of irony, was just a raft on a flat expanse of sand stretching as far as the eye could see. The position of the sun told him it was midmorning, and the relief that would come from it slipping behind Cupid was still hours off. The day was already unbearably hot, but it still wasn't as hot as it had been by the Spire. Wherever they were, this was probably no longer the Burning Sands.

"Selene, could you get a Thermal ward set up?"

Reluctantly, she streamed a thin ward around the four of them, barely enough to cover everything. Lucian suppressed the urge to chew her out for being so stingy with her magic. But he had other things to worry about.

"Serah. Are you okay? Talk to me."

When Fergus splashed some water on her face, she blinked drearily.

"Drink," Fergus said.

Serah accepted the canteen gratefully. Because of the Thermal ward, the surrounding air had cooled somewhat.

"Where *are* we?" Serah asked.

Selene looked over the railing, placing a hand over her eyes to block the sun. "I have some idea."

"I don't see the mountains," Fergus said. "Where are they?"

"It would appear the storm carried us quite a distance south."

She went to the rear of the skiff and lightly stepped out onto the sand. Instantly, she sank. She hurriedly pulled her foot back, nearly losing her dirtied slipper.

"Yes, as I thought," she said. "It would appear we're somewhere adrift on the Sandsea."

"The Sandsea?" Lucian asked.

"It's said to lay south of the Burning Sands, but farther west than the Bone Mountains. So that storm must have blown us southwest."

"Southwest?" Serah asked. "That would mean we've *lost* progress!"

"It would appear so," Selene said.

"How much progress?" Lucian asked.

Looking around, Selene shook her head. "Hard to say. Looks like the Sandsea is all around us, so I'd hazard to guess we got blown pretty far off course. We didn't reach the mountains in time."

That much was obvious. "How do we get out of here, then? Will this raft sink? And which way is east?"

"Well, left of Cupid's eye is always east. That's how we get out of here if indeed we can even move. As for sinking, I can't say. It would appear the raft has enough surface area to float, thankfully."

Lucian looked east but saw nothing but a flat expanse of undulating sand in that direction, as well as waves of heat that made it difficult to see. "I've got nothing solid to tether us to. How are we supposed to move?"

"We must abandon the boat," Fergus said, getting ready to hop the railing.

Selene grabbed him by the arm. "I wouldn't do that if I were you. The sand is so fine you'll sink right to the very bottom. If there even *is* a bottom."

Lucian looked over the side to see that sand almost *eddying* as if it was water. It was probably some combination of extremely fine sand and low gravity. It was downright eerie to look at. As Selene had said, the raft must have only floated because of its wide base.

"We're stranded," Serah said.

"Some sails are still connected to the masts," Lucian said. "Can't we use them to catch a breeze?"

"With what wind?" Fergus asked.

Fergus was right. The air was utterly calm as if there had been no sandstorm at all.

"It might not always be windless," Lucian said. "We can take the canvas of the torn envelope and stretch it out. Is there a way to create wind with magic?"

"We'd have to create low air pressure on the side of the sail in the direction we want to go," Selene said. "We could also create a gravity point a few meters away from the bow."

"A gravity point?" Serah asked. "I'll fray if I try such a thing for a long time, and my ether supply isn't enough to brand it. I don't have the rotting Orb of Gravitonics."

Selene shrugged. "Just trying to help."

Serah's face went even redder, but she said nothing.

Fergus cleared his throat. "We have to figure out a solution that uses one of Lucian's Orbs. Both Serah and Selene will need to take turns with the Thermal ward, at least until the eclipse."

"That leaves Binding and Psionics," Lucian said. "The surface of this Sandsea seems much too unsteady to tether."

"Why not diffuse the focal point to disperse the weight?" Fergus asked. "That's how this raft is floating, after all."

Yes, that was an idea. Creating a wider focal point would use more ether, but there was also less boat to pull along.

"I can give that a try," Lucian said. He looked at Selene. "How long can you hold your Thermal ward?"

Her face was showing some signs of strain. "Maybe another hour or two. Serah and I will need to work in shifts."

"Why not work in confluence?" Fergus asked.

"Not on your rotting life," Serah said.

Lucian didn't want to counter that. It would be easier on both of them, but it required mutual trust. There was no way in the Worlds either of them would let the other control their stream.

"We need to go east," Lucian said. "And unless I miss my guess, we should hit these Bone Mountains we saw earlier. Eventually."

"Well, it's not like we have anything else to go on," Serah said.

"What's south and what's west of here?" Lucian asked.

Selene shook her head. "South will give you more of this for a thousand kilometers before you hit the Sea of Eros. West will just take you back into the Burning Sands. Same for the north."

"The Sea of Eros?" Lucian said. "At least it's water."

"We'll run out of water long before we reach it," Selene said. "And the Sea of Eros is just as dangerous as the Rift Sea and the Burning Sands, if not more so. Our only hope is east."

"Well, we better get started, then."

Lucian reached for the Orb of Binding, creating a focal point far wider than what he was used to. That took a lot of magic, and his mind reeled at having to use so much. His Focus felt . . . *slippery*, unable to hold on to the massive stream effectively. But there was no other choice. If they didn't get moving, and soon, they would die out here. The tension in the tether held, and the raft glided across the fluid surface of the Sandsea, creating a wake of ripples.

They proceeded in this way for several hours, Lucian always feeling as if he was about to reach his limit. But he kept pushing on, knowing he had no choice. When the sun dipped behind Cupid, it lent a great deal of reprieve, and the temperature dropped at least twenty degrees centigrade. They would have a couple of hours of shade before the sun emerged from the planet's other side. The eclipse illuminated Cupid's rim with orange radiance, revealing stars that would have normally stayed hidden during the day.

Cupid's eye was only barely visible, as the planet was

mostly dark. Lucian continued to stream the raft across the Sandsea. The surface more viscous than water, producing a great deal of drag. But at least they were making progress—however slowly.

Fergus broke Lucian from his concentration. "I just did an inventory of our supplies. We probably have water for a week with careful rationing, and food for two weeks."

Lucian nodded. "Better than I expected." He glanced up at the canvas envelope, which was flapping uselessly. "If there's no wind out here, maybe we can turn it into a tarp. Anything that gives us a bit of shade."

"I'll see that we get started on that." He looked around at the fine, shifting sand. "It's hard to tell just how fast we're moving. Or how far we have to go. Can you keep this up for seven days, potentially?"

Lucian felt a tinge of annoyance. It seemed Fergus was doubting his abilities. But before he could say as much, he realized that his harsh reaction made little sense. Fergus was only concerned about his well-being.

Lucian's shoulders sagged, especially as he remembered the Voice talking to him during his delving. "I'm tired, Fergus. I won't lie. I know the Orb can supply the power. The only question is, can I stream it?"

"You must do whatever it takes to survive. Just as each of us must."

Lucian knew he was right. As much as he hated to admit it, he wished he had taken the Sorceress-Queen's lessons more seriously. If he had asked more questions, had tried to learn, he might be up to the task. But he had let his stubbornness get in the way.

He cleared his mind, trying to remove all extraneous doubt. He allowed everything to burn away until nothing remained but his Focus, the Septagon through which all magic flowed. He thought back to what the Queen had told him. Efficiency mattered. It wasn't only raw power that gave a mage strength. It was Focus. It was proficiency. And as Vera had taught, it was also about having an unassailable base of beliefs that emotion or circumstance could not shake.

What did he want? To escape, yes. But deeper than that, what was he doing it all for? He didn't desire the power of the Orbs, but no one could take that burden away from him. No one he trusted, anyway.

He thought of Emma. If he could escape this world, he might someday see her again. Mixed in those thoughts was Serah, too. Serah, who he wanted to keep safe. Serah, for whom he had growing feelings. Where did she fit into all this?

It was all so confusing, and besides, there was no point in thinking about it at the moment. There were bigger concerns to address.

"Does anyone else see that?" Fergus asked, pointing into the distance. "Looks like some sort of pole or something."

Lucian strained his eyes, but couldn't make out anything. He realized from Fergus's normally dark eyes, now glowing green, that he was using Radiance to see.

"I see nothing," Serah said, joining them at the bow. "Maybe Lucian can Bind it."

"I can't Bind it if I can't see it."

"True enough," she said. "Do the usual? Set a beacon on it, Fergus."

"It'll come into view soon enough."

Fergus's eyes resumed their normal brown color. Ten minutes later, they became green again as he sought the pole.

"It's gone!"

Lucian looked at him, confused. "What do you mean, gone? We haven't shifted course, have we?"

"No, I'm looking right where it's supposed to be. There's nothing."

"There it is!" Serah said. "Off to the south."

Everyone turned in that direction, to see something that looked like a pole sticking out of the sand, almost as far as the horizon.

"It wasn't there before," Fergus said. "What in the Worlds could it be?"

Selene's face had become pale or perhaps strained from her holding the Thermal ward earlier, which she had let lapse since the beginning of the eclipse.

"What?" Lucian asked. "Don't leave us in suspense."

"I've heard stories of the Wyrms of the Sandsea," she said. "I only thought them to be wild tales. Things my father told us as children by the fireside."

"Wyrms?" Serah asked. "You're joking."

Lucian's eyes went back to the "wyrm," only to find that it was no longer there. For the creature to be that tall at that distance, it must have been large indeed.

"Animals *live* here?"

"Yes," Selene said, coming to join them. "Stonefish, mostly. But the wyrm is the most dangerous predator this side of Psyche. People hunted them to extinction, at least in the Westlands. But beyond the Bone Mountains, things become hazier. Wilder."

"So, are we dead?" Fergus asked.

Selene watched him, unflappable and unfazed. "Probably."

5

5

AS LUCIAN TETHERED them toward the eastern horizon, the wyrm only drew nearer, clearly stalking them. The thing was faster than Lucian could pull the raft. Within minutes, it would be close enough to strike.

"Ideas on how to stop it?" Lucian asked, trying to keep fear from creeping into his voice.

"My laser shall tear it to shreds," Fergus said.

"You can't stream a laser powerful enough to rend a wyrm," Selene said. "You might chip away at its rocky exterior, but not much else."

"I'll blind it, then."

"It's said they don't see properly, so it would probably have little effect," Selene said. "They detect tremors in the sand. Likely, our position is being broadcast to every wyrm in the area."

Lucian scanned each of the four horizons, but so far it seemed as if this wyrm was the only one. And it was tall. The portion sticking above the fine sand was a dozen meters, at least. It arced in and out of the smooth sand, making directly for the raft.

"It's too large for me to hurt with my Gravity Magic," Serah said.

"I have an idea," Selene said, utterly calm. "But it depends on getting the monster directly behind the raft."

At the speed that thing was going, Lucian knew it would be a tall order. "What's your idea?"

Already, Selene was acting. "I need water. All of it."

"*All* our water?" Fergus asked, aghast. "What for?"

"There's no time to explain."

Serah and Fergus fetched the water, which was gathered in a single barrel that had somehow remained intact and onboard, while Selene was doing something that made even less sense than her previous order—she was ripping off all the gems on her dress. Lucian watched in shock as all of them came off—pearls, rubies, and diamonds. Such was her ferocity that she even tore the fabric away at points.

"What are you doing?" Lucian asked.

Selene ignored him as she separated the diamonds from the rest of the gems. Fergus and Serah returned with about ten canteens of water, adding them to the barrel. Selene dropped the diamonds into the water, her face a study of intense concentration.

"I'm not even going to ask," Serah said.

"Carbon, hydrogen, oxygen, nitrogen," she said. "All of it accounted for. I can set a brand behind the ship. I designed the brand to take those four elements and bond them into as much TNT as possible. It should all happen in a millisecond. Then, Serah, I'm going to need you to light it the instant the wyrm is over it."

Lucian's eyes popped. "You can do that?"

"Can you light it on my word, Serah?"

Serah nodded. "Yeah. No problem."

Selene turned back to Lucian. "You need to speed up the raft. The wyrm is on a course to intercept us. It needs to be behind us if this is to work."

Looking to the south, Lucian could see that much was true. The wyrm was now close for them to see its dark gray coloring, along with the tall spikes lining its back. Its head was rocky and angular, a giant spike protruding from its head. There was no evidence of it having any eyes.

Lucian drew as much ether as he could from the Orb and pulled the skiff faster. If he drew any more, he would delve again, something he couldn't afford unless circumstances forced him. He never wanted to hear the dark Voice again.

Looking to the south, the skiff was gaining some distance on the wyrm. But Lucian's Focus strained with the effort. He couldn't keep this up forever, and already his vision was darkening from the pressure.

"That's it," Selene said. "It's falling in behind us now."

Lucian chanced a look behind to see the wyrm not a hundred meters away. It dove in and out of the fluid sand, completely silent in its approach. That was more terrifying to Lucian. If it were dark, they might have never known it was coming. It seemed a monster of this size should cry out and roar, but all it did was chase them down relentlessly.

"We have one shot at this," Selene said. "Get ready."

She stood at the stern with the barrel. The diamonds from Selene's dress would supply the carbon necessary to create the TNT, while the water would supply hydrogen and oxygen. Oxygen was also naturally abundant in Psyche's atmosphere, along with nitrogen. Lucian wasn't sure how Atomicism worked, but it seemed a powerful Aspect indeed that it could take all these different objects and recreate them into a volatile explosive using a single brand.

The wyrm's posture changed as it neared the skiff. Its long neck shot out of the sand, extending rapidly toward the back of the boat. Its mouth opened, revealing rows of knife-like teeth and an elongated, forked tongue. The mouth became level with the surface of the sand, widening as it zoomed nearer the raft.

Selene threw the barrel overboard, and it became wrapped in an aura of orange light. It bobbed for a moment on the surface of the sand. The open mouth of the Sand Snake would swallow it in moments.

"Now!"

Serah shot a fireball. It flew across the surface of the sand, hitting the orange-tinged barrel at the exact moment the wyrm swallowed it. For a moment, Lucian thought Serah had missed. But then a massive explosion resounded, blowing the wyrm's head apart. Chips of rock and bone flew into the air as a wave of heat blasted outward, pummeling the back of the raft as fire and heat bloomed upward. Though the explosion had obliterated the snake's head, the momentum of its long, massive body caused it to dive deeply into the sand, creating a wave of sand that rose to carry the raft with it. Lucian watched in awe as the body, at least fifty meters long slowly sank into the depths of the Sandsea.

"I . . . can't believe that worked," Selene said.

Serah and Fergus watched, too shocked for words. Lucian wanted to let go of the Orb and allow his Focus a break, but he knew he couldn't do that. That explosion would draw every wyrm in the Sandsea right to their position.

"Good work," he said. "Let's hope there's not any more of them."

Everyone gathered at the bow, Selene hobbling with exhaustion. Whatever she had done, it had taken a lot of magic. For once, no one was arguing, and the four of them stood united. Lucian supposed almost dying had a way of doing that.

"Up ahead," Fergus said.

Lucian's stomach dropped. "What now?"

Fergus flashed a toothy grin. "Salvation."

Lucian peered into the distance. Though it was hazy, he could see a long line of spikes extending from north to south. It could be nothing other than mountain peaks.

Lucian heaved a sigh of relief. "Why'd you have to word it like that? You nearly gave me an aneurysm."

"The Bone Mountains," Selene said. "Passing through them will not be easy by any means. They are as far as anyone on Psyche dares to go."

"What does that make us, then?" Serah asked. "The most daring of all time?"

"I'm just saying there may be people there, however few," Selene said. "And probably not the kind you want to meet. Exiles, ruffians, hermits on the edge of society."

"You never said why they're called the Bone Mountains," Lucian said.

She shrugged. "Their shape, mostly. The mountains are tall and spindly, many rising to a wicked point. They resemble a ribcage with the points sticking up. And they are what we have to pass to reach the Fire Rifts."

"And beyond that, the Westlands," Serah said. She narrowed her eyes. "I think I can see them now."

Lucian supposed the Sandsea would end soon enough. He couldn't say he would miss it.

———

THEY PULLED THE RAFT "ASHORE," where the fluid sand ended and rippled out onto the black, volcanic rock. And that rock extended for kilometers toward the Bone Mountains rising in the east.

Lucian saw what Selene had meant about them looking like a ribcage. Their slopes were long, curved, angled upward toward cruel points. They crowded against each other, forming a solid wall running from north to south as far as the eye could see. It reminded Lucian of the Mountains of Madness, but these were nowhere near as tall. He wondered what tectonic conditions produced mountains like these. They didn't seem natural at all.

"Well, we have a day of water left, give or take," Fergus said, dragging the last of their supplies. "Turns out we missed a couple of canteens, lucky for us. We still have food for about two weeks." He scanned his surroundings, his chest heaving from exertion.

Lucian's throat was already dry. "Food is less of a concern than water. Maybe we can all have a drink now. I'd say we earned it."

"Don't worry about water," Selene said. "Food is the main issue."

"What do you mean, don't worry about water?" Fergus asked.

She looked at everyone, her expression matter-of-fact. "When you urinate, do so in an empty container. Urine is ninety-five percent water. That should last us a while."

Serah's expression widened, horrified. "You want us to drink our piss?"

Selene scoffed. "Of course not. Filtering out everything that *isn't* water is elementary for an Atomicist. That should make our reserves last a little longer. It might taste . . . strange, but it will be pure water. Of that, I assure you."

Lucian couldn't help but smirk. "Sounds like you're speaking from experience."

Her cheeks colored. "I've read reports. Nothing more."

"Sure you have. How come you didn't mention this earlier?"

"It's a matter of last resort. Any use of magic can be taxing, especially creating enough water for four people. Anyway, shouldn't we get moving?"

"As soon as we divvy out these supplies, yes," Fergus said.

"I've already packed most of the food. For our clothing, unfortunately, we must continue wearing what we have."

Lucian looked at Selene's tattered dress with pity. If he had something for her to cover with, he would have given it to her. She'd roast alive under the cruel sun once it emerged from behind Cupid, which could happen at any moment.

"We'll just have to find shelter during the day like we've been doing," he said. "At any moment, the sun's going to show up. Thankfully, it won't be too long in setting after that, but I'd rather avoid the sun if possible."

It might have been Lucian's imagination, but it felt as if Cupid's position had somewhat shifted in the sky. Rather than being directly above them, it was now more off to the west compared to when they had been at the Spire. It wasn't much, but it was progress.

Once Fergus had distributed the packs, the four of them faced the distant, spindly mountains, rising high under the eclipsed starlight. Lucian looked back at the ramshackle skiff. Beaten and nearly falling apart, he supposed that it had held up well, despite its appearance.

Despite their exhaustion, they headed east in search of shelter.

6

THEY MADE it nowhere near the mountains by the time the sun reappeared, but the evening air did much to filter out its heat. No longer in the Burning Sands, the sun was not as harsh.

They traveled on an upward trajectory across rough flats of igneous rock made from some lava flow in the distant past. Or at least, what Lucian *hoped* was the distant past. Smoke tinged the upper peaks of the Bone Mountains, smoke that might be coming from volcanoes. Psyche was known for its tectonic activity, especially in the Fire Rifts. Those would be just beyond these mountains.

Lucian wasn't sure how they would cross those. He remembered passing them over in the *Zephyr*. The hellish cracks in the ground had been a curiosity and gone after a couple of hours, a mere blip in their journey west. Unfortunately, that wouldn't be the case going east.

As the sun went down, they sought an overhang to shelter in. When Lucian collapsed on the ground, completely spent, everyone else joined him. All fell asleep right there, heedless of anything but their need for rest.

LUCIAN WOKE up to the first rays of light stretching across the shadowy, hellish land before him. On the horizon, he could see the smooth line of the Sandsea, though there was no sign of their skiff. It would only be a tiny dot on that expanse. They were probably halfway into the mountains by now, and Lucian couldn't wait until they had left the dreaded sands of Psyche behind for good.

He got started on the cooking. It felt wrong to use water as a base for the morning soup, but Selene had said she could make more. Making water from urine was more than disgusting, but he had to trust her word on that. Unless they happened upon a freshwater source, it was just a fact of life.

The aroma of soup awakened the others. From time to time, one of them would take the piss jug and go off into the morning to take care of business. They would get quite the collection soon enough. Eventually, that stash would run out, and they would have to find a source of potable water. Even if hydrogen was the most abundant element in the universe, it was in short supply on Psyche outside its small bodies of water, which were hundreds of miles away. Selene and her Elemental Sensing had detected none so far, and until she did, piss water was their only choice.

Lucian was hazy on the details of Atomicism, but he remembered how Talents Isaac and Hamil had turned a plain stone into a nugget of pure gold. He knew the greater the difference of one element from another, the harder it was to transmute. Permanent transmutation was the hardest of all. The only way he could see her creating water was by finding a decent amount of lithium in the surrounding igneous rock, which Selene *might* flux into hydrogen long enough to bond it with the oxygen in the atmosphere.

Then again, all of that sounded complicated and beyond

Lucian's reckoning. It felt bad having to rely on Selene for practically everything, but it made him glad he had spared her life. Without her, they would still be in the Burning Sands, and perhaps even dead.

They ate quietly, each making sure to slurp every drop of broth they could. Lucian was still thirsty, but rationing as they were, there was nothing to be done about that.

All they could do was head east. Head east, and hope to find water.

They scrambled up rock faces for the next couple of hours, which was exhausting and backbreaking work. The sun was hot, but not torturously so in the higher elevation. Once they were halfway into the foothills leading into the Bone Mountains, Selene paused.

"I'm sensing some water nearby," she said. "I think over there."

She pointed toward the south. Lucian followed her finger but saw nothing but mountains and black rock.

"You sure?"

"Fairly sure. If we walk a couple of hours that way, I'll be even more sure."

"Lead the way, Selene," Fergus said.

They fell in behind her as she picked a path across the roughened rock. That she was still *going* after all this told Lucian she was no soft noble. The Queen had likely selected her for her innate strength along with her magical talents. Even with the tattered dress and impractical, jewel-sequined slippers, she set a fast pace. Lucian was having trouble keeping up with her.

From time to time, Serah would bridge the larger gaps with antigravity discs. As they made the distance, Selene became even surer.

"There's a promising source of water over here," she said. "We're getting close."

"Could you teach me how to sense elements?" Lucian asked.

She pursed her lips. "I would not. Atomicism is dangerous magic, and I've seen the way you've handled your Orbs. There is no room for carelessness."

"That's . . . harsh."

He heard Serah's voice in his head. *She just doesn't want you to kill her with it.*

That makes no sense. I could kill her anyway if I wanted!

She's not on our side, in case you haven't figured that out. Do you think she'd just give up her secrets for no reason? That's the only thing she has over us. It gives her power.

Lucian saw what she meant. And as much as he hated to admit it, it *was* a smart move on Selene's part. It kept her indispensable.

The four of them crested a rise and immediately ducked when they saw what was on the other side. Lucian got a flash of a small stone home, nothing more. And a thin stream running beside it.

"Someone's *living* out here?" he asked.

"Like I said," Selene said, "this is as far as human habitation goes. And it's only people that are not accepted in Westland society. Frays, criminals, Burners. People you would rather not meet."

"Well, we need that water," Lucian asked. "Is anyone home?"

"I can have a look," Fergus said. He poked his head above the rise, scanning the other side for a moment. "Only infrared signature is a fire inside the cabin. Nothing in the shape of a human body."

"So he could be anywhere," Lucian said.

"Or she," Serah said.

As they were deciding what to do, Lucian heard the last sound he expected. And it reminded him of the sheer terror of his first night on the Mad Moon. Everyone's eyes widened as the wyvern shriek rebounded off the cliff faces. It was impossible to tell just where it was coming from, but it seemed close.

"No shelter out here," Serah said. "Looks like it's going to be a fight."

"We could stay hidden," Lucian said.

"It would smell us out," Fergus said. "Best to meet this head-on and hope for the best."

Lucian didn't like those prospects. In tandem, the four stood at the top of the ridge. There, they saw the wyvern approaching from the direction of the mountains and heading right toward them, black wings spread wide and long neck extended. It seemed to catch a whiff of them, angling for a direct attack.

Lucian reached for his Focus. He had no choice but to face what was coming, to kill the creature that would surely kill him.

"Wait," Fergus said. "Someone's riding it!"

"What?"

Lucian kept hold of his Focus but streamed nothing. Fergus was right. Someone *was* on the wyvern's back, leaning forward into the beast so as not to fall.

And that wyvern wasn't coming for them. It was simply landing beside the stone house next to the stream. And now the rider was sliding off. He wore a plain gray cloak and bore a shockspear, though, at a distance, Lucian could tell he was an elderly man. He had a wrinkled face, and his beard was long, gray, and scraggly.

And the wyvern stood directly behind him, its violet eyes glowing.

"It's Psionically possessed," Lucian said.

Selene raised her hands, which instantly became wrapped in orange light. "What are we waiting for?"

"No!" Lucian shouted.

He reached for the Orb of Psionics, and by sheer instinct,

THE CHOSEN OF THE MANIFOLD

formed a block around her Focus. The orange glow surrounding her hands was extinguished. Her eyes widened, and her face became a mask of affront.

"What are you doing?" she screeched. "We're at his mercy now!"

"He hasn't attacked us," Lucian said. "Not yet. If he wanted to hurt us, he would have already."

"Fool," Selene said. "*No one* out here is friendly. The worst of the worst live beyond the Bone Mountains and the Fire Rifts!"

"Lucian's right," Serah said. "He hasn't attacked us yet. But he sure as hell will if we take the first shot."

Selene seethed, balling her hands into fists. But she didn't offer a counterpoint.

"I'll talk to him," Lucian said. "I'm the one risking our necks, after all."

"We all go," Fergus said. "We're all in this together."

Selene's face was red, either from anger or sun exposure. "If you wish to kill yourselves, be my guest."

Could Selene be right? Lucian couldn't doubt himself now. He just wasn't going to kill someone unless they tried to kill him. For all he knew, this man might be a help to them and was powerful, judging by how he controlled that wyvern.

Lucian started down the slope, heading in the man's direction, who remained standing by his beast, completely still.

7

WHEN LUCIAN APPROACHED, he resisted the urge to place his hand on his retracted shockspear. He wanted to reach for the man's Focus, if only to get a feel for his primary if not outright block him. Elder Erymmo had mentioned it was possible to do that. But the man might perceive that as an attack.

If this man was powerful enough to control a wyvern, it was safe to say he was probably a Psionic. Lucian already had Psionics warded, knowing full well that the Queen was out there and looking for him. He strengthened his ward, all the same, streaming more magic from the Orb of Psionics. The positive glow of magic surrounding him steadied his nerves.

One thing he had discovered was that the Orbs did not make brands and wards more powerful, per se. They only did so as long as he held the Orb. As soon as he let go of the Orb, a ward or brand would lose all the strength the Orb rendered. For the most part, he had to rely on his inner strength when working with passive streams.

Lucian committed most of his ether to the ward, wanting to

be sure this man couldn't beat him. He could always draw more with the Orb of Psionics if need be. To Psionically control a wyvern, the man's possession brand must have been powerful indeed, or at least something designed with great skill. Lucian wanted to scan the Psionic brand controlling the wyvern with his Focus, to learn how he might do such a thing himself. But the man might perceive that as a threat, too, and it was a breach of decorum to do that without permission. It was about as bad as seeing someone naked.

It didn't seem the man was testing Lucian's ward. He was utterly calm as he waited beside his wyvern, wearing nothing but a dusty, travel-worn cloak.

Serah and Fergus were right behind, and Lucian hoped neither of them was trying to feel him out. Lucian hoped his ward would be enough to cover all three of them. Selene was out of sight behind the hill, safe from direct magical attacks.

"This is close enough," Fergus said quietly. "He can send that wyvern right at us."

The thought hadn't escaped Lucian. But unheeding, he stepped closer. The wyvern was even larger up close. From its talons to the top of its pointed head, it was at least ten meters—far longer than the two that had attacked Lucian. Serah's eyes widened, her face pale despite the heat of the day. Even Fergus's hand was trembling as he clenched his shockspear tighter. The hooded old man remained still as a statue.

Lucian stopped, leaving about twenty meters of space between them. He had to remind himself that the man was the threat, not the wyvern. But the wyvern was so large that its shadow fell across the three of them. It gazed emptily, its only movements coming from its ribcage, from where it drew breath.

Lucian knew he had taken a dangerous gamble. Even with the Orbs, this could end badly.

"Lost?" the old man called out.

That booming voice took him by surprise almost as much
as a roar from the wyvern would have.

"Something like that."

"I haven't seen a party of Seekers come out this way in years.
If you're looking for the materials to sail the Sandsea, I haven't
got them. They felled the last trees years ago."

"We're not going to the Sandsea. We're coming from it."

Fergus looked at Lucian a moment, giving him a look of
warning he didn't understand.

The man squinted at them. "*From*? Then you've gone
farther than most. How did you outsail the Great Wyrm?"

"We killed him," Lucian said. "One of us used an atomic
brand."

The man grunted. "If that's true, then you are more capable
than most. The Great Wyrm eats almost every party of Seekers
that sets out from these shores. My humble home is the last
stop before their eventual deaths." He looked up at his wyvern
companion. "Some have tried to tame these wyverns to fly
across, but none can weave a possession brand like mine for
these beasts. And even if they did, wyverns have no interest in
going beyond the shores of the Sandsea."

"It's impressive that you're riding one," Lucian said, hoping
the conversation would turn away from himself. This old-timer
seemed to understand much from little information. If he
already thought them a group of Seekers, and he knew they
had come *from* the Sandsea, it might not take him long to
conclude that they had found the Orb of Psionics. "How did
you come to live out here?"

He shrugged. "That's a long story, and I won't tell it until I'm
sure of you. This spot is the best on this side of the mountains,
as far as I've explored. There's water, and food if you know
where to find it. Akhekh here certainly makes hunting in the
mountains easier." He peered up at the hill behind the three of
them. "Why is your friend hiding?"

"She thinks you're going to kill us," Serah said.

"Yes. I felt her streaming earlier. I could sense her power. So, the one who blocked her must be even more so." His eyes went to Lucian, but thankfully he didn't press the point. "Don't mind Akhekh. He's been with me for a while, now. He won't do anything without my consent. As far as myself: my name's Jagar. Some call me Old Jagar, but I ended up outliving most of them. So, the joke's on them."

"I'm Lucian," he said. "This is Serah and Fergus."

Jagar gave a grim smile as he eyed the top of the rise again. "Go get your friend. Tell her I'm prepared to forgive her, as these parts can be dangerous. I have plenty of food and water, provided you don't make a nuisance of yourselves. If you tell me a bit about your travels and give me enough news to sate my curiosity, then I'll consider that payment enough. I get little in the way of visitors out here ever since the Seekers stopped coming ten years ago."

"You have our thanks," Lucian said. "We'll be back with Selene."

"I'll be here," Jagar said.

———

IT TOOK some convincing to make Selene see sense. Only then did Lucian unblock her, an action which would take her a while to forgive him for. If at all.

When all four walked into the cleft with the stream and tiny cabin, the wyvern was still there, standing beside the house like a guardian, seeming to not want to move for anything. Did Jagar *always* have a possession brand active on the monster? He would have had to. It would be nice if all four of them had wyverns to fly, but Lucian didn't know if he had the stomach for it. Holding *four* possession brands was probably well beyond his abilities, especially considering those brands would be limited to his natural pool of ether unless he held the Orb of Psionics the entire time.

They stood before the entrance of Jagar's house, the stones uneven and mortared with mud. The "door" was nothing more than a screen of reeds hanging from the frame. There was no way to knock, so Lucian brushed them aside to reveal a small, cozy space with a central hearth surrounded by several wooden stools. A small cot lay in the right corner, while an assortment of bronze tools and weapons hung on the wall—a variety of hammers, a saw, several spears and bows and quivers of arrows, a hoe, a pickaxe, a scythe, among other instruments. Jagar had lived here a while and intended to stay. That much was clear.

Remembering what Selene had said, Lucian wondered if this Jagar was an exile, and if so, what he had done to earn the punishment of living far beyond the edge of civilization.

"Make yourselves at home," he said. "Might be a bit before I have something fit for eating."

His voice was raspy and weak because of his age or lack of use. Lucian had experienced the latter after his months-long term on the prison barge. To his shock, he realized all that had happened two weeks ago. It seemed like a lifetime after everything they had gone through.

They took up the stools, Selene most tentatively of all. Jagar did not comment on the tattered state of her clothes. He dug in a chest for a moment and retrieved an old cloak. Not rich vestments, and travel-stained, but well-woven.

"You'll burn alive without the proper cover out there."

For a moment, it looked as if she might not accept. In the end, though, she gave a terse nod before throwing the cloak over her bare, sunburned shoulders.

That action alone told Lucian everything he needed to know about Jagar. At least for now.

"Thanks for taking us in."

Jagar shrugged. "No need. Something any decent person would do."

"Survival must be hard out here," Serah said. "That you've made it work is impressive."

He shrugged again. It seemed to be his default expression. "It's a life. Peaceful. Quiet."

Jagar seemed to be a man of few words, which was fine. He spent the next few minutes throwing ingredients in the pot hanging over the low flame, which contained a random assortment of vegetables and a few pieces of freshly butchered meat. Much like the stewpot at the Volsung Academy, it seemed to rarely, if ever, come off the fire.

Lucian ended up dozing, even if he knew he should be on his guard. There was a wyvern outside, after all. But something about the smell of the stew and the calming ambiance did a number on him. He felt safe here. Others were doing the same, and it was only then that Lucian realized how truly exhausted he was.

When he opened his eyes, a bowl of stew was sitting in front of him on the stones surrounding the hearth. Lucian took his first bite. It was the best thing he'd tasted since the Accounting Feast back in Kiro.

There was enough for seconds, and even thirds. Lucian ate until his stomach felt as if it would burst. Despite the limited resources of his home, Jagar seemed to have no reservations about sharing his bounty.

Lucian was about to thank him, but in opening his mouth, he let out an enormous belch. Selene looked at him, horrified, while Serah and Fergus laughed. The old man's dark brown eyes twinkled, and he seemed to take that as compliment enough.

"Rotting good stew," Serah said.

Selene's eyes narrowed at the use of profanity, but no one else seemed to mind.

"Agak-agak stew, we call it here on Psyche," Jagar said. "Just throw whatever you have in the pot, and more often than not, it comes out tasting sublime."

Fergus rubbed his belly. "I'd eat more, but I'm stuffed."

Jagar said, giving a gap-toothed smile. "I'm glad. Thought *you'd* eat me out of hearth and home."

Lucian laughed at that. It felt good to have a bit of humor after everything they had gone through.

"Now's the time to pay your part," Jagar said. "What's your story? How did you come from the Sandsea without me seeing you pass? Did you go by the North Trail to the Burning Sands? Can't be. It wouldn't explain how you came back by the Sandsea route . . ."

Lucian didn't know what Jagar was talking about regarding the North Trail. He shared a look with Serah and Fergus while Selene just stared into the flames unhappily. From Fergus and Serah, he got the sense that they would back up whatever he said, truth or lie. Lucian didn't want to tell the whole truth, but neither did he want to lie, especially after receiving Jagar's hospitality.

"We were part of an expedition with the Sorceress-Queen, I guess you could say," Lucian said. "We were on her airship, *Zephyr*. A sandstorm caught us and the ship went down."

At the mention of the Queen, his expression seemed to darken, but it passed quickly, like a small cloud over the sun. "A sandstorm? Yeah, those will get you. Probably the reason most Seeker parties don't return, if not the Great Wyrm."

"We pieced some of the airship parts to make an air skiff," Lucian said. "Unfortunately, *that* got caught in a storm, too, and landed us right in the Sandsea."

The old man frowned. Was he already starting to suspect something was off?

"Anyway, we pulled ourselves over here. And lucky for us,

Selene is a good Atomicist and could sense the water source. That's how we found you."

His expression was stony as he ruminated over the story.

"Is something wrong?" Serah asked.

"Well," the man said gruffly, "you don't have the look of Mage-Knights about you, but I supposed you could've lost your clothes in the crash."

"We're not Mage-Knights," Lucian said. "I'm an off-worlder. As is Fergus, too, but he's lived here a long time. Serah and Selene are both natives, but neither is a Mage-Knight."

"That's the part I'm having trouble with. I was testing you a bit, there. It's clear you're not from this world, and it would seem all of you come from different backgrounds. So, how did you find yourselves in the Queen's employ? We Westlanders don't hide our hate for the Queen, so you have balls to admit you're working with her."

If Lucian told him anything more, he might guess the truth. "Well, we weren't working with her out of choice. The Queen thought we might lead her to the Orb of Psionics."

Fergus and Serah looked at him in surprise, but Jagar just gave a knowing chuckle. "And you, being an off-worlder, knew just where to find it, where hundreds of Seekers over the decades didn't."

Lucian looked to the others, hoping for backup.

Fergus cleared his throat. "We're Rifters. At least, Serah and I are. Selene is from the Golden Vale."

"Yes. I surmised that much. Serah especially has the drawl of a Rifter, though yours is an accent I can't quite place."

"Irion."

"Irion. Academy-trained, then?"

Fergus's expression darkened somewhat. "Something like that."

"I studied at the Mako Academy myself, though that was far before your time. Was just another fool young mage who joined Xara Mallis. One of hundreds of them. The Academy life was never for me, and her cause seemed noble. Let's just say I've learned a thing or two since then." He stared into the flames in reminiscence. "I don't regret it. Had I not gone, I'd be a shriveled old man on that cloudy, dismal world even to this day, if not dead. I couldn't have left it fast enough."

"Well, you've got plenty of sun now," Lucian said.

Jagar gave a deep laugh. "That I do. Now, your story has me curious. I don't think you're lying to me, but I don't think you're telling the whole truth, either. Naturally, I'm wondering why."

Lucian saw this man was keen on him earning his dinner. But he also couldn't tell every random person who he was, or what he had. Eventually, they'd run across someone who'd attack him for his Orbs. Lucian didn't think Jagar would do that, but one day he might make the mistake of telling the wrong person. He had already faced betrayal with Osric in the Darkrift.

"I'll tell you more," Lucian said. "Everything I know. As long as you teach me how to brand a wyvern like you."

Jagar dismissed him with a hand wave. "Pshaw. No one can brand like me, boy. Not even the Sorceress-Queen herself. At least for animals."

"Maybe if you showed me, I could learn, too."

Jagar shook his head. "Not a chance. Although, if you could do it, it would shorten your journey across the Fire Rifts considerably. Because that's where I assume you're headed, no?" At Lucian's nod, he continued. "But you'd need *four* wyverns, and possessing even one is tricky enough. The brand will require most of your pool if you're as decent a mage as I think you are. All your friends would have to pull it off, too."

So, it wasn't a matter of the brand being complicated, but simply the fact that Jagar couldn't conceive of them having the expertise to brand four. And finding four wyverns would be troublesome enough. They'd have to come across them in that exact amount, no more or less, and that just would not happen.

"How did you catch that one, then?" Lucian asked.

"Skill," he said. "And a bit of luck."

"Well, Lucian could probably brand one if you just taught him how," Serah said. "He's one of the best Psionics I know. It's why the Queen used him to feel out a path to the Orb."

It took everything for Lucian not to wince.

But Jagar just gave a rueful smile. "And how did *that* work out?"

Her shoulders sagged. "Not good."

Selene was watching Lucian from across the fire. The look of mischief in her green eyes reminded him much of Queen Ansaldra. "But he truly is powerful, Mr. Jagar."

"Just Jagar," the hermit said.

"Jagar." She seemed to test the name. "Well, he impressed the Queen greatly. He even saved a woman under her direct possession."

Lucian nearly spat out his drink as Jagar watched him shrewdly.

"Is that so? The tale becomes more incredible by the minute because not just anyone can do that." Jagar paused, stroking his beard. And then his face lit with realization. "I know. Or at least, I suspected all along. From the moment I first saw you."

If it was this easy for every stranger to figure out he had an Orb, there was no way Lucian could find them all.

"You found what you were looking for out there," he said. "The only part that makes little sense was how you got to it before the Queen."

8

LUCIAN WASN'T sure where to begin. He knew at this point he might as well tell Jagar the whole thing. Then again, he had done the same thing for Osric in the Darkrift, and he had betrayed them. Even if it had all worked out in the end, there was no guarantee it would this time.

"What do you think you know?" Lucian said. "I'll tell you if you're on the right track."

"You found the Amethyst of Starsea, the one sought by all the Seekers." He nodded as if to confirm that. "I figured someone, someday, would find it. For years, I've been the last stop for most of the Seekers setting out from the Golden Vale. At least, for the South Trail. Fewer than a quarter would come back from the embarkation point on the Sandsea. Of course, I always tried to convince them not to risk their necks for something that wasn't a sure thing. But you know how young people are. They dream of glory. As I once did."

"I don't dream of glory," Lucian said, looking into the flames.

"Then what do you dream of?"

"I don't know."

"You don't know?" The old man chuckled. "You must dream of something, lad. If you don't, life won't be worth living."

Lucian thought about his old life. He hadn't been happy in that dingy condo in Miami. It had been downright miserable. Where would he be now if he wasn't a mage? Working somewhere in the League bureaucracy, assuming he passed his civil exam, saving up for a down payment on a ship to travel the Gates, a dream that was out of reach and useless. His dreams were different now. His dream now was to be free and do what he wanted, and to *be* who he wanted. Of course, that was impossible. He had responsibility, now. His trials had forced him to become a person he never dreamed he could be.

And he might be the rotting Chosen of the Manifold, fated to put his life on the line to save the entire galaxy.

He didn't want that to be his dream. He just wanted it to end, but he saw the truth staring him in the face. It would *never* end, and he had to finish the job if he was to earn his rest. That thought alone made him feel a cold despondence such as he had never known.

"I just want freedom, I guess," Lucian said, so quietly that it was almost a whisper. "To get off this moon. To make my destiny."

"You're a man, now," Jagar said. "No matter where you are in the Worlds, a man can't truly be free because he has a responsibility to others. But that's not a bad thing, and freedom isn't the highest possible good, as so many young folks think. Service to a noble cause is. Hang in there, son. You'll get the hang of it."

Lucian wished the others would look away because being called "son" just reminded him of the father he had never truly known. Maybe they'd think his watery eyes were from the smoke rising from the flames. He hoped so.

"I guess I had no one to teach me about that," he said. "I always thought I had to look after myself. Because no one else was going to." He thought about it a moment. "Guess I have some thinking to do."

"Well, you've found your way enough to find an Orb," the old man observed. "With that Orb, you'll have strength no other mage has. Don't use that strength to help yourself. There are many people out there who need help. People who need a hero."

Lucian scoffed. "I'm no hero."

"Says who?" Jagar said. "There's only one person who gets to decide who you are. That's you. The question is, do you want it? Do you want to help people, or don't you?"

"I want to help everyone who's sitting around this fire right now." He thought of Emma. "And others I've met along the way."

"That's a start," Jagar said, "but you've got to think bigger. You need some beliefs, son. You've got to stand for something or you'll fall for anything."

Jagar was annoying him. "Yeah. I'll think about it. For now, though, I need some shuteye."

"Floor's open," Jagar said. "Cot's mine, though."

"We're . . . to sleep on the *floor*?" Selene asked. "Don't you have some spare bedding?"

Jagar laughed. "You have the look of a proper Mage-Lady about you. I don't know how you found yourself out here."

"Not by choice, I assure you."

Jagar looked at Lucian questioningly, but Lucian was just too tired to do any explaining right now. That could wait until later. He wanted to sleep the rest of the day away, and all night, too. Hell, maybe they could just hole up here until Vera came.

But something about what the old man said nagged at him. He could be whatever he decided. He needed beliefs. What *did* he believe in, besides saving himself and those who had become his friends? Were those things not enough?

His gut told him no. The truth was too much to think about

right now. Too much a burden. A responsibility, as Jagar had put it.

He was responsible now, not only for the lives of his friends but for the lives of the entire human race, as grandiose as it all sounded. He held two Orbs, two Jewels of Starsea. And if he didn't find the rest, terrible things he couldn't even fathom were going to happen.

They weren't comforting thoughts to fall asleep to.

———

WHEN HE AWOKE, the fire was low, and the sound of snoring filled the small cabin. Out the open doorway, Lucian could hear the wind blowing across the rocks, along with the gurgle of the stream.

He rolled over and tried to sleep some more when he noticed Serah's spot was empty.

He got up and headed out the door, brushing aside the reeds in the doorway. He found a star-studded night sky, with the white giant cupid taking up most of the western sky. Its eye, as always, pointed the way east.

There was plenty of light to walk to the stream, where he saw Serah bathing in the river. He turned around to head another way, but she seemed to sense him there and waved him over. He followed the slope down, sitting on a rock by the stream. In the middle of the stream, Serah's head was the only thing Lucian could see.

"You never miss an opportunity, do you?" she called.

"And *you* can never miss an opportunity to make fun of me."

She smiled. "Well, of course. Someone has to keep you on your toes. You make it easy, I have to say."

"Well, repartee has never been my forte."

"Oh, but you must learn. It usually means something very exciting is about to happen."

He couldn't help but smile. "Rotting hell. I can never keep up with you."

"And you never will." She watched him for a moment. "Are you just going to stand there gawking, or do you plan to join me?"

Lucian had to admit a dip in the cool water would feel good, even more so with her. But the wyvern standing guard outside the house made him nervous.

"I don't like having an audience."

She laughed. "Trust me, he doesn't care. The water's fine. No eels or leeches. This is choice stuff."

Lucian wasn't sure what to do. The answer seemed obvious, but he was also afraid of enjoying himself too much with her. How could he not, as beautiful and confident as she was? If he went down that road, he might not come back from it.

"Cat's got your tongue? I'm just inviting you in for a friendly bath."

"It's . . . not that." Lucian wasn't sure how to explain it to her. "I guess I'm just . . . being careful."

"Careful? Careful about *what*? You Earthers are so prude. The more dangerous thing is your grimy, dirty, stinky self."

"All right. Fine."

He felt strange taking off his clothes with her watching him. Almost as strange as the statuesque wyvern with the violet eyes staring him down. Stark naked under the planet light, his body was all muscle, lines, and angles as if chiseled from marble. Lucian wasn't sure when that transformation had occurred. Serah just stared at him, for once not having anything to say.

Lucian hurried into the water, never minding the cold. He didn't feel confident in himself. The last time they were together, the cabin had been dark, but under the light of Cupid, there was nowhere to hide.

"Get over here," she said.

Lucian pulled her close. The water was cold, but where her skin touched his, it was warm. Losing himself to her would be the easiest and most natural thing to do. Everything in him wanted to go in that direction. He couldn't think straight, but all he could think about was someone walking out of the cabin right now. They'd see them easily enough. Maybe he was as prudish as Serah had said.

At his silence, she kissed him, and Lucian responded in kind. But as Serah's movements became more passionate, he broke it off. "Maybe we can just . . . talk for now."

She pouted. "Talk is boring. When are we ever going to get a chance again?"

Lucian supposed that was a good point, but he wasn't sure he could separate the emotion from the act. Something Serah seemed to have no problem doing. Either way, it was a dangerous game, especially when so much was on the line. Going deeper with Serah would make things more complicated. It might even be a distraction. It wasn't just a matter of feelings, because he *wanted* to.

Then there was something else Lucian didn't want to talk about. Serah was fraying. He already liked her more than he wanted. He could stop this right now, and it would be less painful in the end. He couldn't bear the thought of having to watch the disease take its course. It would be bad enough watching that as a friend, but as a lover, it might be enough to kill him.

He turned his face away, hoping she couldn't read his thoughts. But he knew there was not much chance of that.

"Look," she said. "I'm an adult woman. I know what this means. I feel you're just trying to protect my honor or something."

"It's . . . not that. I'm trying to protect myself." She watched him, and he made himself meet her blue eyes. "I'm not sure I can do this without it becoming . . . more *real* for me, I guess."

"And why are you afraid of that? You'd rather just be miserable and go on your Orb hunt with me at arm's length?"

No, he didn't want that. But sometimes, what one wanted and what one needed wasn't the same thing. Then again, for all he knew, maybe she was right.

"Just . . . not now," he finally said. "I have a lot going on in my head. Too much to take anything else on."

She didn't seem to be happy about that. "Okay, I guess I'll give you a pass. For now."

With a sudden smile, she dunked her head underwater. What in the Worlds was she doing? He was getting worried, until a few seconds later, when she surfaced.

"Feels nice," she said. "You should try it."

He dunked his head, too, resisting the temptation to open his eyes. That would just make his former resolution more difficult to stick to.

He came up, feeling as if most of the dirt and grime had fallen off his body and hair.

"So," she said. "Is that all that's bothering you?"

It was hard to put words to his feelings. "I guess Jagar got inside my head today. I feel . . . frustrated. Inadequate. Like I'll never be strong enough to do what I have to."

She snickered. "All that rot about responsibility? Yeah, I can see why you'd fall for that." She put a finger on his chest. "Noble Lucian Abrantes."

"I'm not noble."

"You are now. When we met, you were a scared little boy I could hardly respect. You were strong in magic, sure. But you've changed since then. You're like . . . a hero or something, now. When you saved me from the evil Sorceress-Queen, I nearly fainted."

"Well, you saved me, too. You're giving me too much credit."

"Maybe," she said. "Maybe not." She narrowed her eyes and imitated Jagar's raspy voice while placing a finger on his chest. "Only *you* get to decide your fate, young mage."

Lucian grabbed her shoulders and dunked her underwater, her giggles cut off by water. When she surfaced, she was still laughing.

"You can't take *anything* seriously, can you?" he asked, smiling.

"Maybe you're just too serious. What's life without humor?"

"Not *everything* is a joke."

She shrugged. "It can be. I have to say though, it's somewhat inspiring."

"What?"

"You." She watched him for a moment. "All I've ever cared about is taking care of myself. I feel like we're alike in that way. But lately, maybe I'm catching some of this nobility disease, too. Dare I say, I might care about saving the rotting universe, too. Just a little, and as long as it's not too difficult to do."

"Well, it will be difficult. You can be sure of that."

"Don't you feel like things are different, now? Like you've changed?"

"Maybe. I don't know how I got here. I don't remember ever making a choice."

"Well, most people don't change by choice. They're forced to by circumstances. Maybe your journey is just beginning. It'll be interesting to watch, is all I'm saying." She looked back at the shoreline. "All right, this water is getting damn cold."

She emerged from the stream, and Lucian watched as she dried herself under Cupid's light. It seemed only fair since she had so luridly stared at him. Unlike him, though, modesty didn't seem to be an issue.

He dunked his head one more time before following her back to the cabin as the wyvern watched their passage.

9

THAT NIGHT, he dreamed of the Golden Palace of Dara. Fear paralyzed him when he realized the Psionic ward he'd set was no longer active. This time, though, he would control his fear. She could hurt him only if he allowed it.

He found himself in a dark room, the only source of light a glowing throne that held a thin, shadowed figure. Though Lucian could not see the Sorceress Queen's features because of that radiance, he still knew it was her.

"Afraid to show your face?" he asked. "If you even have a face to show."

"Lucian Abrantes. Chosen of the Manifold, Vigilant of Binding and Psionics," she said. When she spoke to him, the voice that left her differed from what he was used to. Before, she had used Selene's voice, clear and young and powerful. Now, it sounded old, and very weary, but the intonation was the same. "We are far from through with each other, it would seem."

Lucian felt his hackles rise. "We could be if you wanted it. Leave me and my friends alone."

"Oh, come off it. Lucky for you, I am merciful. I'm willing to overlook everything that's happened because there are far more important matters to attend to. These are matters you cannot run or hide from. Nor can you run and hide from me. Even after everything, I'm not your enemy. The Manifold means us to work together. If not by choice, then by destiny. It would be far better to do that with a cooperative spirit."

"Sorry, but *I* control my destiny."

An aura of coldness radiated from her. "If that is your belief, then you will be in for a rude awakening. You hold two Jewels of Starsea, yes, but you still don't know how to use them."

"I used them well enough to defeat you."

"A bit of luck, nothing more. It's as if you have some knowledge lost to all other mages." Though he couldn't see her, he could feel her small, victorious smile. "I wonder why that is?"

"I don't know what you're talking about."

"You don't? Well, you'll learn soon enough. You still need me, even if you don't realize it yet. I have something you desire, after all."

How could she know that? She was bluffing. He remained silent.

"Just imagine what we could accomplish working together," the Sorceress-Queen said. "It's not too late. My training. Your power. The resources of this world. I could teach you to take control of the Wardens above us. You could use their fleet to finish what the Starsea Mages started. Hundreds of Mage-Lords and Mage-Knights at your command. I have seen visions of the Swarmers and the destruction they will unleash. Now is the perfect time to strike, to enact our vision, to change the system for the benefit of all humanity. We could become what Xara Mallis and Vera Desai only dreamed of. Of course, it all begins with finding the rest of the Orbs. Of fulfilling your destiny as the Chosen of the Manifold."

"I'll never work with you."

"Tell me, what *is* your plan for the Orbs? Is the future you envision so different from mine?" She scoffed. "You probably don't even *have* a plan for the future."

Lucian *had* a plan, but he couldn't let her bait him into revealing it. Again, he remained silent, a lesson he'd learned well from his time with the Transcends. The only power she had was that which he gave.

"Imagine," she said. "What could you do if only you had the proper mentor?"

"Not interested. I don't deal with murderers, especially murderers who kill my friends."

The Queen was silent as she considered this. "What happened to your friends is . . . regrettable. They fought bravely, but in the end, they attacked first. I had no choice but to defend myself."

Lucian realized from her wording that she believed both Cleon *and* Fergus were dead. He didn't bother correcting her. The less information she had, the better.

She continued. "Remember, it was *you* who betrayed *me*. You agreed to be trained by me, and instead, you took the Orb and used it against me."

"I'm not a puppet to dance on your strings, Ansaldra," he said. "You are a powerful Psionic and an expert manipulator. But the last thing you are is a victim."

Her manner grew even colder. "Such insolence. You cannot change destiny."

"And you can't presume to *know* destiny. If you try to come after me again, I have the power to stop you. And the power to protect my friends."

"Oh, do you believe that? You don't have the full measure of me yet, Chosen. At the time of our brief battle, I was exhausted from surviving the maelstrom and fighting your friends down below. Unlike you, my power is my own, and I have no Orb to serve as a crutch. I don't doubt you can stream significant power. But I also believe your Orbs will not obey you if you go off your prescribed path. You are the Orbs' guardian, nothing more or less. What are you without them?"

"I won't let you sow doubts in my mind," Lucian said. "I know who I am. I am sure of my mission. You can fight that if you wish, but I suggest you don't. It won't end well for you."

"And how do you plan to leave Psyche? Only *I* can show you the magic that will make that possible." At Lucian's silence, she continued. "And of course, you will have no recourse but to work with me for another reason. I hold the purest translation of the *Prophecy of the Seven* in the Worlds, save for the original penned by Arian himself."

Yes, there was that. And Queen Ansaldra saying that only proved she *was* expecting him. If he wanted that prophecy, he might have to work with her. Either that or steal it with a very elaborate heist. But that would be almost impossible if she expected it.

"So," the Queen said, "our time together has not passed. Of course, I would rather us work amenably with one another, if only because the Manifold demands it. A new Mage War is coming, whatever your wishes. The mages must inevitably rise and take the reins of humanity. Unless, of course, you agree with the League that Psyche is the proper place of any mage not content with wearing the yoke."

As much as Lucian hated to admit it, he did somewhat agree with her there, though he didn't want it to come to war. From his history lessons, humanity could not survive a conflict as violent as the Mage War again, especially with the threat of the Swarmers. The Swarmers, who the Oracle of Binding had called the *Alkasen.*

"What say you, Lucian? Are you ready to see sense? Too much is at stake for this stubborn state of mind of yours."

"I don't trust you," Lucian said. "I never will."

"I should say the same for you. After all, your friends

attacked my men with a Thermal brand at the Spire's entrance, one so cleverly crafted that it escaped even my detection. It was enough time for them to kill even Mage-Lord Kiani, one of my most trusted generals."

Lucian almost told her Kiani was better off dead, but he refrained. "You should know that we never intended to work with you. We only did so because you forced us. You just can't stand the fact that we can do this on our own, *without* your help."

"You are so very wrong. That will become apparent in time. You need *The Prophecy of the Seven*, as pure a version as you can get your hands on. And only I can train you to use the Orb of Psionics to interpret it, not to mention help you leave Psyche altogether."

Lucian couldn't help but be curious. "What's your plan for that?"

"Oh, I won't tell you that. Not until you are standing before me, humbled and ready to work for the betterment of all Magekind."

"Well, dream on, then. I can find my way off Psyche. Now, I would appreciate it if you stopped interrupting my dreams."

"Well, no doubt where you are in the Burning Sands, you will need all the rest you can get. I'm doing what I can to reconstruct a vessel worthy enough to make the journey. Believe me, when I'm your only lifeline out of that trackless waste, my terms will not be as merciful."

She leaned forward in her seat, and for the first time, Lucian got a vision of the face he had so briefly seen in his mind during their duel. It almost stopped his heart cold. Her visage was thin and severe, mottled with the sickness of the fraying. Her thin lips curved upward in an unsettling smile, while her violet eyes shone challengingly.

"You have become very arrogant indeed, Lucian Abrantes.

And as my father told me many times, pride goes before the fall."

With that, the dream ended.

———

THE NEXT MORNING, Lucian remained quiet as Jagar prepared breakfast. As they ate, they discussed their plans for traveling east.

"We will need plenty of food and water," Fergus said. "From what you've told us, Jagar, the passage through the Bone Mountains will take a few days at least, at which point we will be at the western edge of the Fire Rifts. After that, we'll have no choice but to follow this South Trail through the whole thing."

"That is so," he said. "That part should take two to three weeks, assuming you don't get lost."

"Are you willing to guide us?" Serah asked.

He waved his hand in dismissal. "I don't think so. I have enough food to spare for you to make it that far, which is all I can do. I've lived my life, or what I've cared to live of it."

"What *did* you do to get sent out here, if you don't mind me asking?" Fergus asked.

"It was . . . years ago. I was banished from my village in the Westlands, and I'd rather not live anywhere else. This life is fine by me."

"Well, I understand if you don't want to show us the way," Serah said. "But could you at least teach us how to brand the wyverns? It would help us far more than the food."

"It isn't simple, and the results could be disastrous," Jagar said. "There are different species of wyverns on this world. The wyverns of the Bone Mountains are among the most intelligent and friendly to humans, though *friendly* is a relative term when discussing wyverns. The wyverns of the Fire Rifts are smaller, less intelligent, and less numerous. You can ride them, but not as easily. Less of a mind to take advantage of. This world belonged to the wyverns before we came along."

"We took it from them," Serah said, somewhat sadly.

"Brute beasts," Selene said. "They would feel no sentimentality at tearing any of us to shreds, so it is only right to return the favor."

Serah's eyes narrowed, but Selene seemed oblivious.

Jagar seemed to ignore her point. "I have something of an . . . agreement with the wyverns of the Bone Mountains. They are not a unified force, and very often have skirmishes with one another. One of the wyvern clans allows me to control the minds of some of their thrall wyverns, in exchange for certain favors. I won't go into details. But my agreement does *not* include allowing other humans into the knowledge they've entrusted to me. If I ever allowed that to happen, I would lose trust with them forever." He shook his head and grunted. "I've already done so by revealing this much to you. My agreement with them ends if I ever leave the purview of the Bone Mountains."

"Would you consider guiding us if I told you the full truth?" Lucian asked. "Of why we were in the Burning Sands, and what's at stake if we don't make it out of here alive."

Jagar scrutinized him, one eye squinted, which made his face appear even more wrinkled. "Well, I won't stop you. I assumed you to be another glory-seeker and one who found what he was looking for, against all odds. But if there's more to the story, why didn't you tell me before?"

"Only because doing so in the past has led to betrayal. But if telling you the truth convinces you, then it's worth the risk."

"I doubt it'll change a thing," the old man said. "Just being honest with you."

It was quiet for a moment around the fire as everyone waited for Lucian to begin.

"I'll tell it all the same. I don't think you could even get an advantage by betraying us." Lucian looked at the others. "You guys can fill in the gaps. But the only proper way to start this is from the beginning."

Over the next few hours, Lucian told Jagar the full story. The relevant details, anyway. The old hermit's eyes popped when Lucian revealed the more surprising details, especially about Starsea, the Orbs, and the cycle of magic that had returned—culminating with Lucian's realization that *he* was most likely Arian's prophesied Chosen of the Manifold. It felt ridiculous to say that aloud, even if he had been thinking about this stuff for months.

Lucian took a drink of some tea Jagar had made during the telling. His throat felt parched and scratchy. The others had filled in details that Lucian missed, and they answered most of Jagar's basic questions.

Now Jagar just watched the fire. He reached into a nearby basket filled with some green leaves Lucian couldn't identify. He rolled them into a ball and started chewing.

"You might need these, lad," he said, rolling another ball. "You others as well."

"What is it?" Lucian asked.

"It's called *ayah*," he said. "A leaf that grows wild in the Bone Mountains. It'll calm you, steady your nerves. It can set bad feelings and many pains aside. At least for a time."

"Is it addictive?"

"No more than coffee."

"Coffee is right addictive," Fergus pointed out. "We grow it in the heights of the Riftlands."

Jagar nodded. "Just a friendly offer, but it helps to loosen minds and tongues."

Serah accepted a roll, as did Lucian, though Fergus and Selene refrained.

Lucian popped the roll of leaves into his mouth before he could second-guess himself. The taste was bitter, almost sickening. But he forced himself to chew. The calming effects of the leaf had to be good for anyone to endure this bitter taste.

"Takes some getting used to," Jagar admitted, "but you'll come to prefer it, eventually. I grow very fine *ayah* in the foothills here."

Over several minutes, Lucian felt his mind relax. It seemed easier to grab hold of thoughts and put them in the proper, logical order. Jagar, too, seemed ready to share more.

"It's time you know who I truly am. My full name is Jagar Tengiz Ashiz. I don't expect any of you to recognize that name, but once, long ago in what seems to be another life, I was Lord-Consort to Queen Ansaldra herself in the early years of Psyche. We ruled together for the greater part of two decades, until one day, I didn't like the way things were going. She exiled me to the Westlands before the Westlands exiled me to this place at the edge of the known world. And it's time you heard my full story, which I would not have shared before. Because of what Lucian has said, things have changed. And it's time you heard the full reason."

10

"WAIT," Serah said. "You *married* her?"

He nodded. "I still am married, if we're being strict about it. We had nothing like an official court back then, of course, so two people's word was enough to make a holy bond. Nor have either of us unbonded those words, though I have thought it in my heart many a time." He chuckled darkly. "It was her ire that got me sent here. She forever banished me beyond the Mountains of Madness after that fateful day, where I lived for a while before they also banished me beyond the Bone Mountains. Maybe I could go back if I wanted, but I've accepted this is my lot. I've been here for the past twenty years, though it's hard to remember sometimes. Haven't had travelers in a while to give me the time or date."

"The year's 2365, I think," Lucian said. "Possibly 2366."

"That's how it is here, cut off from the rest of the Worlds," Jagar said. "If you don't live in Dara or the Golden Vale, where they measure such things, then time for you is the moving of the sun and the cycle of the stars and planets."

"Why *did* you get exiled, exactly?" Lucian asked. "That must have not been a simple thing for Ansaldra to do, even given the type of woman she is."

Jagar chuckled darkly. "Interesting words. *Type of woman.* Well, from what you've told me, she's far gone. She's not the same Ansaldra I married, and she hasn't been for a long time. She was a beautiful woman. No one could hold a candle to her when we were young. Xara was mighty jealous of her during the days of the war. We were all young, then. Young and dumb. But not Ansaldra. She was sharp-witted, ambitious. With the failure of the Starsea Mages, she still wanted to make the best of things, to give the mages hope. She had grand plans for Psyche. She wanted to make this moon into something, something where mages and non-mages alike could live in dignity. Something changed about that, though, about forty years back, though I've lost the count of years. She started talking to that Oracle, Shantozar. I don't know what they talked about, but those conversations were only accomplished through great Psionic power and seemed to poison her mind. Not to say this isn't her fault, somehow. We all have a choice in how we act, in the end. I'm just saying it's a cause."

Lucian nodded. "From what I understand, the old Vigilants of Starsea had little in the way of morals. Maybe that's when she started changing."

"I think you're right in that, lad. But I won't pretend that wasn't my goal, too, once upon a time. The years have convinced me otherwise. Anyway, I was the only one who could talk sense to her. Or, so I thought. She scared the rot out of everyone else. Terrible things were going on in those days. Slavery of the non-mages, elevating the power-hungry, creating the class system of Mage-Lords and Mage-Knights to rule over everyone who didn't have magic." He shook his head. "You know what I think? I think she's trying to make the whole rotting *moon* like Starsea, as the prophecies said."

"What do you mean by that?" Serah asked.

"Well, before she completely lost it, she tried to rope me into her ideas. I'm ashamed to say I went along with them . . . for a time. Before it became too much. I sort of lost myself back then. Anyway, that's neither here nor there. As I was saying before I started rambling on, she shared some of her conversations with that Shantozar. How his ideas and knowledge would allow Dara to rise to the stars." He shook his head. "Well, that's when I knew I'd lost her, and she was no longer the woman I married. I tried to talk sense into her. Told her I could no longer live with myself with the things she had me doing. It was clear I was just a tool as her mind got warped with prophecies, visions, and dark ideas. Most went along with her. Those who didn't, she banished, or worse. She exiled most of her detractors to the Riftlands, which in those days was far more dangerous than it is now. The worse cases were cast beyond the Mountains of Madness, and few survived that journey. Besides me, her Psion, Jalisa, also turned against her."

"You know about her?" Fergus asked in awe. "She's an Elder in my village!"

"Is that so? Well, this moon is a small place. When Lucian was telling his story, I knew her to be the same Jalisa, but I didn't want to interrupt. I'm glad she's alive and well. Anyway, once Ansaldra completed her translation of *The Prophecy of the Seven*, her Psion, Jalisa, had her revelation, too, discovering the location of the Orb of Psionics. Naturally, Ansaldra wanted to keep that information to herself and use it for her ends, as well as claim the credit. But before Ansaldra's ambitions could come to fruition, Jalisa betrayed Ansaldra, spreading those lines of the prophecy far across the surface of Psyche. Oh, how Ansaldra hated *that*. Well, Jalisa was wily and got away, and at that point, Ansaldra was so paranoid that she tried to get all her old friends killed. Many tried to escape across the Mountains of Madness, where there was one of the old religious colonies, though trying to get there in those days was a death sentence since the Pass of Madness had yet to be completed. I saw the writing on the wall, then. I knew running was what I should do, but being the dumb, hopeful man I was, I stayed behind, hoping she would change. We were both in our forties then. I wasn't as young, but I was still foolish, at least looking back now."

"Did she try to kill you?" Lucian asked.

"I thought she would. But she never really did. One day, though, I went up to her and said I couldn't stand it anymore. How it broke my heart to see what she had become. Well, we had fighting words. She begged me to stay but made no promise that she would change. She had made her choice, then: power and her vision for the future. She said another man was coming someday, a man of great destiny. As much as she loved me, she had to stay true to the vision, or else that Starsea Cycle you talked about would be the end of us all."

Lucian felt a coldness at those words. He didn't have to ask who that man was. It wouldn't take long for Jagar to connect those dots as well, as Lucian had omitted that part of the story.

"So, with a heavy heart and many lost years, I left her. In retaliation, she exiled me beyond the Mountains of Madness. Like the Riftlands to the east, the Westlands in those days were far wilder than they are now. No law and order, ruled by petty warlords, living like animals. One could reach it using the Moon Path, which runs down by the Moon Sea. And that dark way is dangerous."

Lucian supposed this "Moon Path" was the same thing as Slave's Run. "How did you get there, then?"

"I didn't take the Moon Path. She expected me to die that way without having to go through the trouble of killing me herself. I had Akhekh."

"Wait," Serah said. "*That* was the same wyvern who helped you escape?"

Jagar nodded. "Indeed. Wyverns live a long time. At least, this one does. They say the Wyvern King of the Bone Mountains has lived since before the Blood Storm marred the surface of Cupid. Anyway, before Ansaldra had gone too far off the deep end, she wanted to see if I could train the wyverns for battle. Well, I obliged, heading up her army and seeing if the beasts would listen to me. And I learned quickly that not just *any* mage could ride them. Only powerful Psionics could, and even then, it practically guaranteed your death unless you knew what you were doing. Well, I went to the wyverns, knowing I was dead either way. And to my surprise, I could communicate with them Psionically and they helped me. But only after I agreed to help them overthrow the Daran Empire. Only then would the Blood Storm go away, at least according to their prophecies. I was so bothered by what my wife did, I agreed, if a bit reluctantly. But that reluctance has gone away as the years went by, as I fought against my spouse over the fate of this world. So, that's how it came to pass that Akhekh helped me cross the Mountains of Madness."

"Bring down the Daran Empire," Fergus said. "*That* is an undertaking."

"We tried twenty years ago in the Westlands," Jagar said. "After years of preparation. And we failed."

"What happened?" Lucian asked.

"The Darans built the Pass of Madness. For the first time, Voidside and Planetside were joined. On the east, the Queen had combined most of Psyche's population, except the Far Riftlands. But on the west were the descendants of the first colonies who lived an isolated existence. Ansaldra and her Mage-Lords conquered the east side of the mountains a long time ago, but the Mountains of Madness proved an impossible barrier. But Ansaldra was interested in the west, not only to add to her strength and bring Psyche under her full control, but because of the Orb of Psionics. The Great Wyvern Kingdom, of which Akhekh was once a member, used to exist in the Mountains of Madness, so even travel by the Queen's airships was impossible. At least, until she carved out enough territory to pass unimpeded. I digress. Once Akhekh brought me to the west, I warned the colonies there that one day, the Queen and her Mage-Lords, Mage-Knights, and hoplites would pour through the completed pass." He let out a tired sigh. "Some believed, but most didn't. But in the end, it didn't matter. It was a slaughter. The Queen's army razed Kalm to the ground, the only city of any note. And it was razed again during the Western Insurrection, just a few years ago. Oh, they hate the Queen there. But I had failed them, and they needed someone to blame for that failure. The new Lord of Kalm, Queen Ansaldra's puppet, exiled me to this place. It was a mercy. Queen Ansaldra later assassinated him for not delivering me right to her court. If he hadn't done that, I'd likely be rotting in the depths of her dungeons in the Mountains of Madness to this very day."

Everyone remained quiet as they thought of Jagar's story. Lucian couldn't help but feel bad for him. Whatever Lucian had experienced, Jagar had experienced far worse.

"Sounds like you did all you could," Serah said.

"Well, resistance against Dara was a fool's hope, anyway. So, that's the long and short of it. That's why there's no place on Psyche for me to call home. All of that happened over twenty years ago, sometimes as much as forty years ago. I've nearly put it out of my mind, at least until you young folks came along, stirring up old memories. That said, I hold my promise to the wyverns fulfilled, and they to me. They know I've done all I could. They've seen how I've suffered at the hands of my fellow men, and so of all men, they pity me. If ever there was an opportunity to strike at the heart of Dara, I would still consider my oath unfulfilled. But that opportunity has not yet come."

Lucian immediately saw what he was getting at. "Jagar, if

THE CHOSEN OF THE MANIFOLD

you help us, then you would be closer to that goal. The Sorceress-Queen will not rest until she has me in chains or even dead. For whatever reason, she's convinced she needs to control me to take Dara to the stars and get revenge for the Mage War."

"From what you've told me, it seems she believes that to her core, and it lines up with everything she told me all those years ago. She is right that you have a central role to play. Fate, destiny, the Manifold, whatever you want to call it, has a part for you. The only question is, Lucian my lad, what *you* see your role to be?"

"That's the thing," he said. "There's still a few months before Vera comes, and given the Warden blockade, that's not a sure thing. If she isn't able to come, then I'll have no choice but to go after Ansaldra and her prophecy." He looked at each of them. "I haven't mentioned this yet, but she came to me in a dream last night."

"The ward wasn't set?" Fergus asked.

"It was stupid, I know. But I also haven't been warding myself since my duel with her. And things have been pretty insane these last few days ..."

"Whatever the case, you must continue to set it," Fergus said.

"I will from now on."

Lucian then told them the details of the dream—a dream that was evidence that the Queen was far from through with him. Said aloud, its contents were far more disturbing than he realized.

"We have learned something important," Jagar said, once Lucian had finished. "Ansaldra believes she and this Chosen will be united, working together toward the enactment of her vision."

Lucian shuddered. "That's *not* going to happen."

"Well, it's quite clear *she* believes it will happen. And she will stop at nothing to ensure that it does."

"She's coming after you," Serah said. "She won't find you at the Spire, but she might figure out the rest if she finds the missing airship parts. Her search would lead her to the Westlands."

Lucian couldn't argue with that logic. "She doesn't know about Vera. That's our one saving grace." He looked at Jagar. "The question is, if we try to hide, will she be able to find us? Would it be possible to hide out here?"

He shook his head. "I only grow enough food to feed myself, with a slight surplus. I don't have enough to go around for months on end, nor is there even the arable land to farm more. I'm afraid you must go to the Westlands, as difficult as that journey will be. There are towns there, scattered as they are in the hills and around the oases. But of course, if you go far enough, there is the City of Kalm on the Surin River. You might lose yourself in its alleys, hiding in plain sight."

"Is that the big town we passed over on the way here?" Lucian asked.

Jagar nodded. "It's the only major city in the Westlands. There are others, but they are scattered. Kalm is the primary population center, for little can survive the Westlands that's not on the Surin. The Surin itself flows south and empties into the Sea of Eros, which wraps around most of the moon."

"So we have two choices," Lucian said. "Try to hide somewhere in the Westlands where we might go unnoticed. Or, go after the Queen and steal *The Prophecy of the Seven*."

"You have a third choice," Selene said, coming out of her silence and drawing everyone's attention. "To work with the Queen as prescribed. That's probably the easiest way that will give you everything you want, at least for the moment."

"That's not happening," Lucian said. "I thought you hated her, anyway."

"I do," she said. "I'm merely pointing out the alternatives."

"Well," Serah said, tersely, "after everything we've gone

through, after Cleon, it's a given we'd never consider that viable."

Selene gave a little shrug and resumed her former silence.

"Selene has a point," Jagar said. "You're not busting in there and getting the prophecy unless *she* allows it. And that will not happen until she's sure beyond the shadow of a doubt that you will be of use and under her control."

Lucian scoffed. "Well, since that won't happen, doesn't that settle it? I'll have to learn to get along without the prophecy."

"But you can't," Selene said. "As someone who has studied *The Prophecy of the Seven*, it's a necessary component toward finding the rest of the Orbs. Arian himself reveals as much. He wrote it to help the Chosen. You simply can't leave here without it."

"I've found two Orbs so far," Lucian said. "And I haven't exactly been looking for them."

"But you can't expect *all* the Orbs to be found that way," Selene said.

"Why not?"

She looked at him as if he was stupid. "True, you got lucky twice. I suppose it's possible to bumble through the galaxy and find them just by following your whims. But I don't buy it. Perhaps the Manifold directed you here not only to find the Orb of Psionics but to find *The Prophecy of the Seven* as well. And not just any translation, but one that is among the purest translations in all the Worlds, penned by the most powerful Psionic."

Lucian didn't bother telling her Vera was the most powerful Psionic, at least per Transcend White's words. Perhaps they were equally matched, or maybe it was a matter of debate.

"You must want me to fail, then. You heard Jagar. I can't get in there unless the Queen allows it. And to be honest, no one here has convinced me that this is something I need to do. All *I* need to do is wait out the Queen."

"That alone will be hard enough," Jagar said. "Even in the Far Westlands, the Queen has Psionically branded agents in any village of note."

"The Eyes of Ansaldra," Serah said with a shudder. "I've only heard stories about them, none of them good."

"The Eyes?" Lucian asked.

"They are spies and assassins that watch her empire for any signs of trouble. She almost certainly would have told them to watch out for us."

"She can also communicate with them instantaneously," Jagar said. "As soon as any of them sees someone matching your description, or the description of Selene, then the full might of her army and mages will fall upon you."

"So the safest option is to stay here. Only you say there isn't enough food for all of us."

"On that point, I cannot budge."

"Well, how are we supposed to survive, then? We can't go into any town without risking getting caught."

"It will be a challenge," Jagar admitted. "Unfortunately, that's a bridge you'll have to cross at some point."

To Lucian, that didn't sound reassuring. There was a long silence as everyone considered the options.

"I have to say," Fergus said. "If we had *The Prophecy of the Seven*, it would make finding the rest of the Orbs easier. That's something we eventually need to do, right?"

Lucian couldn't be hearing him right. "Absolutely not. We're going to get captured or killed. And assuming we get off this moon, there are other places we can find the prophecy."

"Like where?" Serah asked.

"The Volsung Academy, for one," Lucian said. "I read part of a copy there myself. I . . . can't exactly recall what I read. I went into some sort of trance. I remember reading about the

Orbs, secrets of Starsea and creation, and . . ." He shook his head. "It's escaping me. It wasn't much, but there was certainly nothing about where the Orbs might be."

"That might be in another portion of the prophecy," Selene said. "Or the copy you were reading might have been incomplete." She paused thoughtfully. "Would the Volsung Academy give it to you, assuming you could get there?"

Lucian laughed. "Probably not, since they are the ones who exiled me here. But I have a friend on the inside who might get it for me."

"*Might*," Selene said. "You don't know whether they'd risk their necks to give you an artifact so prized. And you cannot compare the purity of this version with the purity of the Queen's. One we know the value of, the other we don't."

Lucian had to admit her point was good. "Well, I won't risk it. There's nothing you can say to convince me it's a good idea."

"I'm with Lucian," Serah said. "It's a foolish idea."

"Whatever you decide, Lucian, I'll support you," Fergus said. "We've learned a lot here, but perhaps it would be best if we tabled the discussion for now. We have a long way to travel, and it's not even certain we'll make it to the other side in one piece."

All went quiet, though Jagar seemed the most sullen of all. Something was going on inside that mind of his. Lucian resisted the urge to ask, knowing that the old man would speak in his own time.

At last, Jagar looked up, his firm gaze meeting Lucian's.

"This is most unusual," he said. "You came from the west, where no one does. You've told me a story that is the most remarkable thing I've ever heard in my eighty-four years of life. I'm an old man, beaten down by life, with no real reason to go on save to draw another breath." He stared into the flames. "My mind rails against it. But deep down, I know that this is not the end of my journey. I'm an exile, though I tried my best. But I don't want to die with my head in the sand, old and forgotten in this blasted landscape. I want to die looking my enemy in the eye. I want to die with dignity, knowing that I tried something . . . even if I'm not sure what that something is."

What was Jagar saying? He watched him in shock as the old man lifted his head and sat with a noble bearing, despite his years.

"Lucian," he said. "I don't know if you're the Chosen of the Manifold. All I want to say is, I feel it's right to offer my services to you . . . if you'll have me."

11

LUCIAN COULD ONLY STARE at him in shock, and even Fergus's and Serah's mouths were agape. Selene watched him coolly, her eyes calculating a new balance.

It was a moment before Lucian could find his words. "Of course you can come. We need all the help we can get."

"What are you hoping to accomplish by coming?" Selene asked neutrally.

Jagar shook his head. "I don't know. Answers? Vindication? To go out in a blaze of glory?" He chuckled. "The reasons don't matter, as long as I'm sure. And I'm most definitely sure."

"That's good enough for me," Serah said.

Fergus looked at him, eyes suspicious. "I welcome you as well, Jagar Tengiz Ashiz. However, others have promised to aid us as well and betrayed us. I will never allow such a thing to happen again."

Lucian remembered Osric in the Darkrift. Could Jagar be trying the same thing? He supposed it was possible, but he didn't think it likely. His tale was too wild to *not* be true, at least mostly. And Selene had joined them as well, though that was more out of necessity than any willingness to trust her. In Lucian's mind, *she* was the one they needed to monitor.

"I can think of no one better to get us out of this mess," Lucian said. "Whatever your reasons, welcome aboard."

Jagar gave a regal nod.

"Out of curiosity," Lucian said. "Where are you from, originally? What is your primary?"

"My primary is Psionics, as you might guess. And I am originally from Alsan."

"Alsan?" Serah asked.

"A small Border World," he answered.

"Alsan is firmly a Mid-World now," Lucian said. "Has been my entire life."

"Huh," he said. "I've lived most of my life here. What a joke that is."

"What's going to happen to Akhekh?" Serah asked.

"Akhekh will be fine. He'll head on back to the mountains, near to where we'll be going. Hopefully, he'll tell his friends not to bother us."

"So, what you're saying is we would have died trying to cross the mountains without you?" Selene asked.

Jagar shrugged. "It's likely."

"And you would have just let us . . . go?"

"Well, I would've warned you to be careful."

"Well, that's a relief," Selene said, all but rolling her eyes.

"You're seriously coming with us?" Lucian asked.

"Well, I might not be if you young'uns keep asking me that."

It was hard to tell if he was truly angry or just being grumpy.

"Well, that settles that," Serah said. "When are we going?"

"It's best if we moved out soon," Jagar said. "The weather can be fickle out this way."

"You mind taking the lead?" Lucian asked.

"There's no other way to do this. No one's come down the

South Trail in years, so that doesn't bode well for it being passable. Still, we'll just follow it and see what we find."

Within the hour, they had filled their leather packs with as much food as they could carry. As they got ready, Lucian realized it could not be easy for Jagar to leave his home for twenty years. Once he, Fergus, Selene, and Serah went outside, Jagar remained in the house for a while, for so long that Lucian thought about getting him. Akhekh waited outside, not seeming to have a care in the Worlds.

When Jagar emerged, he went over to the wyvern. "Goodbye, old friend. Something tells me this might be the last we see of each other."

To Lucian's surprise, the wyvern gave a regal nod, a strangely human gesture. He wondered if that was natural, or something it had picked up from Jagar.

Jagar motioned them all back a few paces, and Lucian saw why. As soon as Akhekh had space, he charged forward. He and everyone else ducked as the wyvern launched itself with its two powerful legs and took to the sky. The great wyvern flapped its wings broadly, heading toward the spindly Bone Mountains.

"Thought I saw my life flash before my eyes," Fergus said.

"There will be plenty of time for that in the days ahead," Jagar said.

Without so much as a backward glance, Jagar headed off into the hills, following an old lava flow eastward.

———

JAGAR CERTAINLY KNEW his way through these hills. There was no hesitation as he picked the most efficient path across old lava flows. By early afternoon, Cupid once again covered the sun, plunging the land into eclipsed darkness. Lucian watched the shadows gathering in every dark nook where a wyvern might be hiding. He felt safer with Jagar with them, but surely he couldn't be a friend to every wyvern on the face of Psyche. However, the old man didn't seem to be concerned in the least. He whistled an old-timey tune as he led the way through the mountains, the base of his shockspear clacking off the rocks.

"Not a care in the Worlds," Serah said, falling in beside Lucian.

"Yeah. He seems . . . happy."

"Maybe he's glad to have an excuse to get out of here."

Lucian wasn't sure about that. "He could have *always* gotten out of here. I think he's happy because he feels free for the first time in a while."

By the time night fell, they were walking through a dry gulley between two nearly vertical mountains. The bareness of the ground and the canopy of the stars above made Lucian feel as if he were standing on the surface of an asteroid, not a planet. They had gained a bit of elevation, so it was cold up here. But Jagar didn't seem concerned about any threats, though he told Serah to create a branded fire near the cave entrance they took shelter in.

"How much longer till we're through?" Lucian asked.

"Oh, couple days, give or take. I haven't taken this path in many years. Nor have I seen any come down it since the Western Insurrection."

"Sounds like we're going to die," Serah said.

Jagar just chuckled at that. Lucian didn't think there was anything to laugh at.

They cooked over the fire and settled down to sleep shortly after. Serah went off into the night, Lucian supposed to answer the call of nature. But when he woke up in the middle of the night, she hadn't come back.

He walked out of the cave, keeping his hand on the retracted spear at all times. He entered a narrow cleft, so similar to the rifts on the opposite side of Psyche. He reached for his Focus, trying to get a sense of where Serah had gone. Radiance wasn't his strength, but he knew enough to seek her Focus. Assuming she wasn't warding it, he would find her.

He felt something back toward the west, the direction they had come from, and followed the trail. After a quarter of an hour of walking, he found her sitting on a rock overlooking the dried lava flows that spread for tens of kilometers toward the west, toward the very edge of the Sandsea, hidden by the curve of the horizon.

She was examining her arm, and upon seeing him, jolted and hid it from view. Her eyes narrowed as if he had caught her in a private act.

"What are you doing, following me like this?"

Lucian stayed where he was. "You okay?"

Her stiff posture thawed a bit. She turned toward the west, hiding her face from him. "I don't know. Can anyone be okay, given the circumstances?"

When Lucian came closer, she didn't turn to look at him. It felt as if she were hiding something, but why would she do that?

"Is it okay if I sit down?"

She shrugged. "Be my guest."

He joined her, trying to leave some space between them. Her arms were no longer exposed. Like Selene, Jagar had given her a dusty, worn robe for protection from the desert.

Lucian didn't want to ask since clearly, she was hiding her arm, but he couldn't pretend that it wasn't there.

"Is it worse?"

She stiffened a bit and then nodded. "It's been hurting all day. Burns something fierce. I've got no Karealas sap, and neither does Jagar. Rotting hell, *that* was embarrassing to ask."

She hung her head and didn't meet his eyes.

"I'm sorry," Lucian said.

She shook her head. "I'd show you, but even *I* don't want to see it."

"That's fair. I mean, is there anything else we can do for the pain?"

"Not a rotting thing." She reached into her pocket, retrieving a ball of *ayah* leaves. "He gave me this, but chewing it just makes me sick. So, I have a choice between feeling sick and slightly in pain, or being clear-headed and in a great deal of pain."

Lucian wasn't sure how to comfort her. "That's terrible."

"I . . . just need to weather it. Immolations are pure bitchery, that's for sure."

"Where could we get some Karealas sap?"

"Well, you can only find the tree in the Darkrift. They don't grow in the light. And they don't grow on this side of the Mountains of Madness, as far as I know. We might find some in an apothecary in Kalm, but that's weeks away. I doubt they'd carry such a high-value item in the smaller villages."

"Makes sense. Well, we'll pass through this Kalm place, eventually."

"Seriously, it's not worth the trouble. I can manage fine. Besides, I'm feeling better. Maybe you're taking my mind off things."

"I seem to have that effect."

"Huh. I wouldn't get *too* confident."

"You can't let me have a victory, can you?"

"Sorry. I'm just a winner."

She scooted closer until their shoulders were touching. "Strange to say, I feel better, though I don't feel you solved anything. Honestly, I just want not to care about it. Acknowledging it just makes it harder to deal with."

A lump formed in his throat, and he was at a loss for words. "That's the thing, though. How could I not care?"

"And what's that going to get you? I know I'm going to die someday. All this sympathy won't make it any easier. Either stop caring or make a move. I know you think you might hurt me by getting more real. Or hurt yourself. Well, whatever you're doing now is worse."

"I don't understand," Lucian said. "After our conversation on the *Zephyr*, I wasn't sure you wanted that."

"I just said that because I thought we were going to die. I didn't want to make things worse. But we survived, and now there's a chance things might be all right. At least for a while. I just . . . want you there for me. I don't want to face the darkness alone. Do you?"

Lucian had to admit he did not. "Serah, nothing is going to happen to you. I won't let it. You're worrying over nothing."

She went quiet at that. It took her a moment, but she reached for her left arm, pulling back the sleeve of her robe. The pink, mottled skin now extended from her wrist to just below her elbow. What had once been a small blotch was now taking up most of her arm.

Seeing that almost made Lucian's heart stop. Tears came to his eyes when he realized it *wasn't* nothing. That was just him in denial.

"You see it, now. I don't have much time left."

"How has it grown so fast?"

"I overdrew three times to attack the Queen's gravity brand. I thought that alone would kill me."

Lucian felt guilty for that. He had allowed the Queen to escape by saving Selene. In the end, they had needed her, but he hadn't known that at the time.

She let the sleeve fall back down. "I understand if it scares you. I understand if it revolts you. If that's the reason you're hesitating so much—"

Lucian leaned forward and kissed her. Serah responded in kind, and Lucian felt the desperation in her lips' movement. After a time, she pulled back and rested her head on his shoulder. When silent tears stained his neck, he said nothing, only stroking her back.

"It'll be okay," he said. "We'll figure this out. Just take it easy over the next few days. Don't overdraw. Don't stream more than you have to."

"I'll have to do what I have to do, Lucian," she said, quietly. "No way around that."

Lucian knew she was right. "I can't let you die. Not after how far we've come. The fraying must end. And it must end soon. We'll find a way off this moon. We'll get *The Prophecy of the Seven*. I will move the Worlds to see you healed."

"Okay," she said with an embarrassed laugh. "That's cheesy."

"I don't care what it is. We have to believe it's possible, or it never will be."

"Told you."

"Told you what?"

"You're a rotting hero, now."

"Whatever. Let's head back. None of this moping."

As they walked back to the cave, she seemed in better spirits. It was something, and he wanted to do everything he could to protect that.

12

LUCIAN STILL COULDN'T SLEEP. He'd set his Psionic ward, so he wasn't worried about the Queen.

He just couldn't get Serah's fraying arm out of his mind. How could he protect her from that? Was there any way to slow it down? Lucian was afraid he'd never find all the Orbs in time to save her. That was likely to take years, and Serah's condition was advancing far faster than he thought possible.

Lucian didn't care how he did it. It just had to be done. Not only for her but for every mage in the galaxy.

The Sorceress-Queen of Psyche claimed she could help him, and teaming up with her might speed things up. If it was enough to save Serah, Lucian could see himself doing it, even if it started another war. The fact he'd potentially let billions die just for a chance to save Serah scared him. Would such a massacre be the greatest good, at least according to the Queen's twisted morality?

There had to be another way, but what? Maybe Vera knew something, but he didn't really know if he could trust her. Like Ansaldra, she had been a member of the Starsea Mages.

Then again, Jagar had been a part of the Starsea Mages, too. Even if he was remorseful, was it a double-standard to trust him, but not Ansaldra?

Lucian wasn't sure *what* to think. Ansaldra was a known evil, at least in his mind, but Vera could be so much worse if half of what Transcend White hinted about her was true.

Vera was his ticket off this world. She had a spaceship, and presumably a way to run the Warden blockade and escape this moon for good. He had to trust that, otherwise, she would have told him such a thing was impossible.

Whatever he did, he needed *The Prophecy of the Seven*. Without that, he might not find the rest of the Orbs. Vera could help him decode it, as strong as she was in Psionic Magic. Together, they could find all the Orbs without Ansaldra's help.

Everything was unknown and dubious. And time was of the essence. At the rate Serah's wound was spreading, she wouldn't last long at all. Perhaps not even a year.

Lucian's stomach sunk at the prospect. But there was a fire in his belly, a determination to succeed at all costs. He had found something personal to fight for, and if there was a way, he would find it.

He only hoped his will was enough.

———

As THE NEXT MORNING DAWNED, Jagar led them through the ravine with impossibly high walls, directly east toward the rising sun. It was cooler up here in the heights, for which Lucian was grateful. It was dry, too. It seemed the entire Planetside was a desert, one that grew more extreme the farther west one went. He was ready to see water again, to see life that wasn't hostile to humanity.

But before that could happen, they had to cross the Fire Rifts.

Already, he saw signs of it. A moonquake shocked him with its suddenness, several rocks breaking from the canyon walls and tumbling to the ravine floor. In the middle, they were in no real danger, but it was a sobering reminder that wyverns were not the only threat out there. Judging by how thickly the broken rocks and boulders filled the ravine, this erosion had been happening for eons.

The going only became rougher, and the debris had piled so high that they were skirting the rim of the ravine. Lucian was wondering if the old hermit had lost his way. But he methodically picked his way east, avoiding the bits that would have forced Serah to use her Gravitonic Magic. For that, Lucian was thankful. Perhaps the old man knew what she was struggling with.

It was a miracle Jagar had survived this long, especially since it didn't seem as if he held back using magic, like Linus and Plato. The Elders of Kiro had talked of stream purity, so perhaps his Psionic Magic was pure enough for him to last this long. It wasn't a question Lucian could ask, at least for now.

They camped that night in a narrow cleft, well-sheltered, with no signs of any threats. The next morning, they set off again, the elevation sloping downward as they came out the eastern side of the Bone Mountains.

In the early afternoon, they reached the sheer edge of a cliff. The ravine dropped hundreds of meters below, where the fiery glow of magma radiated upward. From where he stood, Lucian couldn't feel its heat, but it was plenty hot from the sun beating down on them. Now lower in elevation, the day was proving uncomfortably warm.

"Looks like hell itself," Fergus said. "And there's no way across!"

"Well, I said it would take two weeks at least," Jagar said. "We need to travel farther north to find the passing."

"What if the lava in one of those rifts explodes while we're here?" Serah asked.

Jagar watched the fires below. "Well, we wouldn't be the first to die from such a thing. We must stay as far from the edge as possible. The last thing we need is a moonquake to send us a-tumbling in."

As if in answer to that, Lucian noted a tall plume of smoke beyond the horizon, a smoke that tinged the very air gray, diffusing a sulfurous stench that was difficult to ignore.

"The sooner we get through this place, the better," he said.

Jagar kept walking, and they kept following.

They spent the entire afternoon following this great rift. At points, the magma below would suddenly churn and shoot up flares of fire and heat that reached uncomfortably high, enough for Lucian to feel the heat of it.

"Almost enough to singe my boots," Fergus said.

"It would be the last thing you felt," Jagar called back.

Another rumbling shook the ground. Jagar fell flat on his face, spread-eagled. Everyone followed his example. The ground was warm with the heat below, and it took a few seconds for the vibrations to elapse. Only then did Jagar stand again.

Even as Lucian was staring wide-eyed down into the rift, Jagar carried on, whistling his tune as if nothing unexpected had happened.

"Balls of steel, that one," Serah said.

Selene harrumphed at her irreverence.

Jagar finally called a halt, at a place where the rim above the cliff widened enough for them to back a decent distance away from the edge.

"We'll walk the Fire Path tomorrow," he said over the usual dinner of campfire stew. "It will be the most dangerous part of our journey, for if the fires act up, there's only so much a Thermal ward can do."

104

"What do you mean?" Selene asked.

"If the Fire Rifts decide to be active, the magma will surface, and fast."

"I can tether us across the more dangerous bits," Lucian said.

"Yes, that is something I'd figured. Still, you won't be able to do it in every case, and in particularly bad eruptions, even that won't save us. My suggestion is to hold off on any streaming until necessary."

"Sounds reasonable," Lucian said.

Even if the Orb's power was theoretically limitless, the last thing the group needed was for Lucian to lose his Focus at a pivotal moment. He could easily be incapable of getting five people out of a tight spot once exhausted. Besides, he didn't want to draw so much ether that he delved the Manifold again. That was where the Voice lurked.

Everyone settled down for sleep, to prepare for the hardest day yet.

———

THE DAY BEGAN EASILY ENOUGH, simply following the rim of the rift. After a few hours, though, Lucian noticed what he could only describe as a natural dam of rock that bridged the rift, what seemed to be the only possible way across. This "dam" descended into the rift, making a rough U-shape, where at the bottom it was probably no higher than ten or twenty meters above the surface of the lava. This had to be the "Fire Path" Jagar had referred to the day before, and it was easy to see why it was so-named.

By the time they stood before the entrance, Lucian could see that this narrow path was only a meter or two across in most places, and was anything but smooth. On the left, the lava was lower in elevation by about ten meters, so it was the right side they needed to worry most about.

"Maybe I can pull everyone across," Lucian said.

"This is just the first of many, lad," Jagar said. "Save your concentration. We might need it for later."

Lucian went quiet, deciding to trust the old man's expertise.

They descended, and with the descent came the heat. It baked Lucian's skin, and if it got any hotter, they'd have no choice but to set a Thermal ward.

Once they'd reached the bottom, Lucian was feeling faint, and this was no place to be passing out. They climbed the rest of the way out without incident, the entire passage taking almost an hour. The air at the top was mercifully cool, but the land ahead revealed more cracks and crevices, all of which glowed with the molten red of lava.

"Lovely," Serah said.

Jagar was right. This was just the beginning.

13

THE MOONQUAKES WERE the worst part of crossing the Fire Rifts. Lucian could endure the heat because there was nothing as bad as that first rift. But the passages were so precarious that it was easy to see how anyone might fall.

On the first night during the crossing, they camped on a plateau rising above the rifts below, and the next day was much the same—zigging and zagging their way across a landscape riven with fiery chasms under a dark, bilious sky tinged with smoke. Lucian could see how that which had taken them a couple of hours to pass in the *Zephyr* would take them two weeks or more on foot.

They were several hours into the day when Jagar came to a sudden stop before the next chasm. It appeared as if there had once been a way across, but it had collapsed in the middle, creating an impossible gap to traverse. At least, a gap impossible to cross without Binding Magic.

Jagar frowned as he stared at the crossing. "We've got some hard choices to make."

Lucian stepped forward. "How is it hard? I can tether us across one by one."

"Aye, I'm sure you could. However, that would not be wise."

Serah arched a suspicious eyebrow. "What *aren't* you telling us, Jagar?"

It was clear from his reaction that he was hiding something. Everyone watched him for an answer.

"I didn't want to tell you because I didn't want to scare anyone."

"Scare us about what?"

"The wyverns," he said. "While they are not magical beings, they can detect magic when it's being used. Especially if it's a sizeable amount."

Lucian felt his face redden from anger. "And you're telling us this *now*?"

"I didn't want to cause undue worry. Small amounts are fine, but it's hard to know where the line is. But if you use that rotting Orb, it'll draw every wyvern here like rift adders to blood."

"What does that mean, then?" Serah asked. "I thought you were good with the wyverns."

"Not the fire wyverns. They have something of a rivalry with the Bone Mountain wyverns, and let's just say if they found us here, things would not go smoothly."

"You should have told us this," Lucian said.

Jagar shrugged. "Maybe so. Knowing it doesn't change the equation. This is the only way back to the Westlands, unfortunately. We're going to have to divert our path north or south, and no matter which way we choose, that brings us closer to fire wyvern territory." He thought for a moment. "To remind you, these fire wyverns are smaller and faster. They're red, and the skin can stand up to the heat of the rifts better. They also hunt in large packs and are of lower intelligence than Riftland wyverns and mountain wyverns, which are more or less the same species. These are a different breed altogether. They will kill us without hesitation."

"What do we do, then?" Lucian asked. "We can't use magic, and changing our course will just bring us into their territory, anyway."

"It's a hard decision," Jagar said. "I vote to change course because using magic will draw many of them on us all at once."

Lucian sighed. This was just what they needed. "Okay. So north, or south?"

"North is the direction we need to be angling for. We can link back up with the South Trail from there."

"Well, if it's all the same," Serah said. "Is there anything we can do to keep out of sight?"

"Not much at all," Jagar said. "Fortunately, like most wyverns on Psyche, their eyesight isn't the best, for which you can be thankful. However, if we get too close, they'll have other ways of detecting us, usually by sound or smell. It would be safest to not sleep in the open."

"We must do what we have to," Fergus said. "Lead on."

Selene remained silent, though her eyes were angry and her cheeks flushed. She, too, hadn't liked Jagar holding back information.

Jagar turned toward the north and gazed into the distance for a moment. When he set off, the others fell in behind.

———

HOURS PASSED with no discernible change. They followed the rugged edge of the rift on their right, while the distance ahead revealed nothing that could be a threat. The only thing of note was a molten red glow on the horizon, a glow that grew brighter as the hours passed.

"What is that?" Lucian asked.

"The Great Volcano," Jagar answered. "The main abode of the fire wyverns."

"Do we have to go past it?"

Jagar shook his head. "There should be a way east soon, but we have to get closer first. No way around that."

"And there's a good chance we'll get caught, isn't there?" Serah asked.

"Yup."

"I'm not a fan of suicide," Selene said. "Have Lucian pull us across."

"Well, it sounds like you like the idea of suicide," Jagar said. "That would guarantee it."

Selene retreated into her silent shell as they continued.

Lucian got the vague idea that Jagar might be friends with these wyverns, and delivering them on a silver platter for some unknown reason. Osric had done the same, after all. But there was no reason Jagar would do that. At least, not that Lucian could see. He didn't think he was lying to them, though he couldn't have explained why.

They came to a sort of promontory jutting out over a lake of lava. To bypass the lake, they'd have to skirt around, but there didn't seem to be any clear path. There were cracks three to five meters in breadth surrounding the whole thing. Lucian knew he'd be able to jump them in Psyche's gravity, but he wasn't sure about Jagar, or even Selene, who had the shortest legs of them all. Serah could easily give everyone a gravity assist, but would that use of magic be enough to alert the wyverns?

These thoughts seemed to run through Jagar's mind, too. "We'll jump what we can, and use magic for the rest. My Gravitonics is fair, but it would be better for Serah to bridge the gaps. She can do so efficiently."

She shared a look with Lucian. He caught a brief flash of fear, but it was only a flash. It didn't seem as if anyone else saw it. He would use Gravitonics himself, but he didn't trust himself to do it as well as her. It was one thing to risk your neck with gravity discs, but another thing to hold them long enough for others to use safely as well. Serah was the only one among them who could do the job right.

"My time to shine, then." She stepped forward until she was at the five-meter gap. She raised her hands, which were wrapped with a silvery aura of magic. A moment later, three equidistant discs appeared.

Jagar was the first across, and the rest hurried behind. Lucian gave Serah a worried look before he crossed. She followed behind, allowing the stream to die and the discs to disappear.

They proceeded in that way for a while. Every chance he got, Lucian stared in the Great Volcano's direction. It rose halfway above the horizon, and so far, things seemed to be quiet. For now, all it belched was acrid smoke, not wyverns.

After several hours passed, they had left the volcano well behind. But now they stood before a new obstacle that seemed impossible to cross without magic.

The land simply fell away, revealing a new rift, far wider than anything they had yet crossed. Peering down, lava flowed hundreds of meters below, and the expanse to the other side stretched *at least* ten kilometers. Lucian thought that if Psyche had a Grand Canyon like on Earth, then this was it.

The only time Lucian had tethered something so far was the air skiff to the distant Bone Mountains. And doing that had caused him to delve. From what he could see, there was nothing obvious to latch on to. The distance was too great, especially with the heat waves rising from the rift. It was probably beyond Fergus's skills to set a light beacon that far, and even if he managed it, it would take several hours to get everyone across one at a time. Enough time for the wyverns to fall upon them.

"It's impossible," Lucian said. "Even if I could set the tether, I'd exhaust myself after getting just one person across. I'd have to rest and stream another across hours later."

"Not to mention the wyverns," Serah said. "What do we do? Is there any other way?"

Jagar's head fell, defeated. "I've got nothing."

Selene marched up to him and stuck a finger on his chest. "What do you mean, *nothing*? You led us out here, Jagar Tengiz Ashiz. Get us out!"

"I . . . suppose we could head back south. Hope to catch the end of this rift, where the South Trail goes. But there are no guarantees."

"It's getting late," Fergus said. "It might be best if we just slept on it."

"Sleeping will do nothing," Selene said. "Can we not try going farther north?"

"We could," Jagar admitted. "I don't know what lies up that way, though."

Selene looked as if she were ready to scream at him.

"Someone needs a nap," Serah said, her voice low.

Selene whirled around, her chest heaving. "I'm hot, I'm tired, and I'm *sick* of incompetence. I've been as patient as I can, but I've had enough. I just want to get home!"

She fell to her knees and started sobbing. To see this transformation of the normally cool and collected Selene was shocking. Lucian wasn't sure how to react. He saw her then as she truly was—a young woman who was in way over her head. He supposed that was all of them, but she had reached her breaking point soonest.

It was Fergus who ended up offering her a hand. And to Lucian's surprise, she took it.

"I'm with you," he said. "But we can't break down. Not now. We need to put our heads together and figure this out."

To Lucian's surprise, Selene fell on his shoulder, seeming to want comfort. Fergus was in the awkward position of having to soothe her, but from his face, it seemed he had sympathy. Perhaps because of her many contributions so far, Lucian had expected too much from Selene. She was strong in magic, but that didn't mean she was anywhere near prepared for this gauntlet mentally.

"It'll get much easier, assuming we can get out of the Fire Rifts," Lucian said. "I've decided I want to get that prophecy. I know it means going right into the lion's den, so to speak. But I don't see any other way. If I'm to find the rest of the Orbs, I'm going to need a guide. The *Prophecy of the Seven* is the closest thing we have to that. All of you have followed me this far, willingly or not. No hard feelings if you decide to not help me there. I'm grateful for the help I've had so far. But that's what I'm going to do."

All of them watched him. He felt awkward, as he did anytime he gave one of his speeches. But he thought it was important they know where his head was at. Serah needed to be saved from the fraying, and for now, that was his immediate and visceral reason to go on.

"We should find some shelter, as Fergus said," Jagar said, breaking the silence. "There will be time to discuss all this later. When we're safe."

No one argued as he led them to a ledge, under which was a cave mostly hidden from view of the surface. Within that cave was a small, natural tunnel exiting into the rift itself. Lucian followed it, finding a ledge that overlooked the fiery chasm below. Looking north and south along the rift's length, there didn't seem to be any other obvious way across.

No one spoke much after that. There didn't seem to be any way out of this situation. At least, nothing that didn't require Lucian to stream each person across one by one over many hours or even days. The recovery time for his Focus was the bottleneck, and it wasn't something he wanted to test.

One thing was obvious. If there was another way, they needed to find it, and soon.

14

LUCIAN AWOKE FEELING the worst he had in days. The hard travel was taking its toll. Everything ached, and the hot, dry air infused with the smell of brimstone made him feel as if he were literally in hell. He coughed, and no matter how much he did so, it seemed he could never get enough of the particulates in the air out of his lungs.

They couldn't waste any more time here. He had to do something he had never done before—get five people across this chasm.

Fergus would have to go last, though. He needed to set the concealment ward, which hopefully would be enough to cover Lucian's streaming and make it undetectable to the wyverns. That meant getting Jagar, Serah, and Selene across first. Fergus could go over next to last, and Lucian last of all. That would probably be the hardest part because the passage itself would take at least ten minutes with the distance, and once Fergus was over, Lucian would have to do it all over again with no break. And without Fergus, the concealment ward couldn't cover him, making him a sitting duck.

He supposed it might be possible to tether them both over at the same time. He'd have to wait and see how difficult it was to do one person at this distance.

Lucian explained his thoughts over breakfast, and everyone just stared at him. That couldn't be a good sign.

"We must be patient," Fergus said. "The farther you set your focal point, the more magic it's going to take. And at this distance, it's probably beyond the bounds of possibility. Yes, with my Radiant Magic, you'll see well enough to create the focal point. But to be frank, such a thing would stretch even my abilities." He shook his head. "I can't get behind this."

"Nor I," Jagar said. "It's a great idea, but it's riddled with problems. We shouldn't have to do this."

"If we go north, we're going into fire wyvern territory," Lucian said. "Hell, we already *are* in fire wyvern territory. We could wander around here a few more days, or maybe even get caught doing so." He looked at each of them. "I say we take the chance. Our supplies are limited, and we can't afford to wander around aimlessly."

"I'm with you," Selene said. "The sooner this is over, the sooner we are back in civilization, the better. It's not like this is our last obstacle. We have more mountains to contend with after the Fire Rifts, and then we can say that we are in the Westlands. And the Westlands is a vast expanse. While flat, they are extremely dry and inhospitable in their own right. We probably can't even rest until we reach Kalm. I might even get access to my accounts and buy us airship passage to Cuzin or Laris."

"Wait," Lucian said. "There are airships besides the *Zephyr*?"

Selene nodded. "Airships are the dominant form of intercity travel, at least in the Daran Empire. Mage-Knights make good money by converting water into helium, and the Imperial Airways Company controls that helium. Which of course is owned by the Queen."

"That's too risky," Fergus said.

"We could disguise ourselves and use pseudonyms. Make ourselves look like Westlanders from Kalm. Most of our skin and faces would be covered, anyway."

"That's too far ahead, but it's an interesting idea," Lucian said. "What do you think, Serah?"

She sighed. "I don't know. Neither option seems good, so I'll just say do what you feel is best."

It seemed it would be up to him once again. "I say we go for it. Of course, if Fergus's training doesn't work out, we can always just go back to the original plan."

Jagar nodded, though his wrinkled expression seemed to be somber. "So be it."

———

FERGUS AND LUCIAN stood above the ledge of the rift. They had to test if this could work first before risking anybody's life.

One thing Lucian had neglected in his mental calculus. Fergus couldn't both stream a light beacon *and* a concealment ward. By the time he set the ward, there wouldn't be enough ether to set a beacon. So, Lucian had to use his Radiant Magic to see afar using a sight ward. That would likely use most of his available ether, but Lucian could still stream using the Orb of Binding since it wouldn't draw upon his natural pool.

Now, he just had to learn to set a sight ward properly.

"Expand your Focus," Fergus instructed. "You're thinking too much like a Binder and a Psionic, not a Radiant."

"Whatever that means," Lucian said.

"Not to say Radiance doesn't benefit from a narrow Focus," Fergus went on. "For example, the Focus becomes narrower than most Aspects when you're trying to stream a laser. Incredibly draining, that, and it requires so much ether that you can only do it as an active stream for as long as you can hold it. But

I digress. Most Radiant Magic requires you to expand your awareness outward, to be cognizant of your environment. Can you try to set the sight ward again? Assuming you can manage that, the rest should prove simpler."

Lucian did as Fergus instructed, accessing his Focus and reaching for the Radiant Aspect. Rather than opening an active stream, he designated *all* of his available ether to Radiance, using it to increase his sense of vision. For a moment, details sharpened with unusual clarity—first nearer to him, and then much farther. The others watched from the cave entrance nervously.

But by the time the ward was powerful enough for him to see halfway across the rift as clear as he could in front of his face, the ward collapsed. Lucian shook his head. "I can't get it to work."

He felt his ether return to him, infusing into his Focus—so long as he didn't set the ward, he received most of it back.

"Well, then you'll have no choice but to hold an active stream. Whether you can do so for the allotted amount of time remains to be seen."

"I just need a trial," Lucian said. On the ledge before them was a rock, about half a meter across. Lucian could tell from its size and composition that picking it up on Earth would have been difficult. He hoisted it up, finding it decently heavy. "This is about the mass of a human body. If I can get this across, I should be able to get a person across, too."

"I can't argue with that logic." Fergus peered across the rift. "All right, then. Stream Radiance when you're ready. I have the concealment ward set."

Lucian nodded, standing at the ledge and drawing a deep breath. He needed total and complete concentration. He reached for his Focus, for the Radiant Aspect. He had to hope an active stream would be enough to get the rock across. He enhanced his vision until ether was burning at an alarming rate. There was no way around that, though. This was what he had to do to finish the job. He streamed until he could see a large boulder on the other side of the rift through the haze of heat.

He opened Binding, locking in the focal point. He deepened his Focus until nothing but the image of the Septagon dominated his vision. For this amount of magic, he simply couldn't be present in the Shadow Realm. With luck, he wouldn't dip into the Ethereal Background directly, skirting that transition between Shadow and Manifold. But if that had to happen, then there would be no stopping it.

He could only hope Fergus's concealment ward kept his magic from being detected by the fire wyverns. The others watched nervously from within the cave.

With the focal point set, Lucian set the anchor point on the rock next to him. The rush of Binding Magic became a torrent, entering a tether that now extended ten kilometers long. A gut-wrenching sense of nausea twisted his stomach, not from the Binding stream, but the Radiance stream. Just knowing he had to continue streaming Radiance at this rate, a tertiary Aspect, filled him with doubt. And he had to do so for minutes on end.

At last, there was enough tension for the rock to shift on its own. It flew across the rift, though Lucian was barely aware of its mass racing along the tether. He existed in that state for a while, unconscious, unaware, except for the two streams he had opened. The Radiance stream seemed in danger of slipping away at any moment, while the Binding stream held strong and true. But if the Radiance stream failed, so too would the Binding stream. His vision faded from the strain, as the world began being replaced by blue lines feeding into the tether, and green lines into himself.

He was already slipping away from reality, the first sign he was about to delve. He had never done that while streaming a non-Orb Aspect, and the results could be disastrous. Perhaps even enough to fray him. He couldn't go back there, but the rock still had a fair distance to fly.

He knew what he should do—let go of all his streams immediately and admit defeat. But the rock was close, and to admit defeat possibly meant *never* getting across this rift.

So, he buckled down, determined to finish the job.

A sense of dread overwhelmed him as the Ethereal Background manifested before him more fully, as reality faded completely. The Voice would come back at any moment, and this time, he wouldn't be able to escape it.

His entire body felt as if it were burning, but he couldn't give up. Not when he was so close.

Just when everything was an inferno, he detected the Voice trying to connect with his mind. But just before it connected to Lucian's Focus, something yanked him back.

The rock fell just short of the other side of the rift and into the fiery chasm below.

Lucian let go of both streams and blacked out.

15

WHEN LUCIAN AWOKE, the sky was darker, meaning he had been knocked out most of the day.

He groaned and instantly found both Fergus and Serah above him.

"You rotting idiot!" Serah said. "Did you not hear us screaming at you?"

He didn't have the heart or energy to respond. "It almost made it."

"We're *not* going through with that," Fergus said. "You haven't looked outside yet."

"What do you mean?"

Lucian turned and looked.

In just a few seconds, several flashes of red zoomed by the cave entrance. Lucian felt icy dread.

"They found us?"

Fergus held a finger to his lips. Lucian hadn't noticed how quietly the others had been speaking.

"They don't know we're here," Jagar said. "They could be

searching for us, or they might use this rift as a sort of highway. They live most of their lives down here, after all."

"Or, we could unwittingly be near a fire wyvern colony," Serah said. "Or whatever you would call it."

Lucian stood, heading for the cave entrance. Serah tried to pull him back, but he wasn't worried about being seen.

He didn't want them to lose their last chance to get out of here.

"Lucian, what are you doing?" Serah asked.

He crouched low, watching the line of wyverns continue on their way. It was impossible to count the number, but there were at least fifty. Far too many to handle, even with two Orbs. Or more likely, there *was* a way he could handle them, but he was simply too inexperienced to see it.

He waved Jagar to come out, and the old man reluctantly stood behind him.

"I know what you're thinking, lad. It'll take guts, that's for sure."

"Is it doable?"

The old man was silent for a while, considering. "I can probably control one. The rest will depend on you. How good are you at following streams? Are you recovered from earlier?"

"As recovered as I'll ever be. We're stuck here, and if we wait for exactly five wyverns to come along, we'll be waiting forever."

"They always travel in large packs like this, anyway. But every group has a small contingent to guard the rear. The size can vary, but it's usually two to six wyverns."

"That's perfect," Lucian said.

"Yes. But it'll have to be at least five or more, or nothing will come of it. They are too small to carry more than one person."

Looking down the rift, it seemed as if the end of the train was coming, though it was impossible to see the rear guard.

"Can they sense our heat or even us talking?"

"Fire wyverns' senses aren't as finely tuned as rift wyverns," Jagar answered. "However, their sense of smell and sound is far better than a human's. We should be safe against this ledge, as the wind is not carrying our scent. What we have to be concerned about is streaming. As soon as we do, they'll know where we are quick enough."

"I can stream a concealment ward," Fergus said.

"That will help," Jagar said, "but it will only get us so far. If we ever reach the point of controlling five wyverns, it won't matter. Your ward will not be enough, no matter how strong you are."

"I say let's do it," Lucian said. "We're not getting out of here unless we make it happen."

"You are rather confident in your abilities."

Lucian didn't know where that confidence was even coming from. He had barely got that rock across the rift, and he had no reason to believe he could possess *four* wyverns' minds effectively. And yet, he was utterly confident he could do so. He couldn't wait until he was reaching for the Orbs, until that unadulterated power was flowing through him again.

With a start, he realized *that* was the source of his confidence. It was not his confidence at all, but his intense need to feel the power of the Orbs again.

"This is suicide," Lucian decided. The next words would hurt to say. "Maybe we should try to find another way."

"I'm glad you said that, lad. Now . . ."

A moonquake shook the ground, immediately making Lucian and Jagar drop to the ground and back away. The lava in the rift trembled and bubbled, issuing long tongues of flame upward. A blast of hot wind hit Lucian, circling like a vortex within the rift.

And that wind was circling back toward the wyverns, carrying the scent of humans with it.

"Inside!" Jagar said. "There's no time to lose."

They backed inside the cave, but it was already too late. Not a minute later, reptilian screeches echoed throughout the rift.

THE SIX WYVERNS at the tail of the procession changed course, swerving around and flapping in their direction. It was a good half minute or more before the other wyverns turned around as well, but to Lucian's relief, not all of them did. It seemed they "only" had about ten to contend with, while the six that had originally broken away were a fair distance in front of the rest. Somehow, they had to take control of five of them while handling the sixth, all before the other four caught up.

"Can we handle it?" Lucian asked.

Jagar watched with widened eyes. "Well, we're dead if we *can't*. You'll have to read the brand I set perfectly, and to brand the others as quickly as you can." He gave Lucian a sidelong glance. "That rotting Orb of Psionics better be as strong as you're saying it is."

Even Lucian wasn't sure he had what it took to brand five wyverns. Screeches now echoed through the fiery rift, and with that signal, almost all the wyverns had turned around by now.

Jagar faced the others. "Listen up! We only get one chance at this. If we don't make it work, we're stuck here until the day we die. Those wyverns will never let us escape, and whatever ones we kill will be replaced. Worse, their younglings are small enough to force their way in here. We might kill a lot of them, but not all."

"They're almost here," Serah said.

"Prepare yourselves to fight if we fail. As soon as a wyvern lands, get your ass on its back and hold on for dear life!"

All of their eyes were wide, but they nodded. Even Selene.

"Follow my lead, lad," Jagar said. "I've got the magic to snatch up one, but it'll be up to you to grab the rest. If you were

THE CHOSEN OF THE MANIFOLD

lying about the Orb of Psionics, now's your chance to come clean so we can go down fighting like men."

"No lie," Lucian said. "I'm ready when you are."

"I don't think you are, but I appreciate the confidence."

Lucian was ready, reaching for the Orb of Psionics. He could feel a ripple in the Ethereal Background as Jagar streamed, directing his Focus toward the lead wyvern. Jagar used Binding as the shell, for which Lucian was grateful. With both the Orb of Binding and Orb of Psionics, he wouldn't suffer any side effects from overdrawing. He could follow the streams exactly, and as long as the Orbs supplied the ether, they could get out of here. Assuming they could get on the wyverns quickly enough before the rest caught up.

As Jagar streamed, Lucian immediately saw that the brand was both powerful and complicated. Jagar was a powerful mage in his own right to execute it. It reminded him greatly of what the Sorceress-Queen had done to control Selene, with minor differences. The Psionic stream itself contorted on itself in various shapes, the purpose of which Lucian couldn't guess. All he could do was copy it and hope for the best. He deepened his Focus, drawing deeply from both Orbs, something he hadn't done since his battle with the Sorceress-Queen.

Immediately, the Shadow Realm faded, replaced by a matrix of blue and violet lines. He could see the outlines of the wyverns approaching in slow motion, and could detect Jagar's Focus capturing the mind of the first one. Thankfully, the Binding stream itself was simple—nothing more than a circling of blue magic designed to keep the extremely complicated Psionic stream in place. Lucian saw why Jagar hadn't been sure of their chances. Lucian would not only have to get it right once, but *five* times, for each wyvern leading the pack.

He set his focal point on the second nearest wyvern. To brand all four at once would simply take too much magic, even with the Orbs. Four separate dualstreams in tandem would use sixty-four times as much ether as a single stream, something that would be impossible for him to execute. He'd have to brand each wyvern in succession using a dualstream, and would have to hope that both the Orbs of Binding and Psionics granted him enough power to finish the job. He wouldn't just have to brand the wyverns, but keep hold of both Orbs long enough for them to land safely on the other side of the rift.

Lucian first created the Binding shell, holding it in place on the focal point. This part was easy enough, but once he added the Psionic component, the magic would become more difficult to control.

He then streamed Psionics, following the intricate design of Jagar's stream exactly. He intensified his Focus, seeing in his mind's eye the complicated lines and commands designed to take control of a wyvern's mind. He didn't understand *how* they all worked in tandem. He just had to trust that it would.

Magic roared out of him, Binding and Psionics melding to create the first brand. Lucian directed the wyvern to land on the ledge next to where Jagar's wyvern was already waiting.

Three more to go.

Lucian quickly saw that there was no way he could do each one in time. But maybe the work would go faster now that he had done it once. He pulled more ether from the Orbs, felt the fresh infusion of magic to replace the supply tied up in the first brand. With the Orbs, he could continually expand his available pool. What he didn't know was how long he could hold the Orbs. As soon as he let go, the size of his pool would retract, making it impossible to maintain most, if not all, of the brands.

He had no choice but to hold the Orbs and not let go, for as long as it took to cross this rift and send the wyverns on their way.

With his second wyvern branded, there were now three left, including the sixth one that had to be dealt with before they could mount and fly off. He had to concentrate on the task at hand. The wyverns were too close now, just seconds away. In his peripheral vision, he could already see the others climbing on their mind-controlled mounts. Jagar's wyvern was already flying off with him on it, so Lucian permitted the other two possessed wyverns to follow, which carried Serah and Selene. All three were safe and away.

Now, he just had to get a ride for him and Fergus, the only two left. He heard Fergus's voice shouting something, but Lucian was deaf to it.

He would have to finish it all with one last burst of magic. Two dual streams, one for each wyvern, that would burn ether at sixteen times the rate of a single stream, all while two of his possessed wyverns were getting farther and farther away, becoming more difficult to control ...

There was no way around it. He commanded the Orbs to give him all they had, to hell with the consequences.

There was a moment of sudden calm, like the first nanoseconds before the ignition of a fusion bomb. And then boundless magic exploded within him, seeming to obliterate consciousness itself. The Shadow Realm was all but gone. Nothing of reality no longer existed. All that remained was the Manifold. In this place, he could draw and direct as much ether as he wished, behave like a god, at least regarding Psionics and Binding. Ether here in the Manifold was like hydrogen in the universe. Abundant, everywhere, requiring only the right hand to guide it into creation.

He formed the final two brands seamlessly, ignoring the feeling of dread overtaking him. This had to be finished, and quickly. The violet and blue lines coalesced and converged on the two brands, the magic pouring through Lucian in a flood of pure power. It discharged until *he* ceased to be, his consciousness floating in a void ...

The shadow fell upon him, and Lucian knew no more.

16

WHEN THE DARKNESS FINALLY FADED, Lucian found himself in a square-shaped room, with walls of gray stone lined with columns of runes stretching from the floor and upward into infinity. There were no doors and no viable exit.

A shadowed figure stood before him, wearing a billowing black robe and hood that masked his features, with a long black cape that fell to the floor. Darkness obscured his head and face. He looked the part of the grim reaper.

"At last, we meet," the man said, his voice smooth and friendly, but bearing ominous notes. "Probably not the encounter you expected. And yet this encounter was inevitable."

"Who are you?" Lucian asked, feigning confidence. "What is this place?"

The man chuckled. "Do you not know? The Manifold has manifested this place. And you are not here. Not really. Your mind is, and since your mind cannot conceive of itself without a body, nor can it conceive of another being without form, it created you and me. Thus, we are speaking now."

"What are you talking about?"

Though he could not see the man's face, Lucian knew he was smiling coldly. "You find yourself in a prison. A prison created by the Manifold to guard itself against one thing."

Lucian knew this man wanted him to ask what that was, but he didn't.

The man leaned forward, his form leering and dominating. "It's guarding itself against me."

The man suddenly thrust his hand forward, a hand wrapped in violet, Psionic light. It pushed Lucian against the wall, hard, knocking the wind out of him. In his panic, he reached for the Orb of Psionics, only to find it wasn't there.

The man stepped closer, his footfalls heavy on the black granite beneath. "Missing something?"

Lucian reached for his Focus instead, ignoring the Orb. But before he could do so, the man blocked him quickly and expertly.

"Pathetic. Are you *truly* the Chosen of the Manifold fated to bring the Orbs together?"

"What happened to them?" Lucian gasped. "How did you take them from me?"

The man chuckled. "You can't take what truly belongs to you. And the Orbs ... *all* of them ... are mine."

Lucian realized then who he was dealing with. "You're the Immortal."

The man forced Lucian to the floor with his magic, in a posture of supplication. His Focus became unblocked, but the man had already turned. No, not a man. He was an *Ancient*. A Builder. Or whatever they called themselves. They looked remarkably human, but perhaps Lucian's mind was only creating a human figure since he could conceive of nothing else.

"I'm not here," Lucian said. "This isn't happening."

"Stop saying foolish things. Of *course* this is happening. Stand up."

Lucian stood. There was nothing to gain by disobeying.

The Immortal finally turned, seeming to regard him for a moment. "You are right. I am the Immortal. Or at least, I was. But for our purposes, you can call me the Ancient One. I must admit, you've done well so far. Surprisingly well. The Orb of Binding and the Orb of Psionics are under your stewardship. But there are still five waiting to be found. You must find those five and deliver them to me." He leaned forward menacingly. "Or have you forgotten your promise?"

Lucian thought back to all that time ago, to his metaphysical exam at the League Health Authority. That was the first place he'd heard this voice, and it wouldn't let him go until he had made that promise.

"I haven't forgotten. But then, I didn't know what I was promising."

"Promised it was, all the same. Veer from that promise, you will fumble in the dark and be dead in an instant. From whom do you think your knowledge of magic derives? How do you instinctually seem to know exactly what to do, how to create such a complicated Psionic brand with almost no practice? It is not only from the Orbs that you gain your mastery."

"What are you talking about?"

"I am the Orbs, and the Orbs are me. Long ago, I infused myself into them, you might say. And the more of them you gather, the more powerful I become."

Lucian felt an icy dread and knew it to be true. But most of him was still in denial. "You're not here, though. You're in the Manifold."

"Wherever you carry those Orbs, you carry me as well. Indeed, even before you gained the Orb of Binding, I had marked you for my purposes."

"How? Why?"

"That isn't for you to know. Not yet. Your fate is to obey. You must continue on your quest to find the Orbs. You must bring them to the Heart of Creation, where the physicality of the Shadow Realm meets the reality of the Light Realm. Beyond the First Gate, created in the days of the Forerunners. Where magic came into the Shadow for the first time, and where the universe changed forevermore."

Lucian remembered his conversation with the Oracle of Binding. *She* had wanted him to do the same thing. Was she on the same side as this Ancient One?

The Ancient One gestured all around. "This is the Light Realm, which you can only see because of how deeply you drew from the Orbs. Indeed, the more you draw from them, the more inseparable we become. It is in this place from which the Manifold springs. From here, magic flows into the Shadow Realm through the First Gate—*your* reality. The closest word you might use to describe this place is . . . Heaven. Yes. That is quite fitting. For upon death, this is where the Focus of every mage goes. Upon my death in the Shadow Realm, it was where *my* Focus went." The Ancient One paused, seeming to consider his next words. "I don't expect you to understand, though. It is a mystery beyond you."

"I already know what I'm supposed to do," Lucian said. "The Oracle of Binding told me to bring the Orbs here."

"Did she, now? Well, that's unexpected. Rhana is . . . an interesting one. Yet you have no choice but to complete your task. If you wish to stop the Starsea Cycle, you must gather them. But by doing so, my power shall fully awaken, and I can break free of this forsaken place. And when that happens?" The man leaned forward, all but cackling gleefully. "I will take back what is mine! You are out of options, Lucian. You must bring the Orbs here, to me. It is the only way you can save your race from complete and utter destruction."

"I'll just not gather them, then."

"You don't understand how this works," the Ancient One said. "If you choose that path, the *Alkasen* will destroy humanity. The *Alkasen* despise magic. They believe it unnatural, an abomination to their sense of purity. They cannot conceive of a universe with it. Therefore, they must destroy it. And they *will* destroy humanity until every one of you has perished. As they did to the Lords of Starsea, the people of my race."

"I'll find all seven and just keep them," Lucian said. "I'll become the new Immortal. I don't need to give them to you."

The Ancient One chuckled. "There is only *one* Immortal, Lucian. *Me*. Do you know why your reality is called the Shadow Realm?"

Lucian had to admit he did not. "I never questioned it."

"That shows a regrettable lack of curiosity. Well, I shall answer. A shadow can never do what it wants, can it? Solid matter casts the shadow. Likewise, Lucian, your world is a shadow, of which you are a part. It is but a reflection of the true world, the Light Realm. The Realm in which *I* exist, in which the Focus of all mages exists."

"I thought the Focus existed in us," Lucian said. "Like a soul or something."

"You are woefully ignorant. Your Focus exists in both you *and* in the Light Realm. It is the bridge between Light and Shadow. All of this is beside the point. If you gather the Orbs and choose to exist in the Shadow Realm, then the Orbs, being objects of Light, will have their effect on me, the one who last claimed them. The one they *truly* obey. I will break free! I will gain control of the Light Realm and force you to do as I wish. If I move, then you, too, will move. You are my shadow."

"I'm no one's shadow," Lucian said. "You're wrong. I will claim the Orbs, and they will be mine alone."

"You cannot do so without *becoming* me, Lucian. Just as *I* became the First Immortal."

What was he talking about? "What do you mean, the First Immortal?"

"The Gate Builders were not Starsea, but a race far more ancient than even us," the Ancient One said. "They were the Forerunners."

The Forerunners? "Wait. Starsea didn't build the Gates?"

"Oh, no. The Forerunners did. The Forerunners built the First Gate and all the Gates after that. From the First Gate, they connected Light and Shadow Realms. The one who became the First Immortal entered the First Gate and returned with the Orbs. It is . . . unknown how long Forerunners lasted. Untold eons, most likely. But, disaster struck in the same way it struck the Ancients. They went mad with the fraying, and presumably, the *Alkasen* arose and eradicated them in the same way they eliminated us. And they will eliminate humanity."

"They went mad, too?" Lucian asked.

"Yes. They did. The First Immortal, somehow, lost the Orbs, birthing the Starsea Cycle. The Aspects of Magic, joined in a single Focus, cause magic itself to behave correctly. As it should. But when the Aspects are separated, magic is broken. Magic remained so until eons later when I gathered the Orbs again."

"Wait," Lucian said. "The Immortal never dies. So what happened to the First Immortal?"

"No one knows. But he and I are one. For I made the choice, upon gathering the Seven, that I would become him, and he would become me. To keep the Orbs in the Shadow Realm, to rule Starsea as its Immortal Emperor, you would have to consent to become me and to also become him. Three would become one. You would keep some of yourself, but you would also forget yourself. As I forgot myself."

Lucian felt his mind bending at this point. He would have to give up himself, to become this Immortal who, at least according to the Oracle of Binding, ruled the original Starsea

Empire with cruelty. So much so that his subjects rebelled and destroyed him. There was no way Lucian would allow that to happen.

"That leaves one choice," Lucian said. "To bring the Orbs to the Heart of Creation and to destroy them."

"Destroy them?" The Ancient One laughed. "They cannot be destroyed—only returned and left forevermore. And that would doom your race to a slow and agonizing death. It would be . . . apocalyptic. Billions would die as the Gates shut down, as magic itself disappeared from the face of the stars, never to return. Of course, you couldn't return to the Shadow Realm, either, and would have to spend eternity separated from all you know and love. More than that, you would have to do so knowing, for eternity, that you caused billions of deaths resulting from the choking of interstellar trade. Your homeworld, Earth, as well as its parent star system, would weather the storm. But for all those other worlds?" The Ancient One let the question hang in the air. "They would retreat into barbarism. Many would die outright without the lifeline of the Solar System."

"And what happens if I do what you want? I give them to you?"

"That is the path of least pain," he said. "The ones I fight here care nothing for your race. They only want me gone, and they don't care how many lower lives die in the Shadow Realm to achieve that. What do gods care for the pain of mere mortals? The only way they can gain ultimate victory is by having you bring the Orbs to them at the Heart of Creation, from where all existence sprung."

Lucian wasn't sure how to answer. Nor did he know how he was going to explain this to everyone else. Assuming he even got out of here alive.

"I wish to leave these Ancients to their heavenly games," the Ancient One said. "I wish to take the Orbs and save the galaxy. I wish to drive the *Alkasen* to extinction. Under my stewardship,

THE CHOSEN OF THE MANIFOLD

humanity would thrive. Of course, you are welcome to keep the Orbs for yourself. My mind, as well as the mind of the First Immortal, would fuse with your own. Indeed, the transition has already begun. It is inevitable."

"What do *you* care about humanity?" Lucian asked. "You only care about saving yourself, getting out of this prison."

"That is so," the Ancient One admitted. "But what I want is best for humanity. The question is, what will you decide?"

Lucian didn't even have to think about it. "I will certainly not help you. Why should I believe any of this, anyway?"

"Why have you believed *anything*? I have followed your journey—I can gain glimpses of what's going on in your mind. And the more Orbs you gather, the more you will hear my whispers, and the more I can see the world through your eyes. You came to this place because of how deeply you drew from the Manifold. Imagine how much clearer the Light Realm will become once you hold more. At even five or six Orbs, I daresay you will hardly know yourself anymore. I'm not sure how that will work for you. I found all Seven at once. I knew mortality in one breath, and godhood in the next. You must discover things on your own because even I don't have all the answers. But everything I've told you is the absolute truth. The Oracle of Binding, Rhana, lied to you, Lucian. If not overtly, then by omission. She's here now, fighting her battles, scheming her schemes. Not all agree with her. Shantozar himself has aligned himself to the Shadow Realm."

"My reality isn't the Shadow," Lucian said. "*Yours* is."

"How little you understand. Don't you see that this conflict between Light and Shadow has existed for millions of years, between those who are dead and those who are living? The Forerunners wish for the Light to prevail, for the Shadow Realm to be cut off from the blessings of magic for all time. They seek to keep these blessings for themselves."

"Why?" Lucian asked. "What does it matter to them?"

"Because the Forerunners, and those among my race loyal to them, believe the creation of the First Gate was a mistake, that Light and Shadow should have never joined. But as long as one in the Shadow Realm holds the Orbs, Lucian, Light must obey Shadow. They do not wish to share that power, instead opting to create their realities without a thought or care for the realm they deem inferior. They are selfish, Lucian. They have drunk of magic deeply, and though that fount is endless, they don't wish to share it."

"You're not telling me everything. That much I can guess."

"Of course I'm not. You are not ready for such knowledge. Besides, our time draws short. You drew deeply of the well of the Manifold, but even that draught cannot keep you with me forever. The time will come where you will wish deeply for my knowledge. I may or may not answer."

Lucian shook his head. "You're crazy. *This* is crazy. What am I supposed to do with this information?"

"As I told you from the first, Lucian. Find the Aspects. Bring them to me. It is the only way to save your race."

At that moment, the dark chamber faded, and Lucian's mind snapped back to reality and the Shadow Realm.

17

WHEN LUCIAN AWOKE, he was in the sky. The ground passed beneath him, a rough patchwork of mangled hills and twisted valleys and canyons. The sky above was dark, filled with stars, with Cupid looming in the western sky.

He blinked twice before feeling himself fade again. When he opened his eyes again, the tinge of dawn illuminated the eastern horizon, spreading across a flat expanse of red sand. The wyverns were still flying steadily east. Despite being asleep, Lucian felt the Orbs' presence radiating in his mind. The beasts were firmly under his control, and he could feel their presence, so strong that it was hard to know his thoughts. His Focus felt weary—all he wanted to do was let go. But he knew to do so would be everyone's death.

Thirst tore at his throat. Hours must have passed since he had delved the Manifold. Somehow, he had created brands so powerful that he could hold them even while unconscious. So long as he kept his Focus open to the Orbs, his pool would remain large enough to maintain them. But he didn't know how long he could hold on for. He didn't have a choice in the matter.

It was as if he were grappling the end of a cliff. At some point, his Focus would give out.

No matter the strain, he could not allow that to happen.

He reached for his canteen for a much-needed drink. They had been traveling long enough for his muscles to go stiff and his bones to ache. The only reason he hadn't slipped off was because Fergus, he supposed, had cinched him snugly between two of the wyvern's spikes, enough to secure his hips. Coupled with clasping the ridge just below the back of the wyvern's neck, he was in no danger of falling, even with the undulations of the wyvern's body below him from the flapping of its wide, leathern wings.

He reached with his Focus, feeling the brand on the wyvern carrying him. It was still strong and locked and would last for many hours yet—so long as he kept hold of both of his Orbs. For the first time, he looked to his right, counting four other wyverns carrying each of the others, with Jagar and his wyvern to his immediate right. All were asleep. Of the sixth wyvern, there was no sign. Presumably, they had left it behind, or perhaps someone had killed it.

Once Lucian drained his canteen, he surveyed the surrounding land. Looking back, there was no sign of the Fire Rifts at all, although there was a line of brown mountains, only the peaks of which were visible above the horizon. Before those mountains rose endless hills and valleys, which would have been brutal to traverse on foot.

Directly ahead, the hills evened out into a flat expanse of desert—what Lucian presumed to be the western border of the Westlands.

As they left the hills behind, the others woke up, relieved to see Lucian alive. While he was unconscious, they would have had no way of knowing whether he was alive or dead.

Jagar sidled his wyvern closer. "Good to see you alive, lad."

Lucian hardly had the heart to respond. His unwanted

audience with the Ancient One had shaken him to the core. How to even *explain* that to everyone? He would have to wait until they were all on the ground. Whenever that was.

His voice came out raspy. "How much longer will these brands last?"

"I've had to refresh mine once already, but yours are still holding strong." The old man's eyes popped. "The power of the Orbs!"

All Lucian could do was nod. "It comes at a cost, trust me."

Jagar nodded toward the red expanse ahead. "Those are the Red Sands. We'll need to fly over as much of that as possible before we dismiss the wyverns. They're about to collapse from sheer exhaustion. There should be a town nearby if things haven't changed."

Lucian saw what he meant. The wyverns seemed to be flying quite lethargically, hardly able to keep their wide, leathern wings flapping.

"How long has it been since the Fire Rifts?"

"Oh, at least half a day, and probably more. We flew all night long, and now it's morning. Hard to say how much distance it's been, but a fair amount. This has knocked off weeks from our journey for sure. The Seekers' Trail has Warna Oasis as the last stop before the Badlands, the hilly area right below us. Warna should be around here. Somewhere."

When Jagar veered away, Lucian closed his eyes. He just couldn't deal with this, nor could he process what had happened to him. Yes, he had two Orbs, but he could never use them again as he had. To do so would just send him back to the Ancient One's prison. But that begged the question of who imprisoned him. Were they the godlike beings the Ancient One had mentioned? It could be no one else. All of it was beyond comprehension, so much bigger than he'd imagined. Shadow Realm and Light Realm, the war within it, all the information the Ancient One had given him. How much was to be believed? Was he fated to *become* the Immortal as soon as he gained all Seven Orbs?

Even if Lucian didn't want that to happen, he still had to find the Orbs to stop the fraying. To stop it from destroying Serah. There had to be more options, but something about the Ancient One's words had a ring of truth. Had Rhana, the Oracle of Binding, lied to him, or had she merely held back information? Was she the one he should be wary of, not the Ancient One?

He had never been more confused. He simply couldn't think about it—at least, not now.

"There!" Serah shouted, pointing into the distance.

Lucian saw a glimmer of water on the horizon, reflecting the light of Cupid in the west. That must be the oasis Jagar was talking about. Tall trees surrounded it, and there was even a village crowding around its banks.

To Lucian, it was life. And the wyverns he controlled were flagging, and his brands had to last long enough to send the beasts far away before they could turn around and attack.

Lucian directed the wyverns toward the water. The wyverns knew what he wanted from their Psionic connection. Jagar's possessed wyvern followed Lucian's.

If anyone was watching from that village, there was nothing they could do to hide their wyverns as the morning brightened. Lucian had them land about a kilometer away. As they sidled off, grabbing their gear, Lucian thought about keeping them branded there as an escape option, and probably would have if he weren't so exhausted. He couldn't risk it, though. Jagar certainly couldn't hold his possession brand forever and had to commit an enormous amount of ether in refreshing it.

He and Jagar shared a nod, seeming to understand what needed to be done without saying a word. Within a moment, all five wyverns were running across the sand. They leaped from the ground and took to the air, flying far more quickly unencumbered toward the west.

"Keep a hold of your brands until you can't anymore," Jagar said. "As long as they're a decent distance away, they're too exhausted to turn back and take their revenge."

Watching the wyverns depart, Lucian saw that was so. Though he could keep sight of the wyverns as they shrunk into the distance, at some point, the brands slipped from his control. And as soon as they did so, the wyverns did not change course. No longer holding his Orbs, Lucian stumbled with weariness. An extreme sense of vertigo made him sink to his knees, landing on the hard sand beneath.

The others gathered around him. The sun beating down was hot, but nowhere near the intensity as the Burning Sands or even the Sandsea. Still, the sooner they found shade and shelter, the better.

Fergus helped Lucian up, and the five faced east, where the oasis village, Warna, sat baking in the morning heat.

"Do you know how far Kalm is from here?" Lucian asked.

Jagar nodded. "It's been a couple of decades at least, but yes. I can lead all of you there. I'm afraid that the journey won't be easy, but far less dangerous than what we've done so far. Aye, it'll take a couple of months on foot, and no less."

Lucian would have quailed at that if he wasn't so exhausted. For now, it was just a brute fact, the reality they had to bear along with everything else.

Lucian understood that everyone's reasons to go on were different. Jagar wanted vengeance. That was easy enough to understand. As far as Selene, she wanted revenge, too, and failing that, to leave the group at the earliest possibility. But where would she go after that? She didn't have any family, and the only place that was home to her before—the Golden Palace of Dara, as the Psion of the Court Atomicist, Nostra, was off-limits. That would certainly put her in the Queen's path again.

Lucian wasn't sure what Fergus wanted, either, but for now, it seemed he wanted to help Lucian, avenge Cleon's death, and fulfill his oath to the Elders of Kiro by ending the reign of Ansaldra, if possible. That was a lofty goal Lucian wasn't sure would come to pass. But with Jagar having the same goal, and perhaps Selene too, they might have a shot. For Lucian's part, his next step was finding *The Prophecy of the Seven*. Serah would help him with that, not only because it was her only hope of curing herself, but because she believed that she and Lucian shared the same fate. That was far different from when they'd first met when she had only agreed to guide them to the Dark-rift, and no more.

Lucian was too tired to think about it. He followed the others as they trudged east toward Warna Oasis.

———

WHEN THEY ARRIVED at the outskirts of the dusty town, a group of six men blocked their path, all garbed in heavy dusters and wide-brimmed hats to shield themselves from the desert sun. Almost all bore bronze spears and shields, and one of them even had what looked like an old impactor rifle, a weapon Lucian knew to be illegal inside League Space. How had they gotten one of *those*?

Jagar's voice entered his mind. *Ward Psionics, boy. Ward it strong.*

Lucian did so without question. The impactor worked by applying pure kinetic energy at range. And that usually meant the target's brains and guts exploding in every direc-tion, depending on the gun's power settings. The weapon looked old, but Lucian didn't want to take any chances. He warded Psionics as strong as he could manage while still leaving some room for active streams, opting not to reach for the Orb yet.

Reaching with his Focus, Lucian didn't sense any magical ability in them, but a mage could be in the village behind them.

The chief man with the impactor stepped up, spitting on the dry ground. "Who are you, and what're you doing out here? Give me an answer I don't like, and the five of you will bleed out your guts on the sand."

Jagar took a few steps forward, holding up his hands in a placating manner. "Peace, friends. We mean you no harm. We just want to pass through, get some water, and even pay you for your trouble. If that's amenable to you?"

"What you got to barter with?"

Jagar offered a winning smile "Gems. We'll trade you a generous amount for access to your water and food, and shade to sleep the day away. We'll be out of your hair by evening, of that I assure you."

The man's wrinkled brow scrunched in skepticism. "And who are you, to have gems? You find something out in there in the Bad Hills?"

"Perhaps," Jagar said. "Now, what do you say? Why don't you put down those weapons? We don't want any trouble."

The man's gray mustache twitched as he surveyed each of them one by one. At last, his shoulders relaxed, and he pointed the impactor rifle at the ground. "You better show me them gems so I know you're not blowing hot air."

Jagar smiled and took another step forward. "Friend, no need to put on a show here. I know you're a good man, having to put on a tough act to scrape by. Like all of us must. We mean no harm to you and your people."

"You still haven't told us who *you* are, or who *you're* with. And until you do, not another step forward, old man."

"He's that exile," another man said, about the same age, though he sported a full beard. He spat on the dry ground.

"That there's Old Jagar Tengiz Ashiz. I could swear it, though he's gotten on in years."

"Old Jagar, eh? Well, that certainly changes things." The mustached man kept his gun lowered, though it seemed he had a mind to raise it again. "Well, you know you ain't allowed in these parts, a mean old wizard like you. The Bad Hills is the farthest you can go and no farther."

"Times have changed," Jagar said. "I have my reasons for coming back, and I won't let anyone stop me."

"What reasons might those be?"

"Certainly not to rob the humble folks of Warna Oasis on my way to Dara."

"Dara?" The mustached man scoffed. "You have a ways to walk before you get there!"

"I intend to get there, by hook or crook. I offered you more than a fair price for your water."

"Water's worth its weight in gold out here," the mustached man observed. "Not a drop to be had for *hundreds* of kilometers around, besides us."

Serah stepped up. "And yet, it would seem you have plenty of it. Are you so lacking in hospitality?"

Two of the men had the grace to look ashamed, but the mustached man's sun-beaten face only hardened. "We've become what we had to. We help our own, not strangers. It's a rotting damn shame, but what can you do?"

"You could just trade with us fairly," Serah said. "We're going to die without water. What do you think is going to happen if you don't give us any?"

The mustached man caught her drift. "Is that some sort of threat, missy?"

"I know you don't want to fight. We don't either. What we offered is more than fair."

Jagar opened his pack, taking out Selene's tattered dress. Or rather, Queen Ansaldra's dress. The sunlight danced off rubies, sapphires, and emeralds sewn into the fabric. The men of Warna Oasis gawked.

The mustached man spit. "Ain't worth a bucket of piss out here."

Lucian could tell that the man was bluffing. And it appeared Jagar saw that as much as well.

"Two of each," Jagar said. "Rubies, sapphires, and emeralds. Imagine what price that'll fetch over in Kalm if any of you have a mind to make the trip that way. That's animals you can buy, along with food and other things you no doubt need to replace."

"*Five* each," the mustached man nearly spat. "And as much water as you can carry."

"I'll give you three," Jagar said calmly. "But only if you let us stay the night. We're exhausted after our long journey through the Bad Hills."

The man played with his mustache, seeming to consider. It didn't seem as if any of them were aware of the wyverns, which was probably for the best. "Confound it. All right, then. You've got yourself a deal. Hand me them gems upfront."

"You get one of each now, and two when we leave," Jagar said calmly.

The man grunted, then nodded. "All right then. Fine. You seem the honorable type. For an exile, I mean."

Jagar stripped the Queen's old dress, and there was still plenty on there to bargain with down the road. The only question was, would these men's greed overwhelm their sense? Lucian felt none too safe staying here when it was clear they wanted *all* the gems. He just hoped they were smart enough to let them sleep the day off. But it would be necessary to set a watch all the same.

"I thank ye kindly," the man said, once the trade was complete. His eyes glittered hungrily as he held up the gems to the light. "Looks authentic enough."

He handed them off to another man, the one who had identified Jagar as the Exile. The man walked back to the village, losing himself among the earthen huts crowding around the water.

"Well, my friends, looks like the inn's open. The oasis is yours, and foodstuffs can be had, too." He gave a slimy, yellow smile, missing several teeth. "For a fair price."

"I'm sure we can agree," Jagar said easily.

The man's smile widened, revealing long, sharp canines. "Hartley!"

At once, a nervous-looking youth approached him, eyes wide and blue. "You want me to take them to the empty hut, Pa?"

"Hold your horses, boy," the mustached man said. "I know you, Jagar Tengiz, but who are your friends?"

"I don't see how that's your concern. We're just passing through. If you won't act friendly with us, we won't with you. Plain and simple."

"Fair enough," the mustached man said. "Well, for what it's worth, you can call me Corley. Hartley's my son, and he'll take good care of you."

"We're ready when you are, young man," Jagar said.

"Hop to it, boy," Corley commanded gruffly.

"Yes, sir. This way."

Hartley led them forward into the village of Warna Oasis.

18

THE TOWN SEEMED DESERTED, but that could have been because of the sun, which was beating down something fierce, causing everyone to take shelter inside. The oasis was wide, as much as twenty meters at its widest point, and surrounded with date palms, the fragrance of which was sweet in the desert air. The land was utterly flat and adobe houses, all one story, crowded near the shoreline in the shade of tree clusters. Anytime Lucian peered into the open entrances, all he could see was darkness. Not so much as a whiff of smoke emitted from the roofs. No one was doing any sort of cooking. A strange thing in a town of this size, during this time of day.

It was hard to say, but Lucian guessed this town was large enough to house a hundred people. Rows of crops grew along the water, with small canals feeding them. The homes formed a barrier around the water, and the only way they could get through was by entering the narrow alleyways. It had probably been an intentional design to protect the water from invaders.

Inside the ring of buildings, no one was out and about, either. Lucian realized that could have been because of their arrival. Out here in the Red Sands, strangers were more likely to be enemies than friends, which explained the unfriendly reception.

At last, Hartley led them to a small adobe home, isolated from the rest of the town. It stood in the shade of date palms, the water of the oasis nearly coming to the door.

"This is where you'll stay," Hartley said. "I can get some of the townsfolk to show you their wares."

"That would be fine, boy," Jagar said. "Thank you."

He gave the boy a small diamond, and the boy's eyes popped. "Th . . . thank you, sir!"

Lucian wondered why he was being so generous before realizing having someone on their good side in this place might not be a bad idea. One never knew when a favor might be needed.

Inside the adobe home, Lucian found ample space, even for the five of them, and inside it was a good ten degrees cooler. Lucian dropped his pack and sprawled out on a cot, one of eight.

"Don't get too cozy," Jagar said. "We should stay alert for the next half hour at least. I don't know if Corley and his posse are going to try their luck."

"They're welcome to try," Fergus scoffed. "We will wipe the floor with them."

"Certainly so, but they could still do something stupid because they don't know what kind of trouble *we* are. Greed makes animals of men."

"True enough," Fergus said.

Despite Jagar's warning, Serah was already lying down and snoring softly, and Selene as well. Lucian was drowsy, too. So much so that it was hard to keep his eyes open. Something about the outside heat, and the almost coffee-like scent of the date palms outside, and the relatively cool shade of the adobe hut, was doing a number on him. And branding the wyverns had exhausted him greatly. Though he no longer held the Orbs, he was all too aware of their presence, both of which seemed to throb in his mind.

He forced himself to stand next to Fergus and Jagar by the door.

"Someone's coming," Jagar said.

A thin, hunched woman in weather-beaten robes was pulling a large, creaky cart behind her toward their house. Lucian suddenly became alert.

"Must be a peddler," Fergus said.

The woman and the cart came to a stop before the open-air entrance. She uncovered the cart, revealing a plethora of goods —pots filled with food, wine, bolts of linen and leather, furs, oil, dried dates.

Jagar went forward and haggled in some harsh dialect. Lucian only understood a few English words mixed in. Once all said and done, he handed over some more gems from the Queen's old dress, and they filled their packs with food and new cookware. It was hard to say, but they'd spent about half of the gems. The old woman's dark eyes sparkled as she gave a gap-toothed smile. She picked up the handcart, and whistling, made her way back to the other side of town.

"I have a feeling she made out better than us," Fergus said.

"You would be right," Jagar said. "However, she had us where she wanted us, and there was little else we could do. Everyone in this town knows the journey we mean to make."

"It's fine," Lucian said. "What matters is that we make it out of the Westlands in one piece."

"Perhaps it's time the both of you got some rest," Fergus said. "I slept well compared to you two."

"No arguments from me," Jagar said, stifling a yawn. "I can hardly keep my eyes open. Even if it would be best for two to stay awake, one will have to suffice. Wake Serah or Selene, if you need a rest. I imagine Lucian is dead tired after controlling those wyverns. I know I am."

"Will do," Fergus said. "Don't worry about me. I have the senses of a sand shrike."

Jagar nodded. "Well, until this evening then."

He went to lie down, and soon he filled the house with his raucous snores. The two women were so tired that they didn't seem to hear him.

Lucian, too, couldn't hold out any longer. He took up his cot. After rechecking his Psionic ward to make sure he'd set it strong, he slept.

———

WHEN HE AWOKE, it was evening. The air was cool and dry, and the others slept around him. All but Serah, who kept watch by the door.

Lucian wanted to sleep more, but couldn't help but feel a deep sense of discontent. A sense of *anger*, even. At what, he didn't know. The feelings didn't have any obvious source. He just wanted to direct that anger at something . . . *anything*.

He had to set that emotion aside before Serah could see anything was wrong. For now, she was completely unaware he was awake.

He reached for his Focus, allowing the ether from the Orb of Psionics to enter him. He reached out to a range of at least fifty meters, poking around to detect what he could. Serah had taught him to Seek on board the *Zephyr*, the act of finding another mage in one's proximity. But Lucian felt nothing beyond these walls. With the flow of ether came a feeling of satisfaction, of calm. Lucian held it as long as he could until the flow of the stream strengthened, threatening to overwhelm him. He cut it off, shaping the ether into a huge Seeking field, one that encompassed the entire town and its environs.

Before he let go, he sensed something. Something was out there in the desert. Another mage, even. But as soon as he detected this magic source, it vanished almost as soon as he detected it.

Serah suddenly turned, her eyes widening. "What are you doing?"

"Using a Seeking field. Why?"

"What for?"

The truth was Lucian just wanted to use magic. Did he *have* to have a reason for it? Before, he felt tired and irritable. What was the harm of streaming? He could stream Binding and Psionics as much as he wished without the fraying taking hold of him, so he didn't understand the accusatory tone of her voice.

"I wanted to make sure we're safe," he said levelly. "Speaking of, I thought I felt something to the south of the village."

"Felt something like what?"

"Another mage. It happened when I expanded the Seeking field to about a kilometer."

"A kilometer?" Serah asked. "That's a lot of magic."

Lucian felt himself becoming defensive. "I did it to keep us safe."

The others were stirring at their heated words, but still asleep.

"Let's take this outside," Serah said. "I need to talk to you, anyway."

Lucian resisted the urge to groan and followed.

The sun was setting toward the west, showing through an alley between two buildings across the still water of the oasis. The water was red, perfectly smooth. More people were out and about now, tending to crops and animals, murmuring in the streets. Smoke rose from chimneys, carrying with it the smell of the evening's cooking. The savory scent of roasting meat made Lucian's stomach rumble. The town seemed to sleep during the daytime, which made sense, considering the great heat of the desert.

Serah took his hand. "You need to understand something, Lucian. Even if you can stream nonstop, you could still seriously hurt yourself. Remember what happened when you branded the wyverns? You got knocked out for a long time."

Just her reminder of that made him think of the vision he'd experienced of the Ancient One. He wasn't even sure how he was going to tell everyone the details of that. Maybe he could tomorrow when all of them were walking and had nothing better to do.

"Something's eating at you. I want to know what."

Lucian sighed. "I guess you're right, in a way. But I felt something out there. I'm sure of it."

"This other mage, you mean."

Lucian nodded. "I could reach again, just to be sure."

Reluctantly, Serah nodded. "All right, make it quick. This time, though, just feel in that direction. Don't encompass the entire town. Even if you have the Orb of Psionics, you shouldn't stream more than you have to."

Lucian nodded begrudgingly. He reached toward the south, using far less magic than before.

And the feeling was the same. *Someone* was out there.

"I was right. Now the question is, who is it, and should we be worried?"

Serah's brow furrowed. "It's time we woke the others."

THEY HAD FULL PACKS, extra clothing, and enough water to make the crossing. Or at least, enough by Jagar's judgment and Selene's abilities as an Atomicist.

152

Over dinner, Lucian told them about what his Seeking field had found.

"What surprises me is you did that with a Psionic ward," Fergus said. "I never knew such a thing was possible. You'll have to show me how that works."

"It's possible," Jagar said. "Damn inefficient, though. It works by Seeking the Focus of a mage rather than the fluctuations in the Ethereal Background caused by mages, as a seeking field using Radiance would do. A lot of times, a traveling mage who doesn't want to be seen wards Radiance diligently, but not Psionics."

Serah took a bite of her stew. "So, Lucian wouldn't have felt anything if he'd tried to use Radiance."

"I've been Seeking every few hours ever since we got here," Fergus said, somewhat glumly. "I've felt nothing. Whoever this mage is, they must be highly capable."

"Well, that answers that," Jagar said. "The question is, what are we going to do?"

"We don't even know whether this mage is a threat," Lucian said. "It could just be a villager who has magic."

"Questioning some villagers, or even Corley himself might be a good idea," Jagar said.

"Or Hartley," Serah said. "He seems friendlier."

"Yes, maybe so," Jagar mused. "We'll have to seek him out." He turned back to Lucian. "You still feel anything out there, boy?"

Lucian reached for the Orb of Psionics, creating the Seeking field once again. Only this time, he felt nothing. "That's strange. The feeling's gone, now."

"Gone?" Fergus asked. "How?"

"Tipped off," Serah said. "How else?"

"That would mean someone's been listening in on us . . ."

At that very moment, the crunch of sprinting footsteps headed away from the house, toward the desert.

Lucian charged out of the house, followed by the others. He was just fast enough to see Hartley disappearing in an alleyway between two adobe homes. That kid was *fast*. And if he couldn't keep sight of him, he couldn't stop him with magic.

"Spears ready," Lucian said.

"Friends!"

Lucian turned and saw Corley and the same men from earlier approaching from the direction of the oasis, opposite where Hartley had run off to. Lucian reached for his Focus, ready for anything.

"Your son was eavesdropping on us," he said. "He started running as soon as we mentioned a mage out in the desert."

Lucian thought Corley's face betrayed the slightest hint of surprise, though it was hard to tell in the gathering gloom.

"Mage?" Corley asked. "What're you on about, son?"

"Answer him honestly," Jagar said. "Or things will get ugly, I guarantee it."

He brandished his spear. Immediately, Corley raised his impactor rifle in defense.

"Now, let's not be hasty," Corley said. "This is certainly just a misunderstanding."

"Rotting hell it is," Serah said, stepping up. "You just *couldn't* be satisfied with what we gave you, so you have to take the rest, too!"

"People have betrayed us before," Lucian said. "Is the Queen around? What are you getting out of this?"

Corley blinked in surprise. "The Queen? What in the Worlds are you—"

Lucian had to move fast. These men weren't a threat, but their impactor rifle could be. Besides making sure his Psionic ward was still strong, he reached for Binding and tethered the gun, pulling it straight toward him. The men exclaimed in surprise—for the first time they realized just who they were dealing with—at least one angry mage, and perhaps five.

"All right, all right!" Corley said. "Rotting hell, there's no need for any of that."

"Talk," Lucian said, taking the rifle and pointing it at the men. "Talk right now."

He surprised himself that he was making a move this bold, but he was so angry he didn't care. He was tired of being betrayed, and he would not let someone hoodwink him again.

"Better tell 'em, boss," one man said.

Corley spat, then raised his hands. "Fine. But if I tell you, I want you gone in the hour. You hear me?"

"I hear you good," Lucian said. "Just stick to the truth."

Corley licked his lips. "All right. It was like this. About a week ago, this man came up into the village. Said he was looking for some friends. Seekers who'd gone after that rotting Orb that's supposed to be out there in the Burning Sands." He spat. "Well, he said he had some nice trinkets for anyone who could point him in the right direction or even anyone who would keep an eye out. He said if his friends came back, they'd likely head here to Warna, seeing as we're the last stop before the Bad Hills."

Lucian's stomach sunk. "That all?"

Corley nodded. "More or less."

"If you've got something more to say, say it," Serah said. "You don't know who you're dealing with."

"*All* of you are mages?" Corley asked. "Well, I don't see the harm in what that man wanted. Just thought I was helping him out, and the price he offered was too good to pass up. You can't blame us for that. Life's hard out here, and the runs we make to Kalm or Juram are all that keep us afloat when the crop's bad."

"Tell us everything you can," Lucian said.

Corley seemed as if he didn't want to, but faced down with five mages and no weapon, he knew he didn't have an option.

"Well, he's a tall fellow. Cloaked head to toe, so I couldn't see his face."

"It was a *he*, then?" Serah asked.

Corley nodded. "That's right. Looked like the rotting grim reaper, wearing all black. Who wears all black out here in the desert sun? Rotting fool, that one. I can't tell you much what he looks like properly, though I could tell he had cold eyes and a sharp nose, and this creepy way of talking." Corley nodded toward the east, or perhaps the southeast. "He's staying out that way. Waiting for you." Corley watched Lucian for a moment. "I guess it's safe to say you aren't friends with him."

Lucian shook his head. "That man is likely working for Queen Ansaldra as an Eye."

Corley's eyes widened. "An Eye? What's an Eye after you for?" Then, his eyes popped even *wider,* if that was possible. "No, don't tell me. I don't want no trouble."

"That's the smartest thing I've heard you say," Lucian said. "If you cross us, you'll pay for it. Are we clear?"

Corley nodded quickly. "Of course, sir. We'd never think of it. Whatever we did, we did it in ignorance."

Serah scoffed. "They knew who we were the minute we set foot into town. They planned to sell us out from the beginning."

Corley didn't offer a counterpoint.

"We should keep them here," Selene said. "On their knees, hands behind their heads. We can't let them out of our sight, or else they might warn the Eye."

Lucian went cold when he realized the truth. "It might already be too late."

At Corley's smirk, Lucian realized he had the right of it. Even now, Hartley was running out into the desert, warning the Eye about what was coming.

They had no choice. The five of them would have to go out into the desert and deal with him.

19

"WHAT DO we do about these men?" Fergus asked. "They're working with the Eye."

"The answer is simple, I'd say," Serah said, her voice dangerous.

Corley's eyes widened at that. "What? You'd think I'd stick my neck out like that? The jig's up for me. That mage, though. He's dangerous, and he's out for blood."

"So, what do we do?" Serah asked.

Jagar grabbed his shockspear and approached the group of men down on their knees. Lucian thought his heart was going to beat out of his chest.

"Please, Sir Jagar," Corley said, all but prostrating himself. "I swear on the lives of my wife and son that I won't lift a finger against you. Nobody else will, either."

Jagar spat. "Honorless cur. Begone."

The man stood, backing away a few steps before bounding off. The others followed as if an army were at their backs.

"I don't think they'll bother us now," Fergus said.

Jagar shook his head disapprovingly. "The sooner we move

out, the better. No doubt that Eye knows about us by now." His gaze took in all of them. "We won't know what we're dealing with until we're dealing with it. Travel close, and ward your primaries. That'll give us good coverage. If he hits us with something that *isn't* our primary, ward it if it's a secondary."

Lucian was glad Jagar seemed to know what he was doing. He stood straighter, seeming taller than he first noticed. For a moment, he seemed to see someone different, a captain who had led scores of men into battle. In his prime, Jagar had surely been a capable soldier, noble and proud, and he knew how to lead and give orders.

Lucian warded Psionics but left Binding unwarded for now. He was most comfortable fighting with that Aspect, but if the need ever arose, he could shield it easily.

"Let's move out," Jagar said. "Hand me that gun, Lucian."

Lucian did so, and Jagar opened the chamber and smirked. "Empty."

"Seriously?" Lucian asked.

"Well, we aren't going to find much ammo out this way. Better drop this heavy thing and carry something worth carrying. Let's go."

THEY HEADED out into the dark desert night, leaving the town of Warna behind. The air felt far colder than it should have, making Lucian pull his robes tighter. Because he was holding a defensive Psionic ward, he couldn't hold another ward of the same Aspect, which meant he couldn't seek for the mage unless he dropped his current ward. Not that creating a seeking ward would be of any use, as the rival mage was probably warding himself against detection.

"I'm sensing nothing," Fergus said, shaking his head. "This guy is good."

"What we can't find by magic, we must find with our eyes," Jagar said. "There isn't much cover in these sands."

"We could be walking into a trap," Serah said.

"No doubt about that," Jagar said.

"Stop," Selene said. "My ward's picking up something."

Her ward? That meant there was Atomic Magic out here.

"There," she said, pointing to a spot just a few meters ahead. "An Atomic brand."

Jagar motioned them to get down. Lucian had never felt more exposed on these flats. He could almost feel enemy eyes watching from some unknown place. But when he looked around him, the sands were empty.

"Take a few steps back," Selene said. "Can't go walking into that."

Everyone followed her command.

"What'll it do to us?" Serah asked. "Wait. Something behind us, too. Some sort of Gravitonic brand."

"He's trying to trap us," Jagar said. "Which means he has visual."

He raised a bony, weathered hand and streamed behind the group. The space behind them suddenly lit with silvery magic, the ground shining with a luminescence that faded quickly. Somehow, the old man had completely diffused the Gravitonic brand meant to hem them in.

Serah's eyes popped. "How did you do that?"

"Run," he said, choosing not to answer her. "We're not dealing with just one mage here."

Lucian didn't have time to question. He ran.

And as soon as they did so, several spikes shot toward them, which Lucian recognized to be sharp rocks. He strengthened his Psionic ward, making it strong enough to cover all five of them. The rocks stopped dead in the air as soon as they hit the ward, though a few sneaked past, impervious. Lucian didn't know how that was possible until he realized that *even* his ward had its limits. Passive streams could only go so far. To create a stronger defense, he'd have to dissolve the ward and replace it with a shield.

He made the switch quickly, pulling more ether from the Orb of Psionics. The very air around them shimmered violet as Lucian raised the shield, all the rocks glancing off the barrier, with some even shooting back toward their attackers.

Attackers. Lucian could see them now, in the distance. Not one, but *five* mages, all of them streaming magic at them.

"Stop running!" Jagar said. "They've shown themselves."

There was no shelter out on these flats, so they had no choice but to fight. Lucian wasn't sure how they'd hid themselves, but perhaps they had buried themselves in the sand. For a moment, each group faced across from each other, about fifty meters apart. The middle mage stood taller than the rest, wearing a black robe and bearing a graphene shockspear, a sign of his status. That one had to be the Eye.

The Eye raised his hand, and a large fireball streaked across the desert straight at them. But a Thermal shield Serah streamed easily absorbed the impact. With a shout, Fergus raised his hand, from which streamed a brilliant line of blue light. The laser stopped well short of the Eye, an aura of green shimmering around him. A Radiant shield. Fergus breathed a curse.

One by one, each rival mage lit their shockspear with electric light. One by one, everyone around Lucian did the same. This must be what happened when a magic fight reached an impasse. The next step was a melee, or perhaps a mix of magic and direct conflict.

"I'll take point," Jagar said.

Lucian reached for the Orb of Binding. It was hard to gauge just who had the advantage here, or how the Orbs would perform in this situation, but he would soon find out.

Fergus stepped up to Jagar's side, throwing aside his cloak to create room to maneuver. Lucian followed his example.

As a unit, the enemy mages *flew* through the very air with spears drawn back, each of them tethering themselves to a focal point right in front of them. Before Lucian could even think to counter those streams, they had covered the distance. Both Jagar and Fergus streamed circular, green shields on their left arms, shields which ate the impact of the enemy shockspears. Serah and Selene hung back, concentrating on streaming magic.

Lucian wasn't sure what the plan was, or even if there *was* a plan. All he knew was he needed to help. Jagar and Fergus couldn't hold off those mages forever. But the tall one hung back, seeming to have eyes only for Lucian.

He streamed from the Orb of Binding but didn't have the time to gather enough ether for a devastating blow. Psionic Magic was already pushing against him—with Jagar busy fighting, Lucian was the only one that could shield that Aspect. He hurried to raise his Psionic shield again, but could not set the stream strongly enough. The force built against him until he flew back in the air, barely keeping hold of his shockspear. He reached for Gravitonics, streaming on his feet to force them to the ground. He landed harder than he intended and almost lost his balance. From his moment in the air, he saw everyone was fighting their own melee, even Selene and Serah, who were doubling up on one of the Mage-Knights, while the three others were facing down Jagar and Fergus. The Eye still hung back, watching Lucian closely. It was from him that the Psionic stream had manifested.

Lucian sensed that all the wards had dissipated by now, and all magic was being used for offense. If Lucian needed to defend himself, he'd have to rely on active streams.

Lucian tethered the Eye's shockspear, yanking it toward him. But blue light flashed off the spear, dislodging Lucian's tether. The Eye approached, resolute in his goal. Lucian extended a hand, streaming a kinetic wave. That, too, the Eye blocked with a shield just in time.

Serah broke away from her combat. Surrounded by a silvery aura, she leaped into the air right over the melee between Fergus and Jagar and their opponents. She extended her spear, coming right down on the Eye. Without even looking back, he swept his violet-lit hand, swiping Serah aside as if she were a fly. She shot into the distance with incredible speed, screaming.

Lucian switched the anchor point to Serah while creating the focal point on him. Serah began being pulled toward him, and he directed her to the ground a safe distance away.

Lucian let go of the stream when the Eye charged, brandishing his spear just meters away from Lucian. Lucian, with Psionics still open, lifted a hand and streamed. It was powerful enough to stop the mage in his tracks, but not enough to throw him back, as he had expected.

One thing was sure; the Eye was good, especially at defending against Lucian's streams. But if he ever got close enough to lock spears with him, Lucian wouldn't last long.

Why were the Orbs not responding in the way he was used to? There was too much fear clouding his Focus, and the Orbs couldn't work properly in that state. He took a few steps back, re-centering himself. The Eye had completely weathered the kinetic wave and was now forging ahead. He drove his spear back, readying a jab. But when he thrust, a fork of lightning emitted from the spearpoint. Lucian predicted the attack before it happened, throwing up a Dynamistic shield. He got a nasty shock that staggered him back, but without the shield, that electricity would have fried him.

Focus.

He reached for Binding again, but all he could see was the Eye getting closer. Serah had landed and was closing the gap between herself and the Eye. With a scowl, the Eye turned to deal with her, his spear pulled back.

Lucian charged forward, streaming Binding Magic along the length of his spear. A blue line shot from the spear's point, latching onto the Eye's ankle. This time, the Eye couldn't defend the attack. Immediately, he lost his balance, giving Serah a reprieve.

But now Selene was in trouble, retreating and unable to deal with her assailant alone.

Lucian switched his Focus, tethering the hands of the Mage-Knight attacking Selene together. He looked down in surprise for a moment. But only for a moment. Selene let out a primal scream as she sunk her spear into his gut. Electricity sizzled through the enemy mage's body as he went stiff as a board, then fell forward on his face never to rise again. Selene gave Lucian a curt nod before aiding Fergus and Jagar with their opponents.

By now, the Eye was back on his feet, reaching out his hands, which became wrapped in fire. Serah extended her own hands, slowing his progress with a gravity disc. With a grunt, the man dislodged Serah's stream, causing her to stagger back. With single-minded focus, he stepped toward Lucian.

This man's Binding and Psionic shielding was unassailable. So much so that he had to have known what to expect. How could he resist what the Sorceress-Queen couldn't? It had to be Lucian's frazzled state. But by now, the three mages fighting Jagar, Fergus, and Selene had gone down, leaving only the Eye. Jagar, Fergus, and Selene surrounded him.

Now not fighting for his life, Lucian found the ether was flowing, and quickly. He reached for Psionics and streamed with all his might. He aimed for the center of the Eye's Focus, which was well-shielded. Lucian's stream met the mage's shield, the two forces locked in conflict. With a final push, Lucian shattered the shield with brute force. He surrounded the Eye's Focus with a Psionic block, just as Cleon had taught him.

"He's blocked," Lucian said, fighting for breath.

The man fell to his knees, dropping his shockspear. He kept his head lowered to the ground.

Jagar was the first to step forward. When he placed the sharp tip of his carbon shockspear at the man's throat, the Eye didn't even flinch.

"Any reason I shouldn't kill you where you stand?"

The man said not a word.

"Who sent you? Do you work for Queen Ansaldra?"

Again, the man remained silent.

Jagar shook his head. "I guess I shouldn't expect a word from an Eye of the Queen. Trained from birth to be loyal unto death." Jagar turned to Lucian. "We must kill him."

"We can't get any information out of him?" Serah asked.

Jagar shook his head. "You'll have more luck getting a stone to sing."

"Let it be done, then," Selene said.

Reluctantly, Lucian nodded. Reluctantly, because he hated the idea of killing. But if what Jagar had said was true, this mage was more of a droid than a man.

But Jagar was not killing the man. Not yet. Lucian got a sick twisting in his gut, especially as Jagar's eyes met his. He knew what he was going to say before he even said it.

"You must learn to do hard things, Lucian. This will not be the first time you draw life's blood with the point of your spear."

Lucian's eyes widened at that. Everyone was looking at him. And deep down, he knew Jagar was right. He had to learn to do this, to take someone's life with his own hand. He had done so before at the Spire, but now, he had to do so in judgment.

The Eye's gaze was murderous. No, this wasn't a man in the ordinary sense of the word. He was a killer. He had only surrendered on the chance Lucian might spare him. And if Lucian weren't blocking him now, he would kill them without hesitation. That might have been his plan.

If there was anyone who deserved death, it was him. If Lucian let him go, this Eye would follow him to the ends of the galaxy. He had probably already communicated Lucian's position to Queen Ansaldra, which would lead more Eyes to him.

The sooner he finished this, the better.

Lucian stepped forward, his hand shaking on the haft of his spear. The Eye smirked at that. He probably didn't think he had the stomach for this.

But Lucian had come far. He didn't relish killing—not in the least. But he would do it, if only because he had to.

He retracted his spear with a thought, then placed the baton near the man's neck. The Eye's breathing was slow, measured, and controlled. How could he be so calm in the face of death? Lucian realized that this man had died long ago, at least in spirit.

A single thought, and it would be over.

Lucian's spear extended, piercing the man's neck clean through. His body went stiff as blood poured out. Lucian retracted the spear and stepped away.

The Eye blinked once. Twice. And then fell forward onto the sand.

It was quiet after that. Lucian shuddered as he wiped the blood off his spear with a piece of cloth ripped from one of the dead Mage-Knights. He cleaned what remained with a small amount of water.

"No simple thing, that," Fergus said. "You did well."

"He deserved to die," Lucian said, his voice weak. "So why does it feel bad to do?"

"Killing another man should never feel good," Fergus said. "But sometimes, it can't be avoided. You meted out justice well.

It's one thing to know a man needs to die. It's quite another to enact the sentence."

Lucian nodded. "We should move on. We have a long way to go, and he probably communicated our presence to the Queen."

Jagar grunted. "Well said."

It was hard to tell, but his voice seemed to carry an additional note of respect. Though Lucian had killed before, this time felt different. It wasn't something that had happened quickly in the chaos of battle. It was something he had to think about first, before delivering the final blow.

They took what supplies they could off the fallen men. They found water, more food, and several gold coins minted in the likeness of the Queen, with a wyvern on one side and an impression of the Septagon on the other. They couldn't carry all the water and food, since they had refilled their packs at Warna Oasis. The mages' campsite yielded more coins and water, so much that they couldn't carry it all. Whatever space they had left was for food and water, which was worth more than gold in the Red Sands.

By the time they finished, half the night had passed. The second half they spent walking east.

With each step, Lucian hoped to put the memories of this place far behind him.

20

EVERY DAY WAS MUCH the same as the last. Red sands, the too-near horizon, with absolutely nothing in all directions.

Maintaining the course east was easy enough. They just kept Cupid behind them at all times. However, it felt as if they were hardly making any progress crossing the surface of Psyche.

"Many people go mad here," Jagar said on the third day. "They say the Red Sands got their color from the blood of those who had died trying to cross it."

"I thought it was the iron content," Selene said. "This is the only portion of Psyche with any tangible amounts of it."

It seemed nothing could faze her.

Lucian noticed the farther east they traveled, the cooler it became. Something about Cupid's presence certainly made the moon's surface hotter. The moonquakes were less out this way, too, though they still happened several times a day.

One week passed. And then two. And then three. After that, Lucian lost track.

Everything was the same, and nothing had changed. Flat

sand, red horizons, and packs that got slightly emptier with the passing of days.

Water supplies were getting low. There hadn't been so much as a puddle or a drop of rain. They kept their faces covered for protection from the dry air. Lucian's lips were perpetually chapped. They had about a week's supply of water, and Selene's elemental detection wards had sniffed nothing out. They had been drinking their atomically filtered urine ever since the second week.

Anytime a large boulder on the horizon broke the monotony, which wasn't often, Lucian tethered them to it one by one. That sped their progress a bit, saving them about half an hour. It probably wasn't worth the effort, but anything to get out of here as quickly as possible. Such was the bareness that Lucian wondered how the people of Warna had even made it out that far, or whether this was the way they traveled to do their shopping in Kalm. Could they just be going in circles?

But that couldn't be. Cupid's place in the sky had never changed. They were heading east. Lucian had to believe that was true, or else the laws of the universe didn't matter. Lucian's feet were sore, and he had wrapped them in his worn boots to protect them from blisters.

One morning, they awoke and traveled east as usual. Lucian thought he saw a large boulder appearing over the horizon. He reached for the Binding Aspect, grateful for some break in the monotony. When he was using magic, everything disappeared but the feeling of streaming. There was no pain in his Focus. He held it most of the day, every day, a kind of meditation that could only strengthen him. He never wanted to be afraid during battle again. And he could only do that by being so deep in his Focus that fear no longer mattered.

As time passed and they continued east, one kilometer after another, more boulders appeared. Sharp rocks covered the entire horizon from north to south.

"The end of our journey is near," Jagar said. "At least, the part of it through the Red Sands."

They paused for a drink, each surveying the horizon. Jagar pulled deeply from his canteen, in defiance with the rationing they had been practicing.

"I suppose there's water in those rocks up ahead if you're doing that," Fergus rasped.

"Aye," Jagar said. "And those aren't rocks. Those are the Spindle Mountains. We'll find water there, and some sparse villages, if we're lucky. They may not speak Standard, but barter is a universal language."

Just hearing those words made Lucian want to leap for joy. He probably *would* have, except his feet were in such pain that he couldn't.

They continued. Lucian wanted to stream again, to bring them even closer to the mountains. But now closer to civilization, using the Orb of Binding so powerfully would only alert the Queen to his presence, just as it had on his first night in Psyche. Unfortunately, that would always be a limitation. She had detected that across half the face of Psyche on his very first night on the moon, and she probably could detect his use of them out here, too. For all he knew, the Queen would have her Mage-Knights and Eyes waiting for them at the first village they came to, either in these mountains or perhaps in Kalm, a logical destination. They would have to be careful.

It took another day before they could say they were in the mountains properly. Like the Bone Mountains, the Spindle Mountains had a curious, needle-like quality, their top halves extremely narrow as they reached into the sky like spikes. Selene detected water, and they found a trickling stream running down the mountains' eastern flank. Though it was a trickle, it was more than enough to refill their canteens and larger waterskins. Once again, their packs were heavy.

Now they had to find food. Lucian's form was thinner than

it had ever been, including his incarceration on the prison barge. His robes hung loosely about him. To his desert-trained eyes, these lands were green and filled with life and water. Plants grew beside the stream, scrubs along the sides of the mountains, and small lizard-like creatures darted from the shade of one rock into another.

What he hungered for was real meat. And for that, they needed to cross these mountains or better yet, find a village.

Jagar was of a similar mind. "If we follow this stream east, we'll find something. Water is scarce enough out here for this stream to be settled on. Somewhere."

As they had so often, they followed his advice. So far, it hadn't led them astray.

Walking along the stream made the going easier. After a few more days, the stream fell over in a final waterfall, at the base of which was a large pool. And alongside that pool was a village, the first civilization they had seen leaving Warna weeks earlier.

Lucian pumped his fist, while Serah did a celebratory dance. Both Fergus and Selene closed their eyes, relief written on their features. Jagar just stared down, calculating. It seemed the journey across the Bone Mountains, Fire Rifts, and Red Sands had aged him all the more if that was possible.

"I can negotiate for food," he said. "Likely, they don't speak Standard, and I know most of the major desert dialects." He nodded toward the horizon. "I can't see it for the darkness, but if this is where I *think* it is, then there should be a road leading east that'll take us to Kalm. We have more desert to cross before then, but we've done the lion's share already."

"We should remain cautious," Fergus said, his voice sober. "With people come threats."

Jagar nodded his agreement. "Aye, that is so. No streaming unless we are under threat. And Fergus, if you haven't already, keep us warded at all times."

"I started a few days ago when we found the water," he said.

"Good," Jagar said. "Again, let me do the talking. And perhaps it's best if Lucian and Selene remained out of sight. If an Eye is in this village, then all it would take is one telepathic communication to end everything. We don't know what that Eye communicated before Lucian blocked him, or if he communicated at all. Either way, we must hide our numbers and keep ourselves covered at all times."

"Makes sense," Serah said. "So, where are we staying for the night?"

Jagar nodded toward a ledge above the river. "There would be good. Close to the water, but out of sight. The descent in the darkness would be dangerous without magic. And magic can be detected. We can survive one more day without civilization. Tomorrow morning, we'll go down the cliffs, and Fergus, Serah, and I will go into the village and do some shopping. Selene and Lucian can remain somewhere out of sight. The Queen is watching for our return somewhere along the border of the Westlands. Assuming we can get through the first fifty or hundred klicks undetected, we can escape her net."

Lucian found that to be well-reasoned. "Well, to our last night out of civilization, then."

They set up camp and made a small, smokeless fire over which they cooked a hearty stew, throwing in most of the rest of their ingredients. As they ate, Lucian ruminated over their time since the Spire in the Burning Sands. It had been about a month and a half, maybe even two, and if Vera was as good as her word, she was well on her way to Psyche by now. How much longer remained to be seen, but a typical ship would take about three months.

He wished it were only a simple matter of hiding out here until she arrived. That would be easy enough to accomplish. But without *The Prophecy of the Seven*, they would be flying blind, assuming they could escape. Lucian needed to get his hands on the prophecy, and to do that, he had to go to the heart of the Daran Empire. He would have to face Queen Ansaldra again and steal her prophecy.

It wasn't a thought he could deal with at the moment. Though they were safe from starvation and thirst, new threats loomed. Threats Lucian was not prepared to face.

21

THE NEXT MORNING, it was as Jagar said. They woke early and found a path already carved into the cliffs, which they followed to the desert floor below. Lucian and Selene went south to stake out the rest of the day while the rest went to resupply in the village, taking all the jewels from the Queen's old dress to barter with.

Selene and Lucian took shelter in the shade of a large boulder. Ever since he and Selene's one conversation all those weeks ago at the Spire, they hadn't had a conversation as long. Selene didn't speak unless she had to, and it was hard to tell if that was just her nature, or that she believed herself above them. Lucian would have thought such unusual circumstances would inspire change in her, but there didn't seem to be anything to deflate her air of superiority. Lucian didn't know what it would take to dispel that, but he also knew it wasn't his problem. At least, it wouldn't be when she went her own way.

It was boring, just sitting out there. Selene just stared off into the distance, her green eyes glazed and distant.

"What'll you do once we're in Kalm?" Lucian asked. "Have you thought about it?"

Selene remained silent, her gaze still focused on the far horizon. Lucian thought she was ignoring him until she shook her head. "I don't know."

"If you have nowhere else to go, you can stay with us. At least until you find your feet."

She watched him for a moment. "Have you given any thought to that conversation we had all those weeks ago?"

"Of course I have. It's pretty much all I've thought about outside of survival."

"And?"

"If all this is true about me being the Chosen of the Manifold . . ." Saying it out loud sounded ridiculous. "You were right. If that's who I am, then I don't have a choice, do I? I don't know how I'm going to get my hands on that prophecy, but it's what I have to do."

"I can help you with that. I've lived half my life in the Golden Palace of Dara, after all. Even if I remember nothing from when the Queen possessed me, I still have knowledge that might be of use to you."

"And why would you want to help me?"

"It's not about helping *you*. There's only one thing I want right now. And that's making the Queen pay for what she did."

Lucian nodded. "You and Fergus have a lot in common, then."

"We . . . do." Her cheeks colored a bit. Lucian tried to hide his surprise. Perhaps she wasn't too good for *all* of them. "I've spoken to him about that, and he's set on the Golden Palace, too. Whoever Cleon was, he sounded like an honorable man. The way he died was no way a Mage-Knight should have gone."

Lucian felt a lump in his throat. He thought he'd moved on by now, but just remembering the short time he and Cleon had been friends, all the things he'd learned, all the hardships they had weathered . . . it certainly wasn't easy. "He was a good man."

"Then stab at the heart of the Daran Empire," Selene said. "Avenge his death. Help me kill the Queen."

Is that what Cleon would have wanted? Probably. Then again, toward the end, Cleon had become convinced of the importance of Lucian's mission. And yes, that meant returning to the Golden Palace and dealing with the Queen again. Not her avatar, if she took on another body.

The actual Queen.

"Where is she, anyway?" Lucian asked. "The *real* one, not whoever she's possessing."

"No one truly knows," Selene said. "Most think she's hiding somewhere in the Golden Palace, in the Queen's Tower. That's the largest, rising from the center. No one's allowed in there but her closest advisors and bodyguards. Then again, some say she lives elsewhere. The Daran Empire is vast, and she has palaces and estates all over. She might be in her Summer Palace on the Sea of Eros. She could be on Icemount in the Mountains of Madness. Or, she could be in the Royal Forest, where she enjoys hunting forest dragons."

"Forest dragons?"

"Not to be confused with the wyverns, which stand on two legs. The forest dragons walk on all fours and don't fly. That's beside the point. She could be *anywhere*, Lucian, but I believe that she's in the Queen's Tower."

"I . . . had the sense she was in the Golden Palace when I exorcised her."

"Then that's the most likely location. Jagar might know something, too. He's married to her, after all."

Yes, there was that. All Lucian could think about was, what were the odds? That a storm would blow them off course and force them to land in the Sandsea, and the one place they came out led them right to his little cabin. It was almost enough for

Lucian to believe something *was* behind it all. Vera had always said the Manifold was in control, and the whims of humans mattered little. Or perhaps most people were free, but certain people, like him, had to go along a prescribed path.

He shook his head. "I don't even know where to start. I understand we can get on a passenger airship in Kalm and head through the Pass of Madness that way. But after that?" He sighed. "Is it a matter of walking up to the gates of the Golden Palace and asking the Queen to show herself?"

Selene gave a rare laugh. "Something tells me that if the Queen ever finds out where you are, you won't have to worry about finding her. She'll find *you*."

Following that distressing reminder, their conversation lapsed. They both caught some sleep, and by the time they awoke, footsteps approached from the direction of the village.

Jagar and the others set down the once-again full packs, huffing for breath. "Got swindled out of nearly everything we had. I think those folks could see our plight and knew to take us for all we were worth."

"Your negotiating skills are shit," Serah said, plopping down her bag. "You should've just translated."

"They said it would be an offense to conduct business outside their native tongue."

Serah laughed. "Yeah. You *were* swindled."

"Did you get what you needed at least?" Lucian asked.

"We did," Fergus said. "What do jewels matter as long as we survive this ordeal?"

"Are there any left?"

"Some," he said.

Seeing Selene still on the ground, Fergus lowered his head and offered a hand. Selene's eyes brightened a moment before she took it, allowing herself to be pulled up. Lucian and Serah shared a glance, with Serah shrugging.

"Any news?" Jagar asked.

Lucian shook his head. "Nothing. Just dust and the tumbleweeds."

"Just the *what*, now?" Jagar asked.

"An old American expression on Earth. Should we get moving again?"

Jagar stared off toward the east. "Well, most of the journey's done. All we got left is the Surin Desert. But it's not as dry as the Red Sands, and there'll be plenty of oases and villages on the way. We should be in Kalm in a couple of weeks."

Lucian wasn't sure how to get through that obstacle. A big city meant lots of people. And surely more than a few of them worked for Queen Ansaldra.

But there would be plenty of time to figure that out on the way.

"Ready when you are," Lucian said.

Within minutes, they were walking across the desert northeast toward the road.

———

THE NEXT WEEK, they passed along the empty road through mostly empty towns. They never stopped unless they had to, just long enough to refill their water from a well or nearby stream or oasis, or perhaps to buy some food off a grocer who wasn't too far out of the way. As always, they kept their faces covered, and to Lucian's relief, most other travelers they passed were of a similar mind, so they didn't stick out.

After the first week, the towns grew bigger, and the oases more common. They began almost every day at one body of water only to end up at another by evening. Sometimes they even passed one or two villages in between. Though the lands were bleak compared to the Golden Vale, they were life-filled compared to the wastes beyond the Westlands.

But every step closer to civilization made Lucian feel even

more cautious. Every step brought him closer to his eventual confrontation with Queen Ansaldra.

Despite talking about it multiple times, there seemed to be no clear consensus, much less an idea, of how to get the prophecy other than some sort of heist.

"We must do it at night," Fergus said. "All of us have been to the Golden Palace at some point or another, so we know just how tightly it's guarded."

"Perhaps the best way is with a distraction," Jagar said. "I would say my return after so many years of exile should prove an excellent one."

"What did you have in mind?" Lucian asked.

"Nothing other than a reckoning with Ansaldra. It'll likely end up with me dying. But I can't think of a better way to go."

"You're a strange man, Jagar Tengiz Ashiz," Serah said.

"Maybe so," he said. "But if I can deal the final blow and spare the people of this world her evil, then it will not have been in vain."

"It's true that if Jagar came back, the last place people would think to check is the library," Fergus said. "It just might work."

"The question is how to get in," Serah said. "Is that possible without being seen?"

"Maybe we could try something like the Trojan Horse," Lucian said.

"What's that?" Serah asked.

"I'll tell you later. Maybe we can sneak in inside a cart or something with a secret compartment."

Selene shook her head. "You think it's that easy? They check *everything* before it goes inside the palace grounds."

"No secret passages or anything?"

Jagar's brow scrunched. "In my day, there were plenty of underground tunnels leading into the Mountains of Madness from the palace. But I couldn't tell you where they were now, or even if they still exist."

"I could." Everyone looked at Selene, waiting for her to go on. "Nostra and I conducted a lot of experiments and fabrications in the Mountains. It's where the Labs are."

That had a sinister sound to Lucian. "Labs and experiments?"

"Yes. Various things with chemistry, fabricating materials, that sort of thing. Sometimes, Ansaldra needed something that's not available on this world, such as the helium for her airships, which she also sells to the airway companies, so we'd make it down there. That's just one example. We also create graphene weaponry for her Mage-Lords, and sometimes jewelry. Whatever she wanted."

"And all that occurs in the mountains?" Serah asked. "Why?"

"There's space. There are vast caverns there, and it keeps the more dangerous fabrications far away from her palace halls. And it makes it harder for any within the palace grounds to steal valuable, Atomically-crafted materials."

"So, they are hard to get to," Lucian said. "Then what's the point?"

"The point is, these caverns are accessible from the outside. The tunnels leading into the palace itself are guarded, not to mention warded. If you don't know how to pass through the wards, then you won't get through undetected."

"So, how *do* we get in? Do you know how to get through the wards?"

"Well, what I know will probably be vastly out of date. However, I know several places where we might enter the labs from outside the Palace."

"So, where is the entrance?" Lucian asked.

"Some are within Dara itself. And another we can reach from the Pass of Madness, which is the closest one to us. I've never used that way, though I know where it is."

"The Pass of Madness," Lucian said. "I remember passing

over a town there that was guarding the way. Would the tunnel be somewhere in there?"

"Yes, the entrance is in Passtown. I would have to seek the ward, but assuming it's unchanged, I can seek it out."

"So that's our way in," Serah said. "We use that tunnel, go through the labs, and then the Palace."

Lucian nodded. "While Jagar has his words with Ansaldra, we can nab the prophecy. It could work."

"It's your best shot," Selene said. "Assuming we can find our way to the labs, I still know the Palace like the back of my hand."

It *could* work, but it would mean trusting Selene not to stab them in the back. Lucian wasn't sure *why* she would do that, but trusting the wrong person had hurt him before.

"What's your role in all this?" Lucian asked. "Are you going to be with us, helping us get the prophecy? Or are you going to get revenge on the Queen?"

She shook her head. "I don't know yet. I thought by helping you, I might get closer to knocking the Queen off her throne. She *needs* to be stopped."

"And after that?" Serah asked.

"I haven't thought that far ahead."

"It could work, assuming we can find access to this tunnel," Fergus said. "I've got nothing better."

"The prophecy itself is no doubt heavily branded by Queen Ansaldra herself," Selene said. "Unraveling those brands will be difficult. But since you have the Orb of Psionics, you have the power to undo them."

And hopefully the cleverness, too, though Lucian left that unsaid. The strength of the bear didn't matter if it stepped into a trap.

"That's what we'll do," Lucian said. "Unless anyone has a better idea."

From everyone's silence, he took that as a "no."

They traveled the rest of the day, passing through the largest town yet centered on a large oasis with plenty of adobe buildings lining multiple streets. Some of those buildings even had two stories. Jagar said this town was Aman, a sign they were just another day from Kalm and the Surin River. They passed several inns on their way through and hundreds of people more well-dressed than in the deeper desert. Lucian thought it would be nice to sleep in a proper bed for once, but even that would risk too much. A few kilometers east of town, Jagar took them off-road to sleep under the stars again.

Come morning, they walked again all day, and by the time evening came, they crested the last rise to see on the horizon a massive city lining two sides of a wide river.

After weeks of hard travel, they had made it to the Surin and the city of Kalm.

22

WHEN NIGHT FELL, the Mountains of Madness loomed in the far distance as they walked into Kalm, hoods drawn. The thrum of human life was jarring after so long in the wilderness. On their long journey here, they hadn't passed through a town with as many as a thousand people. Here, there were *tens* of thousands, though it was nowhere near as big as Dara on the other side of the mountains.

A mud-brick wall surrounded the city, about ten meters high, that basked golden under the afternoon sun. Carts drawn by mules wheeled in and out, traders drawn in from the shabby settlements set up outside the walls. A thick pall of dust hung in the air that probably never fell given the rush of traffic. High above the city, an airship lifted off, though it was much smaller than the *Zephyr*. With luck, that would be them soon, and Lucian's swollen feet could finally get some rest.

Jagar gave the gate guard five copper coins they had picked up from one of the dusty villages they'd passed through, and he nodded them all in. Lucian drew his hood closer as they followed Jagar, who walked with purpose down the primary avenue lined with date palms. They joined the flow of foot traffic toward the center of town and the Surin River. From here, the river was not visible, so crowded were the buildings, most of which were three or four stories tall. All the windows were open to the wind, hoping to admit a stray breeze. Hundreds of stalls and vendors lined this main drag, peddling their wares to all the passersby going through the gate. They sold anything from clothing, roasted meat, perfumes, leather bags, jewelry, household supplies, carved figurines, stone idols, talismans, and fish. The smells overwhelmed Lucian's senses.

"Could we not do a bit of shopping?" Serah asked. Even Selene was running her eyes over the goods on offer.

"We're not here for that," Jagar grumbled. "Besides, we spent almost all our gems, and we will barely have enough to secure passage. Unless you mean to *walk* the trail to the Pass of Madness?"

"Our bags are wearing thin," Serah said. "And I could do with some warm food."

"Maybe," Jagar conceded. "If we have time. The aerodrome should be on the eastern side of town, across the river, but it's too late to book a new flight. With luck, we'll be out of here tomorrow."

"And how long will it take to reach Passtown?"

"Most of the day. Weather permitting."

Jagar seemed to only have one thing on his mind—getting to the Golden Palace as quickly as possible to have his words with Queen Ansaldra. That they could be just a *day* from that eventuality was hard for Lucian to wrap his mind around.

"We need to plan more," Lucian said. "We still don't know what we're doing."

"Did we *ever*?" Serah asked.

"Probably not. I guess the key question is how we—"

Jagar raised a bony hand. "No. None of that out here."

"Well, if we're leaving tomorrow morning, where are we staying tonight?"

"I don't know," Jagar said. "Things have changed since I was last here. These buildings are all new, probably because of the Insurrection five years ago. But if Northside is as I remember, then we can lose ourselves there pretty easily. It's not the safest part of town, but between the five of us, we should be able to handle ourselves."

"I'm *not* staying in some run-down hostelry," Selene protested. "I have standards."

"I have to agree with Selene there," Serah said. "I mean, wouldn't it be nice to each have our own beds, just for a single night? Why do we have to rough it every time?"

Jagar's face was the image of forced patience. "*Because*, this isn't about comfort, but safety. I don't know how much five airship tickets will cost, but I assure you it won't be cheap. Besides, we need to fence what gems we have left. No reputable merchant will take them. For that, we need to go Northside."

"Do you have a contact or something?" Selene asked.

"I'm not sure. If he's alive, he'll be pretty old like me. Something tells me if anyone could survive the razing of Kalm, *he* could. He goes by the Desert Fox. Or at least, he used to."

"What's a fox?" Serah asked.

"An animal from Earth," Lucian said. "Small, fluffy, cute, pointy ears."

"Aww."

Jagar growled and pressed on.

They, at last, reached the wide Surin River. It had seemed big from the air when they had passed it all those weeks ago, but from the ground, it was much larger. It was almost like staring across a lake, and a long, arched bridge connected the two sides, high enough to allow river craft to pass beneath. The river had to have been quite shallow for that bridge to remain standing. Either that or perhaps the lower gravity of Psyche made it possible for the bridge to stand without as much support.

From the top of the arched bridge, Lucian could see far across the tops of the buildings, toward the impossibly high Mountains of Madness in the distance. They rose beyond the horizon kilometers into the sky, their spires thin and needle-like, their tops almost lost to the haze of the darkening sky. In just a day or two, they could be beyond them.

When they crossed the river, the east side was even busier than the west side. Jagar turned north, entering the main street following the river. A squad of the Queen's hoplites passed, led by a red-caped Mage-Knight. A Thermalist, then. None spared them so much as a glance. Like the rest of the people, they gave the soldiers a wide berth.

As Jagar led them north, the buildings became shabbier and more dilapidated. The streets were narrow and filled with refuse, and metal bars covered most of the windows. Groups of men skulked in the shadows, or individual people walked hurriedly toward their destinations. Selene watched it all in horror.

"Now you know how the other side lives," Serah told her.

Selene harrumphed.

"Have to say, this is sketchy, even for me," Serah said. "Where are you taking us, Jagar?"

"Nearly there," he said. "Patience. Keep your faces covered and your hands close to your spears."

The groups of rough-looking men ceased their conversation as they watched them pass. It was as if they were being sized up. Lucian hoped it didn't go beyond that.

Jagar paused a moment, seeming to remember something, before entering one of the narrow streets. Just a few buildings down, an old woman dumped a pail of . . . *something* . . . right into the alleyway between. The thin gutter on the side of the road caught some of it, but mostly, it splashed every which way.

Lucian nearly gagged at the smell when they walked by. Fergus's face scrunched in disgust.

"I'll be," Jagar said, his eyes twinkling.

He turned into a doorway on the right, a doorway that looked much the same as any other, aside from some graffiti above the doorframe, in the shape of a fox's head. Lucian followed him to find a dark room lit only by candles, with a rough wooden bar ahead of him that was covered with metal rails. A short man with a mop of gray hair, a prodigious gut, and a balding head stood behind the rails, his face sullen as he wiped down the bar.

"I already told ye," he began gruffly. "If I catch any of you rotting, good-for-nothing miscreants causing me trouble again, the Desert Fox'll hear of it."

"I hope I'm not the miscreant," Jagar said.

The man's head snapped to attention, and his dark eyes narrowed as if struggling to recognize who was speaking to him. "Who goes there?"

"I wish to speak to the Desert Fox."

The man leaned forward, the barest trace of a smile cracking his lips. "Who's asking?"

"You know full well who's asking."

"Aye, I do, you slimy, eely, worthless, waste-of-space, lily-livered milksop. It makes me sick to look upon your stinking, rotting face. I'd throw you out, but I'd infect my hands."

Jagar cracked a smile. "Seems you're alive and well, Fat Guts. I smelled the crust between your belly rolls from the street. It's the rankest compound that ever offended my nostrils, you villainous, faithless, honorless, hornless, spineless, pusillanimous, oath-breaking, sad sack of poisonous, rotting river toad."

The man guffawed. "Why, you no-good, plague-ridden, puke-stained, boil-bursting, hell-bound, three-inched, thick-witted . . ." He shook his head and looked as if he wanted to spit. "Looking on that revolting face after so many years is infecting my very eyes."

The two men stared at each other, and Lucian didn't know who would be the first to strike. But after a tense moment, their lips and cheeks quivered, and both roared with laughter, so much so that tears came to their eyes.

"Jagar Tengiz Ashiz!" boomed the fat old man, unlocking the door and swinging the bar open. He almost jumped on Jagar, holding him in a warm embrace. "It's been too long, my old friend."

"We need help, Dario," Jagar said, returning the embrace. "A place to hide out for the night."

"Yes, I imagine so. You're wanted from the Westlands to the Far Riftlands, from the Mountains of Nohr to the Sea of Eros. I imagine you need money, too, and it's just my sad, rotting luck you dragged your pruned ass right onto my doorstep."

"That's what friends are for, no?"

The old man clicked his tongue, for the first time seeming to notice everyone else. Fergus stood proudly while Serah watched with amusement. Selene just looked horrified.

But it was to Selene that the old man bowed, reaching and kissing her hand as gingerly as if she truly were the Queen of Psyche. "Welcome to my humble shop, my lady. You have a noble bearing about you, and I know this is far from your usual standards. But this shop is a mere face, and I assure you, you will find the accommodations both private and comfortable. Be welcome here, and I can only hope my gentle words now make up for my coarseness earlier."

Selene blinked in surprise. "I . . . would appreciate that very much."

"My name is Dario Farris, though some around here call me the Desert Fox," the man said most nobly, in a far cry from his former lewd words. "I apologize if my conversation offended or infected. It is a joke between Jagar and myself. A password, if you will."

Jagar gestured to Serah next. "This is Serah Ocano, of the Far Riftlands."

"How do you do?"

"Well, well. A most beautiful mountain flower of the Far Riftlands, if I don't miss my guess." Dario kissed her hand as well. Her cheeks reddened as she smiled. "Now, Serah Ocano, which of my bad parts do you like best?"

"I don't know. There are so many to choose from."

Dario smiled graciously and winked before turning to Fergus, who introduced himself. "Fergus Madigan. Captain Watchman of Kiro Village of the Deeprift."

"I believe every word, good captain. You have a capable look about you."

The Desert Fox's eyes met Lucian's, seeming to see him to the core.

"Lucian Abrantes," he said, simply.

"A fellow Earther by your speech," he said. "And what is your claim to fame, to be introduced last of all?"

"I have no claim to fame. Just along for the ride."

"I'm sure you want off that ride," he mused drily. He stepped back, taking in them all. "Anyone who steps behind this bar is a friend of mine. No harm will come to you, though the Devil-Queen herself is out in force and every Eye, Mage-Lord, and Mage-Knight in the Westlands aspires to collect the fat bounty placed on all your overpriced heads."

Hearing that made Lucian sick to his stomach. "It's that bad?"

"Worse," Dario said. "Come. You have nothing to fear from me. Old Jagar and I go way back, to the days of the First Rebellion. Follow me down below, out of sight and sound of passersby. There is much we have to speak of."

Jagar nodded, letting them know they could trust this

Desert Fox. Selene was the first to follow, with Jagar bringing up the rear. Lucian had a bad feeling about this. There was something about Dario's manner he didn't fully trust. Then again, Lucian had been betrayed so many times that he didn't trust *anyone*.

Lucian went down about twenty steps before it opened into something of an underground dining room. A hallway and several doors led farther on, what Lucian assumed to be their accommodations.

"Please, sit down. I can order something from the kitchen and you can tell me everything, for I am most curious."

This man had to be doing well financially if he could afford this underground base and the staff to run it. A servant filled their cups with hot tea sweetened with honey, or something similar to honey on this world, as well as lemon.

Over tea, Jagar quietly told the Fox most of the tale. He must have trusted this Dario implicitly, and Dario was the picture of studious attention, not seeming to miss a single detail. That made Lucian somewhat nervous, but he knew to reach the end of his mission, he'd have to learn to trust *some* people. Jagar had yet to lead them astray.

"That's quite the story," Dario said. "Of course I can help. But after examination, the gems from Queen Ansaldra's dress are too hot for me to handle."

"What do you mean?" Serah asked.

"Such is the craftsmanship that they could have been created by none other than the Court Atomicist, Nostra. It could be traced back to me. I've got a feeling that anyone unfortunate enough to hold those gems will receive a visit from the Queen's Eyes."

Lucian felt his face blanch and noticed a similar reaction among the others. "What do we do, then? We need money for the airship passage."

"Well, I can help you," the Desert Fox said. "And I'm happy

to do so for friendship's sake, and in memory of the failed revolution twenty years back. I'm willing to help however I can in dethroning Queen Ansaldra and freeing the Westlands from her tyranny."

"You and Jagar know each other from the wars against the Queen?"

He nodded. "I've been on Psyche almost as long as Jagar has. I'm no mage, though. Just got tossed here thirty years ago for piracy in the Luddus System. Most of the Mid-Worlds send their trash here. Even if it's not *technically* allowed, the Wardens make an exception for pirates and other space scum and villainy." He flashed a toothy smile. "Of which I was guilty."

"Surprised they didn't send you out the airlock, if you'll pardon me for saying, " Fergus mused.

"Well, I've always been lucky. If anyone could consider living on this hellhole of a moon luck."

"So, you can help us with airship tickets to Passtown?" Jagar asked.

"Oh, without a doubt. I have connections to the Underground in both regards. I can send word to my friends at the aerodrome. You'll have a first-class cabin to Dara if you wish. No questions asked."

"First-class is unnecessary," Jagar said. "And we need only go as far as Passtown."

Selene's eyes narrowed. Imagining her mixing with the riffraff in second-class was unfathomable.

"Well, a private cabin would keep you and your conversation from prying ears. Which might be of more value than the sofas and free spirits."

"Free spirits?" Serah asked. "I'm in."

Lucian smiled, though underneath, he was still suspicious. All this seemed too good to be true, but Jagar seemed to accept everything at face value. Was Lucian just wrong about Dario, or was the Desert Fox outfoxing them somehow? Jagar was a

Psionic, so surely he could read his friend's intentions. Or perhaps he trusted him enough not to.

"Who is your contact with the aerodrome?" Fergus asked.

"I have plenty," Dario said. "The Underground is extensive in Kalm."

"The Underground?" Lucian asked.

"That's what the resistance against Ansaldra is calling itself these days," Dario said. "We can't openly oppose her, so we've gone . . . well, underground. *She* is the ultimate enemy, along with the class system she props up. We will only attain freedom by taking her out for good."

Fergus nodded with approval. "You have my spear arm."

"Same," Selene said, coldly. "Ansaldra must fall."

Jagar nodded somberly. Serah's eyes met Lucian's, and she shrugged.

Dario licked his thin lips. "Lady Selene. Of course, I know who you are. Long have we waited for someone of your expertise to join us. I assume you wish to access the Palace through the mountain tunnels?"

Her eyes widened a bit in surprise. "Yes. How did you know that?"

"That's all there could be in Passtown. Though we have failed in gaining access."

"Only mages in the Queen's employ can access the tunnels," Selene said. "We hope that the pass-wards haven't changed."

"And if they have?" Dario asked.

Selene's face became determined. "Then we will do what we must."

"All of this is moving pretty fast," Lucian said.

"That's how it is, my boy," Dario said, easily. "You wish to get inside and steal the prophecy, while your friends wish to revenge themselves on the Queen. There is no reason both can't happen at the same time."

Jagar had told Dario just about everything, but he had left

out one crucial detail—the fact that Lucian had both the Orb of Binding and the Orb of Psionics. Either Jagar figured it was for Lucian to say, or as much as he claimed to trust Dario, he did not trust him on that one aspect. If it was the latter, then Lucian would need to tread carefully.

Several servants doled out the food, a veritable feast compared to how they had been eating. There was a whole suckling pig, loaves of bread with butter, along with a mountain of potatoes and vegetables served with red wine. The Underground, or at least its top officers, ate well.

They tucked in while the conversation turned to far lighter matters. Lucian ate until his stomach was near to bursting. Despite Dario's charm, Lucian still found himself a bit on guard. Perhaps it was because of that charm that he was cautious. He made a note to check in with Jagar later on about whether trusting him was a good idea.

At last, full of food and wine, they stumbled off to bed. Dario watched them go off genially, raising a hand in farewell, his gut protruding.

Lucian caught up to Jagar and placed a hand on his arm. "Can we talk for a bit?"

"For certain, my boy," he said, his speech slurred a bit. "What's up?"

Jagar led him into an open bedroom, and Lucian could only hope he wasn't making a mistake by sharing his misgivings.

23

THEY ENTERED a small room with a well-made bed lit by an oil lamp, with thick patterned rugs covering the stone floor. Despite the lack of windows, it was more comfortable than anything they had experienced in the last few days.

Jagar took a seat on the corner of the bed. "What's on your mind, lad?"

"You and Dario go way back, it seems."

Jagar nodded. "Aye. Twenty years back, we fought with the Resistance. He rose in the ranks and caught my eye."

"He caught your eye? Were you some sort of leader or something?"

Jagar chuckled. "You might say that. I was the ringleader, leading the whole circus."

"You never mentioned that."

"It was . . . long ago. After the Rebellion, after my exile and my failure, the Resistance became the Underground. There, the Desert Fox made a name for himself, funding the movement with goods pilfered off Daran officials."

"He limited himself to just them?" Lucian asked skeptically.

193

Jagar shrugged. "Well, I can't rightly be sure of that, but it began that way. Who knows how things are now. Old Dario hates the Queen almost as much as I do. Everything he does, he does to bring her down."

"And why does he hate her so much?"

"Well, he lost his wife and kids in the first razing of Kalm. He'll never forgive her for that." Jagar leaned forward. "Lucian, I understand your reservations. Dario is both an honorable man and not. But Queen Ansaldra took everything from him."

Lucian almost let it go there. "You haven't been here for twenty years, Jagar. When I look at how I've changed over the last two, even three years, even I don't recognize myself."

Jagar just laughed. "Some things never change, Lucian. Some injustices set so deep inside the marrow of your bones that they enter your core. Revenge is who Dario is. He will see the Queen undone, no matter the cost."

Lucian made himself nod. "Well, if you say so. I guess we will see how everything plays out."

"Dario might not be much to look at, but that's how he's survived all these years. It's how I knew the Fox would still run the streets of Kalm. This is how we topple this regime once and for all. Then, you will get your prophecy and fly off with your friends into the sky."

It all seemed too neat to Lucian. "No plan survives contact with the enemy."

"That's true. We will need to be ready for anything."

"What does that mean?"

"Get some sleep, lad. Tomorrow will be a long day."

Lucian realized he would not get much more out of him, and he was exhausted. He left Jagar in his room and headed toward his room, finding Serah standing outside his door.

"Did you hear any of that?" Lucian asked.

"Every word."

She followed him into his room. He was glad she wanted to

stay with him, not only for her company but because it made them both safer in this unfamiliar place.

"I don't think you're crazy," Serah said, once she shut the door. "It seems like our hand is being forced, isn't it?"

"Unfortunately. Outside of refusing Dario's help, what can we do?"

"Well, our original plan lines up pretty closely to Dario's," Serah said. "Only I'm not sure how we can get on an airship without money."

"It smells fishy."

"Well, what are the options? We have no money because he can't fence our gems. So the only way we're getting on an airship is if we go through him. And that means we have to follow his plan. Either that or walk some more."

"I wouldn't be opposed to that, to be honest. This way takes too much power out of our hands."

"That's another couple of weeks across the desert and up the Path of Madness. Then you have to get through the gate at Passtown, which is no simple thing when they're going to be checking our faces. Remember, there is no other way across."

"That would destroy me," Lucian said with a shudder. In all this time, he had failed to mention his audience with the Ancient One. Though it had been two months, it was still as fresh in his mind as the day it happened. And he was too exhausted to get into it now. "Won't they check us on the airship, too?"

"I don't know. Maybe?"

Lucian didn't like it, but he felt he was in the position of having to go along with everything. Was Jagar blinded by his past friendship with Dario, or did he simply not care as long as he got his revenge?

"Look," Serah said, reaching for his hand. "I'll talk to Fergus, even Selene, and share your thoughts with them. You're exhausted and could do with some rest. We just need to keep an eye out."

Lucian had the feeling they didn't call him the Desert Fox for no reason. He didn't know what other choice he had.

"It's hard to admit this," he said, pulling her close, "but maybe all this is in my head. Maybe I'm just afraid of going up against the Queen again. To think it could happen so soon . . ." He shook his head. "I'm not ready."

It was a moment before she answered. "Yeah. That might be it."

"She told me in my dream that she was weak during our fight. Which I believe. But if we go back, I might have to face her with her full strength."

"Hopefully, Jagar will be the one taking care of her."

"He's powerful, but he's no match for the Queen. She almost had *me* and I had the Orb of Psionics."

"You've gotten more capable since then. Besides, it's not up to us to take down the Queen, is it? I know that's what Selene wants, what Fergus wants, and what Jagar wants. But what *we* want is different. We just want the prophecy so we can keep finding the Orbs."

"That's true. It makes me nervous that our team is working at cross-purposes."

"Unfortunately, we can't plan every little thing. There are too many unknowns. As you said, no plan survives contact with the enemy. We didn't think we'd make it out of the Burning Sands, either, but we did, against all odds."

"Cleon didn't."

"Is that what you're afraid of? Someone else dying?"

Unconsciously, he held her even closer.

"I see," she said. "Well, I don't plan on going anywhere. We'll get in and out of there fast. How hard could it be to steal a book, especially when the Queen is distracted by her husband's sudden return?"

Lucian couldn't help but laugh. "It all sounds too convoluted to work. I guess we still have to try. That's all we can do, right?"

Serah got up from the bed. "I can go talk to the others. You just rest up, okay?"

She left him there. Such was his exhaustion that as soon as he lay down, he was asleep.

24

THE NEXT MORNING, Dario gave them new, fancier clothes that would make them look the part of first-class patrons on an Imperial Airways airship. Dario also assigned some of his servants to carry their "luggage," which they really wouldn't be using.

Dario led them to the front door but did not proceed any further. There, a well-dressed young man with a trim black goatee waited.

"I must keep a low profile, I'm afraid," Dario said. "I'm entrusting everything to my lieutenant here, Tycho. He's a rising star in our little movement, and you can trust him implicitly."

"Thank you, my friend," Jagar said. "Your help has been invaluable."

Dario beamed. "Of course. Anything for you, old friend."

Things only truly felt real once they were out in the streets. Lucian was thankful there was little traffic, and the walk to the aerodrome took perhaps twenty minutes. Their costumes contained hats, as was the fashion here among the rich, so they wore them low to make passing guards unable to recognize them.

The aerodrome stood past the last buildings in the east of town, with only a small terminal built of adobe standing on an open expanse of desert. There, three airships were moored to the stone landing platforms, though none were anywhere near the size of *Zephyr*. Tycho, along with several of Dario's house servants, led them right to the boarding ramp of the central ship, the largest of the three, which went by the name *Kestrel*. A pretty, blue-uniformed airship attendant waved them directly on board without even checking their passes.

"Safe voyage, masters," Tycho said, with a subordinate bow.

The servants handed over the luggage, which was taken on board by another attendant.

"Welcome aboard," the young woman said. "My name is Lyra, and I will be your servant for the duration of this flight. Please, follow me to your private cabin."

They followed her down a short corridor of paneled wood toward the bow of the ship. They entered the first door on the left, revealing a spacious suite regaled with plates of pastries, meats, cheeses, and pitchers of wine beaded with condensation. Serah immediately went forward and started stuffing her face.

"Our finest cabin," the flight attendant said. "If ever you need anything, ring the bell and I will attend to your needs immediately. I will return when the ship is about to depart."

With that, she shut the door behind her.

"Wow, choice stuff," Serah said, her words muffled by the cheese stuffed in her mouth.

Selene looked at her in disgust. Lucian just looked out the window queasily. Tycho and Dario's servants were already on the road back into town about a hundred meters in the distance. Though he had felt better about things this morning, something about this just seemed off.

Jagar seemed to be of a similar mind. "Be ready for anything, lad. This is far from over."

"What's *that* supposed to mean?" Serah asked, turning her attention away from the food.

"Merely a word of caution. There will be no break between now and then, and I advise full alertness. Things are not likely to work out as planned, and we must be ready for that."

"Just tell us plainly what you mean, Jagar," Fergus said.

"I just want to know if the food's poisoned or something," Serah said.

Jagar shook his head. "The food's fine."

Lucian watched out the window as more passengers filled the ship, wearing humbler clothes than them. There was a sense of unease in the cabin, everyone seeming to catch Jagar's mood. Lucian got the feeling that there was something he wasn't telling them. He almost wanted to call him out on it, but Jagar had already retreated to a corner, where he leaned against the wall, eyes closed.

"Is everything all right, Jagar?" Fergus asked.

Jagar remained silent, instead seeming to sleep, or perhaps meditate.

"Not a good sign," Serah said.

Lucian approached him. "What's going on?"

Jagar finally opened his eyes and met Lucian's gaze. Something *was* wrong, but Lucian wouldn't know what unless Jagar told him. He wondered if he should open a Psionic link, but if Jagar wanted to communicate something to him, he probably would have done so by now.

Lucian reached out with his Focus. But Jagar had warded himself, making it impossible to find a connection. Unless Lucian forced it with the Orb of Psionics, that ward would not break. Jagar's light brown eyes took on a look of warning, a warning that clearly said *not* to communicate anything, either out loud or telepathically. They would only find out what was on his mind when he decided the time was right.

It was at that moment that there was a knock at the door. Lyra popped her head in, giving a professional smile.

"The *Kestrel* is about to embark," she said. "Please find your seats."

When she left, no one bothered to seat themselves. They hadn't done so on the *Zephyr*, so Lucian didn't see the point here. That was when the deck jolted, sending him sprawling. Selene stumbled a bit, while Serah streamed a small bit of Gravitonic Magic to right herself.

By the time he stood, the airship was lifting off at a steady rate. Out the windows, the desert ground fell away with surprising speed. He had only a moment to see the spread of adobe buildings clinging to the river before the *Kestrel* veered east, heading directly toward the Mountains of Madness.

Besides size, the other obvious difference between this airship and the *Zephyr* was speed. *Kestrel* was far slower than its larger counterpart, which told Lucian they didn't have as many Binders on board. Either that or they weren't as talented as the Queen's Binders. They proceeded forward at a crawl, the mountains only getting marginally closer with each passing hour.

It was only by noon that they were well above the lower foothills and angling upward for the Pass of Madness itself. Jagar came out of his doze, his whole body seeming to become rigid with alertness.

"Nearly there," Serah said, coming to stand next to Lucian at the fore of the cabin, where a window looked upon the approaching mountains, a veritable wall of rock. "Are you ready?"

"Well, I wish I knew what to be ready for. Jagar won't tell us."

"Well, he's just hours away from a confrontation with his dear old wife. I'd be queasy, too."

"Are you sure it's not something else?"

"What else *could* it be? He just has the jitters. That's all."

Lucian wanted to let it slide. Then again, sometimes mages, especially those gifted in Psionics, had a sense for when something big was about to happen. Was that from his latent magical abilities, a gut feeling, or even nothing at all? It seemed Lucian was the only one with that premonition. Fergus was eating the food and chatting with Selene. Serah seemed relaxed, seeming to enjoy the scenery. Jagar was the only one besides himself who seemed to be ill-at-ease.

After rising into the air for several hours, the *Kestrel* evened out and approached the mass of mountains ahead, just kilometers away. Behind them, Kalm and the Surin River were well beyond the horizon. The day had advanced enough for the sun to be above the mountains, meaning its shadow was short and didn't fall upon them until they were before the tunnel itself.

Jagar rose from his seat, coming to the window and looking out. It was hard to read his weathered face, whether the emotions churning within were anger, regret, or even fear. As they plunged into the darkness of the Pass of Madness, he signaled for everyone to stand around him.

"Selene," he said. "Are you ready?"

Selene nodded. "Yes."

Jagar gave a slow nod. "Wait for my signal."

Lucian looked from one to the other. "What the hell is going on?"

"Trust me, lad. Unless you mean to trust my old *friend*."

The way he said that made Lucian realize Jagar didn't trust Dario, either, and that something was happening. Something Jagar and Selene had kept from him. He wasn't sure whether to be relieved that Jagar didn't trust Dario, or to be angry that Jagar had left him in the dark.

But this was hardly the time or place. His instincts had not been far off. Something big was about to happen.

Serah and Fergus, unlike Lucian, seemed to take it in good stride and without offense. Fergus had already placed a hand on his retracted shockspear, ready to extend it at a moment's notice, while Serah was doing the same.

"Passtown, dead ahead," Selene said. "Now?"

Jagar nodded. "Now. Follow me. Let's make this quick. And don't kill unless you have to."

"Okay, what is going on?" Lucian asked.

"We're taking a detour, it would seem," Fergus said.

Lucian wasn't sure how he'd surmised that, but he saw that he would have to go along with it. Jagar stood before the door, half-turning his head back. "This ship is not stopping at Passtown, not unless we make it." He opened the door into the central corridor, peeking both ways before emerging. He made directly for the bridge, just a few short steps away from their cabin. Everyone followed him, with Lucian bringing up the rear. He placed a hand on his shockspear, a nervous weight forming in his stomach.

"Sir," came the voice of the flight attendant. "Please return to your cabin."

Lucian wasn't sure what to tell her, but the others were already far ahead, just steps away from the bridge. "Return to your seat. For your own good."

The flight attendant's eyes widened when she noticed Jagar at the door to the bridge. "Hey!" she said. "Return to your—"

Jagar tried the door, which wouldn't budge. With a scowl, he raised his right hand, which became wrapped in violet light. As the woman screamed, he blasted the door to the bridge wide open. Jagar busted into the bridge. Lucian wasn't sure what was going on, but he was a part of it now. He had no choice but to run to the bridge, too.

When he got there, the gray-uniformed Imperial Airways captain with graying, parted hair had his hands above his head, along with his copilot. Jagar was holding his extended shockspear just centimeters from his throat, while everyone else had their weapons out. Lucian did likewise.

"I need you to land the ship on the right side of the pass, inside Passtown."

"There's no space to maneuver here!" the captain sputtered.

"Bullshit." He edged the spear point closer. "Get us low. Right side of the pass, inside the city. Do it if you enjoy living."

The captain gulped. "I . . . do very much, at that. Very well. I'll see what I can do."

The captain moved the control stick in that direction. They sailed over the wall, veering toward the right of the small town occupying the center of the pass, serving as the waypoint between the east and west sides of Psyche.

"Care to explain what's going on now?" Lucian asked.

"A change in plans," Jagar said.

"Obviously."

"Just follow along, and it'll turn out fine. Probably."

Serah looked at him and shrugged. He didn't understand how she could take this so well.

"I assume your friend had questionable plans for us?" Fergus asked.

"You assume correctly," Jagar said. "The greedy bastard sold us out twenty years ago, and it was only upon great reflection during my exile that I figured it all out." Jagar turned to Lucian. "Dario was likely listening to us all the while in the hideout, which was why I insisted you could trust him. The Queen's men and Eyes watch the road to Dara closely out of Kalm, and I didn't think our chances of getting through the Pass of Madness on foot were high." He gave a grim smile. "As soon as I saw Dario, I realized he didn't know what I knew. And I knew his mercenary ways wouldn't resist delivering us right to Ansaldra's lap, especially as soon as I found out about the bounty on our heads." He looked at both the pilot and copilot. "It wouldn't surprise me in the least if these two gentlemen were in on the whole thing, too."

At the reddening of their faces, Lucian saw Jagar wasn't far off in his guess.

"Lower," Jagar growled.

"This is as low as I can go," the captain said tersely.

Lucian looked over the edge and saw they were about ten meters above the village below them. In the lamp-lit streets, he could see people pointing at them.

"Let's get out of here before the hoplites get any ideas," Fergus said.

Jagar gave a curt nod and ran toward the back of the ship, and the others followed. As they neared the exit, two figures emerged from one of the anterior cabins. Their colored robes of red and yellow revealed them to be Mage-Knights.

There was no time to question anything. Lucian immediately raised his hands, reaching for the Orb of Psionics. He streamed a quick and powerful kinetic wave. The force blasted down the corridor, ripping wooden paneling from the walls. A fireball flew from the direction of the knights, but Selene raised a Thermal shield in time to eat the impact. By now, the kinetic wave reached the mages, who screamed as it pushed against them like a solid wall clear down the corridor.

Serah raised her hands, throwing her own fireball back at the mages, but they raised a Thermal shield in time to absorb the impact.

"Stop fooling around," Jagar said. "You'll burn this whole ship down."

A silver disc bloomed beneath Lucian, and his knees buckled as he became twice as heavy. Serah worked to counter the Gravitonic stream, immediately erasing it.

"Amateur," she breathed.

She raised her left hand toward the mages, directing her own disc to spread beneath them. Her frayed arm shook with

effort as it shone more brightly, as the mage in red worked to counter the stream. But he was no match for Serah. Both mages' knees collapsed as the incredible force pulled them down toward the deck.

"I tire of this," Selene said.

She strode forward as the helpless Mage-Knights begged for mercy. Coolly and mechanically, she speared them both. Lucian almost gasped at the brutality and wondered whether it was necessary. But he realized they couldn't leave them alive. Once they were off the ship, those knights would either chase them or report them to the Queen.

Selene returned to the exit, where there was a ten-meter drop to the ground beneath. A sizeable crowd had gathered, but so far, there was no sign of the Queen's men. That wouldn't remain so forever.

"Can we make that jump?" Lucian asked. "Looks high."

"Just pull us down one by one," Serah said. "Shouldn't take long, right?"

Already, Lucian saw a sizeable tower toward which he could bind them. It was close and wouldn't take as much magic as his previous tethers.

He reached for the Orb of Binding, tethering Serah first and shooting her off. After a surprised yelp, it only took her ten seconds to complete the passage. So easy was this that Lucian merely switched the anchor point to the next in line, Fergus, and sent him off right after her. In this way, he had all four of his companions standing at the base of the tower in less than a minute.

Only he remained. He anchored himself and immediately shot off toward the tower, touching down within seconds, landing adroitly with a light step.

"Rotting hell, you're getting good at this," Serah said.

Lucian could only hope it was good enough. "What now?"

"Lead the way, Selene," Jagar said. "Can you feel the ward from here?"

She nodded. "Just barely. It should be on the north side of the pass. I only hope they haven't changed the pass-ward to get through."

It seemed Jagar and Selene had already talked this through. He could only wonder why they had left him out of it, along with Serah and Fergus. But there was no time to question. Selene was already leading them forward, her hood drawn to hide her face from the gathering crowd.

25

SHE LED them through the dark, decrepit alleys of Passtown. Here, there was no natural light save from either end of the kilometers-long tunnel. The only illumination came from grimy gas lanterns, many of which were broken. Still, Selene seemed to know her way through the dark, winding alleyways, guided by a force beyond her.

"Where are you taking us?" Serah asked.

Selene was silent for a long moment, intent on picking the right path. "The Winding Tunnel leads from Passtown to the Atomicism Labs. I've never used them, but I know where they are. If the pass-wards haven't changed, then that's our way forward."

"And if they have? How long did the Queen possess you?"

"About two years, give or take," she said, her voice cold and neutral.

She led them into a wider street with little foot traffic. The wall of the tunnel was directly ahead, including a wide gate about ten meters across.

"Is that it?" Serah asked.

"It should be. It's where I feel the ward strongest." Selene went forward, placing her hand on the gate, which became wrapped in orangish light. Nothing happened at first, and Selene's expression took on notes of frustration. But after half a minute, it creaked open, revealing a path into a dark and foreboding tunnel. Lucian thought he spied stairs just before the darkness became impenetrable.

"That looks scary," Serah said.

Selene went inside, not looking back to see if any of them were following. Jagar was right behind her, streaming a light sphere overhead to illumine the way. Indeed, Lucian saw stairs winding down toward the left into the darkness.

"This will take a long time," Selene said. "Hours, if not days. I can't promise anything. We may have a contingent of Mage-Knights waiting for us at the bottom, and if we flee, we are likely to be boxed in on the top. If any of you wish to back out, now's the time."

From everyone's lack of response, it seemed all of them wanted to proceed. They began descending the stairs, Selene still in the lead.

"Makes you wonder," Lucian said. "Why have a secret tunnel directly to the Palace from Passtown?"

"It's an escape route for the Queen, or so the thinking goes," Selene said. "In case the masses ever breached the Palace during an insurrection."

"Has that ever happened?" Serah asked.

"Not in living memory. The Queen is good at keeping rebellions from springing up, at least on the east side of the mountains. Her Eyes put any insurrection to death before it can fester."

After that, they followed the stairs down for hours in silence. The stairs seemed to descend endlessly, so much so that Lucian was sure it was far into the evening. Just when he thought his knees couldn't take it anymore, the steps came to an abrupt end, revealing a dark tunnel sloping downward. Sometimes the tunnel veered left or right, but mostly it delved straight ahead.

"Where are we, exactly?" Lucian asked, his voice echoing in the tunnel's narrow confines.

"Somewhere beneath the Mountains of Madness," Selene answered. "And still kilometers from the outer reaches of the Atomicism Labs."

"My knees are *killing* me," Serah said.

Jagar was still silent, resolutely going forward with his right hand on the baton of his shockspear.

How long they walked like that, Lucian didn't know. But it was hours upon hours. The tunnel eventually entered a network of caverns, a maze of rock, stalagmites, and stalactites. At some point, they had to stop out of sheer exhaustion and get some rest, so they found a small alcove to camp in away from the main path. Like the Darkrift, there was an entire world of darkness down here, a world that would be all too easy to lose themselves in.

It was hard to tell just how much later they awoke. After a quick breakfast, they made their way back to the main tunnel, until hours later, Fergus broke the silence.

"Something ahead," Fergus said. "Some sort of metal door."

"That would be the entrance," Selene said. "Pray the hike down here wasn't a waste."

Soon enough, they were standing before it. As Fergus had said, it was pure metal, probably quite thick, with no windows to see beyond.

Selene stood before it, closing her eyes and streaming Atomic Magic. Her face was a mask of concentration. She stood like that for several minutes, her brow covered with sweat despite the coolness of the tunnel. Her arms shook, while her shoulders hunched over with effort as her expression became strained, almost agonized.

Just when Lucian was about to tell her to stop, a resounding click sounded from the door. It swung inward, revealing the tunnel continuing.

Selene shuddered and fell forward, and Fergus caught her just in time.

"Selene?" he asked.

From her pale expression and closed eyes, it seemed as if she were out for the count. But her eyelids slowly fluttered open, finding Fergus's.

"That was . . . more taxing than I expected."

"You performed admirably," Fergus said.

After he helped her to stand, she drew a deep breath. "The security in this place is higher than when I was here last. To undo the lock without triggering the alarm wards took almost every drop of magic I had."

"Will there be more doors like that?" Lucian asked.

"Let's hope not, because I can't go through that again."

Gathering herself, she continued into the darkness ahead. Lucian realized then that he had vastly underestimated Selene. She was no soft noble, as he had first supposed, but as tough as any of them, if not tougher. Like Jagar, the need for vengeance was one hell of a drug.

"As long as you know the way from here, we should be good," Serah said.

"I know the way," she said. "I just hope we don't run afoul of my old master."

There was that, too. Ansaldra's Court Atomicist, Nostra, might be down here.

"Will she be down here?" Lucian asked.

"Almost certainly. We can only hope she's spent herself after a long day's work. Otherwise, she will stop this little coup dead in its tracks."

Lucian didn't like the sound of that. But they had no choice but to continue before news from the captain or anyone on the *Kestrel* spread in Dara, which would almost certainly reach the ears of the Queen if it hadn't already.

They continued into the darkness, into the Atomicism Labs buried beneath the Mountains of Madness.

———

THEY ENTERED A SMALL CHAMBER, lit by torches along rocky walls. Several tunnels led out from the chamber, all looking the same to Lucian.

But Selene knew exactly where to go, taking the lefthand tunnel, passing doors on either side. Some were open, and some were not, and of the open ones, Lucian only got the barest glimpse. He spied rows of casks, all labeled in print too fine to read, along with glassware, hearths, forges, bellows, and tools. The only thing he didn't find was people, a fact for which he was thankful.

"We're close to my old quarters," Selene said. "From there, the elevator to the palace shouldn't take long."

She turned down a short tunnel and went to the door at the end. It opened easily, revealing a bare room that contained only a small bed and mattress. Selene stared in shock as if she had expected something far more.

"They . . . took it all. My paintings, my clothes . . . everything from my old life." She stepped into the room, seeming hardly able to come to grips with this reality. "It's as if they've *erased* me."

"They will pay," Fergus said. "We're just moments away from bringing down the one responsible."

"We can't dawdle," Jagar said. "Where is this elevator?"

Selene turned, her gaze haunted. "Not far. The sooner we

get out of here and into the Palace proper, the better. I have a feeling Nostra is skulking about."

They followed her through the empty corridors once again. Lucian couldn't shake the feeling that all this seemed rather convenient. The fires were all still going, so clearly someone was down here tending things. Or perhaps someone had warned them they were coming.

They turned the corner to find an elevator at the end. Selene proceeded straight toward it, streaming a bit of electricity on the door to get it to open.

As soon as those doors opened, a blast wave slammed all five of them back quickly. By sheer instinct, he reached for the Orb of Psionics and streamed a shield, but it was not strong enough to counter the sheer power of the attack.

It was a trap.

"Forgot me, did you?" came a taunting female voice. "My dear Selene, I'm quite offended, because I didn't forget you."

Lucian was the first to recover and Selene next to him. When Lucian looked from side to side, he saw that he and Selene were the only ones standing. The blast had somehow knocked out the others, Lucian's shield only being strong enough to cover him and Selene.

They faced their opponent, a short, middle-aged woman with a pudgy face and graying hair, wearing billowing orange robes. Her eyes were enormous behind her thick glasses, and those eyes blinked at him as they stared him down. The Court Atomicist Nostra looked more like a librarian than one of the highest-ranked officials in the Queen's employ.

"Come to take revenge on me for giving you to the Queen?" Nostra asked.

"To think I once trusted you and counted you as my friend," Selene spat.

There was a brief flash of regret on Nostra's face, but she

quickly replaced it with a smug smile. "Foolish little girl. Do you think I could refuse the Queen's request and keep my head? I didn't *want* to give you up. You were useful. A good Psion."

"Then help us get back at Ansaldra," Lucian said.

Nostra blinked her enormous eyes. "What a ridiculous notion. Who might you be?"

"Lucian."

"Lucian." Nostra snickered. "Not from around here, are you?"

"I'm from a fair distance away."

"Why, you insolent pup! Well, this doesn't concern you. The Queen wishes for Selene to come before her immediately."

"That won't happen. Stand aside. Now."

"I'm afraid I can't do that."

Lucian reached for the Focuses of his friends, hoping to revive them, but it was at that moment that Nostra struck. She surrounded herself with an aura of fiery red energy, and Selene raised a Thermal shield to counter whatever was coming their way. The hue of Nostra's aura shifted to orange. That bubble of orange light passed through Lucian and Selene. The shockwave seemed to have no effect.

But from the widening of Selene's eyes, however, there was a cause for alarm. "She's going to suffocate us!"

Lucian didn't see what she meant, but he found himself curiously short of breath. With a start, he recognized what Nostra must have done—transmuted all the oxygen in the air into nitrogen.

"Counter it!"

"I'm trying! She's warding my efforts!"

There was only one solution, as Lucian saw it. To kill the source of the ward, Nostra herself.

He reached out with the Orb of Binding, slamming Nostra against the wall, hard. She raised a Binding shield, which dampened the effect of Lucian's tether. Lucian increased his magic to match, knowing all the while that Ansaldra would likely detect his efforts. But he saw no other choice. He pressed Nostra so firmly into the wall that she might as well have been a *part* of it. She screamed, unleashing a surprising burst of Binding Magic sufficient to break her free of the hold.

Lucian staggered backward, choking for breath. It had been half a minute now since his lungs had absorbed oxygen. Selene raised her hands and streamed an Atomic wave that blasted outward. Suddenly, the air was breathable again. But it only lasted a few moments. Nostra, with a grimace, streamed her Atomic wave, reverting the air to its previous, anoxic state.

Lucian glanced down at his friends, still inert on the floor. If there was only a way he could wake them up. His hasty Psionic shield had only been enough to cover him and Selene. Would it be possible to revive them with his Psionic Magic?

But he had already drawn too deeply of the Orb of Binding. The fluctuations in the Ethereal Background were probably significant enough for her to notice something, but there was still a hope that the Queen might think they were only Nostra's experimentations. If this battle kept up, then that became less likely.

Lucian held his breath, knowing that panting for more air would only prove useless. He had to trust Selene to revert the air. It was on him to kill Nostra and to do so quickly.

He streamed Binding again, throwing Nostra hard against the wall. Lucian's vision began going dark, his lungs screaming for air. He'd have to get up close and personal, finishing the job before Nostra could finish him.

He extended his shockspear, closing the distance between him and Nostra while keeping the Binding secure. Nostra raised her hands, streaming a fork of lightning from her fingertips. Lucian raised his spear, along with a Dynamistic shield, just in time to fizzle out the attack. Nostra's eyes widened behind her glasses as she prepared another attack—a sudden flash of Radiance Magic that blinded him.

He reached a hand to his eyes, unsure what to do in this situation. All he *could* do was keep the Binding secure. He reached for Radiance, trying to see with magic that which he couldn't with his own eyes. He slowed the stream until he could see a vague, reddish shape, what he knew to be light in the infrared spectrum. Nostra was there, still ahead, penned and trying to break free by streaming a counter Binding.

Selene also proceeded forward with her shockspear out. Nostra squirmed as her former Psion came closer.

"Finish her," Lucian gasped.

His lungs burned for oxygen. There were just seconds left before he closed his eyes, possibly to never open them again. He could feel the Binding weakening in his mind. A few seconds longer, it would be weak enough for Nostra to break free.

Lucian didn't know if Selene could do it. Why was she hesitating?

But then the tip of her spear connected with Nostra's abdomen, the old master's body stiffening with the action. She then slashed at Nostra's neck to speed her death. Tears ran down her face as she turned away from her.

The Atomic brand keeping the oxygen fluxed into nitrogen dissolved, rendering the air breathable again. Lucian sucked in breath after breath, feeling as if he could never get enough air. His vision, too, was returning, allowing him to let go of the ward producing his infrared vision.

Lucian turned his attention to the others, who were just now reviving from Nostra's first Psionic attack. Serah blinked drearily while Fergus was up on his feet in seconds, shockspear out. He advanced toward Selene, who had blood on the lower part of her dress.

"Selene," he said. "Are you okay?"

She gave a shaky nod. "The blood's . . . not mine." She glanced back at Nostra. "I . . . can't believe I could do that. She was my friend. Once."

"Are you all right, Selene?" Jagar asked.

"Physically, yes."

"What the hell just happened?" Serah asked. "All I remember was this wave blasting out at us."

"A catatonic brand," Jagar said. "They trigger from being stepped on or the creator setting it off. It must have activated when we opened the elevator. Nostra likely meant it to incapacitate all five of us at once." Jagar looked at Lucian. "Lucky for us, someone was thinking fast."

"I shielded Selene and me, but it seems I couldn't get it powerful enough to cover everyone."

"Even shields take time to deploy properly," Jagar said. "Brands work more or less instantaneously, so your reaction time would have had to be perfect."

"Either way, we took care of Nostra," Lucian said. "We should keep moving. Ansaldra might figure out Nostra is dead."

Nostra was likely Psionically branded, and Ansaldra would sense that connection had vanished, eventually. If she hadn't figured it out yet, then the five of them had a tiny window of opportunity to advance into the Golden Palace.

"This elevator will take us straight up?" Lucian asked.

Selene nodded. "It will take us to the Palace's lower reaches."

"And that will be my cue to go after Ansaldra," Jagar said. "I'll take the blame for everything down here. That'll give you four enough time to grab the prophecy."

"As soon as Lucian finds the prophecy, I'll find you," she said. "My need for revenge is as much as yours."

Jagar nodded, seeming to accept that.

With a start, Lucian realized he just had minutes left with

both of them. After they went off to find the Sorceress-Queen, he would likely never see them again.

But there was no time for sentimentality. Already, they were advancing, stepping through the open doors.

Selene, with a shaky hand, streamed a small bit of electricity into a nearby panel. The doors closed, and the elevator shot up.

The five of them kept their spears out. There was no telling just what was waiting for them on the other side.

26

THE DOORS SLID OPEN, revealing a dark, cool chamber that appeared to be a cellar. Rows of casks and crates extended as far as the eye could see. Selene led them off to the right immediately, seeming to know exactly where to go.

"This is a recent addition," Jagar said, his voice low.

"They say the stocks under the Golden Palace are substantial enough to last five years," Selene said. "The only way to take this place down is from the inside."

"What lies above?" Jagar asked.

"The Passage of Mirrors is directly above us," Selene said. "It connects the east and west wings of the Palace."

"That was under construction when I left," Jagar said. "The East Wing was the only one completed."

"The East Wing they call the Old Palace. It's where you'll find most of the living quarters and private areas. The West Wing is for more public spaces—the throne room, various halls, Ansaldra's library. From both, we can reach the Queen's tower."

"I don't remember seeing the library last time," Lucian said. "Just a lot of hallways and the airstrip."

"That's on the extreme west of the Palace," Selene said. "If you went as far as the Evening Hall, where Ansaldra holds most of her nighttime gatherings, then you were just short of the library. Which is quite extensive."

"So, how do we get there without getting noticed?" Serah asked.

"Well, these cellars are little used, but extend under almost the entire Palace. Soon, it will be necessary to go upstairs, as this is the lowest level of the Palace itself. No one comes down here except to go down to the labs, and no one spends time there except Nostra."

"Well, she won't be there anymore," Serah said.

Selene ignored that statement, leading them to a set of stairs. They followed her up to an upper landing, a stone tunnel extending far in both directions. Both ways were empty, though heavy wooden doors lined both sides.

"The dungeon," Selene said.

"Perhaps we can bust out some of these inmates," Serah said. "Create a distraction."

"That could cause more harm than good," Jagar said. "I'll be distraction enough."

He headed off toward the right on his own and didn't seem concerned that he wasn't being followed.

"Not so much as a goodbye," Serah said. "Nice knowing you!"

Jagar turned back a moment, half-turned his shaggy head in their direction. It seemed for a moment he might say something, but in the end, he went up a stairwell with his shockspear in hand.

The four of them turned and went the opposite way, ostensibly toward the library, though everything looked the same down here. It was too quiet as they made their way forward,

Selene picking turns at random. At one moment, they paused at the sound of footsteps, but they weren't approaching them. After a couple of minutes, they resumed their walking.

"This one," Selene whispered. "Leads directly into the anterior stacks of the library. Barely anyone goes back there, but the Queen has the prophecy on display in the middle of the library and under guard. We can only hope that Jagar draws the guards away."

"How can we get out once we grab the prophecy?" Lucian asked.

"That I'll leave up to you," Selene said.

"This all seems *rather* precarious," Fergus said.

They went up several flights of stone steps until they reached an archway that opened into a stack of books. Lucian could hardly believe they were actually here, against all odds, and seemingly undetected. But that would not last forever, especially as Jagar made his presence known.

They proceeded forward in between the dim bookshelves. They encountered not a single soul, at least until they heard shouting emanating from beyond the stacks, along with the clanking of armor, signifying a group of soldiers running. They paused for a moment until it was clear the sound was going away from them.

"Seems like they've discovered Jagar," Serah whispered.

Selene raised a finger to her lips in warning. Serah glared, but Selene was already turning around and leading them on.

They entered a wider lane between the books, which led to a wider atrium ahead, an area that had to be the central hub of the library. They followed Selene until they had reached the atrium, where a display case with a worn book inside stood.

But that was not the only thing greeting them. A somewhat hunched and unassuming woman stood with her back to them, wearing a dark gray cloak.

A woman who could be none other than Queen Ansaldra.

IT WAS FAR TOO late to run. They crouched, preparing to fight, each warding their various Aspects in an expectation to fight to the death.

But when the old woman turned, the face wasn't Ansaldra's at all, but someone Lucian knew all too well. And he felt great shock upon seeing it.

Vera gave a small, cunning smile, a smile that sent shivers down his spine. The four of them stood facing her for a good ten seconds, none of them wanting to be the first to speak. Lucian realized at that moment that they didn't *know* this was Vera, none of them ever having seen Ansaldra herself, except for maybe Selene.

"Vera!" Lucian said, running forward. "How in the Worlds did you get here so fast?"

"This is Vera?" Serah asked, only relaxing slightly.

"Never mind how I got here. I *am* here, and that should be good enough for you."

"Do you have your ship?" Lucian asked. "It's time we got out of here!"

He watched her in shock and disbelief. How was this possible? She had at least another month before arriving. But all that would have to come later.

"We can't leave just yet," Vera said coolly, turning back toward the prophecy. "Not before we liberate this very important piece of information."

"I don't understand. I can break the glass if need be."

"It's not so simple, I'm afraid. Come, stand here. Consider this with me."

Hesitating only slightly, Lucian stepped forward, unsure of what she wanted. She didn't break her gaze away from the tome.

"We have little time," Fergus said.

"A fact of which I'm aware, young man. Now, Lucian. Ansaldra is clever, and I wish for you to learn. How do we gain the prophecy without alerting her or dying ourselves?"

Lucian blinked. It looked as if nothing more than glass protected the prophecy. "I don't know. We can't simply take it?"

"I thought I had taught you something about thinking for yourself," Vera reprimanded him. "It would seem the Academy drove that right from your mind."

"We don't have time for this," Lucian said. "Guards could be here any moment. *Ansaldra* could be here, and I don't even know if we can get out of this alive. Is this the time for lessons?"

"Reach out with your Focus. Tell me what you sense."

Lucian saw there was no other way forward, at least for now. He did as she asked since it seemed it was the only thing that would make her happy. He reached for the prophecy. At once, a dizzying maelstrom of Psionic streams and brands assaulted his mind, incomprehensibly complex. If anyone tampered with *any* of those streams, disaster would strike both the would-be thief and shake the very foundations of the Palace, preventing all escape. He saw a vision of that happening as clear as he saw the world before him. To take the prophecy, the Queen would either have to die or at the very least be greatly weakened.

Only one person could undo this brand: Ansaldra herself.

"We need her," he realized.

"That we do. And how do we get her to do what she doesn't want?"

"I can think of a few ways," Serah said. "Threatening to gut her like a rift eel is one."

Vera regarded her icily. "And who are you, so wise in diplomacy?"

Serah opened her mouth until she realized she was being slighted.

"I don't know that, either," Lucian said. "She's only motivated by one thing that I've seen so far."

"And what is that?" Vera asked.

"Working with me. She thinks I'm this thing called the Chosen of the Manifold. Does that sound familiar to you?"

"Does she think that? Well, if that's true, then I can see why she wishes to align herself with you. But all this remains to be seen. We need information, and for now, there's only one place to get it."

Vera regarded the others for a moment. None seemed to know what to say, even Serah, who always had *something* to say.

"I assume all of you are helping Lucian. I won't ask for the details. Our time is limited, and we must find Ansaldra quickly. There's been a disturbance in the Palace, a shifting in the Manifold that tells me things are fast coming to a head."

"Jagar will reach her soon."

Vera's eyes widened ever so slightly at that. "Jagar, you said?"

"What, you know him?"

She seemed flummoxed, if ever so slightly. "This has become . . . more interesting. Hopefully, we will be quick enough to keep the both of them from doing something stupid."

27

NOW, it was Vera who led them through the halls of the Golden Palace, seeming to know the way, as if she had been here before. For all Lucian knew, she had, though people said no one had ever escaped Psyche since its inception as a prison world. Then again, if there was anyone who *had* escaped, it would have probably been Vera. She seemed to have no problems slipping through the Warden blockade, after all.

Certainly, the name Jagar meant something to her. Which made sense, if Jagar had been a part of the Starsea Mages along with Ansaldra herself. These were connections Lucian had never considered. But for now, he couldn't think about them. Things could come to a head soon, and he needed to be ready. He didn't reach for either of his Orbs, but he was conscious of them, knowing he might need to use them at a moment's notice.

They rounded a corner, entering a long hallway, about ten meters tall and about as wide, where the walls themselves were all mirrors. It was dizzying to see, so Lucian kept his focus ahead, where a contingent of the Queen's hoplites, led by a couple of Mage-Knights, disappeared from view around a corner. For now, it seemed as if they were the least of the security's worries.

Vera led them around the corner, down a short hallway that led into a wide atrium. This atrium Lucian recognized to be the place he had waited just before the soiree all those weeks ago. For now, it was empty, though he could hear shouting coming from the Evening Hall itself.

Once inside, Lucian found Jagar, surrounded by well over a dozen Mage-Knights. Jagar stood, spear out, and expression grim. Jagar broke his attention to acknowledge them, his eyes widening slightly upon seeing Vera. Yes, it seemed he recognized well who she was, which made sense, if the both of them were a part of the Starsea Mages. However, Jagar had never mentioned knowing Vera while Lucian had told his story, something he found odd.

"What in the Worlds brought you here, Vera Desai? Meddling in something you have no business meddling in, would be my guess."

"I should say the same for you. I should have known this disturbance was your doing. You've always tried to accomplish by the spear what you could have done with a few simple words."

Jagar seemed to consider this for a moment and broke into a grim smile. "Well, they say it's hard to teach an old dog new tricks. The only trick I'd like to know is how you got onto this blasted moon."

"Keep your spear out of other people's bodies, and you might live long enough to find out."

"As you wish." Though Jagar retracted his spear, the guards surrounding him did not do the same.

"The violence ends now," Vera said. "You will lead us to Queen Ansaldra at once."

One guard, who had a purple plume in his conical bronze

helmet, stepped forward. His voice was harsh, probably to cover his trepidation. "I'll tell you the same as I told him, my lady. Ansaldra is receiving no unlooked-for visitors."

"We are not mere visitors," Vera said. "I am a friend of the Queen's, and if you attack any of my companions, you will answer for it personally."

Such was the weight of Vera's words that the grizzled guard's eyes widened and his Adam's apple bobbed. "Of course, my lady. They say she's in the Tower, but we aren't rightly sure of that."

"What do you mean? If you don't know for sure, then who does?"

His face blanched. "Er . . . Jarvis Tian, my lady. He's the master of the Palace, the castellan. He's who we answer to."

"Then lead us to him at once."

Lucian remembered Jarvis, who had helped him get ready for the soiree. The Queen must have deemed Lucian someone important if she had entrusted that task to the master of the Palace himself.

"I've met him before," Lucian said. "Short man, bald head, bushy mustache. He seemed pretty harmless."

The guard nearly sputtered, as if he begged to differ, and that made Lucian reevaluate things. Perhaps he had underestimated the man greatly.

"I can lead you to him directly," he said at last. "It seems it's my head either way."

"You have sense enough to see that, at least," Vera said. "Lead on."

The guard turned to the rest of his men, puffing out his chest. "You heard the lady. Spears away, form ranks behind me!"

The guards rushed to obey, leading them out of the Evening Hall and deeper into the Golden Palace.

LUCIAN NEVER WOULD HAVE IMAGINED it would end up like this. He still couldn't believe Vera was here, of all places, and weeks before he expected her.

"How did you find me?" he asked.

"I will explain that in due time. For now, let's focus on this meeting."

The area beyond the Evening Hall was even more finely appointed than outside it. Lavish paintings, plush carpets, and gold-trimmed hallways led deeper and deeper into the Palace. They ascended a wide spiral staircase, with archways on the left and right sides that led into vast chambers of interior offices. Lucian guessed they were now entering the bottom of the Queen's Tower, which rose high above the rest of the Palace. Far above them, the Sorceress-Queen of Psyche awaited.

But the guards paused before a wide, golden gate barring passage further up the tower. Lucian realized, somewhat hopelessly, that escape from here would be impossible. This staircase seemed the only way out, and other guards had gathered, marching behind them as if they were escorting a party of prisoners.

For all he knew, they were prisoners, though Vera didn't seem to be the least bit concerned. That steadied his nerves if only a little.

They paused before the golden gate and didn't have to wait long for Jarvis to appear. His expression was neutral as he descended the stairs gracefully, his chin upturned and posture regal. From the arrogant tilt of his head, it seemed he was looking at them with his nostrils as much as his eyes.

"The Queen will see you now," he said disdainfully.

Everyone moved forward, but Jarvis did not open the gate.

"No, no," he said with a small, victorious smile. "Lucian,

Vera, and Jagar only. The rest must stay down here for . . . safe-keeping."

"Absolutely not," Selene said, her cheeks reddening. "I command you to let me through!"

"You are no longer the Queen," Jarvis said.

It was hard for Lucian to believe that this man was the same one who'd gotten him ready for the soiree.

"Do as he says," Vera said.

"I don't want us separated," Lucian said.

"The Queen will not meet with you otherwise," Jarvis said. "How can she guarantee friendly behavior without an act of good faith on your part?"

Lucian weighed his options. If the Queen had ordered Jarvis to do this, then there was no other way forward. Not unless he wanted to fight. Maybe with the Orbs, and Vera especially, it was a fight they could win. Then again, Vera herself was not in favor of that, nor did Lucian relish the thought of having to kill dozens of men just to make a point, especially when a few of them might go down.

"We won't attack the Queen," he said. "You have my word on that."

"I'm afraid there's no other way forward."

"We will do it," Vera said. "No harm will come to your companions, Lucian."

"You can't guarantee that," Lucian said.

At this, Vera remained silent. Lucian ground his teeth as he watched Serah helplessly.

"If you hurt any of them, I will bring this entire Palace down," Lucian warned.

Jarvis's face blanched at the threat. Perhaps he knew of Lucian's reputation, or that he held two Orbs. "They will not be harmed, so long as you do not strike the Queen."

"We won't."

Jagar ground his teeth at that, but this had already slipped past Lucian's control. They would have to improvise.

When Jarvis gave a slow nod, the golden gate swung back, revealing more stairs spiraling up to the right. Lucian proceeded forward, following Vera and Jagar. He looked back once more. But they had already rounded the stairs, hiding his companions from view.

Jagar's expression was sour as they ascended the steps. Several times, he glanced over at Vera, but she seemed blind to him.

"When the time comes," he said, "you will not stand in the way of my vengeance."

Vera gave the ghost of a smile. "*Your* vengeance? You truly believe you have the coldness to kill the one you used to love?"

A shadow of doubt crossed Jagar's face before he firmed his features. "I will do whatever I must."

"I suppose, if you are helping Lucian, that you are privy to his reasons for being here."

Jagar clenched his jaw. "I am."

"Then you know how important it is that everything goes right. There are bigger things in the galaxy than your vaunted need for vengeance. Billions of lives are at stake, and hang on to every choice the three of us are about to make. Remember those billions and feel how small you are against them. We must gather our strength, for even when I came to this moon twenty years ago, she was not a foe to be underestimated."

"You never said how you managed that."

"I'm sure your wife will tell you if you ask."

"She's no wife of mine."

"I'm curious as to her thoughts on the matter."

"Well, perhaps that's something *you* can ask her."

Lucian saw that whatever history these two had, it was far beyond him. "Is it too much for you two to not get us killed?"

"It would seem you have grown in confidence since last we

met," Vera said. "The only question is, is there power to back that up?"

Lucian felt the urge to push her using the Orb of Psionics but refrained.

"There is strength enough in him," Jagar said. "He's been through trials and tribulations your warped mind could hardly imagine."

"Indeed? Well, we shall see about that. I look forward to seeing him match up with our esteemed former Council member."

This elicited a dark chuckle from Jagar. "Council member. How long ago was that? *Council of the Wise*, we called ourselves. More like *Council of the Fools*. What are the chances that the three of us would meet, decades after its dissolution?"

"This is not chance," Vera said. "Decades are nothing to the Manifold, and the frailty of human lives and our perception of time are even less of a concern."

"Yes, so you often preach. Though over fifty years have passed since I've seen you, you haven't lost your love for riddles."

Lucian cut in, not content to let these two argue the entire way up. "Why didn't you tell me about Transcend White?"

"Who, Vivienne?"

So *that* was her name. Strangely, it humanized her somewhat. Lucian saw now why the Transcends didn't want to go by their names. It made them easier to sympathize with and far less terrifying. Perhaps the Transcends intended to instill a bit of fear in their subjects. Such fear was necessary to keep their pupils on the so-called Path of Balance.

"It was not your place to know. As far as I knew, you might change your mind in the end and decide to follow me to Halia. To know that there was another like me, one opposed to everything I stood for, would have only confused you."

"Gee, thanks."

"A teacher decides the right time for her student to learn a lesson. And bringing her up would have only led to more questions on your part. Questions that would have muddied the waters."

Lucian wondered what could cause two twins, of all people, to become so hostile to one another. He knew it had something to do with the Mage War. Vera had fought on the side of the Starsea Mages while Transcend White—or Vivienne, Lucian supposed—supported the Loyalist Mages. Even two years after learning about all that, he still wasn't sure which side was right, or even if there *was* a right side.

"Have you not seen her since then?"

"We're nearly there," Vera said, ignoring him. "Compose yourself, and do nothing stupid. We can work this out with no violence."

Jagar growled, but didn't offer a rebuttal.

Jarvis stood before the door, his blank expression seeming to show he hadn't heard a word they'd said. But Lucian knew he had heard every word, whether or not he understood it. He pushed both golden doors open, each with a Septagon engraved in its face, with colored jewels representing each Aspect of magic.

Lucian steeled himself, reaching for his Focus to better ignore the fear pulsating within him.

28

THE OPENED doors revealed a vast chamber that looked immediately familiar to Lucian. This was where he had met with Queen Ansaldra in his dreams. Her shining, crystalline throne stood across the expanse of black marble, about thirty meters across, shining so brightly as to obscure her features. She was a slender silhouette, nothing more, and she leaned back as the three of them approached. She gave no outward sign of surprise as they stood before her, stopping at the center of the room where a Septagon was carved into the floor. A curious force didn't allow them to step any farther, some sort of ward designed to protect the Queen from confrontation.

The three of them faced her for a long time, each side not wanting to speak first. Jagar's face was a mask of anger, while Vera's was one of cool contemplation. In the end, Lucian stepped forward, only to be rebuffed by the ward.

"Yes, Chosen?" Ansaldra asked. "You have something to say? That you have made it this far, across the barren wastes of the Burning Sands, the Fire Rifts, and the Westlands, speaks to your abilities. I'm impressed."

Lucian ignored the praise, which bordered on sounding condescending. "I need your copy of *The Prophecy of the Seven*, Ansaldra."

Her body stiffened a bit at his use of her name without the title. "I thought you might say something like that. My terms are the same as they always have been. You must work with me and help me enact my vision of Starsea."

"That's never going to happen," Lucian said. "I only have one goal: find all the Orbs and stop the fraying."

She cackled. "If that truly is your goal, then your easiest way to achieve it is to set aside your vanity and work with me. This will not work the way you're hoping."

"I could say the same thing to you. You have no special insight into the future that I don't have."

"I will never let you have my prophecy, my most prized possession," Ansaldra said. "You'll stay here on Psyche with me until the end of your days waiting."

"Or the end of yours," Lucian said.

Though he could not see her expression, Lucian got the impression Ansaldra didn't like being reminded of her age. "As you know, I have my ways of prolonging my life. If my mortal body were to die, I would endure as long as I had a worthy vessel."

"That's the catch though, isn't it? You *don't* have a worthy vessel."

"You're right in that I wouldn't have. However, you were kind enough to return her to me. The only surprise is that it wasn't Nostra herself who led you, and my dear Selene, straight to me, as I ordered."

That was when Lucian realized the Queen didn't know Nostra was dead, and more than that, Nostra hadn't been guarding that elevator. She had been waiting to *escort* them into the Palace. She had likely been aware of their coming all along, perhaps as far back as Warna Oasis because of the Eye. Nostra had likely meant to use the catatonic brand to bring them to Ansaldra without issue.

Ansaldra seemed to read all this, and more, as she spoke again. "Nostra's loss is a great blow to my little queendom. If I didn't have other purposes in mind for Lady Selene, I would raise her to take her place. Atomicists don't exactly grow on trees. Though, I doubt she would be a loyal subject, for understandable reasons."

"Enough talk," Jagar said. "Give Lucian what he asks, or there'll be trouble."

"My dear husband. I half-expected you to be dead out there in the Westland Wastes. It quite surprised me to hear that you were not only alive and well, but leading a party east across the desert. A party which included none other than the Chosen of the Manifold himself, as well as the Lady Selene. That Dario *did* promise to deliver you to me, safe and sound, though I heard there was trouble in the Pass of Madness."

Here, Lucian learned two things. Dario was a scoundrel, and the Eye at Warna had communicated to Ansaldra to expect them, as Lucian had guessed. That meant she had known they were coming for almost two months.

Ansaldra continued. "I was rather impatient, waiting and waiting. But it was better to play my cards close to my chest. Why do the work another will do for you, and far better than you could do it yourself? The only part that *has* surprised me is Vera. I hadn't counted on you reaching her with the Orb of Psionics. But even she can't undo my brands on the prophecy, even with the Orb of Psionics. As with twenty years ago, I'm sure she's quite interested in stealing it for herself." Her gaze turned upon Vera. "You've been rather quiet for someone who's made quite an entrance. I don't know how you went undetected by the Palace's wards. I might have the castellan's head for that."

"Save yourself the trouble, and that poor man's head," Vera said. "Not even your wards, Ansaldra, can delay me. As for my being quiet, I learn more by listening than speaking. That's a lesson that I think *you* should have learned by now."

"Oh, save the judgment and sermons. Even after all these years, they are just as tiresome! I don't need you, nor your dead Psion. That's the price of following you, death by nuclear fire!"

Vera's expression was stony, and she said nothing further.

"As for you, Chosen," Ansaldra said, addressing Lucian. "You are in my complete power. Even if you could defeat me at my fullest strength, it would only mean the death of your companions downstairs. My Mage-Lords and Mage-Knights have them at their mercy. I would see you on your knees, begging for forgiveness for your despicable and treasonous acts back at the Spire."

"You were going after the Orb of Psionics, and I couldn't let you have it."

"Please. I was trying to stop *you* from doing something stupid with it. It was *yours*, Lucian. It was always yours. But you are not *ready* for it, nor are you ready to wield the Orb of Binding. You are far too weak, too inexperienced, your Focus undeveloped. A day after gaining the Orb, you used it for a most foolish purpose. How could you have been so *stupid* as to recall Vera to this blasted moon? This woman will destroy you!"

"And you wouldn't?"

"Have you not listened to a word I've said? I wish to work with you. Vera has her own goals and ambitions, and she will bulldoze you to reach them."

"Sounds like someone else I know."

"It's hardly comparable. Did you know she let her own Psion die during the Siege of Isis? If she would not spare Xara Mallis herself for her ambitions, then what will she do to you in the name of progress? She left Jagar and me for the League wolves, and allowed the rest of the Council of the Wise to perish! If not for her, the Starsea Mages could have lived to fight another day. You may have lived your youth in a golden age of humanity, led by the mages. But no, that was never to be. Vera let the Starsea Mages fall, and for that, the League consigned us to Psyche."

Vera remained silent. She had the air of someone just patiently watching someone dig their own grave.

"You have nothing to say to this?" Ansaldra asked her. "For what purpose did you return? If it's for the Orb of Psionics, this young man has found it, as I'm sure you're already aware, and you won't gain it unless you wrest it from his dead body. If it's for the prophecy, then neither shall you have that. There is nothing in all the Worlds you can give me. I've written its words on my heart, and to give them to you would be a sacrilege to my very soul." She stared down at Vera coldly. "What have you to say for yourself? What is to stop me from trying you, traitor as you are to the Starsea Mages? Traitor to all who knew, trusted, and relied on you?"

"I make no apologies for what I had to do, and I don't need to answer to anyone for it, least of all you," Vera said coldly. "There are greater things at work in the galaxy, things of which you are completely ignorant, trapped as you are on this moon. The Manifold is always one step ahead of us, and just as the Manifold fated Lucian and me to meet onboard the *Burung*, it has gathered the four of us here for a special purpose."

"*What* purpose?" the Queen asked wearily.

"The time may come soon where even you, Ansaldra, return to the stars. But that begins by working with me, not against me, whatever your personal feelings."

This seemed to give the Sorceress-Queen pause, to Lucian's surprise. It took her a moment to recover. "Return to the stars? Is *that* the carrot you're holding out? You all but promised victory when the League assaulted Isis. But because of your faithlessness, the Starsea Mages were destroyed." Ansaldra leaned forward, and only then did some of her mottled, wasted face stand revealed outside the blinding light of her crystalline throne. "That, I can never forgive you for. It's been my life's work to rebuild anew, undoing your ruthlessness. And I won't let anyone, least of all *you*, keep me from my goals."

"Then work with me," Vera said. "Give me the boy, as I need him."

"Absolutely not. He is the Chosen of the Manifold."

"It is my sacred task to help the Chosen," Vera said. "I have a ship and can take him from Psyche, where you can offer no method of escape. With *The Prophecy of the Seven* in hand, we can finish the mission to find the Aspects of Magic."

"*I* have my own plans for him," Ansaldra said. "And I can offer him escape if he agrees to work with me."

"*What* plans?" Lucian asked. "You wanted to use the Orb of Psionics to take control of the Warden fleet above us. You said something like that to me."

"I could show you how," Ansaldra said. "With me, you could save not just the mages of Psyche, but the commoners as well. All of us will need to work together to rebuild Starsea anew."

"Fool," Vera said. "We tried it that way, and we failed. The League today is far stronger than it ever was because of the Swarmer menace."

"The Swarmers? What news do you have of them?"

It surprised Lucian that Ansaldra knew anything about the Swarmers, but he supposed some information might have reached her from mages the League sent here.

"The news isn't good," Vera began. "Much has happened in the last two years, since I last saw Lucian."

Two *years*? Lucian could hardly believe it until he started counting the days. He had spent well over half a year on Volsung and had been in transit to Psyche for even longer, though it was hard to tell just how long. Add to that the almost three months he had been on Psyche itself, and it probably all added up to about two years.

"The League is afire," Vera went on. "Kasturi has fallen and the League fights for its very life. It is strong yet, but who can tell whether they will withstand the storm? So far, the bulk of the Swarmers are contained in the Kasturi System, though it is hard to tell whether that is due to League vigilance, or the Swarmers hanging back to prepare some final onslaught. Indeed, smaller raiding fleets penetrate deeply into League Space completely unchecked. Stations have even sighted Swarmers here in the Cupid System, as Kasturi is only four Gates away. It is full-on war, and it's a war the League is losing."

Lucian went cold at the news. It was not something he could even process. It seemed so much worse than the Second Swarmer War five years ago. No, not five years ago. *Seven.*

The galaxy had moved on without him and in a terrible direction.

"Ansaldra," Vera continued. "There is no time to bicker, given the state of things in the galaxy. Time runs short for humanity, and we four may be the only ones with the chance to avert disaster. The Chosen of the Manifold must gather the Aspects of Magic. I fear that is the only way to have enough power to challenge the Swarmers directly, both in the power of the Chosen and by ending the fraying once and for all." Vera turned to Lucian. "Two years ago on the *Burung*, I hinted to you I had an answer to the fraying. Now, you likely know what that answer is. Like you, I seek the Orbs; not for myself, but for the Chosen of the Manifold to gather in accordance to Arian's Prophecy. That is the reason I left the Volsung Academy all those decades ago, the reason my sister and I came to such a terrible disagreement that severed our bond of sisterhood. A severance that continues to this very day. I alone, along with Xara Mallis, saw the truth of Arian's prophecy, or enough of the truth to recognize its importance. I sacrificed everything for the mere chance the mages might not suffer the fraying. Just as the Swarmers destroyed Starsea all those eons ago, they will destroy us. Humanity must unite behind the Chosen. And yes, the formation of a new Starsea is likely a byproduct of that. But we have such a long way to go, and likely, not enough time to accomplish everything. I am only one person, and I need all of your help. If the people will not follow the Chosen voluntarily, then we must force them. To suggest otherwise means the death of humanity."

Jagar scoffed. "The Orbs. I'm done with all that. Lucian here might have a couple, but there are five left to find."

"We *can* find them if you and Ansaldra see fit to see beyond your own selfish ends," Vera said. "I have my notes and gleanings from various translations of *The Prophecy of the Seven*, but we also need Ansaldra's translation. It might be the missing key to find the rest of the Orbs."

"Have you found any?" Lucian asked.

Vera hesitated a moment before nodding. "I have. But only one."

"It's on Halia, isn't it? That's where you said you were going on the *Burung*. It's . . . where you would have taken me."

Vera nodded regally. "Yes. I'm glad that you remembered that. But just as I told you on the *Burung*, it was always your fate to become my Psion, to learn from me directly. Even if that prophecy has yet to be fulfilled, it is close to fruition."

"*What* prophecy?" Ansaldra asked. "I have my prophecy that the Chosen was to come to this world, with an Orb already in hand, and to leave with two, including the Orb of Psionics."

"So you told me that at my last visit," Vera said. "There is no reason both our prophecies can't be true, but we should not believe in prophecy with all our hearts. That is a mistake I've paid for dearly."

"What does this all mean?" Lucian asked. "What's going to happen to my friends?"

Both Ansaldra and Vera ignored that question. It seemed to be the least of their worries, even if it was Lucian's main one.

"What do you suggest we do, Vera Desai?" Ansaldra asked. "What are you willing to give me if I part with *The Prophecy of the Seven*?"

"Two things," Vera said. "The first is to give you what most desire—a way off this world for good."

Ansaldra was silent for a long moment. "I'm listening."

"I have placed Psionic brands on two young Fleet Wardens, including a high-ranking officer, who stopped my ship in orbit. I'm willing to transfer those brands to you to do with as you will."

Ansaldra cackled. "Is that it?"

"You know full well the damage you can do with such men under your control. You can infiltrate the Warden Defense Network and undo it entirely. If you are half as capable as you claim to be, the entire Warden fleet could be under your possession in a month."

"We can't give her that," Jagar said. "To unleash this madwoman on the galaxy would spell our doom. I know little of these Swarmers, but I've heard something of them from some Orb-Seekers passing my cabin over a decade ago. Ansaldra unleashed upon the stars could be a fate worse than that."

"Such is the value of *The Prophecy of the Seven*," Vera said. "I fear we have little choice in the matter. This is what Ansaldra wants most, and she will have it if she will part with the prophecy. A prophecy which she already knows by heart and could simply rewrite from memory."

Lucian could only watch Vera in horror. "She can't *ever* leave this place, Vera. If she did, it would start another Mage War!"

"And we can't leave here without *The Prophecy of the Seven*. Assuming I can verify its authenticity, then my word is my bond."

"That bond is useless," Ansaldra said. "The Starsea Mages

learned what that bond meant over fifty years ago."

"My bond is stronger than even you know, Ansaldra. Perhaps someday, you will see my reasons, but this is neither the time nor the place. You can take my offer or leave it. You could try to kill us where we stand, but you would not be successful. Unless you believe, after all these years, that your skill with magic surpasses mine?"

From the Queen's silence, it seemed she didn't believe that much. "I have to say, your offer intrigues me. However, you mentioned there were two things."

"Of course," Vera said. "Whatever vessel you would like on this world, if it's in my power to give it to you, then it's yours."

"What do you mean by *vessel*?" Lucian asked.

After a moment, Lucian realized she wasn't speaking about a ship, but about a person. She wanted to give Ansaldra another body to control.

And that could only be one person.

29

"ABSOLUTELY NOT," Lucian said.

"Yes," Ansaldra said. "That caps it off nicely. And Lucian was such a dear and brought back the perfect person for the role."

"Leave Selene out of this."

"I assume Selene is one of your companions?" Vera asked. "I wondered what Ansaldra meant when she referred to her."

"She is," Lucian said. "Ansaldra controlled her before I exorcised her with the Orb of Psionics."

Vera's eyes widened slightly, the only betrayal of her surprise. "I didn't know that. If you did that, then the power of the Orb is greater than even I imagined. And the young woman still has her wits?"

"It seems so," Lucian said. "But I won't let her take control of Selene again."

"It *must* be Selene," Ansaldra insisted. "She no doubt wants to take revenge on me, which can only lead to her death, in the end. She has no friends and family, so no one would miss her."

"*We* would. I promised her we'd get her off this world, and I intend to keep that promise."

"Give me Selene, as well as those Wardens, and our deal is complete," Ansaldra said, ignoring Lucian's point.

Vera leaned over. "Lucian, I urge you to accept. One life is nothing compared to what is at stake. Being strong is about doing the hard thing, especially in service to a higher good."

"That's bullshit," he said, not bothering to keep his voice down. "Ansaldra can choose someone else in Dara, or better yet, no one at all. I don't see why you can't be your normal self. Why ruin other's lives?"

To Lucian's surprise, Queen Ansaldra rose and strode forward with a hobbling step and the aid of a cane. Her posture was stooped, and her breaths were wheezing. Once out of the blinding light of her throne, her shape materialized into that of a sickly, elderly woman. And not only that—the fraying mottled nearly every inch of her skin, and a foul smell issued from her person. She could hardly stand on her own feet. Her face was like melted wax, so much so that it was a wonder she was even alive.

"I'm old, Lucian," she said. "And I have many things to accomplish before I pass. To accomplish those things, I need a young, powerful body, gifted in magic. Selene is the best candidate in my queendom and bears an uncanny resemblance to me when I was younger." She cackled again. "I see you don't believe me. Jagar and I were quite the pair."

Jagar merely glowered, not seeing fit to say anything.

Ansaldra strode forward, looking at Jagar, pausing only a few meters away. "For an old fart in the desert, you've aged well. I might forgive your past misdeeds if you were to apologize."

Again, Jagar remained silent.

Ansaldra sniffed. "Typical. You still can't stand being wrong, can you?"

"This is no lover's spat," Vera said. "If you agree to our terms—"

"I've agreed to *nothing*," Lucian said. "Selene stays with us, or I'll bring this entire palace down around us."

Vera stiffened at those words, seeming to expect instant action. But Ansaldra merely laughed.

"You could try. But even the Chosen with the Orb of Psionics could not undo all the wards and brands guarding these walls. There are wards other than Psionics and Binding that would only destroy you, and by extension, your friends as well."

"You're not getting Selene," Lucian said. "The Wardens should be enough."

"Well, if not Selene, I need an avatar of equal strength. Someone strong and healthy, who is the same sex."

That left only Serah, which was even more disagreeable to Lucian. Besides, she wasn't healthy by any measure.

Lucian connected his mind to Vera's. *Are you sure there's no way to get the prophecy without her?*

Vera hissed while Ansaldra smiled. "No, Lucian. There is no other way." Before he could react, she continued. "You're only proving my point. Your ineptitude knows no bounds. You are not worthy to bear the Orbs if you don't even know how to guard your thoughts from me."

"Then what do you suggest? I'm not handing over one of my own. I'll stay on Psyche for the rest of my life before I do that, or fight you again."

"Please. You would not only have to fight me but every Mage-Knight and Mage-Lord in the Palace. That is a battle you cannot win. As for staying on Psyche, I'm afraid Vera would be rather miffed if she traveled all this way only for you to throw it all away out of stiff-necked nobility."

Lucian simply couldn't betray Selene, even if she wasn't the most pleasant person to deal with.

"It's time I said a few words," Jagar said. "This was to be my meeting, and I've let you people prattle endlessly. But now, my patience wears thin, and I will speak my piece." He glared at his wife, standing a short few meters away. "You will not have Selene, nor will you have those Wardens. I would strike you down now, while we have the power."

"No," Vera said. "I've never heard so foolish a notion, so you must put it away at once. No one in this room is dying. Not today, not while I stand. If any of you want to challenge me on this matter, then go ahead."

From the following silence, it seemed as if no one did.

Lucian!

Serah's voice entered his mind. From the lack of reaction he got from the others, he figured she knew enough for only Lucian to hear.

Serah? What's wrong?

They're trying to block us. We need help!

"Ansaldra, tell your men to stand down."

"They are not harming your friends," she answered. "One of them must have tried something."

"I'm warning you!"

"What is amiss?" Vera asked.

"They are trying to block my friends," Lucian said. "Stop. This instant!"

"The time for games is over, Lucian," Ansaldra said. "What do you say? Take the deal. Not even Vera will save you."

Lucian knew the time for deals was over. His friends were in danger, and Ansaldra would do nothing about it. He reached for both of the Orbs. Ansaldra seemed to sense that move, her face betraying surprise as Lucian blasted her away with Psionic Magic. She flew a good few meters before she recovered enough to raise her own violet shield in response. Her advance slowed, stopping her just before the throne.

Jagar surged forward with a guttural yell, shockspear alight with electricity. "Go!" he called. "I'll hold her. With her occupied, you can unravel the prophecy."

It was far too late to rescue the situation. Lucian ran, and with a curse, Vera followed him.

At that moment, Lucian's foot seized. His boot remained glued to the floor as if it were one with it. Not even bothering to counter the Queen's stream, he simply slipped off the boot and continued running. Vera turned, her thin lips curling into a snarl as she raised her hands. An orange and red swirl of light coalesced at multiple points in the air, forming long spears of ice. There were about a dozen of them, glinting cruelly under the crystal chandeliers. Blue Binding magic then connected those sharp spears toward where both Jagar and Ansaldra were dueling, Jagar brandishing his crackling shockspear, while Ansaldra held a green sword that seemed to be streamed from light itself. Lucian didn't know what kind of magic *that* was, but everything was so far beyond him, he couldn't make sense of it.

All he knew to do was warn Jagar before it was too late. "Jagar!"

The ice spears flew at an alarming speed, whistling through the air. Ansaldra screeched, while Jagar turned just in time to raise a Thermal shield. The red barrier petered out, knocking Jagar back a few paces, where he slammed into Ansaldra's very throne. Ansaldra held her shield as well, seeming to not miss a beat as she swung at Jagar's exposed abdomen. That sword would cut him to shreds.

Lucian could not allow that to happen. He bound Ansaldra's sword arm and locked it against the throne. The sword extinguished, and she let out a frustrated shriek.

Lucian! Serah's voice came again. Somehow, she had overcome her block. *They're taking us somewhere. There's nothing we can...*

Her voice disappeared, because her Focus was blocked again, or a worse reason he didn't want to think about.

"We must hurry," Vera said. "Our only hope is those two keep each other busy enough for us to reach the prophecy and unravel Ansaldra's brands. Even with her so distracted, our attempt to do so will probably prove fatal."

Lucian realized, with Vera here right now, the three of them could stop Ansaldra forever before she could ever rise to become a threat again. But with his friends being pulled away, they didn't have time. The thought of Serah dying alone was enough to firm his decision. Leave Ansaldra to the Mad Moon.

It was far past time he left.

But before he could do that, he had to rescue the others and get the prophecy.

By now, Ansaldra had unbound herself, but she was once again dueling her husband. His concentration was intense, and Lucian knew there was no way to extricate him from this situation, and that his battle would likely be a losing one. This was what Jagar had wanted, and Lucian knew the stars would die out and the universe would end before he ever gave up on his goal.

So Lucian did the only thing he could do. He ran down the circling stairs, down the Queen's Tower, with Vera beside him. Though she was old, she had no trouble keeping pace with him, to his great surprise. Her legs seemed to have strength far beyond her frail body. For all Lucian knew, she might be using magic to make up for the lack of physical strength.

Lucian reached out for Serah with his mind, but there was no connection. All he could do was hope he wasn't too late.

248

30

WHEN THEY REACHED the bottom of the stairs, a scream came from around the corner. Lucian ran forward, but some unseen force restrained him.

Vera strode up beside him and watched at him chidingly. "Are you trying to get yourself killed, boy?"

"They're going to kill them!"

"They are many, but there are just two of us. Even if we could defeat the dozens of Mage-Knights around that corner, your friends could easily die in the crossfire. What do you think we should do?"

"That's a loaded question."

"I've merely laid out the facts."

"You're truly horrible sometimes. They'll die anyway if we don't help them"

She gave a small noncommittal shrug. "I am merely focused on my goal: the prophecy, the contents of which could lead to the saving of billions of lives. Valor avails you nothing if you wind up dead."

"Then what do you suggest? Let them die? I won't have that."

"No, I imagine you won't. Follow my lead, and my stream. We shall fall upon them with a storm of Aspects."

Before Lucian even had time to ask what that meant, Vera turned around the corner and he followed.

Far down the cavernous hallway, about fifty meters away, marched a contingent of multicolored Mage-Knights, and between them walked Serah, Fergus, and Selene, alone and helpless. Almost as soon as Lucian caught sight of them, his skin prickled. Vera was already streaming, and he remembered her instruction to follow her lead.

So, he reached with his Focus, joining his stream with hers. Somehow, she seized control of his magic, and Lucian was powerless to do anything with it. It was as if a mighty river was carrying him far away, and there was nothing he could do to control it. Vera reached for the Aspect of Thermalism, along with Atomicism and Binding. As with Queen Ansaldra, Vera formed a dozen or more ice spikes from thin air. But now that Lucian was following her stream, he understood how she did it in a dizzying array of steps that were almost impossible to follow.

With Atomicism, she drew water vapor from the air itself, though there was not enough to form this many ice spikes. To do this, she duplicated the water molecules, tricking the Shadow Realm into believing there was far more than there should have been. Such a task, he saw, would not have been easy for the common mage. Once she had gathered water in sufficient quantity, she used a reverse Thermal stream to cool it until it froze in the shape of the spikes. All this happened in less than a fraction of a second. Finally, she set a focal point on each of the Mage-Knights in the distance, and anchor points on each of the ice spikes. She didn't do this all at once; maintaining that many streams would have been impossible even for Vera. Rather, she shot off each ice spike one by one using the Aspect of Binding, switching so quickly between spikes that she might as well have shot them at the same time. By this point, she had let go of Thermalism, having no further need of it since the water had already frozen. She only had to hold two streams; the Atomic stream to keep the molecular duplication of water in stasis, and the Binding streams to shoot the ice spikes at great velocity.

Some spikes found their marks, while the Mage-Knights blocked or dodged the others. None came close to hitting Lucian's friends.

All this Lucian comprehended in the three seconds it took for the ice spikes to be created and shot at their targets. And almost as soon as they were away, Vera was streaming again. One of the yellow-caped Mage-Knights had reacted quickly, unleashing a long fork of lightning that extended far across the corridor directly at them, despite the long distance. Vera merely raised her hand, creating a yellow ball of energy that not only absorbed the lightning but *reversed* it with greater power than when the Mage-Knight had streamed it. The lightning struck the mage, blasting him backward and causing him to topple two other knights.

This, too, Lucian could read, being a part of Vera's stream. It was hard to tell, but it seemed Vera had done something with magnetism, created with a reverse Dynamistic stream. Lucian had never tried this before, but it seemed to be a powerful defense, though it took a great deal of ether. Lucian felt it ripped out of him and used for Vera's purposes.

By now, the Mage-Knights had fully abandoned Lucian's three friends. They focused on the new threat, but already a quarter of their number had fallen. In response, they raised their shields, along with a Thermal ward to defend against further ice spikes.

However, Vera did not have this in mind. She raised her

hands again, streaming a long white laser at the lead Mage-Knight, right into his shield. Within a couple of seconds, it turned red hot and began melting on the soldier's arm. He screamed in terrible pain, and astounded, the other Mage-Knights cast aside their shields. A fireball issued from their direction, but Vera nonchalantly ate the impact with a hastily raised Thermal shield, just strong enough to mitigate the blast. She was not only skilled at magic but in judging how much to use for each action.

Fergus and Serah were already reaching for some shocks-pears dropped by the fallen Mage-Knights. They engaged the troop of knights from behind. The knights focused on Vera, who they perceived to be the primary threat.

But now that the Mage-Knights had discarded their shields, Vera switched tactics, creating a Binding stream that flung several of the heavy shields right into the thick of knights, knocking them down like pins. Serah and Fergus fell to the floor, as did several of the knights. But once the storm of bound shields ended, the Mage-Knights could not rise. Vera had them glued to the floor with a gravity amplification disc. Indeed, some of their bodies were flattening sickeningly, bone and blood and armor crunching from the extreme force pushing down from above.

What power was this? Lucian could only watch, his jaw agape, as the knowledge of how to do these terrible things passed into his mind. Vera was allowing him to see everything. Only two Mage-Knights were alive who had escaped Vera's disc. Even now, they fled toward the Golden Palace's west wing, beyond the Passage of Mirrors.

But even these Vera would not spare. Violet light wrapped her hands, and she extended them outward, and a violet aura surrounded each of the mages' heads. The two knights faced each other and, raising their spears in tandem, stabbed each other in the neck, slaying each other at the same time.

In less than half a minute, Vera had disposed of two dozen Mage-Knights as if it were nothing. She lowered her hands, and her face was cold in the face of such butchery. Serah, Fergus, and Selene stood alone, bloodied but unharmed.

A moment later, Fergus streamed a shield of light, raising it toward Vera as if he expected her to attack him, too.

"I'm not after you," Vera said, once he and Lucian had joined them. "We must reach the prophecy. Time draws short."

Lucian realized she was right. Even now, Ansaldra might have won against Jagar. And without that distraction, they could never undo the magic guarding the prophecy.

"I see what you meant by a storm of Aspects," Lucian said. "They never had a chance."

"You can learn too someday," Vera said. "Though it never pleases me to be the executioner. It was the only path to rescuing your friends. But there is no time for lessons. The prophecy awaits."

She strode forward with purpose and everyone fell in behind.

WHEN THEY REACHED the library without further resistance, the prophecy seemed so unassuming in its central display case. It might have been some forgotten exhibit in a museum. But Lucian felt a certain power radiating outward, a brand so complicated that he was almost certain he could never undo it.

"This is on you, Lucian," Vera said. "I am weary after that battle. You must use the Orb of Psionics. Ansaldra connected this brand to other brands, traps behind traps, based on all Seven Aspects, most of which will be outside your expertise. If you trigger those traps, I will do my best to undo them. But I can't promise anything." She then turned to the others. "Jump in if you are skilled enough in the Aspect threatening us. Before we're finished, we might have all had a hand in it."

Fergus, Serah, and Selene shared an uneasy look, but there was nothing else to be done. It was this, or go forward without the proper knowledge for finding the rest of the Orbs.

"Stream now, Lucian," Vera said. "Show us what you've learned, and what the Orb of Psionics is capable of."

He tried to ignore the pressure, but everyone was looking at him. Selene's face was paler than usual, while Fergus was solemn. Serah reached for his hand, holding it for a moment before letting go. Vera gave a nod, urging him to begin.

There was nothing left to be done. Either he won *The Prophecy of the Seven*, or he and everyone died in the attempt.

Lucian reached for the Orb of Psionics and felt toward the prophecy. It instantly repelled him, as if trying to combine two opposite magnets. He reached again, with more power, but it just repelled him with the same level of force, but this time, a small blast emitted outward, destroying the glass. A few shards buried themselves in his skin. In horror, he looked around to see the same thing had happened to the others. After a moment, it was clear no one was hurt beyond a few cuts.

"We should stand back," Selene said.

"No," Vera said. "The danger has passed. And we need to be close to the prophecy to keep it from harming us. We would be dead either way." She turned to Lucian. "Whatever you're doing isn't working. Try again."

Lucian tried to push down his annoyance. He refocused himself on the prophecy. He was sure Psionics was the right Aspect to use, but he also knew that if Ansaldra wanted to be tricky about it, she could have used another Aspect entirely. But deep down, he knew it was Psionics.

He had to go about it differently. And then the answer came to him.

Once again, he reached out with Psionics, only this time, he formed a link with the prophecy itself, as if it were another person.

Lucian felt an instant connection, and at once, visions overwhelmed his mind. Kilometers of ice surrounded him, but ahead stood a pair of double doors, along with a sense of imminent danger. The scene flashed, and fire and lava surrounded him. It seemed he was back in the Fire Rifts of Psyche, overlooking a fissure. Deep below thrashed a gargantuan, snakelike creature, black as a starless midnight. The creature faced upward, opening its wide mouth to reveal rows of needle-like teeth, a deep fire within glowing as it spewed flame. The scene shifted, and Lucian saw a shadowed figure hidden among columns. She held in her hand an Orb shining with orange radiance. The Orb of Atomicism. She raised her hand, streaming an atomic blast that immolated Lucian immediately. The scene flashed once again. Now, he stood in a grand chamber filled with many columns, rising high to a sandstone ceiling. Upon an altar shone a yellow Orb, what Lucian knew to be the Orb of Dynamism. Another flash. A magnificent tree stood before him, its branches laden with snow, and Emma stood before it. It was from his dream right after finding the Orb of Psionics.

All went dark after this stream of visions. The darkness coalesced, drawing into a single Orb, which, unlike the others, had no color. It seemed like a void, a black hole that ate all light. Indeed, Lucian wasn't sure it was an Orb at all. The scene widened until he saw a tall metal tower framed by night and starlight, with a large blue-gray planet hanging above. And from that tower issued a voice:

I CLOSE THIS PROPHECY THUS: *find me beyond the Dark Gate. And, if the passing of long years has ended me, I have my prophecy, kept safe in this tower, the only edifice on the moon beyond the Dark Gate that looks upon Nai Shairen, the Cradle of the Ancients. Find me before it is too late. The Chosen of the Manifold will know the way.*

AT THESE WORDS, the vision faded into a dark maelstrom. Lucian opened his eyes only to see that *The Prophecy of the Seven* was no longer there, replaced by a smoking pile of ash.

31

LUCIAN STARED along with the others in disbelief. At last, Vera turned to him, and her gaze was cold and furious. He opened his mouth to respond, but nothing came out.

That was when the very foundations of the Golden Palace shook. Books fell from their shelves, plaster rained down from the ceiling above, and the crystal chandeliers tinkled as their lights flickered.

"Moonquake," Fergus said. "We have to get out of here."

"This is no moonquake," Vera said. "Lucian triggered the trap. And now, the prophecy is gone forever."

Lucian didn't have time to explain that the prophecy might not be lost, that it had communicated at least some of its contents to him telepathically. He clearly remembered everything he had seen. But there was no time to explain all that.

The floor heaved again, sending them tumbling to the floor. The entryway collapsed, trapping them in the massive library. The library, or perhaps the entire Golden Palace, was collapsing on itself.

"There's an opening," Lucian said, pointing to the left of the door. "See that crack?"

A rending had torn itself in the thick granite walls, just wide enough for one person to squeeze through at a time. Any shifting of stone would cause them to be crushed, but it seemed there was no other way out.

They ran forward. Serah went first, sliding through the crack easily. Fergus came next, and then Vera. Lucian was next in line and looked back to see Selene sprawled on her back by the display case.

"Selene!"

She did not stir. Lucian reached with the Orb of Binding, pulling her toward him and pushing her through the crack. Something had knocked her out, making her pure dead weight. The floor rumbled again, and the crack started closing on itself. Lucian had enough time to pull Selene back into the library before the masonry crushed her.

"Lucian!" Serah screamed.

The wall buckled in on itself, cutting off Serah's voice. Lucian drew back, carrying Selene with him. Her eyes were closed.

"Selene. Come on, you've got to wake up."

A large welt marred her forehead. Some piece of masonry had fallen from above and knocked her out while no one was watching.

As the pillars, arcades, shelves, and roof tumbled in on them, Lucian had to figure out something, fast. He reached for the Psionic Aspect and entered Selene's mind.

Wake up!

To his surprise, she roused, as if being shocked from sleep. She stood, her eyes wide and her breaths heavy.

He reached out for the Orb of Psionics, deepening his connection. He drew as much ether as he could, so much that the Shadow Realm itself was falling away, replaced by a matrix of flowing, purple lines. He drew those streams and directed them all toward the wall ahead, about ten meters to the right of where the crack had been. He could only hope the others had tried to escape and were not out there still. He opened another connection to Serah, just to be sure. The ether roared through him because of the second stream.

Serah. You guys need to get out of here. I'll find a way.

Lucian . . .

There's no time. Go!

He cut off the connection and returned his Focus to the wall. He blasted it with a wave of pure kinetic energy. A great fissure formed from the bottom to top with a thunderous crack. Then, he reached for the Orb of Binding and created something he only knew about in theory: a reverse tether. He formed two anchor points, both on either side of the fissure, and connected those anchor points to a focal point floating in between. Those anchor points pulled against the focal point, keeping the fissure open. This dualstream took an incredible amount of effort, so they had to hurry.

"Come on, Selene. Get through."

She picked her way through the fissure, and Lucian followed behind. Once they stood in the corridor beyond, Lucian let go of the dualstream, allowing the crack to close.

He looked down both sides of the hallway, only to find a pile of rubble from floor to ceiling cutting him off from the others. That was if they were still there. He reached for Serah again.

Are you still on the other side?

No. We did as you said. We're almost out of the Palace now.

Lucian heaved a sigh of relief. There was no reason to blast that rubble aside. They could follow this hallway out of the Palace and link up with the others outside.

"Let's go," he said.

He took Selene by the hand because she seemed reticent to move on her own. He could hardly pull her along.

"Selene, what's gotten into you?"

"I . . . don't feel well . . ."

She stopped and stumbled to her knees. Lucian kneeled beside her. That wound was worse than he'd thought. And magic couldn't simply heal someone. Or if it did, he didn't know how.

But he noticed something else. Her eyes had shifted from their usual green to violet, a vacant stare.

No. This couldn't be. . .

At that moment, Lucian flew and crashed into the wall, his head taking a hard knocking. His vision went dark for a moment—it could have been a few seconds, or as long as a couple of minutes. He stood, then fell again, unable to keep his feet even as plaster rained down from above.

With a start, he stood, feeling battered from head to toe. His neck was stiff, and he could barely move it. But when he did, there was no sign of Selene. Just the crumbling hallway. Ten meters away, the ceiling had collapsed, trapping Lucian in the crumbling Golden Palace.

Trapped, except for a small hole in the ceiling, through which he could see a tall tower in the distance, a tower that had yet to collapse. Summoning what concentration he could, he reached for the Orb of Binding, streaming a tether from himself to that tower. Magic did not stream at first; he was too weary, too unable to concentrate. But he would die if he couldn't stream. With that realization, magic leaped from his chest, pulling him along the tether and out of the Palace at an incredible rate. Just seconds later, the hallway collapsed behind him.

As his consciousness faded, the tether winked out. He fell in the slow-motion of Psyche's weak gravity, coming down somewhere beyond the Golden Palace's outer wall. He closed his eyes, reaching with his Focus, trying to tether himself to a nearby building. But nothing came out.

He would not escape alive.

It was at that moment that he was pulled in a different direction, down toward the road leading out from the Palace. He was making directly toward a group of people, people he recognized to be his friends; Serah, Fergus, and at their lead, Vera, who was the one controlling the tether, her hands awash with blue light.

When his feet touched the ground, he could hardly keep his balance.

"We must carry him along," Vera said. "We've got to get moving. We have a very long journey ahead of us, and escape is not guaranteed."

Lucian felt Serah and Fergus propping him up on either side. Hardly conscious, he hobbled down the cobbled street, unable to lift his eyes and see where they were going.

"Where's Selene?" Fergus asked.

Lucian shook his head. Or at least, he attempted to. "She's gone. I . . . think somehow the Queen possessed her again. Selene knocked me out, flung me right against the wall. I was out for I don't know how long."

Lucian felt a sudden wave of nausea and heaved, but there was no food to come out.

"It would seem he's suffered a concussion," Vera said.

"That much is obvious," Serah said. "Where exactly are we going?"

"Not far, I hope," Vera said. "We must get somewhere high where we are visible."

Lucian looked up and saw a tower in the distance. It was a different one than he had latched onto, this one rising from the city itself. Just now he was noticing people fleeing the scene, and others watching in horror. From behind, the massive

Golden Palace was still rumbling, falling on its foundations. Whoever was still inside was unlikely to survive.

"Jagar," he managed.

"What happened?" Serah asked. "Where is he?"

"He's met his fate," Vera said. "Old fool. He might have been of use if he could have seen beyond his own need for vengeance."

"Have some respect," Fergus said with distaste. "We might still save them if we turn back."

"No," Vera said. "Jagar made his choice, and for all my harsh words, I must admit he gave us the opening we needed to find the prophecy. Even if that was for nothing, we at least escaped."

Fergus pulled to a stop. "We must fight Ansaldra! There might still be time."

"They are likely all dead," Vera said, turning back to look at the Palace. "Look!"

Indeed, the final rumblings sounded from the top of the hill, leaving behind only mountains of rubble. Ansaldra had not been lying about guarding the prophecy, but unless she had some mode of escape, then Vera was right. She was dead along with the rest. Lucian found it hard to believe that she would go down with the Palace unless Jagar had delayed her enough to make it happen. He felt a sort of numb shock as he watched the scene, unbelieving that his friends were trapped in there.

His shoulders slumped. "I'm sorry. It was my idea to go in there. And . . . I'm in no state to fight, as much as I would like to."

"I agree," Serah said. "We need Lucian, and if Vera doesn't want to lift a finger—"

"Lift a finger?" Vera asked in disgust. "I've done infinitely far more than I should have for you. Only because of Lucian am I allowing you to journey with us off this cursed moon. Of course, you are welcome to stay, if you both have your vengeance to seek on Ansaldra."

At this, both Fergus and Serah were silent. Things were not getting off to a smooth start with them and Vera, and Lucian was too tired to ease the tensions.

"We must find a way to that tower, or perhaps the top of a building," Vera said, as they pushed down the hill past crowds of onlookers, most of them looking at them curiously. "The tower would be better."

"What's the point of that?" Fergus asked. "Where did you land your ship?"

"In the Mountains of Madness. The plan was to walk there directly, but that's impossible, given Lucian's condition. My ship must come to us, and it can extricate us from this situation if we are high enough off the ground."

"Let's move," Fergus said. He glanced back at the rubble of the Palace, almost far enough behind to be hidden from view. He hung his head. "Forgive us, Selene."

———

NO ONE TALKED as they made steady progress down the hill. They even ran past squadrons of hoplites and Mage-Knights, but the soldiers did not stop them, just supposing they were among the panicking crowds.

But they would get renewed attention when the spaceship arrived. Such a sight would scare the people of Dara, and if the Mage-Knights had their wits, they might even attack.

The chaos lessened as they entered the bustling city streets, where the news was still fresh. Most of the people were trying to get to high ground to get a better view. Likely, that would make getting to the top of the tower impossible, because others would have the same idea. Still, Vera didn't seem to be concerned, leading them in that direction. Lucian stumbled along, only forcing himself forward through sheer force of will. He could only hope Vera had a medical pod on board her ship.

After a time, they came to the base of the tower, a wide, circular structure of golden stone that was dark under the shadow of the hulking Mountains of Madness. To Lucian's surprise, it seemed no one was trying to enter it until he saw two Mage-Knights standing guard outside its double doors. This place was likely the home of an important lord of Dara, and people knew not to bother with it. Still, the knights looked uneasy as they gazed out at the crowds. They knew it was only a matter of time before chaos erupted.

Vera approached the guards with confidence. "Let us in."

The guard Vera addressed hardened his face. "We have no orders to let anyone in, and Lord Hawkin is away on business."

Before either knight knew what was happening, Vera had her hands raised, and violet Psionic Magic surrounded their heads.

"You will let us in," she said, her voice commanding and brooking no argument.

"At once, my lady."

As the guards opened the doors, Lucian noticed a new sound, a high, shrieking thrum that almost reminded him of a wyvern. Looking up into the sky, he saw a shadow in the sky approaching quickly from the direction of the Mountains of Madness. It was hard to tell its size at this distance, but it seemed a fast, sleek craft. Lucian couldn't guess how many creds it cost.

"We must hurry," Vera said, once they stood inside a vast entry chamber.

She led them up a set of circular steps, past multiple floors. As the guard had said, this Lord Hawkin was away, and they met no resistance. By now, the ship's engine outside was an unholy roar, shaking the very stones of the wall and wood of the spiraling staircase.

At the top of the stairs, a trapdoor led to the roof outside.

When Vera tried it, the door was locked. With a curse, she blasted it off its hinges with Psionic Magic.

The four stood on the roof, with the silvery spaceship hovering alongside the top of the tower. Only several meters separated it from the building itself. Lucian wondered just who was piloting it.

An airlock door opened, revealing a whitish light. A boarding ramp extended, connecting to the tower. Serah watched with widened eyes, for the first time in her life seeing a spaceship. She and Fergus helped Lucian on board, and Vera followed closely behind.

And just like that, in a matter of minutes, they were on board.

"You must strap yourselves in," Vera said, calmly. "The Wardens will be upon us soon now that we are out of hiding."

"Strap ourselves what?" Serah asked.

Lucian realized Serah was not familiar with the vernacular. He went to help her find a jump seat set in the wall of this entry area, what appeared to be a sort of wardroom, with a couple of tables built into the wall.

"Help them, Fergus," Vera said. "I'll tell Alistair to get going immediately."

"Alistair?" Lucian asked.

"My pilot droid. Hurry. We aren't out of this yet."

Lucian had neither the time nor the wherewithal to ask more questions. He allowed Fergus to strap him and Serah next to each other before he secured himself in another jump seat across from them. Lucian had little mind to take in his surroundings, such was his pain. But he met Serah's eyes, scared and blue.

"It'll be all right," he said. "We'll be off-world before you know it."

"Yeah," she managed. "That's what I'm afraid of. They say

there's no air in space. That if the door opens, you'll get sucked out and your head will explode."

Lucian couldn't help but laugh. It probably wasn't the right reaction, judging by the shock on her face.

"That probably won't happen." That was assuming the Warden fleet didn't shoot them down, of course. It was probably best to keep that possibility to himself.

The ship shook, and Serah closed her eyes tightly. "I always dreamed of seeing the stars, leaving this place behind. But now, all I'm thinking about is how everyone I've ever known is on this world." She let out a shaky breath. "This terrible, stupid world."

"Space is big," Lucian said. "But as long as you have friends, it's not such a cold, dark place."

"I hope so."

A sudden bout of dizziness hit him. He had to lean his head back and close his eyes. Serah's hand found his.

"How long will it take to get out of the atmosphere?" Serah asked.

Lucian tried to shrug, but the motion was too painful. "Couple minutes, maybe. Depends on the trajectory of the ship."

"You're really hurting, aren't you?"

"I'll be fine. Just a minor concussion. Could've been worse."

At that moment, the ship suddenly pitched and angled upward. Serah let out a scream. Lucian wanted to tell her to relax, that it would be fine, but the words didn't come. They were shooting off so fast that he was sure he would have flattened into his seat without inertial dampening.

He couldn't keep himself awake. When he came to, Serah was looking around, eyes wide open. She was looking out of the nearby viewscreen, which showed Psyche's dark nightside. Above the rim of the planet, looming close, was the white gas giant, Cupid. Already, they were gaining distance from the moon, though it was almost imperceptible.

There was gravity, but it seemed to be coming from the ship's acceleration. He was being pushed back into his seat, and the force was such that he could have unstrapped himself and stood on it sideways if he wanted. It was impossible to know whether the inertial dampening field was countering the force, and until he found that out, it would be best to sit tight. It could shut off at any moment, increasing the force to intolerable levels. At the speed they were flying, that would be a death sentence.

Vera's voice exited from a nearby intercom. "All of you, report to the bridge."

With that order, Lucian knew it would be safe enough to move. He wondered just how Vera expected him to do that when he noticed small indentations built into the deck itself. It wasn't *quite* a ladder, but it should be enough to climb toward the bridge along the deck itself, with the ship's momentum pushing him sternward.

He unstrapped himself and then helped Serah with her harness. She didn't understand how to unlatch the safety belt, but together, they made quick work of it. Together with Fergus, they climbed the indentations in the deck to the bridge, which was down a long internal corridor. Though the force pushing them down wasn't much, the work was still strenuous to Lucian.

Within a couple of minutes, they had made it to the bridge. As soon as all were inside, Vera shut the door behind them. Sitting in the pilot's chair was the droid Vera had mentioned.

"I'm Alistair," the droid said, its long, metallic head swiveling with a whir. Its eyepieces were red, and even if Lucian knew droids couldn't convey emotions, the machine's stare was intense and gave him the creeps. He had never heard of a pilot droid, but that didn't mean they didn't exist. After all, there was

one sitting before him now. A lot of unbelievable things had
happened in the last few hours.

"Strap in," Vera said. "Things might heat up soon."

"What do you mean?" Fergus asked.

"As I feared, our sudden escape has caught the eye of the
Warden fleet. Even now, I'm tracking well over a dozen ripsaw
fighters on our tail."

Lucian knew ripsaws were fast, equipped with the latest fusion
drives and railguns. Their only disadvantage was a lack of range.

"Can we out-fly them?" he asked.

"Assuredly not," Alistair said.

"We will," Vera said. "How long until we are within range of
their cannons?"

"Twenty minutes and thirty-seven seconds, at this velocity,"
Alistair said.

"And how far away from Cupid are we?"

"About five hundred thousand kilometers."

"Can we close the distance in time?"

"I don't understand, Vera. That would mean your certain
death. Something I cannot allow."

"Hypothetically speaking?"

"Hypothetically, at maximum burn, allowing for sufficient
power to the inertial dampening field, we will enter the planet's
orbit in about twenty minutes, give or take a few seconds."

"Perfect. Set course for Cupid, but of course don't enter the
atmosphere. Use its gravity to slingshot us on a course to Ibbus.
Turn off all thrusters after the maneuver is complete to hide
our thermal trail."

"While the *Wayfinder* can survive those G-forces, it is
doubtful organics could survive for more than a few seconds."

"Organics?" Serah asked. "What's the metal man going on
about?"

"He means us," Lucian said.

"I have a plan for that," Vera said. She turned to Serah. "I sense you are a Gravitist. I will need your help in creating a gravity aura to lessen the G-forces of the slingshot."

"I don't know what that means. How long would I have to hold it for?"

"Alistair?" Vera asked.

"Approximately twenty-four minutes and thirty-two seconds."

"That's a rotting long time."

"Together, we can do it. If Fergus and Lucian lend their aid, that's enough magic between the four of us."

"Assuming it *does* work," Lucian said, "can't the Wardens just find us? Where is this Ibbus, anyway?"

"Ibbus is the fourth planet in the Cupid system, its largest gas giant," Vera said. "It's not Ibbus I'm aiming for, but one of its moons, named Kandi. And the Wardens won't be able to find us as long as we give off no heat and transmit no signal. They might guess our destination, but for all they know, we might aim for one of the Gates. More likely, they will lose us when we go beyond the planet's horizon." She shrugged her bony shoulders. "It's our only shot."

"We must do what we must do," Fergus said, staring out the viewscreen at the approaching gas giant. "I never dreamed I would escape Psyche, and I would not have us ripped to shreds before I get to taste my freedom."

"I don't feel so well," Lucian said.

"You must hold on a while longer," Vera said. "You will have several days to recover, assuming we get out of this in one piece."

"I thought we were going to Halia," Lucian said. "Why go to this Kandi, anyway?"

"Because," Vera said, with forced patience, "you insisted on bringing your friends, and I don't have the food, water, or oxygen to keep them alive that long. Halia is a voyage of two months, and I only brought supplies enough for two people."

"Oh."

"Oh indeed. That said, Kandi is an insignificant trade port, more likely to be used by various scum and villainy than honest people. But they will have whatever we need. For a price. The League is not likely to have a presence there."

"Scum and villainy," Serah said with a smile. "We might fit right in."

This observation went unanswered as *Wayfinder* drew closer to Cupid and the Warden ripsaws closed in from behind.

32

CUPID DOMINATED THE FORWARD VIEWSCREEN. So much so that it was *all* Lucian could see. Its baleful storm stood before them, crimson and red, and it seemed to grow larger every passing minute. It might have been his addled state, but he remembered Jagar mentioning the wyvern prophecy that the great storm would only end when Ansaldra was dead. According to that prophecy, she was alive and well.

As they streaked toward the planet, gravity pulled Lucian down. But so far, Vera had not instructed to counter-stream its effects. On the dash, the gravity readout was climbing beyond 1G. From his long time on Psyche, the force seemed almost crushing. And it climbed even higher.

"Rotting hell," Serah said. "I'm feeling woozy."

"You must endure," Vera said. "Even someone who's lived their entire life on Psyche can endure two gravities, for a time."

Serah didn't respond.

Gravity pushed Lucian down into his seat, an oppressive, invisible weight bearing down on his shoulders. The meter climbed above two gravities. But Vera called for no countermeasures. Lucian's heart was already thundering against his chest, struggling to feed oxygen to his brain.

Three gravities. The seats reclined, causing the downward force to act on the back to the front of his body rather than from head to toe. He could see again as blood flowed freely to his brain, but he could see only a narrow sliver of the forward viewscreen. Not that there was much to see, anyway. Just a white mass that was the planet's surface, thousands of kilometers away.

Wayfinder raced along, picking up both speed and gravity. Lucian didn't even know how much gravity they endured, but a glance over at Serah revealed her eyes to be closed and her cheeks quivering. She was enduring ten times what she was used to.

"Vera," Lucian rasped. "We must stream now."

At that moment, Lucian felt a sudden easing of gravity. A silvery disc had blossomed beneath the five of them, including Alistair. Blood flowed smoothly while it became infinitely easier to breathe. He could even raise his head a bit and check on the others. All of them seemed to move, too, including Serah.

"Stream, Serah," Vera said.

"I can just make a ward."

Vera did not comment as Serah streamed her ward over Vera's. Together, the gravity reduced a tolerable amount. If the gravity meter on the dashboard was still reading it correctly—it was now *six* gravities, and still climbing—an amount of force that would have killed them within minutes. But within this small bubble, it must have been a quarter of that.

"Incoming shots!" Alistair said. "I must divert course."

As the meter climbed above eight gravities, Alistair gave the slightest deviation to course, and not a second later, streams of railgun fires blasted past the viewscreen and directly toward the planet's surface. But with that swerving came an incredible surge of lateral gravity, forcing Fergus's arm outside the bounds of the gravity disc. He shouted as his arm plummeted at incredible speed, yanking him against his restraints. He yowled as bone cracked and his arm bent at an unnatural angle.

"It was necessary," Alistair said, his voice emotionless and robotic. "Let's hope we've lost them for good, now."

Lucian wanted to kick that hunk of metal in the head. "Fergus! You okay?"

As Fergus closed his eyes and wailed in pain, Lucian could see the hacksaws dropping far behind on the LADAR screen. They were gaining kilometers on them every second, and they had opened fire as soon as they were in range. That they had ceased firing meant they had to be out of range now. A sign that this was working.

"Keep the anti-grav field steady," Vera said.

Fergus's arm was still outside the gravity field, turning a sickly shade of blue, but Lucian knew there was no hope in moving it. As the gravity ticked above ten, as Vera and Serah's gravity ward struggled to keep the gravity tolerable within their bubble, the arm might as well have been bound with the full power of the Orb of Binding. The gravity meter now read fourteen G's and held steady, and above the anti-grav disc, it must have been at least three.

"My arm is gone," he rasped. "Crushed beyond all use and recognition. I can only hope the marrow doesn't leak into my blood."

"Five more minutes, Fergus," Lucian said. "Hold on. We'll get you to the med pod."

They endured that hell for the next few minutes, but the hacksaws didn't shoot at them again. Even Vera was straining to keep the ward at its fullest strength. Lucian did what he could, but he didn't have the concentration to focus on the stream, and Fergus was no use in his current state. This was up to her and Serah alone.

"Thirty seconds until maneuver is complete," Alistair said.

Those thirty seconds seemed to take an eternity, but at last, the ship eased upward, and the planet below them escaped from view. The gravity reading fell precipitously over the next minute, from fourteen to four. Under the anti-grav field, they were experiencing something equivalent to Earth's gravity. It was another minute before Vera and Serah could release their streams entirely. Only a small amount of artificial gravity provided downward force toward the deck.

"We are in a situation," Vera said. "We have perhaps half an hour before the Wardens can get a ship beyond Cupid to get a lock on us. If they have any ships already on this side, then we might already be dead. We need to power down nearly one hundred percent to have any hope of remaining invisible to thermal scans. The fusion drive of *Wayfinder* is heavily insulated, but of course, insulation does not cover the thrusters. Once we are away from Cupid and the radiation it produces, we'll be easy to pick out."

"What does all that even mean?" Serah asked.

"We will travel with only marginal artificial gravity," Vera said. "I don't know what that will do to Fergus's arm, but it won't help matters."

Fergus winced in pain. "Is there no medical pod?"

"There is. But running it would create an unacceptable amount of heat that needs to be vented into space. That would allow the Wardens to track us the entire way to Kandi. At worst, League vessels in that direction will intercept us."

"Fergus could die if left untreated," Lucian said. "Where does the heat go?"

"It's expelled through the exhaust ports."

"I can set up a reverse Thermal ward," Lucian said.

"You don't have the skill or strength," Vera said bluntly.

Lucian had to admit it wasn't his area of expertise. And Serah had already strained herself from her gravity ward.

Thirty minutes would not be enough time for her to recover. They needed Selene, but of course, that was worse than useless to think about.

"Can you do it, Vera?"

"As I've said," she said, "I've already overtaxed myself. When all of you came with me, you assumed the risk of doing so."

"I have an idea," Alistair said. "Quite simple."

All turned to listen.

"Flip the *Wayfinder* with exhaust ports pointing toward Kandi. The Wardens won't pick up thermal signatures if I point the exhaust ports toward Ibbus."

"Let's do that," Lucian said.

"No," Vera said. "It's too risky. They will see us coming, and our trajectory will reveal us to be coming from Cupid. *No* ships come from Cupid in this system, only Warden vessels."

"That's hypothetical," Serah said. "If there are Warden vessels out that way, won't they catch us anyway, if they are expecting us?"

To this, Vera had no response. He knew he couldn't force her to do this. Only she could command the droid. Fergus's life remained in her hands.

Lucian *knew* she wouldn't do it. Fergus was silent, not even arguing in his defense. He looked so pitiful, lying on the deck and holding his arm. Even his groans were weakening.

But after a moment, she looked at them. Within a moment, they would learn Fergus's fate.

"All right," she said. "Flip *Wayfinder*."

Lucian wanted to shout for joy. Everyone strapped themselves in after making sure Fergus was secure. Not a moment later, the side thrusters flipped the ship, which was still flying at incredible speed toward Kandi and its parent planet, Ibbus.

Once the maneuver was complete, Fergus was out for the count. Lucian unstrapped himself and with Serah's help and

Vera leading the way, pulled Fergus toward the medical pod sternward. Up close, Lucian could see just how bloody and broken the arm was. Though he was unconscious, he was still breathing.

Once inside the tiny clinic, they laid the bloodied and battered warrior inside the pod, and Vera input the auto-surgery command.

"We should be high enough on components for him to make it. He may need additional work on Kandi. If there's anything more advanced than a med pod there."

"Thank you," Lucian said. "We're in your debt."

Vera ignored the thanks. "I must get back up front. Soon, we will see whether all this was a mistake. If I need anything, I'll call. In the meantime, try to get some rest."

She left him and Serah in the clinic, watching Fergus through the window in the pod.

"You think he'll be okay?" Serah asked.

Lucian shook his head. "I don't know. It looks pretty bad."

Serah sat after pulling down a nearby jump seat. "Rotting hell. If this is space, then take me back to the Riftlands."

"It's too late for that now."

"Jagar's gone, and so is Selene. We're dropping like flies." She looked down at her mottled arm before continuing. "And if I keep streaming like this . . ."

She left the rest unsaid.

"We shouldn't have to stream for a long while. You heard Vera. The trip to Halia will take two months."

"Two months." Serah laughed bitterly. "I'm not sure what I'd prefer, two months trapped with that weirdo, or two months slogging across the wastes of Psyche."

"She can probably hear you."

"What's she going to do if she can?" Serah rolled her eyes. "Not a kind bone in that one's body, as we say in the Riftlands."

"Well, she knows where to find the Orb of Gravitonics. That's our lead."

"And you'll have another shiny stone for your collection. And after that, only four more to go."

"Only." And someone out there in the cosmos held at least one of those Orbs, though Lucian didn't know which one. All he knew was that it couldn't be the Orb of Gravitonics. That left Thermalism, Atomicism, Dynamism, and Radiance. The Oracle of Binding had said that the finding of one Orb had kick-started magic and the Starsea Cycle anew.

The only question was, who had found which Orb? Was that an answer Vera might know? If the vision he'd seen while connecting to the prophecy was true, then that would have been the Orb of Atomicism.

"All I know is, this might be pointless," Serah said. "We could have ignored the prophecy entirely. Jagar and Selene both paid the price."

"We don't know for sure they're dead," Lucian said. "Ansaldra possessed Selene, and until I see a body, I won't believe Jagar's gone."

"Either way, it's all rotten. How can we find the other Orbs without the prophecy?"

"Not everything's rotten."

"What do you mean?"

Despite his exhaustion, Lucian told Serah what had happened when he connected his mind to the prophecy, all the visions he'd seen, as well as the words from Arian himself. So clearly did he remember it he could recite them word for word as if the Old Master had scrawled them into his brain.

Once Lucian had finished, Serah shook her head. "You think it's real?"

"I *know* it's real. I just don't know what this Dark Gate is. But apparently, it leads to Nai Shairen. The Oracle of Binding mentioned something about that planet. She seemed to imply it was the homeworld of the Builders. Or the Ancients, rather."

"Any idea where that is?"

"Not a clue. Either it's a planet that's gone undiscovered, or it could even be one of the League planets. Just built over and forgotten."

"And we know it has at least one moon," Serah said. "And that moon has a tower on it, where Arian went with his prophecy. A prophecy that will lead to the rest of the Orbs."

Lucian nodded. "The Chosen of the Manifold will know the way. That's me, right?"

"I would hope so. Otherwise, what am I doing here? Either way, isn't that a good thing? It means the Palace wasn't entirely pointless."

Lucian smiled. "Well, all this seems to be beyond me. Maybe Vera can help."

"Just keep this to yourself, at least for now. It's two months until we reach Halia. That might be enough time to work something out, or to even have more revelations from this Arian."

Lucian didn't think that likely. "I don't know how it worked exactly. Something in Ansaldra's magic allowed me to experience the prophecy as if those visions were happening. Or at least, happening in the future."

"It could all be a lie," Serah said.

"Maybe. But something tells me it's real. That something *meant* me to see it."

Serah smiled. "Destiny and all that."

Lucian didn't like that word. "I guess."

They both looked down at Fergus. By now, the screen had tinted, not allowing them to see his face.

They just sat there in silence. Lucian still felt frazzled from the events on Psyche, and he had a massive headache. Though he had not seen Jagar and Selene die, it was probable that at least Jagar had fallen, while Selene might be in an even worse state. And with Fergus out of commission, and all of them hanging on the edge of death if the League picked up their trail, it seemed far too early to celebrate.

They explored the ship, finding various common spaces, holds, and cabins, enough to crew about twelve people. One of the sliding doors was locked next to the wardroom, and Lucian guessed this must be Vera's cabin. The rest of the cabins were quite spacious, at least by spaceship standards, each containing two beds and two chests of drawers built into the wall. The fusion drive was located aft, and like Vera's cabin, was inaccessible. There was one lavatory, complete with a shower, in the middle of the corridor where the cabins were located. The galley was next to the wardroom and quite cramped. The only cooking instrument was a small oven, enough to fit a few trays of food at a time. No meals from scratch here, just warmed-up frozen food. But that was to be expected. Lucian's stomach rumbled at the thought of food, but his need for sleep and a shower was greater.

He let Serah go first and waited for his turn at the table built into the wall. It was there that he crashed into a deep sleep.

33

LUCIAN AWOKE IN A BED. He didn't understand how he'd gotten here. Someone must have dragged him, and the fact he hadn't woken up from that told him just how exhausted he had been.

He forced his eyes open to see Fergus lying in the bed across from his bunk. Happiness swelled in his chest, and he was about to talk to him until he noticed his even breaths. He must have been sleeping it off. He was on his side, and his arm was in a cast. If the pod had shot him up with as many pain drugs as Lucian suspected, it might be a while before he woke up.

When Lucian went down the corridor, it was empty. There was no sound except for his echoing footsteps and the steady hum of the vents. There was not even a thrum of the engines. They must have still been off as they coasted toward Kandi. He wasn't sure how far away the moon was, but if Ibbus orbited farther out than Cupid, Kandi was likely to be a frigid world.

When he showered, the heavenly feeling of warm water and soap washing away layers of grime, dirt, and even blood was beyond words. The water fell far slower than what he was used to; the gravity in this ship was even less than Psyche's, probably to keep power usage down and minimize thermal exhaust. That they were still alive, hours later, was a good sign. Once done, he dried off and dressed in a nondescript jumpsuit common to most ships. In the coldness of space, it would serve better than robes, and wouldn't stick out in a busy pirate haven like Kandi.

Lucian entered the wardroom to find Vera sitting at the table with a cup of tea. He took up the spot opposite her, and she regarded him coolly with her dark eyes. That the long-expected moment of her arrival had happened in the last twenty-four hours filled him with a sense of disbelief.

Now rested, it was time to get some answers, but he wasn't sure where to begin.

And perhaps because of that hesitancy, Vera spoke first after taking another sip of her tea. "I don't know if you remember, but two years ago on the *Burung*, I told you that the Manifold is one step ahead of us, always." She gave a thin smile. "In these last two years, I've sometimes doubted those words, but I never will again."

"Two years and the first thing you think to tell me is that you were right?"

She chuckled. "I suppose. But only because you were so adamant that I wasn't."

"Well, I'll admit the universe can work in funny ways. According to you, the Manifold kicked me out of the Volsung Academy, the Manifold sent me to Psyche, and the Manifold got me *off* Psyche."

"All that, and more," Vera said. "Your journey is just beginning. I feel privileged to have skipped all the messy bits to arrive now."

"I doubt the mess is over. It feels like it's just beginning."

"Indeed." Vera drained her cup. "That's what we must

discuss. You've been very busy, and I would like to hear how you came across not one, but *two* Orbs, the Jewels of Starsea I've sought ever since before the Mage War."

A large part of Lucian was hesitant to part with that information. Emma's old warnings returned to him along with what Serah had told him not to volunteer too much, at least about his revelations about *The Prophecy of the Seven*.

"I need food, first," he said.

Vera gave her customary shrug. "There is plenty in the freezer. Help yourself."

When Lucian returned with a hot meal five minutes later, he told her practically everything that might be of interest. For hours, he related his struggles at the Volsung Academy and the Transcends' betrayal. Here, he was intensely curious about Vera and Transcend White's backstory, but Vera told him she would tell him that once he was through relating his adventures. He told her about Linus and Plato on the Isle of Madness and wondered how they were doing—whether they were alive or dead, or whether the Wardens had taken them to Psyche as well without him ever knowing. He related his audience with the Oracle of Binding, Rhana, and his first revelations of Starsea, along with her instruction to him to find the Orbs, to gather them all and return them to the Heart of Creation, ending magic and the Starsea Cycle once and for all.

Vera held up a hand and seemed to ruminate. He almost expected her to tell him that was enough, to get some rest, because it was the middle of the night, or rather, the early morning, and he had been talking for hours.

At last, Lucian broke the silence. "What do you think?"

She thought for a long moment before she gave her reply. "If you have it in you to go on, I would hear the rest."

Lucian almost wanted to stop there because of his exhaustion, but he also wanted to get this all out of the way at once. He told her about crashing into Psyche, meeting Serah, and also meeting Fergus, Cleon, and the Elders of Kiro Village, as well as the visions he'd received from Ansaldra. He told her of his mission to find the Orb of Psionics in the Burning Sands, using only a fragment of *The Prophecy of the Seven*. By the time he got to the part of him reaching the Spire in the desert, and his battle with Ansaldra over the fate of the Orb, Vera was listening even more intently.

He paused again here, to rest his throat and to get another meal and a drink. Then the telling continued with their journey back east, meeting Jagar and infiltrating the Palace after discovering Dario's betrayal. He only stopped when he reached the part where he came upon Vera in the library.

Vera asked a few more clarifying questions, and once done, seemed to be satisfied. "I think I have the gist of it."

"What about you, then? What have you been up to in all this time?"

"Well, I don't have a story such as yours. Most of that time I've spent on Halia, following a lead to unearth the Orb of Gravitonics. After much time and excavation, unraveling of mysteries and things forgotten since the fall of Starsea, I've located the temple which holds the Orb."

"That's great," Lucian said. "Where is it?"

"The dark side of Halia, deep beneath the ice. It took over a year to locate, and just as long to excavate. The work was nearly complete by the time you contacted me. I had to drop everything, especially when you mentioned holding two of the Orbs."

"That must have been hard, to pause your work."

"Nothing of the sort. You were merely one string of a grand plan coming together."

"Grand plan? What grand plan?"

Vera gave a small, secret smile. "Why, the end of the fraying and the salvation of humankind. I already knew most of the information the Oracle of Binding relayed to you. There were small snippets that were new information, but nothing that changes anything. Hearing your story, and what you've gone through, only proves to me everything I prophesied on the *Burung*. You have been marked by the Manifold, Lucian, but the Chosen of which Arian wrote cannot be identified until someone holds all Seven Orbs. Until then, it is premature to say *anyone* is the Chosen of the Manifold. Indeed, you would be the *last* one I'd expect to be the Chosen. You are lacking in experience, and so far, it seems you've survived more by dumb luck than any sort of skill."

Lucian resisted the urge to defend himself, even if he thought the assessment unfair. "Someone out there has found at least one," Lucian said. "Someone a long time ago, in the middle of the 23rd century. That's when magic first arose, and when the Starsea Cycle started up again."

"Indeed," Vera said. "That was before my time, as you might have guessed, and I didn't discover that until I'd pored over Arian's lines in the Volsung Academy library. I pieced together fragments of varying versions of the prophecy."

"That must have been long ago."

Vera chuckled. "Yes, it was. But time has a funny way of contracting the older you get. It doesn't seem long ago at all when I first realized the truth. That Arian's Seven Orbs were not the ramblings of a frayed man."

"Did you know him?"

Vera nodded gravely. "Aside from my dear sister, I might be the only living being who has spoken with him. I was a mere Novice at the time of his disappearance. He was severe in his lessons, but always kindly. There hasn't been a Psionic as powerful as him since the dawn of magic, and that includes me."

"He must have been very powerful."

"Indeed, he was. There was a brief time before the fraying was common knowledge, where all seemed possible. *The Age of*

Wonders, they called it. Magic would usher humanity into a new era of progress. I came of age at the proper time for instruction in the ways of magic. In those days, there were no limitations, and the Old Masters—that is, the Seven who founded the Volsung Academy—had, over two decades, delved and learned many things that were possible, things that were done in those days without fear of wasting illness. I came to Volsung then, a young woman confident and determined to learn myself." She smiled in reminiscence. "Back then, *everyone* wanted to be a mage. And why not? We were mighty, both feared and loved, and all held us in high esteem. The mages founded many academies. There was at least one on every world, sometimes even more."

That alone was difficult for Lucian to imagine. It was hard not to be caught up in Vera's nostalgia for an era that would never return.

"I was still a young Novice when the Concordat of Magic was signed."

"What was that?"

Her thin eyebrows arched in surprise. "Do they teach nothing these days? That was the treaty signed between all mage academies, in the year 2280. It was a mutual agreement, sworn by all mages, to use magic only for the good of humanity. It opened many opportunities for the mages to go out in service to the League of Worlds. We were commissioned for special projects. Indeed, most of the so-called Wonders of the Galaxy, such as the Domes of Nessus and the Elevator of Hephaestus, to name a couple, were only possible to create through the use of magic. These days, no one would ever dare anything that great, and not just because of the fraying. But for the next twenty years, as I matured and became a Talent myself, and then finally a Transcend for a very brief period. I can see now, looking back, that I lived in the Golden Age of Humanity."

"When does the Mage War start?"

"I will come to that, in time. There was a kink in this age of progress. And that kink was the fraying. It first started being recognized as a problem that affected all mages well into my Talenthood, in the late eighties."

"You mean, the 2280's?"

Vera nodded. "Of course, most were in denial. But as mages started dropping like flies, rotting from the inside out, many even going mad and murdering those closest to them, it threw everything into doubt. Of course, the Transcends tried to cover it up, but they could not hide such a serious matter. Not for long. A growing faction advocated limiting the use of magic so that the fraying took longer to take hold, until the mages could discover the mechanisms by which it occurred. I was a member of that faction. I saw it as necessary to save my fellow mages, but after ten years with little results, and many dead mages, some of whom were my friends, I sought other answers. Indeed, I was seeking answers as soon as I recognized the fraying as a problem. I dove through the writings and transcripts of the Old Masters, most dead now for at least twenty or more years. I read millions of words of personal journals, minutes, contracts, missives, memorandums, dispatches, letters, and outbound and inbound electronic mail. And I was only scratching the surface."

"What were you looking for?"

"A couple of things," Vera said. "The first being the first mention of the fraying, or something like it, in the Academy's history and lore. The first mention took place while I was still a Novice, by none other than Arian himself. He recognized that many of the Old Masters were wasting away before his very eyes. The Old Masters, if you are not already aware, were the very first mages. And likewise, they were the first to fall to the fraying. Back then, it was easy to write off the symptoms as diseases of age. All except for one died past their sixties. Young, even then, but not strange enough to think anything of it. But

Arian, who was left alone among the Old Masters, found himself the only Transcend of the first generation, the only one who remembered the oldest of days, the only one who had ever known and spoken to those who first took to the stars after the discovery of the Gates. Perhaps it was this loneliness, of being a relic of a generation no one remembered, that drove him to seek answers. That is a feeling I understand very well."

"He delved the Manifold."

"He did. Four times. And each time, he discovered things that are still taught to this day. Or at least, they were by the time I left the Academy. However, it was on his fourth and final delving, the one before he left the Volsung Academy for good, where he wrote his most famous work, *The Prophecy of the Seven*. The only version of which he took for himself. However, before Arian left the Volsung Academy, the prophecy, tragically, was copied by some very bored Talents and Novices who didn't recognize its importance." She chuckled darkly. "It is from these missives that we derive all of our knowledge of his most famous work."

"Wait," Lucian said. "What do you mean, they were copied by bored Novices and Talents?"

"Arian was almost a joke. Seen as senile, his peers, including the less senior Transcends, did not give him the respect he was due. He alone stood against the Volsung Academy's massive projects, including commissioning mages to the League and construction conglomerates for profit. In those days, the Volsung Academy, and most others like it, were money-making machines. It was almost all business, despite the Concordat of Magic the Academies agreed to abide by. Indeed, most in those days thought business *was* the common good. The economy in those days was roaring, and by that point, no major war had touched humanity since the First Worlds' Rebellion in the early 23rd century, almost a hundred years before. Arian was the last who remembered those days, though he was still a young man. His warnings went unheeded. So, once he had written his prophecy concerning the fraying, the Seven Orbs, the Chosen of the Manifold, Starsea, and the coming Time of Madness, no one took it seriously. Including me, to my shame. He left the Volsung Academy then. Many believed he did so out of an old man's spite. The prophecy was only copied a few times, by bored mages who had neither the expertise nor motivation to do the work properly. Arian did not write his prophecy in Standard English. He transcribed it exactly as it came to him during a state of Psionic hypnosis. Unless one reads it in such a state, one can't glean anything accurately."

"When did he leave Volsung?"

"Oh, I was still a Novice. This would have been in the early 2280s, almost a hundred years ago now. As a Novice, they told me not to question it. And I didn't. Not for a long, long time. I questioned nothing until I sensed something was amiss years later. That's when I, as Psion to Transcend Violet, dusted off the old tomes of his prophecy and got to reading. The first thing I noticed among the four copies of the prophecy that remained is that none of them agreed, despite being copied from the same source. I found that most curious, but didn't question it. I wrote a master copy, writing only the parts which agreed with one another, which was perhaps fifty percent of the prophecy in full. I would not learn more unless I cared to delve the Mani-fold, something I didn't dare do. At least, not then."

"What happened then?"

"I did what any good Psion would do. I shared my findings with my master, a woman long dead by the name of Myria. That woman never smiled, but she had the nerve to laugh at me. She told me to put that damn prophecy away, and that she had more important matters for me to attend to. So, being the good Psion I was, I humbled myself and listened."

It was hard to imagine Vera *ever* humbling herself. But if all this was true, then Vera was only slightly older than him when all this occurred. That was also hard to imagine.

"I did my duties as prescribed, and beyond. Like my sister, I wanted to run the show. I thought the Transcends were fools, and I was going to change things. But Arian's words had rooted themselves in my mind. Arian's words, as transcribed by those hapless Novices, most of whom were Talents who were my senior by now. Of course, I questioned them and showed them what had happened, but none seemed to think much of it. It was quite surprising to me that absolutely *no one* wanted to take Arian's words seriously. They had sullied his name beyond all repair."

"How did that change? I mean, didn't this prophecy start the Mage War, between those who believed in it and those who didn't?"

"It did. Though that was over a decade away. Much can happen in even two years, as you well know. Imagine what can change in ten. Anyway, among my supporters, you might be surprised to learn, was my sister, Vivienne."

"Transcend White. *She* supported you?"

"Yes. At least, until she realized what her beliefs would cost her. In the end, she could not tear herself away from the ideology of the Volsung Academy. That was why we fought on two separate sides."

"That must have been difficult."

"It was. But ideas can lead to zealotry, and when one becomes a zealot, family is the least of one's concerns. So fervently did I believe in my mission during the war that I would have been able to kill my twin." She smiled sadly. "Thankfully, it never came to that. But even now, we remain enemies, though we haven't spoken in decades. Not since the war itself."

Lucian watched her, absolutely astounded.

"But you asked how a prophecy no one believed in came to

divide all of Magekind. Well, that only happened because of the work *I* did. I laid aside my fear of fraying and delved the Manifold, seeking answers. The risk turned out to be worth it. Within, I learned much, so much so that upon Transcend Violet's death, they raised me to take her place. I was forty, the youngest Transcend to sit the Amethyst Chair."

"I guess that's the name of Transcend Violet's seat."

Vera nodded. "For two years, I was a Transcend. And I took a Psion, a promising young Talent named Xara Mallis. I shared my findings with her, and I also made finding Arian and his lost prophecy a top priority of the Academy. I began teaching as I saw fit, inspiring a generation of mages to seek the Orbs and end the fraying. For that, they cast me out, and when that happened, to the Transcends' and my sister's utter dismay, many followed me. So began the Starsea Mages, the group dedicated to finding the Orbs and Arian's prophecy. Not a few months later, the Academy Mages convinced the League to annihilate us at all costs. Work had only just begun at our Sanctum on Isis, then a young world of great potential. We decided then that we would fight for our very survival, since our mission was humanity's only hope. Back then, of course, no one could have guessed just how many billions would fall in the fires of war.

"And the rest, as they say, is history."

34

VERA STOPPED SPEAKING, and Lucian could hardly comprehend everything he had heard. For the first time, she had answered almost all his questions.

"If you'd told me all that from the beginning, I might have followed you."

Vera chuckled. "Would you, now? Even if that's true, you were not ready for the knowledge. And you would not have believed me, especially with Emma pushing you another way."

Lucian thought that was probably true. "It's . . . a shame, isn't it? You might have found some Orbs if the Academy Mages had left you alone."

"Maybe so. I've thought about it a lot over the years, but I don't think it would have mattered. The League and the Academy Mages saw our actions as a violation of the Concordat of Magic. For they amended that agreement once all recognized the fraying as a threat. The Edict of Limitation dictated that magic could only be used at need, and never streamed otherwise. Of course, that edict was almost useless, because *any* amount of magic leads to the fraying."

"They teach the Path of Balance," Lucian said. "Stream enough to empty your ether, but not so much that you overdraw."

"It's simple, even tidy, but it's false. Magic begets magic. As time goes on, the more a mage uses their ether, the faster that ether accumulates, thus accelerating the fraying."

"Those two men I met on the Isle of Madness—Linus and Plato—they learned to block their magic completely."

"Self-blocking is known to me. Extremely dangerous, that. They must both be powerful mages, for forming a Psionic block on one's Focus, and committing all and future ether to the maintaining of that block, is not easy to do. That's probably why so many of their pupils died in the attempt. Though you speak kindly of them, and I'm sure they meant well, it's tantamount to homicide. *You* could have died, and had you known the danger, you would have never tried."

"What other choice did they have?" Lucian asked. "It was that or the Mad Moon."

"I don't judge their choices. But forcing it upon others as a requirement for sharing in their resources and knowledge is what I take issue with. That's neither here nor there. Everything regarding magic and its use is a tragedy unless we work together to finish what Arian prescribed so long ago."

"Finding the Orbs. I've found two, and someone out there has found another. So unless you or any of the Starsea Mages found any, that's what we have to work with."

"We might have found all or most, had things been different. During my time at the Volsung Academy, Xara was my star pupil. Young, bright, and dedicated, especially where it concerned the prophecy. Despite being an Atomicist, she wished to train with me."

"That's allowed?"

"It's unheard of these days, but back then, the rules were not as firm. It was still uncommon for a Transcend to take on a

Psion of a different Aspect, but it was something I felt strongly about. Remember on the *Burung*, when I told you that only once, had I felt a fate so marked as yours?"

"Xara Mallis," Lucian said. "That's why you chose her."

"I truly believed in her. She was a bright light, who I came to see as the galaxy's only hope. In her, I saw a mage with the potential to be even more powerful than me. And she was daring and unconventional. She could have never fit in among the conservatives of the Academy. They saw her as a threat."

Lucian remembered Transcend White saying that. He also remembered her putting *him* in the same category as Mallis, though "daring and unconventional" would be the last words he'd use to describe himself.

"You've been on Psyche before," Lucian said. "Can you explain that?"

"I went there twenty years ago, desperate for information. I knew if anyone had discovered new lines of the prophecy, it would be Ansaldra. Many mages focused on finding the Orbs, but Ansaldra had dedicated herself totally to the unraveling of *The Prophecy of the Seven*."

"How did you sneak past the Warden blockade? And how do you have a ship, and if you have a ship, then what were you doing on the *Burung*?"

"For the first question, I can approach unseen through the use of Radiant Magic. Even so, a vessel did catch us, a patrol craft on the far side of Cupid. I was not lying about Psionically branding two Warden officers; I did that so they would send us on our way and not report us. I was prepared to turn over those branded officers to Ansaldra for her help in unlocking the prophecy. So, that explains how we reached Psyche more or less undetected. Of course, things were different when we left Psyche. When Alistair came to pick us up, I was not on board to hide the ship, so the Wardens picked us up."

"Okay, I guess that makes sense. How do you have this ship and what were you doing on the *Burung*?"

"I've had this ship for almost all my life, ever since the start of the Mage War. Of course, I've kept it upgraded since then. With *Wayfinder*, I can go places that interstellar liners can't take me. Places such as Psyche. As for what I was doing on the *Burung*, it was to meet you, Lucian."

"To meet *me*?"

"Yes. I have my prophecies, and inclinations guided by the Manifold. I'm experienced enough that to not question it. I simply do. I wasn't sure who or what I would meet exactly, but as soon as I saw you, walking down the corridor of the *Burung*, I sensed your potential. It was almost the same feeling I got upon meeting Xara Mallis, greater than six decades previously. Further meditations on the Manifold revealed that inclination to be correct." She watched him. "Does that answer your questions?"

"I suppose. You were talking about going to Psyche before?"

Vera nodded. "Yes. I went to find information. But Ansaldra would share nothing with me, blaming me for her confinement on Psyche. That was always her fault. Never accepting responsibility for her own mistakes."

"What's the story behind that?"

"I escaped the Siege of Isis, while she and the rest of the Starsea Mages didn't."

"I'd be pissed, too. You even left Xara Mallis behind. Jagar, too."

"It was not a simple decision. Ethics would have told me to fight to the last breath, to the very end. But I chose not to do that because the stakes were too high."

"That's convenient."

"My decision was simple but difficult. I knew I would face scrutiny for it for the rest of my life by any of my former allies

294

who survived. But *somebody* needed to find the Orbs, and there was no one better for the job than me."

"Of course."

"You can be glib if you wish. But only I had sufficient knowledge. So, I took *Wayfinder*, this very ship, and by some miracle escaped the League blockade. I would say the Manifold preserved me."

"Thank you for your sacrifice."

"If only you knew. But how to make you understand? If I had not survived, I would have never met you. And then you would have never entered the Volsung Academy because my sister would not have been interested in admitting you. And if that hadn't happened, she would have sent you straight to Psyche, and without the Orb of Binding, you may have not survived long enough to find permanent shelter."

Lucian knew all those things were true. "Still wasn't right."

"There is no ultimate right and wrong, Lucian. Right is simply what we decide is important. Anything that stops me from solving the fraying is wrong. And that meant abandoning my friends on that world being rent asunder by the tachyon lances of the League Fleet."

"It's . . . a lot to take in."

"Well, it is time you learned the full truth. Other than Xara Mallis, you know more about me and my mission than perhaps anyone. But I tell you only so we can go forward together in a spirit of mutual trust."

"Fergus and Serah as well."

"Though I'm not sure of them yet, not having spoken with them, I will have to trust your judgment. They would not be following on such a mad quest unless they truly believed in your mission."

"Any ideas who found that other Orb?"

"I don't know. Certainly not me or anyone I know. It

happened long before my time. One of the Old Masters, maybe, or someone who was known to them."

"It could be Arian himself."

"I've thought that many times. But, strangely, he omits that fact in any of his writings, so I don't think it likely. If he wanted to be believed about the Seven Orbs, what better way to do that than show that he *found* one?"

Lucian thought that was a good point. "Well, it can't be any of the Old Masters, then. When someone dies with an Orb, they leave their Orb behind. Someone else would have claimed it. So it's someone who found it long ago who's still alive today, maybe with longevity treatments, or at least someone who claimed the Orb after the original person died. Or even an heir of *that* person. It's that, or they died somewhere dark and forgotten, where no one would find it."

"I've given a lot of thought to all those possibilities. However, it is useless to think about. While I have a lead for the Orb of Gravitonics, so much so that it is practically within our grasp, I know little to nothing of the other Orbs. It's a shame we lost *The Prophecy of the Seven*. Ansaldra's version surely has information I'm lacking, as it revealed the location of the Orb of Psionics."

At this, Lucian felt a bit guilty at keeping information back. And he had plenty of opportunities to admit it. But they had already talked a long time, and now was a natural time to stop. If he wished to share it with her later, he would do so when he was no longer tired.

It was at this moment that Serah joined them at the table.

"Fergus seems to be doing well," she said. "He's awake, and says he feels right as rain."

"Good," Lucian said. "His arm is healing all right, then?"

"He certainly seems to think so."

"I checked the diagnostic shortly before he came out of the pod," Vera said. "A few more weeks and his arm will be as strong as ever. The wound looked more grievous than it appeared."

"All good news," Lucian said. "So how long until Kandi?"

"Two more standard days, give or take," Vera said. "We are shooting like an arrow from Cupid's bow. Not a perfect analogy, but we're making good speed. By the time we get close and engage the thrusters to slow ourselves, we should be far enough away from League interference to not have to worry."

"So, we've lost them for good?" Lucian asked.

"I wouldn't say that, but the *Wayfinder's* trajectory should be dark on all scanners. We'll only be picked up once we're in range of Kandi."

"Can you tell us more about this moon?" Serah asked. "What's it like?"

"An inhospitable hellhole would be too kind a description. However, the Cupid system is little-habited, with no orbital infrastructure save for the Wardens around Psyche. I'm afraid it's our only choice if we want provisions for the journey. I must restock my medical supplies as well. Both will cost a fair deal of credits, isolated as Kandi and Ibbus are, but I see little choice in the matter. Of course, fuel will be necessary, too."

"You must be swimming in creds," Lucian said.

"I've had sufficient time and resources to acquire wealth over the years, which should hardly be a surprise, given my age and abilities. My money is well-hidden and untraceable."

At that moment, Fergus entered the wardroom and joined them. Even if the little table was crowded, Lucian noted he had squeezed next to Serah rather than joining Vera on her side.

"Are you feeling well?" Vera asked.

"Yes, thank you," Fergus said. "Serah and I will repay your kindness for taking us, I assure you."

"Well, your first opportunity will come soon. I will need help securing supplies at Port Kandi."

"Done," Fergus said.

"Introductions and proper explanations will have to wait until later," Vera said, rising from her seat. "If you have questions, you can ask Lucian. I've briefed him on the basics, and he can fill in any gaps."

"One more question, before you go," Lucian said. "Who is that droid?"

"Alistair? He's been with me since the Mage War. I programmed him to pilot this ship far better than any human. Though old, I've kept him maintained and upgraded over the years, same as the ship. At the time I gained the *Wayfinder*, it was one of the only space-to-surface vessels on the market. Now, these kinds of ships have become increasingly common, though still expensive. Upgraded as it is, *Wayfinder* is as advanced as any personal spaceship you'll find in the Worlds. I think you'll see that when we make a three-month journey in only two months. That speed is how I arrived on Psyche long before you expected."

"How fast does *Wayfinder* go?" Lucian asked.

"Its top speed edges just over .04C," she said.

".04C?" he asked. "I thought anything above .03 was impossible."

"As said before, I've done my part to keep it up to date, per Alistair's specifications."

"A useful droid," Fergus said approvingly.

"Now, I must go check on our progress and rest," Vera said. "There will be plenty of time to get on the same page during the journey. Space is difficult to bear, especially for those not used to it. It would be best to prepare your mind. Despite *Wayfinder's* speed, the journey will be long, and will test you greatly."

Vera departed, leaving Lucian, Serah, and Fergus alone in silence.

"What did she tell you?" Serah asked.

"A lot," he said. "I'm still reeling over it a bit."

"Let's hear it, then."

Lucian couldn't bring himself to say everything again. At least, not yet. "I need some time to think. Later today, maybe, but speaking with Vera isn't easy. I need sleep more than anything."

"What about us?" Serah asked. "Doesn't seem she's talking to us much. How do we know she won't dump us on Ibbus?"

"Well, Ibbus is the gas giant Kandi orbits."

"Let's not get technical here. Am I right to be concerned?"

"I won't let that happen. Besides, she says as long as you're committed to helping me find the Orbs, you're fine. Which both of you are, last I checked."

"Not like I have a choice," Serah said.

"I'm committed," Fergus said. "I have nothing else to commit myself to. I lost my place at Irion, my community at Kiro." He shook his head sadly. "I don't even know if they are still alive."

"My father's back there," Serah said. "I don't suppose I'll ever see him again."

Talking about their home just made Lucian think about his own, the one he'd long lost. He wasn't even sure what home *was* anymore. His parents were dead, and his life before becoming a mage wasn't worth missing. There was the Academy, but that was not home, either. He was groundless, forced to wander the galaxy on an adventure he'd never asked for.

Then again, so were Serah and Fergus. He remembered something Vera had told him long ago. The entire galaxy could be a prison if you thought of it that way. Even if the stars were open to him, he felt no freer. He had a single viable path ahead of him. And with the Swarmers back, there was even less time to complete his mission.

"We'll be fine as long as we stick together," Lucian said. "I'm far past the point of trying to do this on my own. You're stuck with me, at least for now."

"I'd always dreamed of seeing other worlds," Serah said with a smile. "Now, a part of me wishes I was back home, even in that cold, dark, stinking cave. Even if that's not a good life, it's something I know. All this . . . *technology* . . . is confusing."

"We'll have plenty of time to teach you about how it all works," Lucian said. "You're going to be shocked at what you see when we land."

"I already am. If warm showers on demand are not the pinnacle of human society, then I can't imagine what is."

Fergus cleared his throat. "As horrible as life on Psyche is, there's a certain simplicity to it. Out here, not so much. Especially now that we all qualify as rogue mages. The League might not know who we are, but they know someone got off Psyche. They could identify Lucian or me, if someone we know saw us, or they thought to scan us through any stray camera. That will always be a danger." He shrugged. "Then again, the galaxy is vast, and the odds of that happening are pretty low. If they don't know to look for us, then they can't."

"Yeah, I don't see us going back to Volsung soon," Lucian said. "Nor Irion, unless there's an Orb there."

Serah looked at Lucian, and from that gaze, he knew she hadn't told Fergus anything about his visions. There would be time for all that later.

"I'm going to sleep," he said. "Let's meet up later today. Try to rest up in the meantime."

He left them there and headed back to his cabin. As soon as he lay down, he was fast asleep.

35

HE WOKE UP LATER RAVENOUS. He warmed up some food with Serah and Fergus and caught them up on everything Vera had told him, and told Fergus about the visions he'd experienced while the prophecy was being destroyed. Vera was still asleep in her private cabin.

It was late by the time he'd finished. And upon finishing, he came to a decision.

"I'm going to tell Vera everything, too. This is something I can't keep from her."

"You can't!" Serah said. "Not yet."

"If not now, then when? I don't think she was lying to me about everything she said. This could be the thing she needs to lead us to *The Prophecy of the Seven*. The *real* prophecy, the one Arian wrote himself. How else are we going to find out about the Dark Gate, Nai Shairen, and all the rest? She has most of the puzzle, but we might be holding the only piece she needs. She's never going to figure that out unless we tell her."

"True," Serah said. "Still . . ."

"Do what you think is best," Fergus said. "It's safe to say

Vera has an extraordinary story, but even when she shared so much of it, we can't be entirely sure of her motives."

"I agree," Lucian said. "I don't agree with her beliefs or all the things she's done. But she believes she's doing the right thing. I just don't see how this progresses unless I tell her, and it's better to tell her sooner rather than later. All those places I saw might even be locations for the Orbs."

"Look at it another way," Serah said. "You have something she doesn't have. It's a card you can play if she ever turns on you."

That was something to consider as well. "If we think Vera's going to turn on us at the last moment, then what are we doing here? We should just stay on Kandi and find another way off that moon."

"If she would allow that," Fergus said. "Besides, from how she's described this Kandi, I doubt Pan-Galactic is flying there."

"She's our ride off Psyche," Serah said. "But it seems we need her to find the Orbs, and our interests align. For now."

"She wants the same thing we want. To find the Orbs. That should be enough."

Their conversation stopped short when the door to Vera's private cabin opened. "I suppose we're all caught up now?"

Serah and Fergus watched Lucian, who hesitated a moment before speaking. "There is one thing I still need to tell you. I think you're the only one who might help me."

"I'm listening."

Lucian told her then of his visions and Arian's words as *The Prophecy of the Seven* disintegrated into ash. He recalled as clearly as when he first saw them, much to his surprise. Somehow, the contents of the prophecy had melded with his mind so that it was now a part of him. If he wanted, he could close his eyes and see it playing out in his mind like a holo-film.

Vera's face was intent at first, and then ashen.

"Did I say something wrong?"

She licked her thin lips. "No. It's just . . . I've waited so long for such a breakthrough. I've toiled for so many countless years, thankless and in the dark. If I had uncovered even a quarter of what you've just related to me, it would have been time well spent."

"So it's useful?" Serah asked.

"Useful? It could be everything! It's obvious what your visions mean. Less obvious is Arian's location, but we might deduce it. Even from what you've told me, we can make an educated guess on where some Orbs might be."

"What?" Lucian asked. "Where?"

"Your first vision of the ice was instantly recognizable to me. For that is the location of the Orb of Gravitonics, on the world of Halia, toward which we are going. The double doors are the most recent part of my excavations, doors that will not unlock until the alignment of planets in that system creates a very specific gravitational pull, an event that happens only once every seven standard years. That event will occur in, you guessed it, a little over two months from now. That ice cavern can be no other place."

"Seriously?" Fergus asked. "That lines up almost perfectly."

"The Manifold works its will upon us, and it is our part to follow. As for the fissure of fire, it is not the Fire Rifts of Psyche, as you suspect. I would hazard to guess it is Hephaestus because that is a world of fire, volcanoes, and seas of molten lava. The fire basilisks are famous there, and they are gargantuan, lithoid creatures unique to that world, with rocky black skin and lengths of up to thirty meters. You probably saw such a creature deep in that rift. One Orb must lie there, in that location. I hazard to guess the Orb of Thermalism."

"And the others?" Lucian asked.

"The others are more difficult to guess at. The Orb of Dynamism must be in some temple of the Ancients, for little can be told, at least from what you've described. As for the tree, that is less clear. That could be anywhere in the Worlds unless you can give specific details on what kind of tree it is. But from your description, it matches nothing I know. It need not be in the League itself. Starsea extended far beyond the bounds of what humanity has colonized."

"What about the figure in black, holding the Orange Orb?" Serah asked. "You skipped that one."

"I did on purpose. It's the Orb of Atomicism."

"Do you have any ideas?" Fergus asked. "That must have been the first Orb found!"

"That is sound reasoning," Vera said. "We could talk about this for the next two months and get no closer to the goal. This other person will reveal themselves, in time. As Lucian follows his prescribed path."

That there was someone else out there, somehow who was seeking the Orbs, too, made Lucian's skin crawl. Would he have to fight them?

"What about that last bit?" Serah asked. "It seems important, too. The black hole and the metal tower against the night sky, and a large planet in the background."

"That is the key part of the prophecy," Vera said. "That is likely Arian's location because he was speaking to you from there."

Lucian's eyes widened. "Nai Shairen. He said it's through the Dark Gate. What does that even mean?"

"The Dark Gate was the only way in and out of Nai Shairen, the Ancients' homeworld. Its moon, Nai Elyn, was holy, its only building a tower where the Immortal and all his house lived in paradise, to be worshipped as a god looking down on his world. It would seem that Arian located it, and he discovered its location through his prophecy."

"He said the Chosen will know the way," Lucian said. "Except I don't know where it is."

"Another mystery," Vera said. "But there is still time to figure it out."

"How do you know all that about Nai Shairen?" Serah asked. "It seems you know something about it beyond Lucian's prophecies."

"I have studied the Ancients for decades and have even delved the Manifold for rumors of them. That is how I knew the names before Lucian told me. Whatever the case, we have leads now. But even with this new information, Halia is the closest world, just two Gates away. And from there, Hephaestus is another two Gates. Or, if we discover the location of the Dark Gate, we can go there to look for *The Prophecy of the Seven*. The original! It's there. It *must* be there, unless Ansaldra laid those words as a trap. But I doubt even she is capable of such trickery."

"It's real all right," Lucian said. "We have the information. The only question is what we do with it."

"For now, sit on it," Vera said. "There's a long time before we arrive on Halia. And tomorrow evening, we'll be docking at Port Kandi, the only outpost of any importance on that moon. Of course, all of this conversation is pointless if things go badly. Let us hope they don't."

36

THE NEXT EVENING, all four of them, plus Alistair, had gathered on the bridge. They had strapped themselves in, preparing to power on full and burn as they approached the smuggler's moon of Kandi. The viewscreen presented a forward vista of the approaching planetary system. Ibbus dominated the screen, a world of deep oceanic blue, carrying two thin green stripes around its equator and a thin ring barely visible against the backdrop of stars. It had forty-two known moons, though Kandi was the only one permanently settled, and the largest, being bigger than even Psyche. Unlike Psyche, it had no atmosphere of note, and various ices, mostly methane, covered it from pole to pole.

"I've requested docking," Alistair droned. "Let's see if there are any open berths." There was a moment of silence before he spoke again. "There are twelve available spots, more or less the same price."

"Which is closest to a supply station that carries all we need?" Vera asked.

"That would be dock 7K. It is operated by Intergalactic Transport Solutions."

"I don't care who it's operated by," Vera said, with a twinge of annoyance. "Is it within walking distance?"

"Yes. I will approve it immediately. It shouldn't take long before the network . . . ah. It's already verified."

"That was quick," Serah said.

"One of the first lessons you need to learn about the wider universe," Vera said. "Money leaves your hand like lightning, but enters like cold treacle."

"Whatever *that* means."

Alistair cleared his throat. It was a strange sound coming from a machine that didn't even *have* a throat. "I've already analyzed our stores, and have located the needed supplies: foodstuffs, water, fuel, and medical."

"The price?"

"12.6204 world credits to restock in full, and 1 credit for the hangar."

Fergus's eyes widened. "12.6? Has inflation been that much during my imprisonment?"

"Not so much," Vera said. "This world is far from typical trade routes. Everything carries a premium."

"Shall I sync the amount in full?" Alistair queried.

"No. Put in the request, and I will pay in person."

"As you wish, Master Desai. The store has accepted the request. The supplies are in a warehouse about five hundred meters from the hangar. A representative will meet us there to accept payment."

"Excellent," Vera said. "The sooner we're off this moon, the better."

No one made any comment about this as the icy moon grew in the viewscreen.

"Is that it?" Lucian asked.

"Yes," Vera said. "It won't be long, now."

The moon expanded with amazing speed. As Vera had mentioned, it seemed like nothing more than a ball of ice. There was no atmosphere to burn through as they descended. The artificial gravity cut out, replaced by the real gravity of the moon. Before them spread a cratered, icy wasteland and a star-filled sky, dominated by the leering blue giant of Ibbus halfway above the horizon. It looked freezing out there, and Lucian wondered if he'd have to wear a spacesuit. That was one thing he had yet to experience.

But it didn't seem as if a suit would be necessary. A couple of thousand meters above the surface, Lucian noted what looked to be a settlement of domes and connecting walkways. He wouldn't have called it a city; such a settlement couldn't have held over ten thousand people. But it was a connection to civilization, however tenuous. For that reason alone, it was a beautiful sight.

"The tops of those domes look like red eyes staring up at me," Serah said. "I don't like it."

"They are perfectly safe, I assure you," Vera said. "I can't speak for the denizens within, however."

"Denizens?"

Vera ignored her. *Wayfinder* lowered itself into the massive crater in which the domed settlement was situated. The surface itself seemed to open up to accept them. The hangar was underground, then.

Wayfinder touched down in a small, ill-lit berth barely large enough to hold it. Ice coated the hangar's outer edges. When the doors above closed, a great wind blew into the hangar.

"What's happening?" Serah asked, alarmed.

"They're pressurizing the hangar," Vera said. "Wouldn't want to suffocate stepping outside, would you?"

A few minutes later, the vents shut off. After this, a door to the interior of the settlement opened. A scraggly young man wearing cargo pants, a thick jacket, and copious tattoos around his neck approached the ship. He seemed to whistle as he stood and waved them to come out.

"It would seem I need to talk to this man," Vera said. "Fergus, I would have you come with me. In rough places, many men would try to take advantage of an elderly woman on her own, and I'd rather keep a low profile and not have to teach them a bloody lesson."

"Understood." He turned to Serah and Lucian. "Will you be all right on the ship?"

"I suppose," Serah said wistfully, looking into the hangar. It seemed she wanted to be anywhere but the ship. As she looked at the young man, he winked at her.

"That rotting bastard," she said. "As if he has a chance with me!"

"We'll be back soon," Vera said. She stopped for a moment. "Oh. Before I forget." She reached into her dark robes and handed Lucian something he had never expected to hold again: a slate. "I've already uploaded mine and Alistair's data. If you need anything, call. No telepathy."

Lucian stared at the slate dumbly. It was old, at least ten years out of date, but it felt like getting a part of himself back. "Why no telepathy?"

"I don't believe there are any other mages here, but if there are, they might detect the fluctuations in the Ethereal Background. It's not a risk I wish to take."

"What's that thing?" Serah asked, looking at Lucian.

"A slate."

"A what?"

"I'll buy more for the rest of you if any are to be had. Remember: keep a low profile. Keep the door locked, but if anyone gets too close to the ship, call me immediately."

"Sure," Lucian said.

Vera and Fergus headed off into the settlement, leaving Lucian and Serah alone with the ship.

"Why did she pick Fergus?" Serah said, somewhat glumly. "I've never been off Psyche my whole life, and now I have to stay on this ship for two more *months*?" She kicked the wall, wincing slightly at the action.

"Judging from what we saw above, you aren't missing much."

"I want to see pirates," Serah said. "Scum and villainy."

"Pirates are the last thing you want to see. Even Vera doesn't want to walk alone here. It sounds like a rough place."

Outside the bridge, four more men wearing company jumpsuits entered the hangar, a total of five including the one Vera had spoken to.

"What're those men doing?" Serah asked.

Lucian shrugged. "They seem to work for the company. See their jumpsuits? ITS. Intergalactic Transport Solutions. They're a mega-corp that operates spaceship hangars all across the Worlds."

"Something's fishy about this."

Lucian had to admit, the men seemed to take a lot of interest in the ship, looking it over as well as up at him and Serah, as if sizing them up. They laughed as if sharing a private joke. If something shady *was* going on, now would be the time for them to strike while Vera and Fergus were away. Lucian didn't know whether he was just being paranoid from always having to fight these last few months, or if it was instinct. Alistair just sat quietly, as if nothing was amiss. Then again, what instincts did a droid have?

"What are those men doing, Alistair?" Serah asked.

"It appears they are looking at the ship."

"Obviously," Lucian said. "*Should* they be looking at the ship?"

"Well, I did not schedule an inspection."

Two men had gone around to the back of *Wayfinder*, while

two bulky men remained in front. They made a big show of making notes on their slates.

"Looks like *they* think you did."

"I would have remembered if I did so," Alistair said.

"I'll go talk to them," Lucian said.

"I'm coming with you," Serah said, brightening.

"Wait!" Alistair said. "Master Desai said not to leave the ship!"

"Didn't she say to call if anyone got too close?" Serah asked.

How could Lucian have forgotten? He picked up his slate. "Call Vera."

There was no answer.

"Maybe the signal can't get out," Lucian said. "That rock wall looks pretty thick."

"Or maybe they're *stopping* the signal," Serah said.

"Why would they be doing that?" Alistair said. "It isn't logical! I didn't order an inspection."

"Serah's right. Something's weird about this. I'm going out."

"I won't allow it," Alistair said.

"Let me out, or they're going to do something to this ship that'll ground us for weeks. Do you want that on your hands?"

Alistair watched him for a moment, his red eyes seeming baleful. "As you wish."

"Let's go," Lucian said to Serah. "Be ready for anything."

"Oh, I *love* a good fight."

"Low profile!" Alistair nearly shrieked. "No magic, no violence!"

"Make sure your shockspear's ready," Lucian said. "We shouldn't have to use it, but—"

"We should be hopeful?"

Lucian sighed. "*Not* the answer I was looking for." They paused before the blast door. "Look, this place doesn't apply, but out there in the Worlds, especially League-sanctioned

Worlds, you can't just go around killing people, even if they are doing something you don't like."

Serah's blue eyes widened as she placed a hand to her mouth. "No. Really? Murder is . . . *bad*? I'm so glad I have you to teach me."

Lucian rolled his eyes. "I'm being serious."

"I'm not dumb, Lucian. You don't have to take me so seriously all the time."

"This *is* serious, though. Just be ready."

"You need to relax." She squeezed his arm. "You're tense and wound up, huh?"

He couldn't help but laugh. No matter the situation, Serah would always be Serah. They opened the blast door and walked down into the hangar.

———

THE BIGGEST OF the lot immediately approached Lucian, a heavily muscled bald man with hard eyes and a fake smile.

"Just in time. The lads and I just finished our multi-point inspection."

"We didn't order an inspection, multi-point or not."

The other men's faces became angry, as if Lucian were trying to cheat them. Such was their act that for a moment he almost believed them.

The man looked at his slate. "Well, says here clear as day that you did."

"Can I see that?"

The man shrugged and showed Lucian his battered slate. Indeed, there was an order form for an inspection, filled out and signed by Vera Desai. Did she *really* order that? No. She said to call her if anyone got too close to the ship.

"Look, buddy, she ordered nothing. She'll have my head if I

pay you a single sub-cred. You can take it up with her when she gets back."

"Oh yeah? The boss will have *my* head if I don't come back with the full eight creds you owe *me*."

"Eight creds?" Lucian laughed. "I can look at a ship for two minutes and charge that much, too. It's pristine, anyway."

"Well, tough. That'll be eight world creds, or there'll be trouble."

"Rot that."

"Rot what?"

Lucian had forgotten "rot" wasn't part of common vernacular outside Psyche. "I said, *rot* that, and you picked the wrong rotting ship to mess with."

The man gave a nasty smile. "Well, that's fine and dandy. Either you pay me ten world creds now—two extra for your insolence—or I'm going to have to get the higher-ups involved. Trust me, you don't want that."

"Lucian," Serah said, "are we still doing this low-profile thing?"

These words seemed to have more of an effect on them than anything Lucian had said. Perhaps it suggested they were dangerous criminals or something.

"I don't have the money," Lucian said. "You'll have to talk to Vera about that. She's the one who signed the contract, right? Do I look like Vera to you?"

"I suppose not," the man said. He looked confused. This wasn't going the way he wanted.

Lucian looked down at the man's nametag. "Look, Bruno, you have a nice hustle here. It's a good idea, but you could work on it a bit. A bit of professionalism could go a long way. Maybe actually go through with an inspection and give a list of details of things that might need to be fixed. Then it would be a bit more believable. Because now, you're not even trying. It's sad."

Bruno's face turned red. He was about to say something, but Lucian cut him off.

"You're not the threat here, and you know it. Vera is someone you don't want to mess with. You saw this ship, how pretty it was, and thought we'd be a nice mark. But you want to know how someone like Vera gets a ship like this? She's stepped on every toe in the galaxy. Sometimes even more than toes, if you catch my meaning."

It seemed Bruno did. "I'll be back, and you'll be sorry."

"You won't, and I won't. Losing face isn't the worst thing. Losing your entire face, though. Can't really come back from that."

Bruno backed away two steps, spat at Lucian's feet, but in the end, he turned around and left. His four cronies followed him, shooting venomous glares at Lucian. Only once they were out of the hangar did they go back on board.

"Wow, that was amazing!" Serah said.

"Well, let's hope they were bluffing. If they weren't, we might be in a bit of trouble."

Lucian called Vera again, and this time she picked up. He put her on speaker.

"Where are you?" Lucian asked. "These guys came in making up some rot about an inspection. They tried to hustle me for ten creds."

"And did you give it to them?"

"I told them to talk to you."

"This is beneath me. Have Alistair pay them. I want no trouble."

"Uh, Vera?" Serah said. "It might be too late for that."

"What do you mean *too late*?"

"Lucian basically told them to fuck off."

Vera was silent for a long moment. "You *what*?"

"They were bluffing," Lucian said. "And I didn't use those exact words."

"Actually," Serah put in, "Bruno, if that is his real name because it sounds ridiculous, mentioned getting some of his friends."

"And you let him *leave*?"

This was getting worse and worse. "Uh, maybe."

Vera sighed. "This is unbecoming of you, Lucian."

"If you had just picked up the slate . . ."

"I was busy. We're almost back. But they can lock us in until we pay the amount in full. If we're lucky, we'll get away paying twenty. If we're unlucky, there will be a lot of dead bodies and trouble and the League might sniff out our location. Why were you not keeping any of that in mind?"

"I don't know," Lucian said, lamely.

"You have much to learn in the ways of wisdom. Pray that this turns out to be nothing."

She hung up.

Alistair's voice emanated from the intercom. "Lucian! Serah! Get to the bridge at once!"

They ran to the bridge, only to find over a dozen men, half of which bore gauss rifles and jury-rigged power armor, entering the hangar.

"Rotting hell," Serah breathed.

Rotting hell indeed.

37

THERE WAS no time to call Vera or rely on anyone else. It was him and Serah against all these men.

"Eight creds is looking pretty cheap now," Serah said.

"Don't remind me. Alistair, is there some way I can talk to them?"

"If you come to the bridge, I can rout you to the hangar's auditory network."

Lucian hurried to the bridge with Serah close behind. As soon as he was inside, the men below had the *Wayfinder* surrounded.

"All right," Lucian said, his voice exiting into the hangar. "We'll pay up. Alistair, can you sync them ten creds?"

"Make it fifty," came an unfamiliar voice. A short, stout man wearing power armor clanked forward and looked up at Lucian. "And it'll be seventy if you give me any more lip."

Alistair muted the mic. "I'm not authorized to give that much."

"Permission to kill them?" Serah asked.

"That's fourteen down there," Lucian said. "Even with magic, one of us could end up seriously hurt, or the ship knocked out of commission."

"What do we do, then?"

"We're waiting," the boss said. "You have thirty seconds before we start blasting!"

"They will not blast this ship," Alistair said. "They want to take it intact. They hope we don't have the credits to pay, and then they will try to take the ship as collateral."

Lucian was calling Vera, but she wasn't picking up.

"Five seconds!" the commander boomed.

Lucian unmuted the mic.

"All right! You'll get your money. For that amount though, Vera has to approve it. She's almost back. I'm just a grunt. I can't give you that kind of money."

"They're stalling," one crony said.

"Stalling?" Lucian asked. "Are you blind? There's four of us and fourteen of you. You have heavy weapons, we don't. This isn't a fight we want. If you're patient and wait for Vera to come, you'll have your creds instead of a starship shot to hell."

"At this rate, I'm going to want the *entire* ship," the leader said. "My patience is wearing thin."

"You crazy? This ship is worth this colony a hundred times over!"

"And what's your life worth, kid? And that droid up there. You'll need to sign over his I.D. card to me, too."

This was spiraling out of control. Lucian tried calling Vera, but when she didn't pick up, he reached out for her. *Vera, you need to hurry.*

Stay on the ship. Under no circumstances go out the blast door!

What's going on?

Stall them. For the stars' sake.

She severed the connection.

"All right, kid," the thug said. "Decision time. What'll it be?"

"I don't know what to tell you. Vera has to approve everything. I don't have her account info."

"Don't play dumb. Tell the droid to sync the creds to the same account where you paid the docking fee."

One man raised his rifle, readying to shoot. Lucian didn't know what kind of damage it could do on the *Wayfinder's* hull, but he also didn't want to find out.

"All right! I'm telling him to sync it."

"I refuse. It's against my programming."

"Alistair!" Lucian said, hoping he sounded convincing. "Please. Do it."

"My master must tell me to do so directly. I'm not allowed to spend amounts above twenty-five credits without her express approval. I'm sorry, but I can't do as you ask."

"We'll take the twenty-five," the boss put in quickly.

"Then all is in order," Alistair said. "Please stand by."

The men outside waited in silence. After thirty seconds, the boss let out a ragged breath.

"What's the hold-up? You have fifteen seconds before we start blasting!"

"That's what he said two minutes ago," Serah whispered.

"What was that, bitch?"

Too late, Lucian realized Serah didn't understand muting and unmuting. But by now, they had run out of time. And he was getting pissed.

"Okay. I've got something for you."

He reached for the Orb of Binding and drew as much ether as he could. He created seven tethers in quick succession, binding the men together in twos. Power armor slammed against power armor, and where the men weren't wearing power armor, the armor crushed bone. A few shots rang out, ricocheting off *Wayfinder's* hull. Whatever the ship was made of, it was tough stuff. Lucian bound the leader, sending him flying up toward the hangar ceiling.

"Psychos!" one of them spat.

"That's right," Lucian said, the intercom still blaring. "Psychos. We're about to get psycho on all of you!"

"Draw their guns away, Lucian!" Serah screamed.

He didn't know why he didn't think of that. He switched the focal point to the ceiling and then bound each of the men's guns one by one. They flew into the air, rendering them weaponless. Now they were running for the doors. But once they'd reached it, it wouldn't open. They pounded on it with all their might, but even with the power armor's enhanced strength, they couldn't beat it down.

"Did you lock the door?" Lucian asked Alistair.

"No. I imagine that was my master."

Lucian didn't have to question him further, because the doors of the hangar above slid open. The men's screams evaporated into nothing as the air whooshed out of the hangar with incredible speed. The draft was so great that it pulled all fourteen men, including those who had fallen, straight up at least ten meters before the moon's low gravity pulled them down again in a slow-motion dance of death. Lucian cringed as he watched some of those men writhing in agony as the cold, airless moon sucked the life out of them. Only two men in power armor had the forethought to deploy helmets, but it was too late. It only took thirty seconds for all the bodies to freeze solid.

Now Lucian knew what Vera meant when she said to stay inside the ship.

The hangar doors closed again, and air rushed back into the hangar. After a couple of minutes, the jets turned off, and the door to the outpost rolled back.

Lucian's slate ringed, and he put Vera on speaker.

"Get down here and help!"

Everyone, including Alistair, rushed from the ship. Fergus

and Vera rolled into the hangar with at least a dozen pallets of supplies. They didn't bother unloading, they simply dragged the pallets directly onto the ship. After a couple of minutes, klaxons blared, but by then, everything was on board.

"Clear us for departure," Vera said.

"Requesting," Alistair said. He was still for a moment. "They're saying the settlement is on lockdown."

"Ask for his account address and offer him twenty creds to open the hangar doors."

Another pause. "He will accept no less than fifty."

"Give it to him," Vera spat. "Twenty-five now, and twenty-five when we're clear of the doors."

Another pause. "He accepts. The transaction cleared."

The blast door to the station closed, and instantly the hangar door rolled back. *Wayfinder* powered on and instantly lifted off, shooting into the void above.

"We're not out of this yet," Vera said. She turned to Lucian. "Foolish is too kind a word for your actions. Instead of leaving peacefully and without incident, we've made a scene that the League will sniff out if they haven't already. And instead of eight credits, we're out fifty."

"We're alive, at least," Lucian said.

"That we are. For now. Whether we stay that way remains to be seen."

"Did you guys get everything we needed?" Serah asked.

"Yes, aside from the fuel," Vera said. "There's a shortage here, and we will need to stop at Archea Station."

"Archea Station?" Lucian asked.

"It won't be like here," Vera said. "It's a stable mid-world, and the prices will be fair and there shouldn't be a supply shortage. It will lengthen our journey by a fair bit, however."

"My calculations say it will lengthen it by eight days," Alistair said. "We are lucky its orbital path will be nearly in the center of our inter-Gate trajectory."

Ten minutes later, *Wayfinder* had left the smuggler's moon of Kandi well behind, and Lucian couldn't have been happier. All that remained was the long journey to Archea Station, and then finally, Halia.

THE MADNESS OF THE MAELSTROM

Two minutes later, the soldier had left the smuggler's moon of Kandi well behind, and the crew didn't have time happier. As they coasted out on long journey to Vektor, Serah, and their hope flared.

38

THEY SPENT the next few days recovering, not only from their ordeal on Kandi, but from the wear and tear of Psyche. Lucian slept constantly, never seeming to catch up. Having steady meals was foreign, and the leanness of his body staggered him. He no longer recognized who he was in the mirror. Lucian learned from Vera that it was October 29 on the standard calendar, and the year was 2366. He had left Earth over two years ago, but he felt at least a decade older.

For the first time in two years, aside from the prison barge that took him to Psyche and quieter moments on the Isle of Madness, he had time to think. For days, all he could do was lie down, sleep, and luxuriate in thought. As he ate, more strength returned to him, and he spent most of his time in quiet meditation. He had troubled dreams, filled with death and danger and fear, old memories he could never cast aside. They were a part of him as much as the new physical scars, of which he now bore more than a few.

Anytime he talked to Serah or Fergus, they talked about

things outside the mission. It was as if they wanted to forget that horror show for good, at least for a time.

After a week of relaxation, Lucian finally felt sane enough to focus on what lay ahead. There was still about a month until they docked at Archea Station, a month Lucian intended to spend learning about magic and the Manifold from the most powerful living mage in the galaxy.

This time, he would not let the opportunity go to waste.

He knocked on Vera's door, and with that action, it felt like stepping back in time two years ago. Only this time, he would inform her of his intent to learn from her. That was if she was still willing to teach him.

The door slid open automatically, revealing Vera sitting in an armchair, apparently coming out of meditation. "Yes?"

Lucian entered the cabin. "I was wondering if you might train me. I've grown since then, and I'm ready to learn more."

Vera watched him closely and with a critical eye. "Are you indeed? What makes you say that?"

"I have a reason to fight now. And as much as I've learned, I still don't know what the hell I'm doing."

"Perhaps you underestimate yourself. And it might be the Manifold is directing you subconsciously, at least until you fulfill your purpose."

That sounded far more ominous than Lucian would have liked. "I know my purpose, something I didn't know the last time we met. I'm supposed to find the Orbs and return them to the Heart of Creation."

"And how does that make you feel?"

Lucian sat in the armchair across from her. "It doesn't feel real, to be honest. I don't think I'll make it that far, for one. The idea of it is incredibly overwhelming." She waited for him to go on. "I think Ansaldra is right, in a way. I'm too weak to use the Orbs. And I was hoping you might train me to be stronger. That's your whole thing, isn't it?"

"Maybe. Who can say what the Manifold wants from you, in the end? You must keep an open mind as to your fate. None can say who the true Chosen is until the end."

"So, you're saying this other person with the Orb of Atomicism could be the Chosen?"

"Possibly. Does that mean you should set aside your path?"

"No. I'm not doing this for me. I'm doing it for people like Serah, people who will fray unless someone gathers the Orbs and ends the Starsea Cycle."

"Well said. I believe you are ready to learn more. But it will require you to set aside all preconceived notions, to take on a different way of looking at the wider universe." She held up a hand, just as Lucian was about to tell her he was ready. "No. Speak not any lie to me. For some things, Lucian, you can never be ready, just as you can never train your mind to bear an inferno."

"What do you mean?"

"I mean exactly that. I require you to walk through fire without being burned. That is what my training means."

Lucian wasn't sure if she was being literal. "Seriously?"

"You are young. Brash. Unwise. You have learned much since our last meeting, but your abilities and character leave much to be desired."

"I'm ready to work on both."

"Indeed? We shall see. Your first test, Lucian, might come as a surprise." She watched him, a note of amusement in her dark eyes. "The path to becoming strong is to take the hardest path. The path you could never imagine yourself traveling."

"What must I do, Vera?"

"Simple. For the duration of your training, you must surrender both of your Orbs to me."

His eyes widened. He wasn't sure he heard her right. "I'm sorry?"

"That is my price. Will them into your hands, and give them to me."

Was this some sort of test? "How does that help things?"

"The relationship between Master and Psion is one of implicit trust. What greater way to test that trust than for you to give that which you most prize? What I could destroy you with, if I so chose? And how can you become strong unless you remove those crutches and learn to stand on your own two feet?"

"This could all be some trick."

"It could. Do you trust me, Lucian, or don't you?"

Lucian had to look deeply into himself for that answer. He knew what he *needed* to do, but the actual doing it was the hard part. "I . . . don't trust you. Not completely."

"And why not?"

"You abandoned your friends on Isis. You warred with your own family over your beliefs. You would choose those beliefs over someone closest to you."

"Because of those sacrifices, many that gave me great pain, you know exactly where I stand. What does that tell you?"

Again, Lucian wasn't sure what she was getting at. It was riddles all the way down with her.

Vera continued. "Once before, I said I don't teach those who are not my students. And I do not teach unless the student recognizes me to be the Master, to trust me in all things implicitly. Magic is far too dangerous, far too complex, for anything less than that."

"But you taught me to question."

"So I did. But now it's your turn to take that critical eye and look right back at the person who taught you to use it. When you look at me, what do you see?"

For the first time, Lucian looked into her dark eyes for more than a second or two. It was no simple thing to do, such was her gravitas and power. But the longer he looked, the more things he saw, and the more things he realized, either through his intuition or Psionic sensitivity. Her gaze was like a winter storm, freezing him to the core. It was like death coming over him, like drowning at the bottom of the Ocean of Storms. He had gotten the feeling before, but it was so buried that he had never made the connection.

Staring at her was like staring at the Ancient One.

"Ah," she said, her lips twitching into a smile. "You see it, now."

"No," he said, unbelieving of what he had guessed. "You're .. . him?"

She looked away, and only then did Lucian feel some measure of relief. "No, I'm not him. But he and I have spoken before, and like you, he has marked me. He is the one behind it all, the spirit I met within the Manifold all those years ago. He directs me in things, sometimes. As he directed me to you."

"You left that part out. You told me the Manifold guided you."

"And so it did. The Ancient One, the Second Immortal of Starsea, is a being of the Manifold. And as the Orbs awaken, he can affect the Shadow Realm more."

"He's dangerous," Lucian said. "And you *voluntarily* speak to him?"

"I do what I must for the sake of humankind. I am strong enough to bear it, though every time I have spoken with him, it has made me doubt that conviction."

His meeting with the Ancient One was something he had kept hidden from her, and yet she had known.

He would probably not get another opportunity to under-stand the Ancient One's motivations, so he shared everything with Vera, everything from his very first encounter with him during his metaphysical exam, to the odd dreams, to the extended audience when he delved the Manifold to possess the wyverns.

By the time Lucian had finished, he felt a certain weight lifted from him. But strangely, that did not make him feel much better. Vera merely watched, in her cool and mechanical way, the gears turning in her head.

"Of course, I knew you had spoken to him," she said. "When I said you were marked, I never said who marked you. The Manifold, yes. But the Manifold is an uncaring entity, the unmoved mover, that which lies behind all. I knew something within the Manifold was interested in you, Lucian, and I knew who it was, even back then."

"But why? Why would he choose me?"

"Must there be a reason?"

"There must be!"

"I'm not convinced. Yours is a . . . curious case, no doubt. And only time will tell as you unravel more secrets."

"I don't want to."

"You must embrace it, Lucian. Do you believe yourself to be the Chosen of the Manifold? It's not a title to be envied." She watched him closely. "It's ironic, in a way. The Seven Orbs would give you ultimate strength, but they will make you a slave to the Immortal's will, make your thoughts no longer your own. How long do you think your mind can withstand the transformation?"

"I don't know. Is there anyone who can take this burden from me? Maybe I'm not the Chosen. Maybe I'm too weak."

"Perhaps. If you wish for *me* to take them, well, I'm afraid that's not my role. As powerful as I am, the Ancient One has clarified that it is my part to teach, and my part to spin webs. An old spider."

"What does he want with me, then? It's just . . . incomprehensible."

"So it is. All we know is what he's chosen to reveal. He wants to use you for his purposes, and his ultimate aim is clear. He desires the Seven Orbs of Starsea. He desires his former power, his empire, to be complete. Just as every one of us desires to be complete, the strongest and best versions of ourselves. Nothing in star or planet, Shadow or Light, will stop him. You are nothing to him, Lucian. And yet, you are everything. I've often spoken to you of power and will. And yet, ironically, there can sometimes be a stronger power in being a slave. Remember that. Though we don't know all the answers, neither is everything lost."

Vera stood and extended her hands. At first, Lucian thought she was reaching for him, but such an act of comfort was not something Vera would do. She was asking for something.

"Are you willing to give the Orbs now, after what I've told you?"

After a moment, Lucian nodded. He knew everything she said to be true. He could not progress in his abilities unless he voluntarily weakened himself. It carried risk. Significant risk. But it was necessary, at least for now.

"I will," he said. "Only . . . I don't know how to do it."

"Only will it to happen, and it will be so."

Lucian stood, extending both of his hands. There was a moment of hesitation, but then he reached for his Focus, where he knew both Orbs to lie. He wanted to embrace them, to feel their power wash over him, to forget everything. And yet, he knew he could not do that.

Instead, he took those Orbs and willed them out of his Focus, into his very hands.

Nothing happened at first, but as time wore on, he noticed blue and violet streams of light spreading down his arms. The blue flowed down the left arm, while the violet flowed down the right. Those lines collected in his hands, brightening until they shone like twin suns. And then the brilliance faded until the deep blue and the deep violet of each Orb stood revealed.

Holding the warm Jewels of Starsea, one in each hand, Lucian felt a certain emptiness, but also the releasing of a burden. For the first time since picking each of the Orbs up, he could not stream those Aspects with reckless abandon. The very thought of streaming without them scared him. Vera was right. These Orbs *had* become crutches. He could no longer stand on his own merits.

Vera extended her hands, and with great effort, Lucian handed over his Orbs. It felt as if he were handing over his children to a demon and trusting her not to roast them.

But Vera did nothing of the sort. She did not absorb the Orbs, throw them, or do anything untoward. She merely wrapped each one in a small blanket and placed them in an old chest at the foot of her bed. That this old, shabby chest could hold such treasures was ludicrous. And yet, it was so. In the end, the vaunted Aspects of Magic were just things Lucian could choose to give away if he had the will to do so. And perhaps that was a lesson.

"Now," Vera said, turning back to him. "Free of false power, you can develop your strength as a mage."

Lucian nodded. "I'm ready to walk through fire."

"Then let us begin."

39

IN LUCIAN'S twenty-two short years, he'd survived one of the roughest parts of Miami, endured the condemnation of the Transcends of the Volsung Academy, had scraped by on the Isle of Madness, had persisted through the Rifts of Psyche, the Darkrift, the schemes of the Sorceress-Queen Ansaldra, along with the Burning Sands and Fire Rifts.

Vera's training, in its way, was far more difficult than all those combined. And without the benefit of the Orbs, he had only his strength to rely on.

"Focus," she said. "You are too impatient."

It was hard for Lucian to stream without the Orbs. He never realized how much he had been relying on them.

"Stop trying to get somewhere. Feel your Focus. Sense the Manifold beyond. Do not depend on emotion."

Lucian pushed down his frustration. No matter what he tried, it was never right. It was like Talent Khairu times a thousand. Vera had no word of praise, only critiques designed to dismantle everything he thought he knew.

"Never stream unless it's from a place of conviction. Never

take a drop of ether for granted. Stop thinking of the Shadow Realm, the reality of flesh and bone. There is only the Light Realm, and it's the Light Realm that dictates our reality. Sense it, engage with it, and there will be nothing that can stop you."

"That's delving," Lucian protested. "It would kill me."

Vera gave a cunning smile. "What have I told you before?"

"Belief makes magic."

"My lessons, my Psion, are of the old school before the Mage War tore Magekind apart. The old school teaches you to cultivate your strength, not hobble it. The Path of Balance you've internalized is . . . *rot*, as you might say."

"But won't unlimited magic lead to the fraying?"

"It might if you do not follow my instructions. The teachings of the Academies are of the lowest common denominator. They don't teach the greater mysteries unless you rise to become a Psion of one of the Seven. The Path of Balance is for Novices and Talents that will never rise above their station. Do you think the Transcends limit themselves, that they would voluntarily keep themselves weak? How do you think they rose so high and are so esteemed by their inferiors?"

"They break the rules."

"*What* rules? The Path of Balance is a lie. But it is also a truth. It is true for some, but a falsehood for others, but they would never teach you this, as it would only lead to resentment and display their hypocrisy. The freedom I teach is a kind of restraint. Most can't handle mastering their own choices, and would rather be told what to do. For this, the Path of Balance serves a convenient purpose. Had you remained at the Volsung Academy, you might have risen high—in two decades, perhaps. Only then would you have learned such things."

"That's not fair."

"Conventional ethics imprison your mind. The higher you are, the richer you are, the more powerful, the more people allow you the privilege of lying."

"I don't like that. Leaders should be the most honest."

"And why do you suppose that?"

"If the people find them out, it will lead to chaos."

"Has it ever? Or do people simply make excuses for their leaders? But I digress. This is a lesson for another time. The rules of the game are that which you make them. If you play by a certain set of rules that lend you an advantage, and your opponent does not, what do you think happens?"

"You win."

Vera nodded. "Not everything is zero-sum, of course. And even the craftiest of manipulators do not foresee all contingencies. Hubris is always a danger, leading to fatal errors unseen until the end. All types of manipulation, Psionic or otherwise, are tools. The tools themselves are not evil. All that matters is why we use them."

"I won't become a liar."

"I never said to become a liar. We must wear many hats, and that is simply the way of the universe. All this to say, put away your old notions of good and evil, honest and dishonest. Only realize what is most important to you. Anything that impedes that is *your* evil, to be eradicated without mercy."

———

ONLY AFTER A WEEK of training his Focus did Vera allow him to stream, albeit in paltry amounts.

"Impure rubbish," she said. "Again."

Lucian wasn't even manifesting the streams into anything useful. Vera seemed only interested in his stream's purity.

"Your mind is too distracted," she said.

"You're making me nervous."

"My scrutiny is nothing compared to what you must go up against."

She was probably right. "How do I stream purely, then?"

"Training. Patience. Remember your Focus, always. Be aware of it at all times. This is not something I can teach you, but something you must discover for yourself."

Lucian heaved a frustrated sigh. "It feels like I'm going backward."

"You are," Vera admitted. "That's entirely the point. You've gone down the wrong path these last two years, so you must go back to the turn you missed. You chose the road going over the gentle plain, rather than the one going up the mountain. While more difficult, the path of the higher road lends greater perspective."

Lucian was tiring of her analogies. "I think I see your point."

"Focus, then. We will try streaming again next week."

When they passed through the Archea Gate, Lucian wasn't there to watch. He was busy training, as he always was, even without Vera watching him.

A knock at his cabin door broke him from meditation. Serah slipped inside and came to sit next to him.

"I'm bored," she said. "There's nothing to do on this ship." She held up her slate. "This thing loses its charm pretty quickly."

Knowing Vera, it likely didn't have any games or even a single holo-film. "I wonder how long we'll be docked at Archea Station."

"However long it takes to refuel. Which I imagine won't take long. Still, there might be enough time to take you out. Show you that there's life beyond this ship."

"Yes, *please*. Can we go to the holo-theater? I've heard people talk about that on Psyche. You get put into a story, expe-

rience it as if it were happening to you. That sounds more like
magic to me than anything I've ever done."

"Maybe we can. I don't know if they have one on the station.
If not, I'm sure there are many things to do. Most things cost
money, though."

"You think Vera would give us some?"

Lucian shuddered. "I don't know. I don't like the idea of
asking."

"Ugh. I'm tired of her. Well, we can figure something out. I'd
be happy just looking around."

As a lifelong Rifter, it probably wouldn't be too hard to
impress Serah. "All right, then. It's a date."

"A date?"

"It means when you go out with someone."

"Oh." Her cheeks reddened slightly. Lucian couldn't help
but laugh.

"What's so funny?" she asked, somewhat heatedly.

"It's not like you to be bashful. I'm just enjoying it."

"Whatever. We can bring Fergus along, too. I'm sure he
needs a break. Are you done with your meditations?"

"Never. If I slack off, Vera will be the first to know."

"Come on," she said, rubbing his arm. "You need a break.
It's a fact that if you meditate too long, you'll turn into a statue."

"Really?"

She nodded solemnly. "I don't want you to become boring,
like the Elders of Kiro. You're a handsome man in the prime of
his life. The *last* thing you should do is meditate."

Lucian was about to respond when there was a knock at his
cabin door.

"It's me," Fergus said from the other side.

"Come in," Lucian said.

The door opened, and if Fergus thought it was surprising
they were together, he gave no sign of it.

334

"Thought you guys might want to see this broadcast. It's live in the wardroom."

After sharing a look, Lucian and Serah followed Fergus there.

Vera was already there, watching the viewscreen on the ship's starboard side. It no longer displayed the cosmos outside, but a news program. When he read the ticker at the bottom, his heart plummeted.

"Swarmers in A.C.," Lucian said, feeling somewhat faint. Just the mention of that system reminded him of his mother, over two years dead.

"A.C.?" Serah asked.

"Alpha Centauri. It's the most populated system outside of Sol. And Sol's neighbor."

Serah's face blanched as the anchor related the facts. A Swarmer fleet had somehow sneaked by undetected and was well on its way to Chiron. It then showed footage of skirmishes between League vessels and the tiny Swarmer strike craft.

"How did they break through?" he asked.

"The primary League Fleet is on the opposite side of League Space, defending the Kasturi Gate," Vera said. "It would seem the *Alkasen* have outwitted them."

"Chiron is a First World," Lucian said. "They would have *had* to have left some defenders. Right?"

"Other than a nominal planetary defense network and the strike craft they house, the planet and its people are utterly defenseless. Evacuations are already underway."

"Evacuations to *where*?"

But Lucian already knew that answer. Only one world, as populated as it was, had the resources to handle tens of thousands of refugees: Earth. While Chiron held tens of millions, there was no way that even *it* had the orbital infrastructure to get that many bodies off-world promptly.

"How did it come to this?" Fergus asked. "If Lucian is right, then this is our punishment for using magic."

"Punishment?" Vera asked. "I would not jump to conclusions. The *Alkasen* are the force associated with the instigation of a new Starsea Cycle. As the Cycle advances and reaches its culmination, they become more dangerous. But we do not know all the details. All we know is that they despise magic, per Lucian's words from the Oracle of Binding and my discoveries."

"It might already be too late," Lucian realized. "If Chiron falls, Earth is next!"

"Perhaps," Vera said. "If Chiron suffers the same fate as Kasturi, then the death toll of this Third Swarmer War will surpass every conflict since the Mage War."

"How many died on Kasturi?" Serah asked.

"It's a little-populated Border World, but several million are presumed dead. The last broadcasts fizzled out over a year ago. I . . . would not go searching the GalNet for that once we are in range of Archea."

"I wouldn't know where to begin," Serah said. "Millions dead . . . I can't imagine such a number."

"It's a reminder that we need to continue working," Lucian said. "People are counting on us, even if they don't know it." Lucian looked at Vera. "How far is Alpha Centauri from here?"

"Four Gates," Vera said. "Archea to Halia, Halia to Volsung, Volsung to Earth, and finally, Earth to A.C.."

"They are in Kasturi, too," Lucian said. "Six Gates away, unless I miss my guess."

"That's correct. It doesn't get more Mid-World than Archea. It's part of the Ring, a collection of forty worlds that more or less surround the four First Worlds and Earth. Either way, we are in no danger at the moment. We should dock at Archea Station within a couple of days. It will take several hours for the ship to refuel. I do not recommend leaving the ship, but if you wish to walk around, I won't stop you. You should know that in times of uncertainty, the worst of society takes advantage, as we saw countless times in the Mage War. For now, the League is strong, and whatever may happen, it can stand for years yet. As long as Earth itself does not fall, nor the Swarmers take the Forge of Heaven."

"The Forge of Heaven?" Serah asked.

"A helium-3 mine and starship fuel refinery in Uranus."

Serah snickered. "I'm sorry, what?"

"It's the name of a planet in the Solar System," Lucian said. He couldn't help but smile, despite the dark conversation.

"I'm sorry, but *who* named it that?"

"That's beside the point," Vera said, with forced patience. "Uranus contains the largest deposits of helium-3 in Sol System, and being the smallest of the gas giants, it was the easiest to exploit. The Volsung Academy Mages handled its making." Her eyes became somewhat distant. "I was there as a young Talent. The chandelier cities surrounding the Forge are a sight to behold, and none of their like has been built since."

"So, this place is of strategic importance," Serah said. "I think I understand."

"So long as it's held, the League will never lack for fuel. And already, the shipyards of Earth, Luna, Mars, and the Outer Moons are assembling an armada such as the Worlds have never seen, even since the days of the Mage War. That said, it means nothing if they can't find the people to crew them, and the ships will not be fully ready for two to three years."

"Will that be an issue?" Lucian asked. "I know there's plenty of people on Earth who don't have jobs. Almost fifty percent of the population."

"It may come to that," Vera said. "So much remains to be seen. The times grow ever more uncertain. But we can do nothing but watch and focus on our work. That's all anyone can do."

40

WHEN THE *WAYFINDER* docked at Archea Station, at what had to be the cheapest berth possible in a tiny orbital station that wasn't even a part of the primary complex, Lucian, Serah, and Fergus stepped out of the airlock and into the shabby hangar after Lucian had retrieved his Orbs. Though he didn't believe Vera would make off with them, he wasn't foolish enough to stake the Orbs on that belief.

Vera approached them from behind. "Alistair informed me the fueling drones won't arrive for another twelve hours because of a backlog. With the Swarmers, there is a serious shortage. That said, Archea Station is centrally located, and you can reach most of the Worlds from here."

"What are you trying to say?" Serah asked.

"If any of you wish to part from this dangerous quest, you will probably not get another opportunity again."

Both Fergus's and Serah's eyes widened at that, and it seemed neither had even considered it as a possibility. Nor had Lucian.

338

"Leaving after learning that the galaxy is going to hell?" Fergus asked. "It would be faithless to leave now."

"Same," Serah said. "I'm on this crazy ride."

"Very well," Vera said. "I will not stop you. Just remember to lie low. With those jumpsuits, you'll blend right in." She considered. "I've given your slate wallets access to a small portion of my account. Don't spend it on needless frivolities."

It was hard for Lucian to not feel like a child getting an allowance, but money was money.

"Go," Vera said. "Be back in eight hours or earlier. And please—stick together. This station has a reputation, but the three of you together should more than handle it."

As they walked off down the shabby, ill-lit corridor, Lucian was glad it was empty. The lights flickered, and the life support vents rattled in a way that didn't inspire confidence.

"Have you been here before, Fergus?" Serah asked.

After several more treatments in the med pod, his left arm was out of its sling, and about as strong as his right. "Unfortunately. Not a nice place to be, and Archea itself is even worse. Or at least, it was."

"When were you here?"

"I first came eight years ago, a posting from the Irion Academy."

"A posting? Doing what?" Serah asked.

He hesitated a moment. "I was a bodyguard for a very rich and corrupt crime lord."

"Seriously?" Serah asked. At Fergus's nod, she whistled.

"That sounds like that should be beneath a mage," Lucian said. He immediately regretted it. "Sorry. That came out wrong."

"It *was* beneath me," Fergus said. From his voice, it seemed there was more to the story, but he didn't want to talk about it.

Serah didn't seem to pick up on that, though. "Who were you guarding? What was his name?"

"It was a woman," Fergus said. "And there's no point in talking about it now. She's long gone."

"Did you kill her?"

"No, I didn't kill her."

"How'd she die, then?"

Fergus's expression was growing irritated. "I'd rather not discuss it."

"Well, if there's anyone that's out for your blood, that's something we need to know before we go in, right?"

Lucian's mind was racing with possibilities. "Maybe you should stay on the ship, Fergus, all things considered."

"Turn here," he said. "This gondola will take us to the primary station."

"Gondola?" Serah asked.

"It's a sort of transport that runs along a magnetic wire. There'll be no gravity, so make sure you're strapped in."

Fergus scanned his slate on an airlock, on the other side of which was the gondola, large enough to seat perhaps eight people. The cost was only five sub-creds, a pittance compared to what Vera had given them. Once seated, they strapped themselves in and shot off. Gravity pushed them back into their seats as they shot toward the station, a rotating torus orbiting a blue-hazed world with a green band of vegetation along its equator. Large lakes and wide rivers interspersed that band, which was likely a forest.

Serah, however, was looking toward the station itself, eyes large. "People built that?"

"A long time ago," Fergus said. "Archea Station is pushing a century now. There are far bigger habitats in the Worlds. They say the L-Cities above Earth collectively hold almost a million people."

"I can't imagine."

Within minutes, they had reached their top speed and were

floating against their restraints. Serah unclasped herself and floated through the cabin, a wide smile on her face.

"What're you doing?" Fergus asked. "You're going to slam into the viewscreen when we slow down!"

"I've got my magic."

"*No streaming.* Irion posts mages here, or at least, they used to."

"Fine."

As Serah strapped herself in again, Lucian turned to Fergus. "What if someone recognizes you?"

"No one will. Mages don't escape Psyche, remember? If they see me, they'll believe their eyes are playing tricks on them. Besides, I look different now than I did then."

"Different, how?" Serah asked.

"I was . . . portlier, you might say. And I had a beard."

"I guess the living was good on Irion."

"I didn't think so then, but in retrospect . . ."

The gondola slowed and connected to its receiving port. The airlock hissed open, revealing a shabby lobby filled with spacers and dockworkers, busy at work loading and unloading various cargo ships. It seemed they had entered a sort of dockyard.

"Where are you taking us, Fergus?" Serah asked.

"I know some bars where our credits will go far. I would have a drink to celebrate my freedom. It's warranted, wouldn't you say?"

"Hell, yeah! Lead the way."

"Maybe just one," Lucian said, thinking of his training.

"Come on, live a little," Serah said.

Serah was going to stick out like a sore thumb. Though she wore a jumpsuit, like the rest of them, there was a wildness to her step and curiosity in her eyes that made her the object of attention. Lucian noticed more than a few dockworkers looking her way, and Serah looked right back.

"Why are all of them staring at me like that?"

A heavily tattooed and muscled dockworker approached. "Hey, beautiful. Ever ride a hover-bike?"

"Leave her alone," Lucian said.

"Oh yeah? You going to make me, runt?"

"Lucky for you, you're not worth our time."

"*You're* lucky I'm on my shift, or I'd knock you clean through the deck."

"Whatever you say, pal."

They left him behind, fuming, heading for a nearby elevator. Fergus hit one of the bottom levels, and the elevator descended.

"Was that man going to fight us?" Serah asked.

Lucian shook his head. "Just blowing hot air. Trying to impress you."

"Impress *me*?"

"He was trying to pick you up," Fergus explained.

"I figured that. I wasn't sure, because the customs here are . . . strange."

"What do you mean?"

"Well, on Psyche, when a man likes a woman, he doesn't shout at her. He makes a gift, usually. Something small, but valuable to the person receiving it. It should be thoughtful and gracefully presented. If the woman accepts the gift, then the man can court the woman. Or, if they both know each other well enough already, they can discuss marriage." Serah looked at him. "Are you seriously telling me that when men like a woman here, they just *shout* at her?"

Lucian laughed. "The desperate ones, maybe. It's called catcalling and in most places, it's frowned upon or even illegal. But normally, when a man likes a woman, he asks her out. If they hit it off, things can proceed from there."

"Interesting. As in, marriage?"

342

"Sure, but maybe not right off the bat. Most people wait a year or more."

"*A year!*" Serah's mouth twisted in disgust. "You could die in a year! If a man made *me* wait that long, he'd be seeing the last of me."

"Really?" Lucian asked.

"On Psyche, we don't have time for waiting. You could die any moment, any day. I would've married young, but . . ." She trailed off. "Never mind about that. No man would want me, now."

"That guy wanted you," Fergus said.

Fergus jumped as a Gravitonic disc jerked him into the elevator wall.

"No magic!" he said.

Serah let him go. "You deserved it."

Lucian couldn't help but laugh. It felt nice to not be serious for once.

The elevator came to a stop, and when the doors opened, it revealed a wide avenue, a commercial area filled with shops, restaurants, bars, and clubs on multiple levels.

"Rotting hell," Serah said, gawking. "What's all this?" She sniffed the air. "It smells so good! I want to eat everything!"

She ran to a nearby food cart. Exchanging a glance, Lucian and Fergus ran after her. She brushed her way to the front of the queue, not seeming to understand the concept of waiting her turn. They didn't have queues on Psyche either, Lucian supposed.

"Young lady," a gruff old man said. "The line starts back here."

Her cheeks reddened. "Oh. Sorry. I'm starving, though."

"Come on, Serah," Lucian said. "Just . . . *try* to blend in?"

That was easier said than done, especially with her staring at every single thing in wide-eyed wonder. Lucian didn't blame her, though. This was about as far from Psyche as you could get, especially the multicultural crowds filtering in and out of store-fronts and bars.

She fell in beside him, and Lucian reached for her arm and locked it into his own, both to steady her and to keep her from wandering off.

"You've got this," he said. "Just follow Fergus's lead." But it was at that moment that he realized Fergus disappeared.

"Over here!" Fergus said, standing in front of a bar with flashing blue neon lights.

They headed over, walking down the tree-lined avenue toward him. Above them stretched viewscreens looking out on the verdant planet below. Several ships streaked by, heading for the planet itself.

When they entered the dingy establishment, they found three open stools at the bar.

"I'll get the first round," Fergus said with a smile. "Barkeep! Three Io volcanoes."

They watched as the experienced bartender deftly mixed an assortment of liquids in three glasses that he lit on fire. Serah's eyes popped as the bartender slid the drinks toward them. Just as they grabbed them, the flames petered out, and the contents within vibrated.

"This won't kill me, will it?" Lucian asked.

Fergus laughed. "Probably not. Drink too many, though, and you'll wish you were dead."

Hours and several drinks later, the bar had filled up, and the conversation was rolling. Only then did Lucian work up the courage to ask Fergus about his past.

"So, what was bodyguarding like?"

Fergus shook his head. "What do you think? It was a waste of my talents and abilities, and when I figured out who Irion contracted me to, I was livid."

"I don't think the Volsung Academy does anything like that."

THE CHOSEN OF THE MANIFOLD

"Well, Volsung subsists on some old grants it got after the Mage War, which they invested wisely. Irion didn't receive such grants, so they run a thriving business where they contract mages to certain companies, groups, and individuals with less than . . . *stellar* . . . reputations, shall we say. If the price is right. It's probably illegal, but nebulous enough for them to get away with."

"That's what they did to you?" Lucian said.

"That's right. They assigned me to guard a pirate named Zheng Yang. The so-called Terror of the Stars."

"Even on Earth, we've heard of her," Lucian said. "People say she's as ruthless and she is beautiful."

"That would have been eight years ago," Fergus said, going on. "When I arrived, well over a thousand vessels flew under her flag. Archea Station and much of the world itself was under her control." He looked around, left to right, to make sure no one overheard them. The blare of the music seemed sufficient to cover their words. "My guess is, new crime lords have risen in her stead, but it would be wise not to speak too loudly about it. She had many husbands, most loyal unto death. Some might still lurk here."

"Husbands?" Serah asked, shocked. "I need to meet this lady."

"If you knew her, you wouldn't wish that. She's the most horrible person I've ever met. Truly, without a soul, and cares for nothing but herself. I witnessed her torture, execute, and ruin the lives of hundreds of people, and through her captains and lieutenants, she's killed thousands more. All to line her greedy pockets with creds. She had no motivation but power and wealth."

Lucian knew Fergus would not have been so bold to speak this, especially here, unless he was deep in his drinking. His eyes became hooded with reminiscence.

"How did she become the Terror of the Stars, then?" Lucian asked.

"She got her start in the brothels and bordellos of the Understation. I'm sure from the moment she entered this galaxy, she went through horrors untold. Either way, I can't speak to that. Through sheer tenacity, manipulation, theft, and sometimes violence, she ended up running quite a few establishments. She ended up blackmailing the right people, and ended up marrying a middling pirate, who she inherited from. Most think she sped along his death, though it's controversial. For all her faults, she actually did like the men she consorted with, but perhaps even she couldn't resist that opportunity. Thank the stars she no longer lives here."

"Wait," Lucian said. "I thought she was dead."

"I never said dead. She's gone. She fled beyond the Border Worlds with all her crewmen and her armada of a thousand ships, with enough supplies to last decades. She kidnapped many people over the years, including women and children, to build her new society. A pirate queendom, if you will." Fergus drained the last of his drink. "I got caught up in all that, like a bug in a spider's web, but when Irion ordered me to guard her all the same, even as she left League Space, I defied their will for the first time in my life. Irion is famed for never breaking a contract, so my actions ruined their reputation. I often wonder how much Zheng Yang paid for my services, but she never told me. It must have been a lot."

"Did anyone try to kill her?" Lucian asked.

"Oh, yes. And I saved her life many times during the two years I guarded her. When Irion exiled me for breach of contract, words were useless. I'm sure they told the League Wardens that I abetted her. They had to dispose of me to send a message to all their mages, and future clients, that they would not tolerate a disobedient mage." He chuckled darkly. "And perhaps I abetted her, in a way. I could have left anytime, gone rogue, but I chose not to. And of course, the Wardens wouldn't listen to me about how the Irion Academy contracted me. For crimes against humanity, they sentenced me to life on the prison moon of Psyche."

"What the hell," Serah said. "That's so messed up."

"But now, I'm a free man. When I heard we were coming here, I thought I'd come back to this bar, where I drank many a night lamenting the chains of Irion's contract. I drank then out of darkness and despair, hoping to drown my sorrows by the bottle." He looked at his empty glass. "Now, however, I drink in celebration. I'm free. Broken, but free."

"You must want to kill her," Lucian said. "Or at least throttle the Transcends of the Irion Academy."

"I'm not like Selene or Jagar," Fergus said. "I understand the need for vengeance and wished for it for a long time. But about the time I joined you, I realized my life could be more than that. So, that's why I'm here. I could go off and seek them out, go out in a blaze of glory. I suppose if I ever ran across her again, and could finish her, I'd do it."

Lucian noticed someone eavesdropping on their conversation—a beautiful young woman with raven-black hair sitting just a couple of stools down. With a smirk, she paid her tab and left, losing herself among the crowds.

"We should head back," Lucian said. "We've had enough. I'm sure your old employer has eyes and ears all around."

Fergus nodded. "That, I don't doubt. I wanted to have a walk around, get a feel for things. To see if something like a ghost of her remained." He gave a small smile. "It seems things are better. People are out and about, and only the older ones seem to walk with a careful step. It will take time, but even giants must fall. I don't need revenge. Fate will have revenge for her far sweeter than any I could devise."

He didn't elaborate, paying the tab and leaving the bar. They stumbled back toward the ship. It had gotten late, and

Lucian's slate revealed the time to be two in the morning. Once they reached the dockyards in the elevator, it was empty and the lights had dimmed.

About halfway back to the gondola, six street toughs emerged from behind some boxes, barring their path. At their fore was the young woman Lucian had noticed in the bar.

"Zheng Yang sends her regards," she said.

At that moment, the toughs pounced, each raising a kinetic pistol, while one wore a shield generator on his back that he powered on. That energy shield, Lucian knew, would deflect kinetic, electric, and magnetic magic.

There was hardly time to react. Lucian reached for the Orb of Psionics, streaming a Psionic shield as strongly as he could manage, just in time to deflect a stream of shots. He extended his shockspear with a metallic whir, along with Serah and Fergus, setting a Dynamistic brand on its tip. Lightning raced along the weapon, collecting at its point.

The toughs' eyes widened, clearly not expecting to deal with *multiple* mages. Fergus, with a shout, streamed lightning from his spear, but it sizzled on the periphery of the energy shield. They fired more shots, and Lucian's shield ate the collective fire easily. Without the Orb, it would have been much harder to maintain the shield. Vera's training allowed him to stream more efficiently than he ever had.

Serah created a gravity disc on some nearby crates, which pulled two toughs that were close. They lost their balance and tumbled to the deck. Lucian, keeping his Psionic shield strong, calmly strode forward, shockspear in hand. Fergus joined him at his side. They had to pass through the shield to use magic to their advantage.

The four villains who remained, among them the young woman, switched for melee weapons, curved cutlasses that glimmered coldly under the energy shield's light. They barred Lucian and Fergus's path toward the man wearing the shield generator. Fergus struck first, spearing one right through the gut. The two that had fallen were trying to stand, but Serah kept them trapped with a gravity disc.

The young woman, not liking her odds, began backing away toward the one wearing the shield generator, leaving two for Lucian and Fergus to deal with. The taller one cried out and charged Lucian, swinging his cutlass with wild abandon. But Lucian, deep in his Focus, sidestepped calmly and thrust his spear, catching the man in the gut. Fergus easily disposed of the other, leaving only the shield-bearer and the young woman who was all but fleeing. The shield-bearer, with a yelp, dropped his equipment and fled as well. Fergus threw his spear with deadly aim, catching him right in the back. Lucian tethered the spear back to Fergus's hand, which he caught deftly.

"The other one's too far," he said. "We need to help Serah."

Lucian let his shield go. One man under Serah's gravity stream was attempting to raise his pistol toward Serah, his hand trembling with effort. Lucian bound the man's gun to the floor just as Fergus strode forward to dispose of both.

With five dead, the young woman was long gone, losing herself among the stacks of crates.

"This isn't good," Serah said.

"Come on," Fergus said. "I don't want to be around when the police drones come."

They headed back to the ship.

41

WHEN THEY RETURNED to the *Wayfinder*, Vera was waiting for them in the wardroom, along with Alistair, who stood by her side. It was the first time Lucian had seen the droid standing. It was probably two full meters at a guess.

"What happened?" she asked, her eyes noting the new weapons and shield generator.

"We ran into trouble," Lucian said. "Someone recognized Fergus from when he used to work here for Zheng Yang."

Vera's eyes widened. "He *what*? Why in the Worlds did you not say anything? You could have jeopardized everything!"

"I wished to see the station," Fergus said. "The odds of someone finding us were . . . low."

"Not low enough. We are still four hours away from getting our fuel filled. What happened?"

Lucian told her then, knowing there was no way out of it, and her expression darkened when he told her of the young woman who got away.

"And no one followed you here?"

"No," Fergus said. "Although it wouldn't take a genius to see what airlock we were heading for. And they knew where to intercept us."

She shook her head. "They will almost certainly track us, and they know who and where you are. Give me one reason I shouldn't dump you right here."

Fergus was silent.

At last, Vera relented. "Pray that she doesn't let that information slip to the League."

"I would doubt that very much," Fergus said. "She has no reason to. However, she will likely inform Zheng Yang. I'm sure she would stop at nothing to see me dead."

"You'll have to relate the details later, as it concerns everyone's safety."

"I will," Fergus said. "I shouldn't have left, but I didn't want to stay in here if I didn't have to."

"We just need to burn four hours, right?" Lucian asked.

"Assuming the fueling drones are on time, then yes," Alistair said.

While they waited, Fergus told Vera what he'd told him and Serah. By the time he finished, Vera was not happy.

"It was irresponsible of you, regardless of your reasons," she said. "Do you not realize the stakes?" When none answered, she continued. "And Lucian, I trained you to be above such things. You certainly knew going into the station was dangerous, and yet you stood idly by, despite what he told you."

"I can't control what my friends choose to do."

"Done is done," Serah said.

"Easy to say. But mark my words, the matter will not end here. But again, I sense a shifting in the Manifold. Another piece, unlooked-for, is on the move."

"Zheng Yang?" Lucian asked.

"She, or someone else, caused by your actions tonight. Therefore, we must be careful. Even the smallest action, the smallest word said in a bar, might be heard by the wrong ears, creating a tidal wave that roars through the galaxy."

At these words, all of them went silent. There was simply no arguing against it. Lucian tried to imagine a future where Fergus was being pursued by this Zheng Yang, if not personally, then by her assassins and bounty hunters who wanted the price on his head.

Thankfully, things remained quiet. By eight in the morning, the fueling drones had refilled the ship with new stores of helium-3, and *Wayfinder* was ready to set out for the next leg of its journey.

It would be eighteen days before *Wayfinder* arrived at Halia. Once they passed through the Trappist Gate, it would only take two days to reach the planet itself. Since Halia orbited a red dwarf, Trappist-1, the orbital distances were tiny, meaning the Gate was a mere twenty million kilometers away from Halia rather than the billions of a larger system.

Either way, the Orb of Gravitonics was close. The prospect of having it for his own seemed unreal. Almost too easy.

Then again, nothing was certain until the Orb was in his hands.

———

VERA PUSHED Lucian brutally in those final ten days. She pushed him until he couldn't stream anymore. It almost felt as if she were trying to punish him, all the more so because she had taken his Orbs again.

But with three days left, and Lucian's mind in an exhausted haze, she reserved her most advanced lesson.

"Today, you will learn to overdraw properly, without the benefit of your Orbs."

Lucian blinked drearily. "I can't go on, Vera."

"Why not? Have you dropped yet?"

"No. But I will soon."

"You must confront your fear. For overdrawing causes you, for a moment, to delve. Is that your trepidation?"

Lucian nodded. "That's where the Ancient One is."

"And why do you fear him?"

"He's powerful, the Immortal of Starsea. And to him, I'm just a pawn meant to bring him the Orbs like some lapdog."

"His power here is limited," Vera said. "But at least Three of the Seven have awoken, and he feels their call."

"What did he mean, that I must *become* him? Is there a way to prevent that?"

"Not by any means I possess. The Immortal is beholden to the Seven Aspects of Magic, as they are to him. No being can possess them without *becoming* him, in the end. It is . . . a sacrifice, not meant for those unready."

"Then how can I return them to the Heart of Creation? If I become him, wouldn't I want to *keep* them? To become a power-hungry dictator or something? There has to be another way. Otherwise, why would the Oracle of Binding tell me to do something that is ultimately impossible?"

"There is much yet to be deciphered. We must table this discussion for another time. Now, reach for your Focus."

Lucian did so, despite his utter exhaustion.

"You must delve, and not allow the poison of ether to touch you. You must allow the fire to not burn. Stream coldly, with no emotion, no fear, no exhilaration. I can say no more. The rest is up to you."

Lucian drew a deep breath and closed his eyes. He reached for his Focus, leaning on the training Vera had given him over the past several weeks. He banished all emotion until there was nothing but the Septagon and its seven-colored Aspects floating in his mind's eye.

And then, through the space in the center, he reached.

A torrent of ether entered him, a torrent untouched by any

impurity of the Seven Aspects surrounding him. Once the ether filled his Focus, he let go.

"Good," she said. "Very good. You are ready, Lucian."

He was about to ask for what when she reached into her trunk and withdrew the two covered Orbs. His heart leaped at the thought of holding them again, absorbing them into himself. But he drove those thoughts from his mind. He couldn't love these things that were loyal to another master. He was only their steward, and could never become attached to them.

Perhaps that was their power. The desire to own them, to use them, to feel their power and sweetness. Perhaps that was what corrupted, in the end.

But it was impossible not to feel some strange longing as Vera revealed the Orbs, their twin brilliance casting Vera's cabin deep indigo. Lucian reached without hesitation, taking one in each hand. As soon as he did so, both Orbs streamed their collective light down his arms and into his heart, until nothing remained but the relative darkness of her cabin.

When Lucian felt for them, they were there, waiting, thrumming like latent hearts. And their manner of waiting was . . . expectant, recalculating a new balance. As if even together, they could not control his mind.

He could never let that happen again. "I am their steward. No more, no less."

Vera nodded. "You understand, then. The principal part of your training is complete."

Lucian blinked in surprise. "So soon? But I feel we've barely scratched the surface."

"I fear our time on Halia will change things, especially when we uncover the third Orb. In four days, the gravitational lock will open, and we will only arrive on the dark side of that world in three days. Time is short, Lucian, and things long-planned for are coming to a head. Prepare yourself. For any possibility. And always listen for the will of the Manifold, thrumming within the folds and streams of the Ethereal Background."

"I don't understand."

"You understand enough to go forward, Lucian." She sat on her bed, clasping her hands. "Go now. I have much to meditate on. I suggest you do the same."

Lucian left her, sensing some change in Vera's mannerisms. A sort of distance that hadn't been there before. He didn't discount it. He knew enough now not to discount the smallest inkling.

A storm was coming. Something was going to happen down there on the surface of Halia, beneath the ice, in the Temple of the Ancients.

Only time would tell what that storm amounted to.

42

THE DAYSIDE of Halia grew in the forward viewscreen, where all had gathered. Tidally locked to its parent star of Trappist-I, Halia's extreme sunward facing side was a desert. A dark ocean, roughly circular, surrounded that hellish land, giving the planet's dayside the appearance of an eye. Surrounding the sea was a black land, the only habitable region of the planet, lands of eternal twilight. Beyond the rim of the world, lost to vision, was Halia's nightside, a cold, glaciated wasteland without end.

It was hard for Lucian to believe that they were here at long last. That in that black land, somewhere, his uncle lived. It seemed pointless to think about now since they wouldn't be seeing each other, and they had only met once. He might as well have been on Terminus, twelve Gates away.

It was on the far side, where the night was darkest, where the Temple of the Ancients lay buried and forgotten kilometers beneath the ice. Forgotten, except for those standing here on the bridge of the *Wayfinder*.

How Vera had found it, Lucian couldn't guess. But there was

no time to question as Alistair piloted the *Wayfinder* toward the dark nightside, cloaked in an impenetrable veil.

A foreboding grew in Lucian's chest as they approached, and from his friends' silence, they felt much the same. In Vera's dark eyes was an eagerness, though her features betrayed no emotion.

They burned through the atmosphere, through an eternal night sky, to find a world of unbroken ice fields extending perpetually in every direction, illumined only by the thousands of stars studding the sky above, diamonds in the black. Lucian had never seen a bleaker sight.

No one said anything as the *Wayfinder* landed in a somewhat sheltered hollow, in the middle of which stood a vertical shaft leading directly down, approximately a meter in width.

"Alistair," Vera asked. "What is the temperature outside?"

"Sixty-two degrees below zero, factoring in wind chill."

"Not as bad as I thought. I only have cold-weather gear for two, so Serah and Fergus must remain behind. Besides, where Lucian and I are going, none may follow."

"Not a chance," Serah said. "I didn't come this far to be left behind."

Her posture was stooped because she had never spent a day in a gravity greater than Psyche's. Halia's gravity was roughly equal to Earth's. She was in no state to go outside. Even Lucian felt heavy and strained.

"The descent is long and treacherous, and not even a thermal ward can shield you from frostbite for long. Besides, it will take you weeks to develop the musculature to combat the effects of Halia's gravity. Lucian, being Earth born, will find it easier to adjust. And his coming is necessary."

"It's all right," Lucian said. "I'll be fine."

"Lucian..."

"We'll be back before you know it," he said. "Vera is right.

The ship is safer. Try to rest up. You were both on Psyche far longer than me."

"How deep is the shaft?" Fergus asked.

"Two kilometers. It warms marginally the lower you go, but not enough. It's not warm enough to go wardless until you're well within the temple."

"We'll hold down the fort," Fergus said. "Get that Orb and get back here."

Serah was facing away, clearly upset.

"Serah . . ." Lucian said.

"Go," she said, her voice hurt. "You've made your choice."

Lucian didn't know what to say. "I'll be back soon."

He and Vera dressed in heavy snowsuits with built-in nano-heating. A thin film covered his face, through which air could pass through, warmed. Likewise, his thick boots had thick treads and built-in heating as well. He was positively burning up inside the ship.

But when Vera opened the blast door, a gust of brutally frigid air swirled inside, far colder than anything he had ever experienced, even in the north of Volsung.

He followed Vera down the boarding ramp and straight for the shaft, delving straight into the ice. He took a glance above, to see a moon about twice the size of Earth's shining with icy blue radiance. It took him a moment to realize that it *wasn't* a moon. It was another world, the fifth out from its parent star. The distances in this system were so short that planets could appear as large as a moon in the sky. And just to the right of that blue planet hung another, farther out, slightly smaller than Earth's moon and its color a sickly green.

From what Vera had explained, the gravity lock would only open in the temple below when all those planets lined up over-head, of which there were four, though Lucian couldn't see the other two, which were more distant. It was a strange concept to wrap his mind around, and it made this place feel utterly alien compared to Volsung, or even Psyche.

"How did you find this place?" he asked.

Vera ignored his question. Either that or the wind made it impossible to hear. When they arrived at the shaft, Lucian peered down into the endless black. Someone, presumably Vera, had chipped handholds into the side of the ice. His boots and gloves had heavy treads, so he probably wouldn't lose his grip. But the descent would be no cakewalk considering his grav-lag.

"The descent will take several hours," she said. "The space is narrow but runs straight down. You can push your back on the opposite wall if you need a rest. I'll go first."

She entered the hole without hesitation. He wondered how an elderly woman of her feeble strength could ever make the distance. But if she could do it, then he supposed he could, too.

He looked back at the ship, where Serah stood watching from the bridge. It was no true window of glass, just an outer viewscreen that was a seamless part of the ship. That viewscreen faded, replaced by the silvery hull of the *Wayfinder*.

Now, it felt as if he were truly on his own. Peering down, Vera had already lost herself to the darkness. And despite the warmness of his suit, he was catching a chill.

He entered the shaft, out of the wind. Their long descent began.

———

IT TOOK HOURS. They paused for breaks several times. Lucian lost himself in meditation, working to calm himself for what lay ahead. Within hours, he would be face-to-face with the Oracle of Gravitonics. They would camp just before the door, just in time for it to unlock hours later once the planets aligned. From his vision derived from the prophecy, he knew exactly what to expect: an ancient temple with ice covering every surface, with long pillars extending upward to a high, ice-encased ceiling.

Lucian wondered why the Ancients would ever choose to build a temple here. Perhaps long ago, this glacier had been a sea, and the planet had spun on its axis. Perhaps it had been some sort of island that had sunk to the bottom of an ancient ocean, or it had even floated on the water. Then once this side of the planet had gone cold, a glacier had buried it from above.

Whatever the case, Lucian couldn't figure it out.

At long last, there was light. Something Lucian found strange. Why would Vera have a light source going for four months?

They reached a sort of bottom, a steep bank of ice, which they slid down. And then, they stood before tall, ancient doors, wrought from gold and silver and carved deeply with runes running vertically from floor to ceiling. These doors alone would be an incredible find, for no other Builder ruin was said to contain writing of any sort.

"The threshold," Vera said. "Come. We are nearly there."

He felt a warning in his heart, something he could not explain. And yet, he also felt a significant source of power up ahead, just as he had felt it at the shrine in the north of Volsung, and as he had felt it in the Burning Sands in the Spire. The Orb of Gravitonics awaited, of that he was sure.

He and Vera went up the high steps and passed into the Temple of the Ancients.

And once they went through, the doors slammed shut behind them.

Lucian whirled around, shaken by the loud reverberation. He pushed against them, and when that failed, reached the Orb of Psionics to give them a mighty push.

"Help me," he said. "I'd rather not die down here."

"You won't," Vera said. "Those doors will not open again until the Orb of Gravitonics leaves its pedestal."

Lucian turned to her. "How do you know that?"

"Because those doors are locked with a Gravitonic Magic too powerful to tamper with. Even for me."

"So the temple locked us in?"

A new female voice joined them. "No. I did."

Lucian turned to see a middle-aged woman standing among the columns of the temple. She wore a dark cloak, had shoulder-length black hair with streaks of gray, and deep olive skin. Her brown eyes watched him with amusement, a smirk playing at her lips.

This woman struck his heart cold. She looked instantly familiar, though he couldn't have said why. It took a long time for him to realize the truth, though his logic railed against it.

It was a face he had never seen outside of history lessons. It was simply impossible that she could stand there before him.

And yet, there she was, plain as anything he'd ever see in his life.

"Lucian," Vera said. "Allow me to introduce you to my Psion, Xara Mallis. She is the Chosen of the Manifold."

THE CHRONICLE OF THE MANIFOLD

43

LUCIAN COULD ONLY STARE in disbelief. Both Vera and Xara watched him, looking for some reaction. All he could think was that this couldn't be real.

But ironically, Vera's training returned to him, calming his panic and helping him make a snap decision.

He reached for the Orb of Psionics so quickly that neither Vera nor Xara were ready for it. But he did not reach to strike at them.

He felt his mind link with Serah's. *Serah! It's a trap! Find somewhere to hide.*

Lucian didn't know if the message got out, but he mixed in an excess of jarring Psionic streams, something he hoped would garble his message from the outside. An outside source cut off his link, a source that could be none other than Vera.

"They cannot help you," she said. "I owe you an explanation. It's . . . the least I can do."

The sting of betrayal was too sickening for words. And yet, it didn't surprise him. The signs had all been there, but he had followed Vera all the same. In the end, did he have any choice but to walk into the trap?

"Does the explanation matter? The two of you mean to kill me and take my Orbs."

"Kill you?" Vera shook her head. "No, Lucian. That's the last thing we want."

Lucian didn't know what she was talking about until he remembered their last conversation.

Time is short, Lucian, and something long-planned for is coming to a head. Prepare yourself. For any possibility.

"Any possibility." He couldn't help but laugh. "I would have imagined anything but this."

He looked at Xara, a proud and regal woman probably in her mid-forties. But the Mage War had ended over fifty years ago with her death. She should be almost as old and hobbled as Vera by now.

That was when the dots connected. Xara hadn't aged, and she had destroyed the planet of Isis with Atomic Magic, along with her Starsea Mages, in an incredible show of force.

There was only one answer that made sense.

"You hold the Orb of Atomicism, Xara. Don't you?"

She gave a small smile. "Very good."

"And you didn't die in the Siege of Isis. Vera did not leave the planet alone."

"Again, good."

"And you were the one to find the first Orb. The one that unleashed the Starsea Cycle."

"That's where you go wrong. Even I don't know who found the first Orb."

So Vera hadn't been lying about that.

"How is this possible? How are you here, and how have you remained hidden so long?"

Xara looked at Vera, as if for permission to speak. When Vera nodded, Xara turned back to him.

"Vera and I located the Orb of Atomicism before the start of the Mage War, on Isis, where we built the Starsea Sanctum. My possession of it was a closely guarded secret, something between Master and Psion. Even my closest advisors might have killed me for it in the end. So, you are the first to learn about it in over fifty years." She chuckled. "It's been a long, strange journey. And I've had to exercise a great deal of patience."

"And you, not me, are the Chosen of the Manifold?"

She nodded. "That's correct. Long ago, when I was mere Psion at the Volsung Academy, Vera had a prophecy that I would be the one to gather the Seven Orbs and lead humanity to victory against an ancient, dread menace. Though we did not know what that meant at the time, it became clear that her prophecy was alluding to the Swarmers, also called the *Alkasen*. I did not immediately believe her, of course. But eventually, I came to see the truth. We left the Volsung Academy to search for the Orbs. We discovered a lead in *The Prophecy of the Seven* that took us to Isis, and it was there that we uncovered it, against all odds. By now, the League had declared war. But even with the power of the Orb, we could not turn the tide."

"Where have you been hiding all this time? Surely, someone would have recognized you."

She smiled. "I'm dead, Lucian. And everyone who fought with me in the war is also dead, or on Psyche. Though you recognized me, others might not, especially since I've aged somewhat. But I won't hide myself for much longer."

"What do you mean?"

"I will lead Magekind, and humanity, against the Swarmers. There is no time for debate. All must fall in line behind me."

"She's right," Vera said. "When we met aboard the *Burung*, Lucian, I immediately recognized your importance. The Ancient One meant you to gather the Orbs of Binding and Psionics, that much was made clear to me after you appeared to me from Psyche, in this very place. But gathering those Orbs was not for your benefit. It was your fate to bring those Orbs to Xara, the true Chosen of the Manifold."

Find the Aspects. Bring them to me. Lucian could hear that voice as plain as his thoughts.

"Were you the voice in my head during my metaphysical?"

Xara shook her head. "I know the voice you're talking about, because I've heard it, too. As has Vera. That is the Ancient One, the being I'm fated to become once I gather the Seven. He was simply guiding you toward your goal. Which, once you give me the Orbs, you can consider complete."

Complete? Was it really to end like this, with him relinquishing his power, his burden? He had dreamed of this moment for so long. At last, he could lay everything down.

But it did not bring him comfort. Not in the least. It made him feel numb and used.

And it made him angry, though that would not help him here. He held his Focus, to better steel himself for what was ahead.

"What are your plans for the Orbs? Are you going to return them to the Heart of Creation?"

Xara shook her head. "Such a task is impossible, and even if it's doable, the likelihood of success is infinitesimally small. The First Gate, through which you must go to find the Heart of Creation, lies deep in Dark Space. That is where the *Alkasen*, the calamity that broke Starsea, abides. We have considered the possibility, but it requires learning the First Gate's location. And given the breadth of the former Starsea Empire, which expanded across as much as a thousand suns at its height, such a search would take many lifetimes."

"That's it, then?" Lucian asked. "You're just going to willingly . . . *become* . . . this evil being who just wants to dominate our reality?"

"Evil?" Xara asked. "The Ancient One is far from evil. He is the champion of the Shadow Realm, of which we are a part. He is our bastion against the unimaginably powerful beings of the Light Realm, who wish for nothing more than to obliterate us. When he breaks free of his prison, when the power of the Seven awakens in full, we will break the Starsea Cycle once and for all. When I hold the Seven, mages can draw endlessly from the Manifold without the fear of going mad. This is what the Light Realm fears. This is why they created the abominations we call the Swarmers. They want us dead, Lucian, and if the Seven Orbs return to them, it would mean disaster for humanity."

"Why do they want to kill us, then? Why does our existence matter? Are we harming them in any way?"

"Long ago, eons before even Starsea existed, the Forerunners bridged the gap between the Shadow Realm and the Light Realm, creating the First Gate, through which all magic flows. But the beings of the Light Realm resented their power being shared with us, who they see as lesser. They resented the First Immortal, the Shadow Lord who dared to defy the Light."

"The Shadow Lord?"

"He who passed through the First Gate. So involved were they with their celestial wars they failed to notice the thief in their midst! The First Immortal, the Shadow Lord, took the Seven for himself, and so brought magic into the Shadow Realm. From magic, they created the Gates and the First Starsea Empire, the one before even the time of the Second Starsea—the Starsea that the Ancients created."

So, this First Immortal had stolen the Seven Orbs. They didn't belong in this reality, and that was how magic entered the universe.

"If the First Immortal stole the Orbs, then why didn't these beings in the Light Realm get them back, if they're truly so powerful?"

"The beings of the Light Realm cannot enter the Shadow

Realm without devolving into beings of Shadow. And so, they created the *Alkasen*. Do you know what they are, Lucian?"

"Monsters. That much is clear."

"Yes. They are not living things, the way you and I think of life. You might think of them as fallen angels. They are thralls of the Higher Beings, banished to the Shadow Realm, cursed to never return until they find the Orbs. They hunt them, Lucian. It was from the *Alkasen* that the Seven Oracles hid their treasures, to guard them until one day, the Chosen of the Manifold, the Third Immortal, would forge the Third Starsea Empire. The Empire Vera prophesied to last until the end of time."

Lucian wasn't sure what to think anymore. "But the Oracle of Binding wanted the Orbs returned to the Heart of Creation, to end magic here forever. That's . . . what I agreed to do."

"That isn't possible," Xara said. "And even if it was, I would not want to do it. With the Seven Orbs, Magekind would be free from the fate of the fraying, the curse the Higher Beings placed on us for daring to use their power. Magic is the best thing to have happened to humanity. Or at least, it has the *potential* to be. But how could you know about the Age of Wonders, the brief taste of what a new Starsea might be like? That could be reality, Lucian. With magic, we could solve the universe's ills. There will be a brief time of struggle until I gather all the Orbs, and of course, the war against the *Alkasen*. But once that's done, Starsea will enter a golden age. With magic, we would rule with power and majesty and justice."

"Not even the Immortal could do such a thing," Lucian said. "It would seem the First and the Second ones failed. And you're saying *you* could succeed?"

"She will," Vera said firmly. "Arian's prophecy speaks of the third and final Starsea, and a golden age until the end of time."

Xara nodded. "With Magekind united behind me, and the League as well, once they recognize I'm the Worlds' only hope, I will fulfill Vera's prophecy and ascend to become the Third

Immortal, the Empress of Starsea. If that means sharing my mind with the Ancient One's, so be it. If it means my suffering, I am willing. Because of me, billions will live, now and in perpetuity, and humanity will enter an Age of Wonders unending."

To Lucian, it sounded too good to be true. Like sheer madness. This was the idea the Starsea Mages had fought and died for? The way Xara told it made it seem like the right thing. And Lucian might have believed that, but for the warning in his heart.

If Xara was right and the Seven Oracles of Starsea wanted to protect the Orbs from the *Alkasen*, then why would Rhana have wanted him to *return* the Orbs to the Heart of Creation? Wasn't that what the *Alkasen* wanted, too? Perhaps she had changed her mind in the long years between the fall of Starsea and the present.

Something wasn't adding up, and Lucian wasn't sure what.

"What do you say, Lucian? Are you ready to release your burden? To fulfill your destiny? Everything has been gathering toward this moment. I have the strength, will, and power to wield the Orbs, and with four, none could stop me. It might even be enough to halt some effects of the fraying. We won't know until I've absorbed them."

"I don't trust you," Lucian said. He turned to Vera. "You kept all this from me. I never trusted you. Not fully. But I trusted you enough to give you the Orbs for a short time. Why did you not just take them and give them to Xara? Why even train me if you were just going to betray me?"

"Betray you? This is no betrayal, Lucian. You would have never come here willingly if I told you who was down here. In fact, allowing you to take the Orbs and their burden would be the greater betrayal. For you are not strong enough, Lucian. Perhaps, with decades of time, you might learn enough to wield them properly. But alas, we do not have decades. We probably do not even have two or three years to work with."

"So what, I'm useless?"

"Far from useless. I would not have trained you if I deemed that. I ask instead that you join us in our quest to find the rest of the Orbs. I believe the Manifold has a part for you to play."

"You mean, the Ancient One."

"As powerful as he is, he is still beholden to higher realities. Not even he can see all ends." She watched him closely. "That is why I didn't take your Orbs, Lucian. It was not my part to take them. I will admit, they tempted me to taste their power. But it would have done no good and potentially ruined my work, decades in the making. The Orbs belong to Xara Mallis, and her alone."

"The Manifold does not have a Chosen until someone holds all Seven Orbs," Lucian said. "You said so yourself, Vera. And so did Shantozar, the Oracle of Psionics, and so did Rhana, the Oracle of Binding. And you just said no one can see all ends, not even the Ancient One. So why could it *not* be me?"

"Do you contend the title then, Lucian?" Vera asked.

"I contend nothing because neither Xara nor I have a claim to the title."

"That's not what I meant. Do you wish to be the Chosen of the Manifold, truly? Do you have fifty years to train to match Xara's abilities? Do the Worlds have that amount of time before the *Alkasen* grind them to dust? Who is better equipped, more experienced, wiser, and a proven leader of men and women? And who did I prophesy holding the Seven, of ending the threat of the *Alkasen* once and for all?"

"Even you said prophecy is a tricky thing. And you've based your entire life around this one. For someone who likes to berate people for being foolish, that was certainly pretty stupid."

"Such insolence. How little you understand. How little you would risk. You could never be the Chosen of the Manifold. You must be reasonable."

"Why not just kill me? Because I'm going to hold onto these Orbs until my dying breath. I'll never let the Immortal rise again. I'll find a way to return them to the Heart of Creation. Maybe I don't want to be the Chosen, but I'm the only one of us three willing to take that harder road." He looked at Vera. "Is that no what you preach so often?"

At their stony silence, Lucian realized his death was an actual possibility. If he gave up the Orbs, they would allow him to save himself and his friends. He hoped Fergus and Serah were hiding somewhere, safe from the cold. He had a feeling they could not open the door into the Temple unless Xara opened it herself.

"Both of you may be more experienced," Lucian said. "You may even be right. But something feels off. I don't trust either of you, and that counts for everything. And I don't trust the Ancient One."

"Are you prepared to die, Lucian?" Xara asked in a soft, dangerous voice. "You don't strike me as the heroic type. And it seems clear, against what Vera opened, that you don't want to help us. We won't force you to help us. So, how about this instead. You can give up your Orbs, and we'll even drop you off at Halisport, along with your friends. How does fifty thousand credits sound?"

Lucian could hardly keep his eyes from popping. That was more money than he could earn in two lifetimes, if not more. He wanted to say yes. Desperately.

Especially when the alternative was dying.

"I don't believe you'd give that to me," Lucian said. "I know too much."

"No one would ever believe you about me. Not until I reveal myself, anyway. It's a significant sum, even for us, but it's also fair. For everything you've gone through. Besides, who can place a fair value on Two Aspects of Magic?"

Lucian knew he could negotiate and ask for more. And they

would give it to him. Despite himself, his mind raced with possibilities for what he could do with the money. It was enough for him, Fergus, and Serah to all have an enjoyable life. If Xara was right, and her possessing four Orbs slowed the fraying, it would give Serah time to live. And isn't that what he wanted? Perhaps it was even enough time for Xara to find the rest of the Orbs, to stop the fraying completely.

And it would be nice to just *not* have to risk his neck. And for what? The impossible chance he could stop *magic*? Xara was right. It was an impossible goal and might not even be preferable to what she outlined.

To say anything but "yes" to the offer, that ridiculous sum of money, was ludicrous, a decision made from stubbornness and pure ego.

And yet . . . it still felt wrong. He wasn't afraid that they would kill him if he took the deal. Somehow, he knew that wasn't in their plans. The offer was legitimate.

He saw both of their faces relaxing, as if they knew his acceptance was a foregone conclusion. Still, the offer warred in his mind with what he knew to be right. Who was he to risk his friends' lives? What would they think of all this? They'd probably kill him if he rejected the offer.

Of course, if Xara and Vera didn't kill him first for refusing. That was the only possible outcome of all this.

Lucian's shoulders sagged. He was the only thing standing between the galaxy and a new Immortal Empress, one whose mind would fuse with the Ancient One's. For all of Xara's words, he knew that would not be a good deal for humanity in the long run. The Second Immortal had enslaved many races, races who had fallen to the *Alkasen* onslaught all those millennia ago. The Oracle of Binding was someone Lucian trusted far more than these two, though he couldn't have said why.

In the end, that decided for him. Was the Ancient One reincarnated in Xara Mallis's body worth fifty thousand credits? Was it worth fifty *million*?

He had no choice but to stand up for what was right, as hopeless as it was. Even if he was standing alone. If he died, he died. He could do no more.

"I'm the only one standing between the two of you and utter madness. Kill me. If you can."

At that moment, with a power he didn't know he had, he drew deeply from both Orbs. And immediately, Shadow Realm fell away.

44

LUCIAN DELVED SO DEEPLY into the Manifold that he could no longer see the Shadow Realm before him. He drew all the ether surrounding him, forming a ward of incredible strength, made not only with Binding and Psionics, but laced with each of the Seven Aspects. As Vera had taught him, he drew without emotion, without fear, surer of his abilities than ever. He became a fountain of ether, all of which created his seven-sealed ward in a rainbow tapestry.

He knew deep down that he was not strong enough to challenge even *one* of them. So, this was his only shot—a ward sealed him with all seven Aspects of Magic, making him unassailable.

Magic glanced off him, like pebbles against a fortress. He recognized those pebbles to be the concerted attacks of Vera and Xara, useless against him. His ward was so large, so powerful, that it was sucking up all available ether, at least in the general vicinity.

There was no ether left for them to break him. And even if there was, Lucian doubted they could do so.

But neither could Lucian move or fight back. He was in an impregnable shell, practically catatonic save for the thoughts in his mind. In this shell, nothing could hurt him or find him, but neither could he affect the world outside.

He didn't know how long the shell would last, but he knew it would endure for a long, long time. And that he had no way himself of breaking it.

So he could do nothing but sense Xara and Vera striding forward toward the locked door at the other end of the Temple, which had opened to reveal the resplendent Orb of Gravitonics. He could see it shining like a silver beacon, a nova of light and endless possibility. He longed to hold it. But doing so would be impossible.

He watched helplessly as minutes passed like seconds, as Xara took the Orb, received the revelation from the Oracle, silent and garbled in his bubble. They came to stand beside him for a moment, talking in low, distorted voices. They were but shadows, hardly decipherable against the static of the Ethereal Background swirling around him. After a time, it was hard to say how long they left him there alone.

Time passed at a steady clip. Hours. Days. Weeks. It was impossible to tell. Time didn't seem to exist here. Here, it seemed the Beginning and the End were all one, and he was just an island in a tempestuous sea of time. He would catch visions in the gray static beyond. People. His memories. The birth and death of stars. Whatever he thought, a primitive version of it would paint itself on the tapestry of the Ethereal Background.

In time, the gray faded, and he noticed two figures standing before him. Something was familiar about them. But he felt their souls, their Focuses, and knew them to be friends.

Lucian? Lucian!

Serah . . .

You're alive! How do we get you out?

Reach for me. Don't leave me here . . .

He felt a connection, something pulling at him. A gray light pierced the ward, followed by a red one and an orange one. From the second figure, larger and bulkier, came four lights: orange, yellow, green, and blue. The lights coalesced for a single moment, dispersing along the perimeter of the chrysalis, unraveling the streams.

Hold on, Lucian. Don't let go.

Lucian didn't. He kept Serah's presence in his mind, never letting go of the Psionic link. He slipped through the barrier, rushing through a maelstrom of gray. Something chased him here. Something dark. But Serah was pulling him back to reality, out of this miserable place where he no longer wanted to stay.

In the next moment, he could see her shape, her face, her eyes. He held onto her. She was something warm after that place of cold and darkness. He wept on her shoulder, not caring about his weakness.

"It's all right," she said. "You're safe."

OVER THE NEXT couple of hours, around a branded fire in the Temple of Ancients, Lucian learned what had happened.

Fergus and Serah had hidden, as he'd told them, getting as far from the ship as they could in the terrible cold before they had to create a shelter in the snow. They used magic to do that, and Serah created a Thermal ward to keep them warm. Fergus created the strongest concealment ward he knew to shield them from Vera, who would surely search for them upon discovering they had abandoned the ship.

Only after they heard the spaceship flying away did they reemerge and head for the shaft. When they reached the bottom, half-frozen, they'd found Lucian before the open door leading into the inner sanctum, where the pedestal that once held the Orb of Gravitonics stood empty. He was suspended in a chrysalis, cast in a rainbow of colors, motionless with eyes closed.

They had been down here three days. And only after three days did Serah connect to him. When this happened, the chrysalis shattered, and Lucian broke free.

After they finished, Lucian told them everything that had happened, and they listened in wide-eyed astonishment. Once done, they sat around the fire, no one saying a word for a long time.

At last, Fergus broke the silence. "Xara Mallis, the Chosen of the Manifold. I don't believe it. Not for one rotting second."

Serah shook her head. "Me, neither. You turned down life-changing money. You risked everything, Lucian." She paused. "Even *us*."

"I'm sorry about that," he said.

"Don't be. You would've been dead to me if you'd taken that money. We came here to save humanity, not sell it out."

"You did well, Lucian," Fergus said. "To my shame . . . I don't know if I would have been as strong. I would not have condemned that choice. However, if you had taken the money, I probably would have lost faith in higher ideals." Fergus put a meaty hand on his arm in a rare show of affection. "Now, I know there are people like you out there. At least one, anyway. That's someone worth fighting for."

"I don't know about all that," Lucian said. "But . . . thanks." He shook his head. "Morals are pointless when we're doomed to starve to death. We've been three days without food."

"Let's . . . not think about that," Serah said, putting her head on his shoulder. "We'll find a way. We always have, right?"

"This situation is worse than the Burning Sands," Lucian said. "We're in the center of the dark side of Halia, a world far larger than Psyche. We have about ten thousand kilometers to go across bleak glaciers under a sunless sky until we reach the warmer Twilight Lands. We have no ship or means of transportation. Even if I were to tether us across the entire landscape nonstop without sleep, we'd starve or freeze to death."

"We have to try *something*," Serah said.

They thought for a while, but no one came up with anything. Lucian started thinking of his mother, then. He didn't know why. How long ago it seemed when she had hoped he might come here because his uncle might help him.

He stiffened. Was it possible?

"Fergus," he said, almost not wanting to know the answer. "When a mage streams radio waves, can anyone pick it up, or just other mages?"

He frowned, confused. "Anyone can, theoretically, but they'd have to be looking for you."

"What if I know who I want to contact, but don't know where he is?"

"Who?"

"My Uncle Ravis. He lives here. He's an exec for Caralis Intergalactic. I don't know what else to do but send out a distress beacon."

"That can be dangerous," Fergus said. "You never know who might answer the call, especially on an undeveloped world like Halia. For all we know, Vera and Xara are waiting in orbit just in case we try something like that."

"More likely they think we're dead," Serah said. "No one could survive out here, not even a mage. And obviously, they supposed Lucian had shielded himself so well that he could never escape. But they didn't count on us still being alive to figure it out."

Lucian nodded. "Let's hope so. Caralis is the biggest megacorp on this world. No one comes to this side of the planet, as far as I know. If we can get a message out, addressing it to anyone in the company but mentioning my uncle by name, saying we found something big . . . someone might pick us up. It's a long shot, but worth a try."

"You think so?" Serah asked doubtfully.

"This is a ruin of the Ancients, long lost to time. My uncle will want to get his hands on it, I'm sure. My mom always used to tell me he'd even sell his mother for the right price."

"I suppose it's safe to say they didn't get along," Serah said.

"Whatever the case, it's something that will interest him. And if we claim we're with Caralis, then he can lay claim to the site as his own and order the company's archaeology division here."

"It might work," Fergus said. "We'll never know until we try."

"I can't mention myself by name, for obvious reasons. But I think if we say all that, he'll come running. If not him personally, then someone close to him."

"Can you trust him?" Serah asked. "To stay quiet about you, I mean."

"He probably doesn't know my situation at all," Lucian said. "Unfortunately, I will have to explain at least some of it, and hope I can swear him to secrecy. What other choice do we have?"

"So, when do we start?" Serah asked.

"We need to get above ground, to make sure the ice above us doesn't block the message," Fergus said. "I can send it out. It makes sense, given that I'm the Radiant."

"Sounds good to me," Lucian said.

———

THEY DIDN'T STAY on the surface long. Just a minute or two before ducking down into the shaft. Serah streamed a Thermal ward to take the bite out of the cold, though it was still quite frigid within its reddish aura. Even under the ward, they couldn't last forever out here.

"I told them what we found," Fergus said. "That we worked for the company, and to bring their archaeology division here as quickly as possible to claim the site. Is that good?"

"Perfect. You didn't mention our names?"

"Of course not."

"All that's left is to wait, then. They'll know where to find us?"

"If they've correctly identified the source of the transmission. We can only hope it's not Vera and Xara coming back."

Lucian had the feeling that they had moved on. Moved on *where* was another question entirely. Likely, Vera was going to use the visions Lucian had shared to gather the Orbs, of which Xara now had two to match his own. It made him sick Xara had gotten the Orb of Gravitonics unchallenged, but he still might reach the others or even the original copy of *The Prophecy of the Seven*.

With that thought, he knew his next goal. To find the prophecy—the *real* prophecy—before Vera and Xara could do the same.

They hadn't waited fifteen minutes when a descending spaceship ripped downward from the sky. It was a bulky cargo craft, obviously a Caralis ship that had diverted immediately from whatever errand it had been on, most likely the closest one to the temple site.

That ship landing on the ice was the most beautiful sight in the Worlds Lucian had ever seen. It was salvation. It was hope.

And it meant things weren't over yet. Not as long as he drew breath.

EPILOGUE

TRANSCEND WHITE usually had no trouble falling asleep. By this point in her life, she had trained her mind to do whatever she wanted it to do.

This night, though, was different. She had been tossing and turning for hours, listening to the gusting of the lonesome north wind outside the tower's walls. There was a shifting in the Manifold's balance. It made her stomach twist as if she were a Novice asked to stand before the Transcends.

Psion Gaius's dignified knock only amplified this feeling. With a sigh, she stood, slipping on her thick slippers. It was winter on Volsung, and no matter how much firewood they imported from Nova Bergen for the Transcends' hearths, it was never enough to take the chilly edge off.

She went down the spiral steps of her tower on creaking knees. Once she stood in her study, she called out with a reedy voice.

"Enter."

Psion Gaius passed the threshold and gave a slight bow. And to Transcend White's surprise, he was not alone.

"Emma Almaty? What brings you here at this hour?"

The young, pretty Talent's cheeks colored a bit as if she had just been scolded, though Transcend White had only been curious.

"There's something that's been weighing on me for a long time, your High Eminence," she said. "For months. I can't eat, I can't focus, I can't sleep. It's twisting me up inside."

Transcend White thought that uncanny, given her state. Perhaps Emma had Psionic premonitions as well, though her primary gifting was Radiance. It was worth exploring. "Well, out with it. What was important enough to interrupt my sleep?"

From the way Psion Gaius was looking at Emma, he hadn't been told. Something about the young woman's manner told Transcend White that it was important.

"Could I speak to you alone, Transcend White?" Emma asked tremulously.

She gave Emma a level stare until, after a moment, she nodded for Psion Gaius to leave. Though he did so without complaint, she could feel his animosity at being excluded. She would have to teach him to control his emotions, especially if there came a day where she was too weak to lead the Academy.

When the heavy wooden door shut behind him, Transcend White nodded for Emma to continue.

"It's about Lucian," she said. "Lucian Abrantes."

Now Transcend White's stomach did a flip, but she made no outward expression of her surprise. She'd dreamed of him lately, as much as she had tried to avoid that. Strange dreams of him traipsing around the galaxy getting into many troubles. As she might expect for one of his kind. The dreams had seemed so real, but of course, they couldn't be real. The young man was on Psyche, or even dead.

"Yes? What about him? I know you were friends, so if this was about our decision—"

"It's not," Emma stammered.

Transcend White looked at her in shock. For a Talent to interrupt her like this was unheard of. Normally, she would have been angry, but such was the poor girl's state that she instead wanted to comfort her.

"Have a seat, child," she said. "You're clearly in a tizzy. Would you like some tea?"

Emma shook her head, her face pale. "No. Transcend White, Lucian is alive. I know he is! He spoke to me from Psyche itself about four months ago. It was no dream. It was *him*."

"Impossible. Not even I could form a Psionic link across such an impossible distance . . ."

"Yet it's true. You know me, Transcend White. I'm an excellent student, and a capable Talent despite my age, and I would have never come to you about this if I didn't think it important, especially in the middle of the night."

"I see." Could she be right? Transcend White didn't want to admit it, but the mere idea of it had the ring of truth.

"Lucian is alive," Emma said, "and also, he's off Psyche now. I saw him in my dream with . . . *you*."

Transcend White felt goosebumps on her arms. "Me? Where? What are the details?"

"That's all I can say. It was this icy chamber, like a cave."

"Volsung, maybe. I can have the Psions scour the Isle of Madness."

"You think he's back on Volsung, now?"

"That's highly improbable, but no stone will go unturned." He couldn't be back here. How could such a thing be possible? She had contacted the captain of the prison barge herself to make sure he was on board and locked away. "Are you *sure*, Talent Emma?"

"I'd stake my life on it. I know he's alive and he's off Psyche. And more than that, he needs our help."

Transcend White thought for a long while. The girl had

382

seen him with Vera. What did *that* mean? Were she and Lucian working together? Did that abominable woman take him from Psyche? If so, for what reason?

Were the Orbs real, and was Vera still working to find them? That prospect alone was enough to give her a chill, though she gave no outward sign of her distress. But from Emma's wide eyes, the Talent seemed to catch some of the feeling.

"You've done well, Emma. If you have any more dreams like this, come directly to me."

"What does it all mean, Transcend White? If I might be so bold as to ask?"

"That's not for you to know. You've been a great help to me. If you have any more visions, come to me posthaste. No need to get Gaius. You have my full permission to come to the Transcends' Level without an escort."

She nodded. "Of course."

"You may go."

Emma stood, her legs shaky, as she went for the door. Once she was halfway out, almost closing it behind her, Transcend White cleared her throat.

"Talent Emma? If you can . . . *speak* to him . . . please tell him to come back here, if he can. If he truly is off Psyche."

Emma nodded. "I will."

She closed the door, leaving Transcend White to stew in silence.

At that moment, Transcend White knew she had committed a grave mistake. She had made quite a few of those over her long years, but none, perhaps, so great as this. They had sent Lucian away, thinking him a danger to the Volsung Academy, like Xara Mallis. The Manifold had marked the young man, as Xara had been. The Transcends had talked long and hard about it, and they had all agreed that they could not make that error again.

And yet, the Manifold had laid all their plans to waste. On

Psyche, he was to bother no one again. Transcend White had not relished the decision, but it had been necessary. Or so she'd thought.

The Manifold meant bigger things for him. Whether those were for good or bad, she couldn't say.

She didn't know if he would ever forgive her. And she didn't know if she could set aside her old woman's pride and ask his forgiveness.

In the end, though, she might have to do so. The stakes were too high. Whatever Vera wanted with him, it wasn't good. And if it had anything to do with Starsea or the Orbs of which Arian prophesied, most especially if the prophecy were *true*, against all odds, it could prove disastrous.

It was on her to correct her mistakes. With the potential resurgence of the Starsea Mages, and the sudden onslaught of the Swarmers, she could only hope it was not too late.

THE END OF BOOK FOUR

THE STARSEA CYCLE CONTINUES IN BOOK FIVE

THE PROPHECY OF THE SEVEN

ABOUT THE AUTHOR

Kyle West is the author of a growing number of sci-fi and fantasy series: *The Starsea Cycle*, *The Wasteland Chronicles*, and *The Xenoworld Saga*.

His goal is to write as many entertaining books as possible, with interesting worlds and characters that hopefully give his readers a break from the mundane.

He lives with his lovely wife, son, and two insanely spoiled cats.

ALSO BY KYLE WEST

Aberration

CPSIA information can be obtained
at www.ICGtesting.com
Printed in the USA
LVHW041213181222
735472LV00004B/399

9 781954 411043